Love in a Time of War

Love in a Time of War

An Army Nurse's Coming of Age Story

Leslyn Amthor Spinelli

Door Creek Press

Love in a Time of War is a work of historical fiction. Apart from the well-known actual people, events, and locations that are included in the narrative, all names, characters, and incidents are the product of the author's imagination or are used fictitiously.

Door Creek Press, Apple Valley, MN

door.creek.press@gmail.com

Cover design: Casey Niederwerfer

Author Photograph: © Bri Heiligenthal

Library of Congress Control Number: 2022909459

ISBN: 978-0-9981124-9-7 (hardcover); 978-0-9981124-8-0 (large print); 978-0-9981124-7-3 (trade paperback); 978-0-9981124-6-6 (ebook)

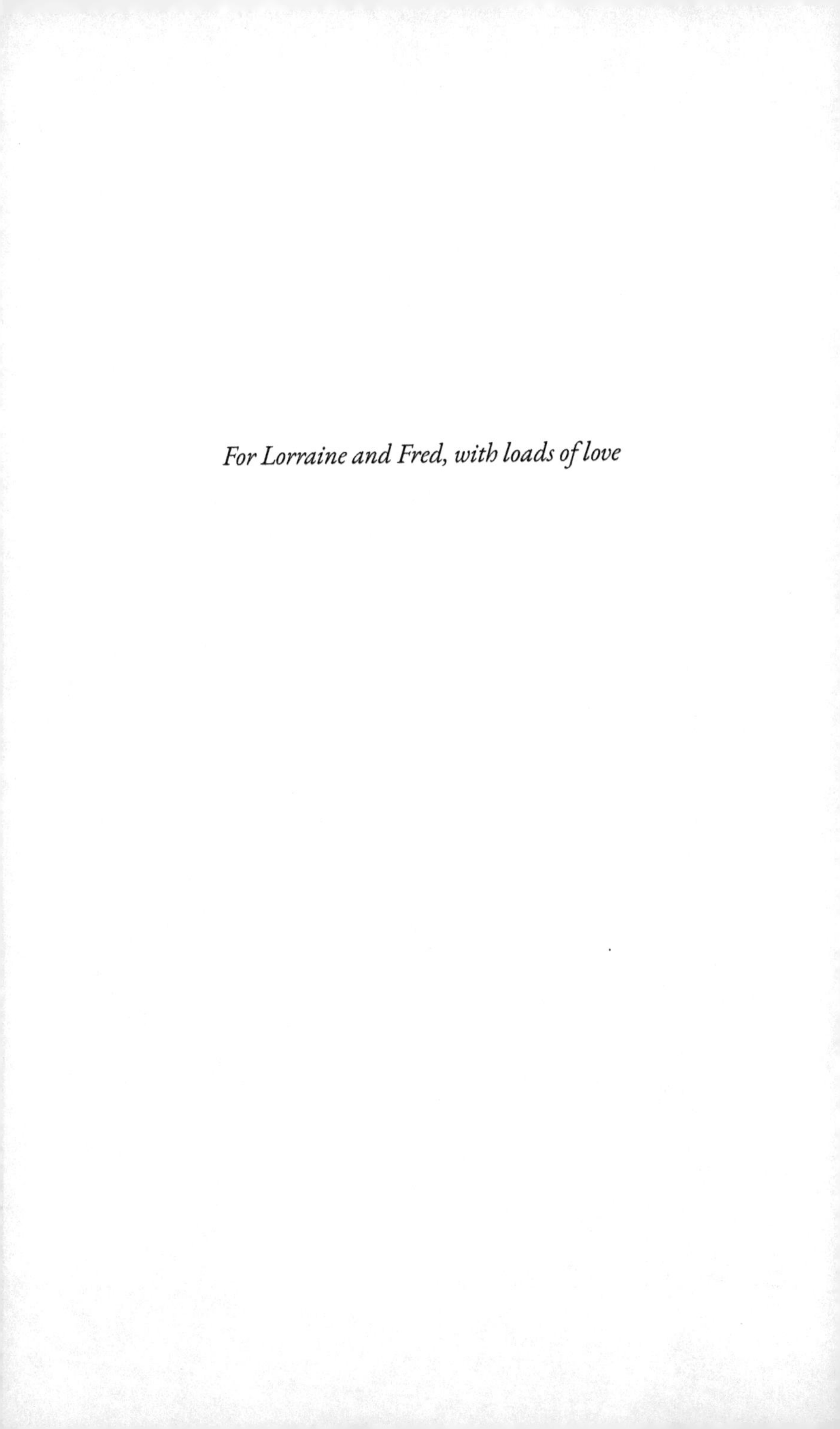

For Lorraine and Fred, with loads of love

Chapter One

March 15, 1943

SHE SHIVERED, THE DAMP COLD BLEEDING THROUGH THE fibers of her lightweight coat as she hurried down the track to board the Hiawatha. She'd left her winter clothes packed away in storage since she wouldn't need them where she was going. She knew she might be uncomfortable along the way, but she could stand discomfort—anything to get out of the three-county area where she'd spent her entire life.

She'd ridden a train only once before, traveling with a friend to Madison on a special trip to celebrate their graduation from high school. Today, that foray felt like ancient history.

Her heart swelled upon seeing the train's first passenger car painted red, white, and blue and bedecked with a Buy War Bonds! banner. Though the car looked full at a glance, she decided to climb aboard anyway.

Stumbling up the steps under the weight of her jam-packed overnight case, she felt her cheeks flush. *Auspicious beginning,* she thought.

"Careful, Miss," the porter said as he extended a hand to take the bag. And when she reached the top he added, "If you move quickly, you'll find a few empty seats in the third car to your left."

She passed through the first two cars and into the next. Halfway down the aisle she spied a vacant pair of seats and slipped gratefully into the one next to the window. The train was already stuffy and smelled of woolen outerwear that hadn't been thoroughly dried. The slight draft at the corner of the pane of glass felt refreshing.

She looked out the window, staring unabashedly at a group of about ten people surrounding a uniformed sailor. They took turns hugging and kissing him and stroking his cheek. An elderly man brushed away tears when the sailor at last broke from his embrace. The serviceman—who couldn't have been more than nineteen years old—glanced over his shoulder as he walked toward the train, blotting his nose along the way.

Her own send-off at La Farge bus station had been decidedly less demonstrative. She'd bidden farewell to Joey weeks earlier. And gas rationing had precluded her sister and aunt—her two closest relatives—from accompanying her to the train station in La Crosse. Neither of them was comfortable with goodbyes: they'd given brief hugs and sniffled a bit, and by the time she'd reached her seat on the bus, they had already gone.

Now she saw more passengers hustling toward the train and checked her watch. They were due to leave in five minutes.

"Is this seat taken?"

She glanced up to see the young sailor whose farewell she'd witnessed only moments earlier. "No. No, it's not."

He threw his duffel bag on the overhead rack, leaned down, and extended his hand. "I'm Sean M-murphy—from Minneapolis."

"Louise Dietrich from La Farge, Wisconsin," she said—accepting the young man's clammy hand—then turned again toward the window.

"I've never heard of L-l-la Farge," Sean said. "Is it c-c-lose to any towns I might know?"

She sighed, not altogether silently. "About a two-hour bus ride southeast of here—right back in the direction we're soon headed, but there's no train depot there."

"So you've already had a l-l-long day," he said, reaching into his coat pocket to pull out a crossword puzzle book. "I'll l-leave you alone then."

Louise stifled a twinge of guilt for rebuffing his attempt at conversation. Her seatmate on the bus had talked incessantly throughout the ride, and the strain of listening had drained her. Now, she wanted nothing more than to keep to herself.

By the time they'd reached Red Wing on their journey to Chicago, Louise was fast asleep.

She woke with a start when the train's whistle blared at a crossing, envisioning the horrific accident eight years earlier: her uncle and four cousins had been killed when their car was hit by a train. *I'll bet* that *whistle sounded just like this one.* She shuddered and rubbed her temples, trying to erase the picture in her mind's eye—the mangled mess they'd witnessed only half an hour after it had happened. *Did I just scream?* she now wondered and turned toward her seatmate.

"Are you okay?" he asked.

"Uh-huh," she said, then looked more closely at him and saw the collection of tears in his eyes threatening to spill down his cheeks. Instinctively she reached over and took his hand. "Oh my goodness, are *you* okay?"

He wiped his nose with the back of his free hand. "I thought I was, but I guess not...saying goodbye is just so hard. And I keep crying."

"I take it you were home on leave?"

"Yes. For my father's funeral. Home is in St. Paul, but my grandparents wanted him buried in the family plot in La Crosse. We did that this morning."

"Oh, I'm so sorry," she said, then gently extricated her hand and offered him a tissue from her purse.

"Thanks."

Far too familiar with bereavement, Louise knew it would help Sean to talk about it. "Had your father been ill?"

"Uh-huh. He'd reenlisted in the Navy the day after Pearl Harbor, but when he went for his physical, they found he had a tumor in his brain."

"How awfully unfair. Did he undergo treatment?"

"Uh-huh. He had surgery and did okay for about a year. When he went into a coma a couple of months ago, I went ahead and enlisted. There wasn't anything I could do for him at home, and I know he wanted me to serve."

"Is your mom still alive?"

"Yes. And l-luckily, she's got her parents and my three older sisters to help out."

"That is lucky." Louise swallowed the lump in her throat. "I lost my mom when I was just shy of fifteen. My dad died a year and a half later, and all my grandparents were gone by then. My younger sister and I were pretty lost. I guess we still are."

"Where'd you live after your folks died?"

"My parents owned a small dairy farm about two miles outside La Farge. When Dad got sick—he had had a few small strokes before the massive one that killed him—his cousin and his wife moved in to take care of us and the farm. They treated us okay, but it wasn't the same as having parents. We barely knew them, and they didn't know how to help us with our sadness. Plus, they had kids of their own to tend to.

He stared down at his lap. "If you don't mind my asking, how old are you now?"

"I'll be twenty-two in a couple of weeks," she said with a half-hearted laugh. "Almost an old maid. And you?"

"Eighteen and a half."

She winced. "All you young boys going off to war, it just

doesn't seem fair. Are you at least meeting nice fellows in the Navy? I mean, boys you can call friends?"

"Yes, I'd have to say so. When I first got to Great Lakes Naval Station, it was hard. You might've noticed I stammer a little when I'm nervous, and I was really nervous then. But two guys in my group spoke up for me when I was getting razzed about it, and we've become pretty close. They tell us we'll be assigned together when it's time to ship out."

"That's great. So far, I only know four people who'll be in my unit—"

"W-wait a minute. You mean to say *you* enlisted?" Sean asked.

She chuckled. "I sure did. When I graduated from nursing school there were lots of recruiters urging us to sign up. I was kind of at loose ends and really wanted to help in the war effort. Beyond buying bonds, I mean. I considered joining the Navy, but—honestly—the Army Nurse Corps recruiter was more encouraging. I go in as a second lieutenant with pretty good benefits. And they say they'll keep us away from the actual fighting."

"They sure as hell better. Pardon my language."

Louise let out a laugh, bringing half a smile to Sean's face. "As I was saying," she continued, "the people I know will be in my unit graduated from the same nursing school as me, and I'll be traveling with one of them from Chicago to Los Angeles. The whole unit got orders to report to March Field in Riverside, California, so I guess I'll meet the rest of them in a few days."

"Are you nervous?"

She paused a moment. "A little. But more excited than nervous, I think. The only place outside the state of Wisconsin I've been is Winona, and that hardly counts. I'm eager to see the world."

"Yeah. Me, too. But the news from other parts of the world is pretty scary sometimes," he said, his voice cracking a bit.

"Hey, why don't we write to each other? We could cheer each other up and talk about the awful Midwest winters we'll be missing. It'd be fun to hear where you get stationed and about all the kids you're meeting."

"Th-th-that would be nice," he said. He ripped a blank page from the back of his crossword puzzle book, wrote his name, service number, and current address on it, and handed it to her.

"I haven't gotten my service number yet, but I'll write you when I get settled." Louise immediately questioned her impulsive suggestion that they correspond. *You can't make friends with every fragile young soldier or sailor you meet—the hospital wards will be full of them,* she told herself.

But this is different.

"Thanks for talking with me," Sean said. "It really helped, but I don't want to be a pest. I'll work on a few easy puzzles to take my mind off things and leave you alone."

"Okay."

Louise turned again to the window. The sight of the snow-covered hills and valleys stretching for miles and miles mesmerized her, and she dozed again. At the Portage depot, several passengers collected their bags and left the train.

When the train began moving again, Louise realized that few new passengers had gotten on. No one hovered in the aisles for a vacant seat. She remembered the admonishment her classmate Anna—a year older and ten years more worldly—had given her when they made their plans to meet in Chicago: "Don't just stay in your seat the whole way from La Crosse. Visit the club car!"

She stretched her arms and stood up. "It looks as though every-one's got a seat. If you wouldn't mind saving my spot, Sean, I think I'll go use the ladies' room and then grab a beer in the club car."

He jumped to his feet, allowing her to pass. "I'd be happy to."

"Can I bring you anything to eat?"

"No, thanks. My sister packed a dozen sandwiches and three batches of cookies. I'll gladly share when you come back."

"I'll look forward to it."

Louise took several deep breaths to calm her nerves as she made her way to the club car. Though she'd been to bars frequently enough to feel comfortable in them, she'd never gone alone and could hardly afford to spend her meager savings on frivolities like drinks. But she remembered Anna's assurances, "There'll be loads of fellows dying to buy you drinks! Believe me, a blue-eyed blonde with a sweet figure like yours is gonna turn heads. All you have to do is walk in and find a seat."

She pushed open the door to the smoke-filled car and took a moment to survey the scene. Not an empty chair in sight and several groups of people—many in uniform—stood in clusters already engaged in conversations. Her resolve instantly dwindled, and she'd just turned to leave when a dark-haired man wearing a leather bomber jacket caught her by the elbow. She spun around and glanced at him warily.

"Don't you dare leave already," the man said with a smile. "It's not as crowded in here as it looks, and it'd be a cryin' shame for you to miss out on the fun." He removed his hand from her elbow and extended it. "My name's Hank Duke. What's yours?"

She felt a spark of electricity as she shook his hand and her cheeks reddened. "Louise. Louise Dietrich."

"Pleased to meet you, Louise. C'mon and let me introduce you around."

She followed as he led her halfway down the car to a bunch of servicemen gathered around two club chairs, one occupied by a young brunette woman with meticulously styled hair and the other occupied by a disheveled and obviously inebriated sailor. The brunette sized Louise up without missing a beat of the story she was telling. Hank grabbed the sailor by the upper arms and pulled him to his feet. "Time to vacate this chair, buddy. There's a lady present who needs a seat."

"Get your goddamn hands off me, asshole," the sailor mumbled and stumbled away.

"Ain't that just like a Navy man?" Hank asked the fellow

aviator standing beside him, who guffawed in response. "Louise, this is my buddy Sam and he's going to the bar to get the next round. What'll you have?"

"A beer is fine, thanks."

"We're celebrating my promotion," Hank said, "so I think something stronger than a beer is in order. How about a sidecar?"

"Um, okay."

By the time the train crossed the Wisconsin/Illinois border, having consumed two sidecar cocktails and half a club sandwich, Louise felt decidedly more relaxed. She'd laughed at what seemed like a hundred jokes and had gotten the inside scoop about what to expect if she was sent to the Pacific or the European Theater. The brunette—a civilian from Chicago named Betty—had even wished her well on her journey.

Hank ushered her back to her coach seat and, while Sean Murphy stood awkwardly in the aisle waiting for her to be seated, bade Louise farewell with a prolonged kiss. "You're a swell kid," he said. "I hope our paths cross again." He gave a small salute and was gone.

Feeling slightly tipsy and weak-kneed from the kiss, Louise slid into her spot at the window. "Sorry," she said to Sean, "I didn't realize I'd be gone so long. And I should've invited you to come along. There were kids in the club car who were no older than you. Getting served, I mean."

"It's okay."

They passed the remainder of the ride in silence. Louise promised to write and gave Sean a sisterly hug before they exited the train.

Chapter Two

Louise couldn't help staring upward as she entered the Great Hall at Union Station in Chicago. For one thing, the architecture and the sheer magnitude of the building were designed to draw eyes toward the skylights, the chandeliers, and the elaborately carved marble ceiling. For another, her friend Anna had instructed her to wait under the clock—mounted high on the wall—at the Canal Street staircase. She felt uneasy as she looked around, unable to find the appointed location. The station was crowded and intimidating, and Louise was never more aware of the sheltered, small-town life she'd led. She glanced at her watch—she was to have met Anna a half hour earlier—and a wave of panic overtook her.

Holding her purse tight to her chest and trying not to bump into anyone with her overnight bag, Louise followed a group of passengers she hoped were headed in the right direction. But as they dispersed in front of her, she was forced to stop again to get her bearings. On the verge of tears, she finally tapped a kindly-looking gray-haired gentleman on the shoulder. "Excuse me," she said, "could you point me toward the Canal Street staircase."

"Of course, my dear," he replied, turning her gently around by the elbow. "Go right, just past that second pillar. You can't miss it."

"Thank you," she murmured and hustled toward the pillar. Rounding the corner, she immediately spotted Anna at the bottom of the stairway—decked out in a stylish red wool coat and hat.

Anna had been in the Chicago area visiting relatives for the past two weeks and, judging by her outfit, had spent at least some of that time shopping. Not a conventionally pretty woman, Anna accentuated the positives: her wavy brown hair was always perfectly coiffed, her makeup was flawless, and she wore the latest fashions, which looked great on her lanky frame. Louise couldn't help feeling mousy by comparison, though she was genuinely ecstatic to see Anna's familiar face in this crowd.

She ran up to her friend and gave her a quick hug. "I'm sorry I'm late."

"I just got here myself," Anna replied. "It took forever for my grandfather to find a place to park. And for me to convince him he didn't need to see me all the way to the train."

"I'm sure he means well," Louise said. "I'd be glad if I *had* a grandfather to see me to the train."

"I suppose you're right," Anna said, looking somewhat chagrined.

Louise felt a pang of guilt for having chastised her. Then, determined to change the subject, she said, "Golly, that coat and hat are fabulous—like something out of *Vogue*! I thought you weren't bringing any winter things, though?"

"Silly, isn't it? Especially since my grandmother couldn't manage to get any ration coupons for shoes to go along with them." Anna stared down at her well-worn black pumps. "Still, she insisted—and agreed to pay the postage to ship them home if I get sent to the South Pacific."

"That's what I'm hoping for," Louise said, linking arms with her friend to walk toward the platform. "Someplace exotic that I'd never get to see otherwise. 'Course, I guess anywhere would seem pretty exotic next to Vernon County."

Anna winked. "So true!"

ANNA HAD VOLUNTEERED TO PROCURE THE TICKETS, and Louise had briefly worried they'd have to vie for seats on the long journey west. She was relieved when their California Limited porter led them to assigned spots in one of the Pullman cars. "My name is Franklin," he said as he stowed their overnight cases, "and I'll be here to serve you during your travel. Please let me know if you need any assistance."

"Thank you, Franklin," Anna replied. "The first thing we need is directions to the club car."

The black man's eyes crinkled at the corners. "Yes, ma'am," he replied. "It's the fourth car down on your right, and the dining car is right past it. Just tell me when you'd like to dine, and I'll schedule your seating."

When he left to attend to passengers down the aisle, Louise leaned over and whispered, "Franklin's so nice. I can't believe we have such good service."

Anna drew a tube of lipstick and a compact from her purse and began primping in front of the tiny mirror. "C'mon. Let's go see what the service is like in the bar."

As had been the case on the Hiawatha, they found the club car abuzz with people and only a couple of them women. Though Louise was poised to hang back, Anna pulled her toward a group of about eight sailors and asked, "Who'd like to buy us some drinks?"

The tallest of the bunch, a ruddy-faced blond standing at least six-three, staggered over and put his arms around their shoulders, sloshing beer on Louise's back. "The name's Mikey, sugar," he said, "and I most certainly will. Who're you?"

"I'm Anna and this is Louise. And thanks for the offer, Mikey, but maybe one of these other gentlemen might have an easier time navigating to the bar."

"Pardon our friend, ladies," a shorter bright-eyed redhead chimed in. "Mikey's been drinking since Philadelphia. I'm Dave."

After making introductions and discerning everyone's preferences—everyone's, that is, except Mikey's—Dave trotted off to get the next round.

And so began the four-day, three-night journey to Los Angeles.

The seats had already been converted to bunk beds, separated from others in the compartment by heavy curtains, when Louise and Anna returned to their assigned car. "Up or down?" Anna asked with slightly slurred speech.

I should volunteer to take the top bunk, Louise thought, gripping the ladder with white knuckles. But a tsunami of nausea overcame her the instant she lifted her right foot, swiftly washing away her magnanimity. "I think I'm gonna be sick," she mumbled, sinking onto her knees.

As if by magic, Franklin appeared with a metal basin in his hand. "Here, miss," he said, handing it to her and guiding her by the elbow. "Let me see you to the ladies' room."

A stout, matronly woman dressed in a chenille bathrobe buttoned to her neck came out of the restroom, scowling as Louise —whose sober self would've been mortified—pushed past her and ran into the closest stall. Using her last scintilla of willpower, Louise made it to the toilet before disgorging the several drinks and the sandwich she'd consumed that evening, utterly oblivious to Anna's arrival.

"You okay?" her friend asked from the next stall during a pause in Louise's retching.

"I'll...be okay...just gonna stay here awhile."

Anna washed up and brushed her teeth, then asked again, "You sure you're okay? I can stay here if you want."

"Just go..."

After the stomach spasms ceased, Louise sat on the small bench in the ladies' room, a cool, wet towel pressed to her face, until she felt reasonably confident about walking the length of the car.

She found Anna snoring heavily from the top bunk. Louise gave a silent prayer of thanks as she collapsed onto the lower bed and placed the basin beside her pillow. *Why'd I let Dave talk me into "just one more" drink so many times? I'm never gonna be that stupid again*, she thought as the rhythm of the rails lulled her to sleep.

LOUISE AND ANNA MADE THEIR WAY TO THE DINING CAR for the nine o'clock breakfast seating—apparently Anna had had the wherewithal to tell Franklin of their preference before retiring —grateful for the waiting carafe of steaming coffee. Louise took a tentative sip to test the temperature, then swallowed three aspirin with the next. "Remind me to stick to beer from now on, okay?" she said. "My head is killing me."

"I don't feel so good either," Anna replied, "but I stopped after my third Tom Collins."

The friends looked up as the waiter directed two more passengers to their table—a small man and the woman Louise had almost bowled over en route to the bathroom the night before. The woman recognized her. Wearing a black wool dress with a pearl-encrusted cross necklace, her gray hair pulled into a tight bun, she sat across from Louise. "I have to give you a piece of my mind, young lady," she said. "You should be ashamed of yourself, stumbling through the sleeping car like a common drunk. I found it very upsetting to watch, and it took Raymond here a long time to calm me down. Your mother would be so disappointed."

Raymond stared at his lap as though wishing he were anywhere else. "Now Sylvia," he mumbled, putting his hand atop hers. She shook it off and began looking around the dining car.

Louise's face flushed with shame, and tears stung her eyelids. She couldn't speak.

Anna's hand shook as she moved her coffee cup from her mouth to its saucer, clinking it loudly and spilling coffee in the process. "For your information, my friend and I have enlisted as army nurses and are headed off to war," she said. "Her mother is deceased, but I know she'd be nothing but proud of her daughter. And she'd sure as heck understand a little harmless over-indulgence."

Sylvia—clearly unappeased—proceeded to summon the waiter. "We need to be moved to another table," she demanded.

"I'm sorry, madam, but these are the last two available spots for this seating," the waiter replied. "There'll be room at ten o'clock if you prefer to return then?"

"Why, I never..." Sylvia began, gripping her napkin in a tight fist.

Raymond took a deep breath and said, "We'll stay, thank you." Then, turning to his wife, he added, "I believe you owe these young ladies an apology, dear. They're embarking on a journey to serve their country and have every right to kick up their heels a bit."

Her face blotchy with anger, Sylvia bounded from her chair, nearly losing her footing as the train entered a curve in the track. "I'll do nothing of the sort," she sputtered. "And I've lost my appetite." With that, she stormed down the aisle toward their seats. As fast as one can storm in a swaying train car. Anna covered her mouth to stifle a smirk, and even Louise managed to breathe easier.

The trio ordered breakfast, which Raymond insisted on buying. "It's twenty-five years ago, almost to the day, when I left to join the army," he said. "I was only eighteen and nervous as the dickens...and I would've been even more nervous if I'd known what was ahead. I can only hope things go easier for you. It should, you being ladies and all, but you never can tell. Uncle Sam's right hand doesn't always know what his left hand's doing."

Louise would remember those words many times during the course of her enlistment.

TRUE TO HER PROMISE TO HERSELF, LOUISE CONSUMED nothing more potent than beer throughout the remainder of the trip. And instead of joining Anna in the club car, she accepted Raymond's offer to sit with him in the observation car while his cranky wife napped through the New Mexico desert. He told her about his service in the Great War, but the faraway and sometimes vacant look in his eyes told Louise he was sparing her many of the awful details. That realization made her more than a little uneasy. *What have I gotten myself into?*

Chapter Three

March Field

A CONVERTED SCHOOL BUS TRANSPORTED THE TWO women and twenty-two men from Union Passenger Terminal in downtown Los Angeles to March Field—about sixty-five miles east—bouncing along the dusty highway. Almost panicky with the increasing temperature inside the bus, Louise leaned over to rest her elbow on the metal frame of the open window. "Yow!" she shrieked, yanking her arm away. "It burned me."

"And we're like sitting ducks in this rattletrap," Anna said. "Let's hope it doesn't break down or we'll get fried by this blasted sun."

The freckled young private nicknamed Red, who'd ushered them onto the bus and sat in the seat in front of them, turned around and grinned. "Not to worry, ladies," he said. "It's just around the next bend and over a bit of a rise."

A few minutes later, the bus struggled up to a vast plateau in the picturesque mountains and drove through the main gate of the sprawling base. Palm trees, manicured lawns, and vibrant tropical plants surrounded the buildings, many of Spanish Mission architectural design. "There's the hospital where you'll be working," their guide told them, pointing to a large two-story stone building. "There's the chapel and the gymnasium...and over there're the barracks...and the PX—the post exchange. You can't see the airfield or hangars from here, but they're huge."

"It's like its own city," Anna marveled.

"You've got that right," Red said. "I heard the other day that the population's up to around sixty thousand. And lemme tell you, only a small fraction of 'em are women. You're gonna have more suitors than you can imagine."

Anna beamed. Louise's stomach grew queasy. Not in the market for a suitor, she hated to face the task of turning them away. It was one thing to have a few drinks in a group setting but an entirely different matter to deal with individual men bent on romance.

At the administration building, Louise and Anna presented their enlistment papers and medical examination reports to the Women's Army Auxiliary Corps attendant wearing a name tag that read FIELDS, seated behind a heavy wooden table. She checked her clipboard. "You're in luck—only a handful of other women from your unit have arrived so you'll get a good choice of rooms in the nurses' quarters." The WAAC showed them a rudimentary floor plan of the building in question. "I'd suggest the first floor because it's cooler, and several doors down from the bathroom where it's a little quieter.

"We have our own rooms?" Louise asked incredulously.

"Uh-huh. But mind you this'll probably be the last time in your whole enlistment, so make the most of it."

Anna chose her room quickly. Louise studied the diagram more closely and selected one across the hall from her and next to a room with the name "Frankenburg" penciled on it.

"Good choices," Fields said. "Red'll be back with the bus in a few minutes to take you over there. You can unpack and wait for your CO to come by with further instructions. Her name's Captain Riley. Kind of a hardnose, I hear, but she's also supposed to be fair. Here are your passes so you can move freely around the base. You'll return to this building tomorrow to get dog tags and uniforms."

LOUISE SAT ON THE SINGLE BED IN HER SPARTAN, STUFFY room with her open suitcase beside her, staring out the window. They'd been told there'd be rigorous training before they received their overseas orders, which she found more than a little unnerving. She saw plenty of people bustling around the base, and they all looked much more physically fit and confident than her. *What if I can't do it?*

Anna walked in a few moments later, mopping her brow with her hankie. "You haven't even started unpacking?"

"I guess I was just daydreaming."

Anna took a handful of underpants from her suitcase, carried them to the dresser, and put them in the middle drawer.

As she reached back into the suitcase for some stockings, Louise spoke up. "Thanks for trying to help, Anna, but I'd rather put my things away myself. I know how I like things organized."

"Suit yourself, then," her friend said, turning to go, "but I'd get a move on if I were you. I'll be in the common area. I saw a radio and a few magazines to keep me occupied until Captain Riley shows up."

Without a word, Louise began to unpack and moved the underwear to the top drawer. *Anna means well, but I can't wait to make some new acquaintances—hopefully some who aren't so forward.*

She'd just pushed her empty suitcase under the bed when she heard a knock on the door jamb. "Yoo-hoo, I see I've got a new neighbor," said the diminutive brunette who poked her head into the room. "I'm Gladys Frankenburg, but everybody calls me Frankie."

Louise couldn't help staring at this pixie-like woman with sparkling brown eyes, a button nose, and her hair in a ponytail. "Glad to meet you. I'm Louise Dietrich. And pardon my saying so, but you don't look old enough to have graduated from nursing school...I'm sorry...I shouldn't have said that."

"Don't worry about it," Frankie said with a laugh. "Everybody says that. And I'll have you know I'll be twenty-two in May."

"I've got you beat—I'll be twenty-two in March," Louise replied. "It'll be weird celebrating so far from home. Which is La Farge, Wisconsin, by the way."

"I'm from Wisconsin, too—Janesville. I guess almost everyone assigned to the 44th General Hospital is from the Midwest. There're a couple of gals who graduated ahead of me at my school who signed up and will be in our unit, Dot Albrecht and Bertha Shoemaker. I heard they're getting in tomorrow."

"Have you met our CO yet?"

"Uh-huh."

"And?"

"And, she seems pretty much by the book. But then again, I'm not usually a rule breaker, so we'll probably get along okay. If you're done here, why don't we go to the lounge and wait for her there?"

FRANKIE, ANNA, AND LOUISE WERE SITTING ON THE sagging couch in the nurses' common area listening to the news on KFI-Los Angeles when Captain Sheila Riley appeared in the doorway. An imposing figure—tall and solid with short hair, graying at the temples—she commanded the room merely by her presence. Louise saw her first and struggled to her feet, unsure whether a salute was in order. "At ease, ladies," Riley said quietly. "You're not officially on duty yet, and we don't have much time for formalities in the nursing corps. I'm Captain Riley, your CO, and I'm guessing you're Dietrich and Krause."

Louise shook her extended hand. "Yes, ma'am, I'm Louise Dietrich."

"And I'm Anna Krause."

"Glad to have you both aboard," Riley said, "although I can see we Irish will soon be outnumbered by you Krauts. My God —'Frankenburg,' 'Krause,' and 'Dietrich' in this room alone! They'd better not send us to the European theater, or the majority of my nurses might defect."

Louise glanced toward her companions to judge their reactions, but neither appeared ruffled. Louise had felt her blood pressure skyrocket at the word "Kraut."

"Have a seat," the captain said. Without missing a beat, she reached in her jacket pocket and produced a package of cigarettes, lighting one and sinking into a chair by the window. She inhaled deeply and let out a slow stream of smoke. "I've had a long day, and it feels good to get off my feet for a minute. The 44th's doctors and I have been busy making plans for the unit, and we've gotten a full orientation of the base hospital. Tomorrow's set aside for paperwork and handing out uniforms and equipment, and you'll be starting to work the following day—eight-hour shifts, four days a week, for the foreseeable future."

"Are any of the patients battle casualties?" Frankie asked.

"Just run-of-the-mill hospital cases at this point—the kind you'd expect at a base housing about seventy thousand trainees. But who knows how far afield the evacuation chain will extend as this war goes on?"

"Will we have other assignments while we're here?" Anna asked.

"You'll have training and drills on the fifth day and two days off. Be at the admin building by 0900 tomorrow and we'll get started. Frankenburg here can show you around."

Riley stubbed out her cigarette in the amber-colored glass

ashtray on the end table, rose from the chair, and strode to the door. "By the way, you're welcome to eat at the officers' club tonight if you want, but you'll be *expected* there at 1800 hours tomorrow. They're having a dinner for the 44th's doctors and nurses." And she was gone.

Louise let out the breath she hadn't realized she'd been holding. "Didn't you hear her calling us Krauts?" she asked. "It makes my blood boil."

"I heard her," Anna said, "but I think you're overreacting. What d'you think, Frankie?"

Their new friend shrugged. "I guess time will tell."

"I hope you're right, Anna," Louise said. "One thing's crystal clear—she's not going to remember our first names."

"So I gather, Dietrich," Frankenburg said with a wink. "Let's get dressed and head to the club. I could use a little drink."

"All right," Louise said. "And maybe we can practice using military time. She lost me at '0900 hours.'"

"It's simple," Anna said as they headed down the hallway toward their rooms. "Midnight is 0000 hours, noon is 1200 hours, and our six o'clock dinner tomorrow night is at 1800 hours."

Simple for you, maybe, Louise thought. *But it will take me a while to get it through my head.*

Half an hour later, the three women joined a group of five nurses from the second floor and walked en masse to the officers' club. *Safety in numbers,* Louise thought, tamping down her jitters about being on display in the mostly male club. Frankie put her arm around her shoulder as they walked. "Relax," she said. "Most of the male officers are still on duty so we'll have a chance to get settled before the onslaught."

Frankie was right: the only people in the club were the bartender and four older gentlemen sitting at the bar, oblivious to their arrival. "Welcome, ladies," the bartender said as he dried a highball glass with a crisp white towel. "Pick a table and I'll come over in a sec to take your orders."

The women looked at each other tentatively until Anna spoke up. "How 'bout that one by the window? It's big enough for all of us."

True to her pledge, Louise ordered a beer, and Frankie and another of the nurses followed suit. The rest chose mixed drinks, though Anna announced she only intended to have one.

By the time they'd finished the first round, the women were chatting like old friends and hardly noticed that male officers were arriving in a steady stream. When someone played Glenn Miller and the Andrews Sisters' "Don't Sit Under the Apple Tree" on the jukebox, the nurses began singing along. A few moments later, two Air Corps pilots doffed their bomber jackets and came over to pull Anna and Louise to their feet to dance. Louise felt her cheeks flush but let herself be swept up in the moment. Another pilot cut in just as the song was ending. "No fair," he said. "May I please have a whole dance?"

Benny Goodman's "Jersey Bounce" was next up on the box. "Sure," she said. "This is one of my favorites."

"Mine too," he said. "By the way, I'm Jesse van den Berg, but everybody calls me Dutch."

"Pleased to meet you, Dutch. I'm Louise Dietrich...and Lord only knows what nickname I'll end up with here." She couldn't help noticing the dimple in his cheek when he smiled.

Dutch waved off three other officers who tried to cut in. He twirled and dipped her as the song came to a close, and Louise was surprised to find herself at ease in his confident arms. "May I buy you a drink, Louise?" he asked, guiding her off the dance floor by the elbow.

"Sure. A beer would be great."

"Ah, a woman after my own heart," he replied. "C'mon with me to the bar so no one else manages to spirit you away."

She glanced at the table where she and the other nurses had

been seated and realized everyone was on the dance floor. She followed him, first to the bar and then to a smaller table away from the jukebox. "So, tell me about yourself, Louise..."

Dutch's eyes never left hers as she related the abridged story of her life, and he teared up when she mentioned her parents' deaths. "Aw, I'm sorry," he said. "I can't imagine losing both my folks within such a short time...and while you were still so young."

"Thanks. I guess that's why I'm so close to my little sister Etta —her real name's Henrietta, but no one ever calls her that. She's thirteen months younger and if you can believe it, way shyer than me. She's thinking about joining the women's naval reserve."

Louise paused to take a sip of beer. "Now it's your turn. And don't omit anything." The moment the last four words left her mouth, she felt a pang of guilt. After all, she'd neglected to mention a rather important detail.

"I'm a PK—a preacher's kid, that is—from Michigan," he began. "I was an only child 'til I was fifteen and my sister came along—"

"Ahem...hope we're not interrupting anything important." They looked up to see a guy approaching their table with Anna in tow.

"Hey, Alex," Dutch said. "Louise, here, and I were just getting to know one another. What's up?"

"This is Anna," Alex said. "She and I are gonna get a table for dinner and wanted to know if you'd join us."

Louise shrugged in response to Dutch's questioning look. "Okay," he told Alex. "We'll finish our beers and join you in about half an hour."

Forty-five minutes later Louise looked at her watch. "Gee, you're so easy to talk to. The time just flies by. But I need to use the ladies' room and we told our friends we'd be there at six—0600 hours, I mean."

"No, you mean 1800 hours," he said with a laugh.

She felt her cheeks flush. "Oh, my goodness, I can't believe I goofed *that* up. Our CO just ordered us to attend a welcome dinner here tomorrow at 1800 hours, which is obviously six p.m."

"Don't worry about it—we all made those mistakes early on." As he stood to pull out her chair, a lock of blond hair fell over his forehead, and Louise had to resist the urge to brush it back.

"I have to say I'm regretting our promise to join Alex and your friend to eat," Dutch said as they walked away from their cozy table.

Louise primped in front of the ladies' room mirror a tad longer than usual. *For someone not looking to get involved, you're sure expending a lot of effort to get your lipstick just right.*

Dutch stood waiting outside the door and offered Louise his arm. Her stomach fluttered as she accepted it and allowed him to lead her into the dining room. Alex and Anna were already seated at a table with four other people, including two of the nurses Louise had come with. "We decided to wait for you kids before ordering dinner," Alex said, "and we were just about to give up on you."

Dinner was a loud and jolly affair, followed by more dancing. Louise gradually came to enjoy chatting with her many partners, though she felt a wave of relief when Dutch cut in for a slow dance shortly before last call. "May I walk you back to your quarters?" he asked.

"I promised I'd walk with Frankie—"

He raised an eyebrow. "I certainly hope Frankie is a girl."

Louise giggled. "Her real name is Gladys."

"Okay, then. May I walk *you and Gladys* home?"

"Sure."

"I understand you've got the dinner tomorrow night, but may I have a few dances with you afterward?"

"I'd like that."

. . .

When Frankie and Louise strode down the hallway to their rooms, one of the doors opened to reveal a shapely redhead wearing a baby doll nightgown. Frankie gaped, while Louise ran into the room and hugged her. "Vivian! I wondered when you'd get here."

Vivian's wavy auburn hair danced around her face as she laughed. "I did, too. The train was delayed in New Mexico—we just sat on the tracks for three hours looking out at the god-awful desert. I was afraid I'd get demerits or something for being late, but I guess the powers that be understand unpredictable rail travel."

Louise motioned for Frankie to come in. "This is Gladys Frankenburg from Janesville. Frankie, meet Vivian Vogel—from my graduating class at St. Francis Hospital nursing school."

"Gosh, I'd give anything to be as tall as you and have such gorgeous hair," Frankie said.

"Believe me, being tall isn't all it's cracked up to be," Vivian replied with a rueful smile. "Boys don't seem to like being towered over, and if one more person tries to call me 'Red' or 'Rusty,' I'm afraid I'm going to deck 'em. You should be glad you're petite."

"I don't know about that," Frankie said. "Hey, I'm gonna go back to my room and let you two catch up."

"G'night," Louise said.

"She's swell," Vivian said as Frankie closed the door behind her, then plopped on the bed and scooted over so Louise could join her. "The barracks seem fine. What about the food? And our COs?"

"Well," Louise said, "the only meal I've eaten since I got here was at the officers' club, so I can't vouch for the military food..."

"The club. How was it? Were there lots of handsome men?"

Louise giggled. "So many, in fact, that my feet are sore from dancing. I met one in particular who was really cute. He walked me home."

"Do tell."

When Vivian ran out of questions about Dutch, she asked, "And the COs?"

"Captain Sheila Riley is the nurses' CO. She came by this afternoon to meet me and Anna."

"And?"

"I don't know quite what to make of her yet."

Vivian raised an eyebrow. "What do you mean by that?"

Louise pretended not to hear the question.

Chapter Four

THE FOLLOWING DAY FRANKIE LED LOUISE, ANNA, AND Vivian to the mess hall for breakfast—eggs, hash browns, bacon, and strong coffee—and then to admin by the appointed time.

The women all groaned at the sight of the uniforms being issued: light blue shirts and skirts, dark blue jackets and caps, maroon ties, brown shoes, and gray gloves.

"Good Lord," Louise said when she tried hers on, "I feel like a clown in this getup. Our patients are going to laugh themselves silly when we walk in."

"I hear a lot of the boys stay in the hospital here for two or three months," Frankie said, "so they deserve some laughs—even at our expense."

"Easy for you to say," Louise said. "The uniform looks so cute on you nobody'll even think it's funny."

They stood in line to have their dog tags made, chatting amiably. But when Louise's were finished and she placed the chain bearing her tags over her head, she couldn't help but shiver.

"You okay?" Anna asked her.

"I guess so. It just hit me when I put these things on," she said, fingering the metal tags, "that this is serious business. They use them to identify dead soldiers, after all."

"I know what you mean. Those recruiters at St. Francis Hospital played down the danger and hooked us with all their flag-waving and 'see the world' talk. But one of the guys I was dancing with last night told me his sister was a Navy nurse stationed in the Philippines when the Japanese attacked there the day after Pearl Harbor."

Louise wrinkled her brow. "Was she hurt?"

"Apparently not then," Anna said with a sigh. "But she was transferred to Corregidor with 'Dugout Doug' MacArthur before he evacuated, and it fell to the Japanese last year. The Navy told the family that she's missing in action. She could be a POW or she could be dead. A nurse, for heaven's sake—supposedly stationed far from harm's way."

Louise shivered again.

Frankie walked up to them, oblivious to the nature of their discussion. "Hey, you two," she said, "they've posted our first duty schedule. Let's go have a look."

About twenty nurses swarmed a bulletin board, vying for the perfect view of the list. Frankie, too short to see over the shoulders of her peers, walked around the group and ducked in front of the board. "Louise," she called over her shoulder, "you and I drew the day shift for the first three weeks."

"What about me?" Anna asked.

Frankie looked again. "You're on days, too," she said.

Vivian Vogel was assigned the evening shift.

When they got back to the barracks and neared their rooms, Frankie let out a whoop. "Glad you finally made it," she called to two women lugging suitcases down the hall. They stopped in their tracks and rushed over.

Frankie hugged them, then turned to her new friends. "These are the folks I was telling you about, Dorothy Albrecht and Bertha

Shoemaker, but they go by Dot and Shoe. Dot, Shoe—meet Louise Dietrich, Anna Krause, and Vivian Vogel."

Everyone helped carry the newcomers' luggage to their adjacent rooms, and all but Anna—who begged off with a headache—chatted in the hallway. "I told you Dot looks like Doris Day, didn't I?" Frankie said to Louise and Vivian. "What do you think?"

"Oh, stop it, Frankie," Dot said before the others could respond. "You say that just 'cause I'm blonde and look pretty wholesome. That's where the resemblance ends, and heaven knows I can't sing."

"Who'd you tell them *I* looked like?" Shoe asked Frankie, jostling her elbow.

"Uh...you don't really resemble anyone famous," Frankie replied, clearly flummoxed.

In fact, Shoe *was* somewhat nondescript. Short and wiry, with light brown hair, hazel eyes, and a face full of freckles, her most striking feature was her genuine smile. Louise liked her immediately.

"Well, we'd better unpack and head over to get checked in," Dot said. "I heard we're supposed to be shipshape and at dinner by six."

"I think you only have to be 'shipshape' in the Navy," Vivian teased, "but they told us full dress uniform."

"And wait'll you see the uniforms," Louise added. "They're not the most flattering things someone could've come up with."

"Remind me why we signed up again," Shoe said to Frankie.

MOST OF THE 44TH'S THIRTY-FOUR NURSES AND SEVERAL physicians were present and in uniform for the reception dinner at the officers' club that evening. Some had worked together before. During dessert their commanding officer, Lt. Colonel Frank Weston, a convivial man and well-respected doctor from the University of

Wisconsin, gave a rousing speech geared toward team building. Afterward he worked the room like a bride at her wedding, introducing himself and personally welcoming each member of the unit. "We'll probably be here for a few months to staff the hospital until they decide where to send us," he said. "Use this time to get to know each other and figure out how we can work best with one another. My door will always be open and I'll welcome your suggestions."

His voice took Louise back to her childhood, when her father was alive to give his infrequent but sound advice. "I like him," she whispered to her tablemates after the CO moved on to the next. "He reminds me a little of my dad."

"Oh, for crying out loud," Anna said with half a sneer, "we need a decisive commander, not a father. This guy probably doesn't have a clue how to run a unit. Otherwise, why would he ask us for suggestions?"

"Aw, give the man a chance," said Dot, one of the older graduates of Frankie's nursing school. "The medical corps is growing by leaps and bounds—out of necessity—and there can't be that many docs who have military experience."

"I agree," Frankie said. "And I think he's kinda handsome—"

"Talking about me, Frankie?" Dutch van der Berg asked, putting his hand on Louise's shoulder.

"Uh...no," Frankie said, flustered. "But I guess my comment *could* apply to you, too."

"I gotta stop fishing for compliments. It's unseemly," Dutch said, then turned to Louise. "Lt. Dietrich, may I have the pleasure of a dance or two?"

She glanced at the surrounding tables and realized none of the other nurses were leaving their seats. "I'd like to, but I'm not sure our reception's over yet."

Dot turned to the table behind them where Captain Riley was seated—clearly disengaged from the conversations around her. "Excuse me, Captain," she said, "are we free to get up and socialize with folks from outside our unit now?"

A look of surprise flashed across Riley's face and she, too, looked around the room. "Feel free," she said. "Dinner's over."

Dot swung back to the table. "Cap'n says it's okay, Louise," she chirped, clearly pleased with herself.

"But you'd better send some of your fellow aviators over here for the rest of us, Dutch!" Anna said. Louise cringed.

"Yes, ma'am," Dutch replied, his expression deadpan.

En route to the dance floor, the couple detoured toward the bar where several other pilots from Dutch's unit stood talking. "There're some pretty young nurses in the dining room who would love to shake a leg," he told them. "Their reception's over, and Lt. Dietrich here would prefer not to be the only lady on the dance floor."

Louise sensed the color rising up her throat and bowed her head shyly. But when Dutch put his arm around her shoulder and whispered, "Sorry to put you on the spot, honey," her trepidations melted away.

Dutch led her flawlessly to Glenn Miller's "I've Got a Gal in Kalamazoo," and Louise felt as though she was dancing on a cloud. When he held her more closely to the slower Bing Crosby song, "I Don't Want to Walk Without You," she drank in the scent of his Old Spice cologne and wished it would never end.

It did, of course. "I hate to let you go," he said, "but I see my friend Alex sitting by himself, and I promised him I'd introduce him to a friend of yours."

"He's not fond of Anna?" Louise asked, remembering the two had been paired at dinner the evening before.

Dutch shook his head. "Not so much. But Gladys Frankenburg seemed awfully nice when we walked home last night and I think they might hit it off."

Louise grinned. "I think so, too," she said, surveying the room. "She's over near the piano dancing with that really tall guy."

"I see her. I'll go cut in. You get Alex and bring him over to us, then we'll switch partners."

Chuckling and feeling not one iota of self-consciousness, Louise approached Alex's barstool and grabbed him by the hand. "C'mon. There's somebody you've just *got* to meet."

As predicted, Frankie and Alex seemed immediately smitten. After several more songs, Dutch and Louise coaxed them to a four-top table for drinks. But when Bing Crosby began crooning "Moonlight Becomes You" and Frankie cried, "Oh, I love this song!" they were off again.

Dutch beamed. "Looks like we did good."

"Y'know I love this song, too," Louise said, surprising herself at being so forthright.

"Well then, let's not let it go to waste."

Chapter Five

Louise and Frankie were assigned together on the base hospital's surgical ward and reported to the charge nurse, Captain Callahan, to begin their first shift. The stocky middle-aged woman with thick ankles and peroxide-blond hair, invited them into her small cubicle of an office and motioned them to the two olive-drab folding chairs opposite her desk. "Coffee?" she asked.

The young nurses nodded and watched as Callahan swiveled toward the table behind her and filled two mugs from an electric Sunbeam Coffeemaster. "My mom's been bugging my dad to buy her one of those since it was invented," Frankie said.

Callahan winked and replied, "Life is too short to drink bad coffee and, believe me, you'll get plenty of that in the army. I'm a lifer, and I can probably count the good cups of coffee I've gotten in a mess hall on one hand."

They sipped in silence for a few moments. *This* is *good*, Louise thought.

"Let's drink up," Callahan said. She drained her mug in two large gulps, stood, and moved toward the door. "I want to show you around before the doctors begin their morning rounds."

Louise's coffee was too hot to follow suit. She waited until the charge nurse stepped into the hallway and set her mug on the desk. Frankie did the same.

"You two will attend to the fifty patients on this floor and the one above it," Callahan said as she led them into a long, narrow dormitory containing about sixty beds. To a man, the waking patients stared at the young nurses, and several let out catcalls.

Louise felt her cheeks flush, and Frankie looked equally uncomfortable. "Boys!" Callahan yelled, albeit with a smile. "Hold it down, or they might be tempted to be late with your pain pills."

After a tour of the ward and its supply closets and cabinets, the captain showed them the staff break room and where to stow their sack lunches. Two men, probably in their mid-twenties and dressed in orderly uniforms, stood chatting. "Lieutenants Dietrich, Frankenburg," Callahan said, "meet your ward boys, Corporals Gillespie and Thompson."

The four exchanged glances before Callahan jerked her head in the direction of the door. "They're heading back right now to finish toileting the patients," she said. Without a word of acknowledgment, the two orderlies hightailed it out of the break room.

Louise could hear them grumbling under their breath in the hallway and glanced at Captain Callahan to see if she'd heard it as well.

"Close the door, please, Lieutenant Dietrich," the captain said. "I might as well alert you to the problem right away." Then she paused and stared out the window for what felt to Frankie and Louise like an eternity.

Does she want us to ask what the problem is? Louise wondered.

Finally, Callahan sighed and said, "As you probably know, since Pearl Harbor, the Army Medical Department has been gearing up for war on so many fronts. They've established training programs for medical corpsmen who'll be on the battlefields with our soldiers. Gillespie and Thompson are recent graduates and they're itching to get into the action. They'll operate with quite a bit of autonomy in the field and probably be called 'Doc.'

"Instead, they find themselves here—emptying bedpans, changing diapers, and cleaning vomit from the floors. The worst of it is, they have to take orders from the nurses who all outrank them and are virtually all women."

"I guess I can see why they'd be a little disgruntled," Frankie said.

"Nevertheless," Callahan replied, "they're in the Army and there's a chain of command for a reason. I don't want you two to tolerate any insubordination from them. Or even any insolence. And whatever you do, don't do their work for them. They're here to assist *you*."

Thankfully, Captain Riley and two doctors—Captains Connelly and Edwards, who Louise and Frankie had met at the reception—showed up to do rounds, and the discussion of the orderlies' attitude ended.

Since Connelly, Edwards, and Riley were already familiar with the hospital, Captain Callahan excused herself. "I've got to attend to a patient in the isolation unit," she said. "If you need me for any reason, send one of the ward boys to get me."

She was gone before anyone had time to respond.

"Callahan runs a good hospital," Connelly said, "though it's a little too regimented for my taste." Then, turning to Captain Riley, he said, "Sheila, until we learn all the rules, please let us newcomers know if we're breaking protocol."

Riley gave a curt nod in return.

I don't think she likes being called by her first name, Louise thought, *even though they're the same rank.*

The doctors made a special point to include Louise and Frankie in their discussions as they checked on patients. The orderlies were conveniently on the opposite side of the dormitory during the rounds.

When the doctors and nurses stopped at one bed, they found

the patient—a twenty-one-year-old soldier recovering from surgery for a ruptured appendix—writhing in his sleep. Connelly put the back of his hand to the soldier's forehead, but he didn't awaken. "I'm guessing his temperature's over 102. Corporal Gillespie," he called to the closest orderly. "Come here a minute, please."

Gillespie joined the group somewhat tentatively.

"Any idea how long he's been like this?" Connelly asked him.

"No, sir," the corporal replied. "I emptied his catheter bag about half an hour ago and he seemed to be sleeping peacefully."

"Thank you, Corporal," Connelly said. "Sheila, please bring me a three-milliliter syringe of Pentothal. We'll give it to the patient in small doses until he's calm enough to examine."

Captain Riley turned to go. "Dietrich and Frankenberg, come with me so I can show you the procedure for dispensing medications," she said.

By the time the nurses returned with the injection, Gillespie had gotten a basin of water and was wiping the patient's brow with a wet cloth. "It's good he's already got an IV," Connelly said. "I'd hate to have to start one with him squirming around."

The first injection into the IV failed to calm the patient, but the second one did the trick. The gathered staff breathed a collective sigh of relief. Gillespie helped the nurses turn the patient on his side to take a rectal temperature. "Uh, 103.2," Louise said as she removed the thermometer.

"Let's increase the sulfa dosage to treat possible escalation of infection and give him a shot of morphine in case the writhing was from pain," Connelly said.

"And let's hope we don't have to open him up again," Captain Edwards said.

The rest of the rounds went routinely. The patients stared at the young nurses but, perhaps due to the presence of two male doctors, refrained from inappropriate comments or gestures.

After their CO and the doctors left the ward, Louise whispered to her friend, "How do you think we should approach Gillespie and Thompson?"

Frankie shrugged. "They seemed fine with the docs," she said, sotto voce. "Maybe they just get peevish with Captain Callahan."

"Let's hope."

As the morning progressed, though, the women couldn't help noticing the orderlies' icy looks and how they kept their distance.

Around noon, one of the patients, Private Hunter, who was one week post gall bladder surgery and still in considerable pain, summoned Louise. "Excuse me, Lieutenant," he said, "but I really need to pee and I can hardly sit up, much less walk to the latrine."

Louise replied, "You're not supposed to get out of bed. I'll have one of the corpsmen bring over a portable urinal."

She took a white enamel urinal down from a shelf and approached Thompson. "Corporal, would you please take this to the patient in bed sixteen?" she asked in the politest tone she could muster.

"I was on my way to take my lunch break," he replied and turned to walk away.

Louise felt her hands clench. "The patient shouldn't have to wait on your account," she said. "Feel free to have your lunch *after* you attend to him—that is, as long as Corporal Gillespie will be on the floor in case we need help with something."

When Thompson spun around to face her, she momentarily feared he would slap her. With reddened cheeks and his eyes ablaze, he said, "You're trying to tell me Gillespie and I can't eat together?"

Swallowing the bile rising in her throat, Louise replied, "That's exactly what I'm telling you."

"No one else has ever told us that."

Louise glared at him. "Well, *I'm* telling you now. We can revisit the issue after Lt. Frankenburg and I become familiar with the ward and our duties here," she said. "And after you both show us your willingness to cooperate."

Thompson grabbed the urinal and stormed toward Private Hunter.

"And don't you *dare* take this out on the patient," she called after him.

Louise's knees felt rubbery, and she struggled to walk toward Frankie without grabbing the furniture for support.

"What's the matter?" Frankie asked her. "You're white as the sheets on these beds."

Louise took her friend by the elbow, steered her outside earshot of any patients, and summarized the kerfuffle.

"Earlier you asked how we should approach the corpsmen. I guess you decided," Frankie said, with a laugh.

"It's not funny."

"I know. And I'm proud of you for taking a stand. It would've come to something like this eventually—and Captain Callahan told us not to take any of their guff."

"Where's Gillespie?" Louise asked.

"He finished helping me bathe a patient and said he was going to eat lunch."

"Did he ask if it was okay with you?"

Frankie shook her head.

"Then I'd better go tell him our new rule before he comes looking for his cohort," Louise said, clearly dreading the task.

"Maybe it'd go over better if you and I agreed not to take our lunch breaks at the same time," Frankie suggested.

With considerable apprehension, Louise went into the break room, grabbed her lunch from the refrigerator, and took the seat directly across the table from Gillespie. "Mind if I join you?"

"Uh…Thompson usually sits there," he said, craning his neck to look for his partner.

"I understand," Louise said, "but Lt. Frankenburg and I are just learning the ropes of this particular hospital and unit, and we decided that while we're on duty at least one of us—assisted by at least one of you—should be on the ward at all times. Meaning we'll need to take turns eating lunch." She unwrapped and took a bite of the egg salad sandwich the mess hall cooks had prepared earlier that morning, then paused for his response.

Silence.

I can out-wait him, she told herself and took another bite.

"This isn't fair," he sputtered. "And you're just trying to pull rank on us."

Louise sighed. "I know it's not *fair*," she said. "I've only been in the Army for a couple of days and I can already see lots of unfairness." She thought she noticed Gillespie's expression softening a bit as she spoke. "You and Corporal Thompson trained hard to become medics and to do important work, yet you're stuck here doing the menial tasks we *ladies* order you to do. And to top it off, the charge nurse refers to you as 'boys.' That would sure irk me."

The corpsman's anger had dissipated entirely by the time she finished. In fact, he looked like he might cry. *These guys are as emotionally discombobulated as we are*, Louise suddenly realized.

She scooped up an errant glob of egg salad with a fork and put it into her mouth, giving him a moment to collect his thoughts.

"Okay," he finally said. "I can live with your new rule for a while."

"Can you also get Corporal Thompson to understand?"

"Probably."

Louise reached across the table to shake on their agreement.

"One more thing," Gillespie said. "Could we keep Captain Callahan out of this? She's already got a list of beefs with us, and I wouldn't be surprised if she's planning some sort of disciplinary action."

"Sure. But you may be surprised to know she understands more than you think about the unfairness you're experiencing."

He shook his head. "I doubt that."

During the remainder of their lunch break the two made

typical small talk, and—much to the astonishment of their coworkers—they returned to the ward smiling.

ON THE WAY BACK TO THE BARRACKS AFTER THEIR shift, Louise told Frankie more about her talk with Corporal Gillespie.

"I'm really impressed with how you dealt with the situation—especially calling out Thompson," Frankie said. "I wouldn't have had the gumption."

"I usually wouldn't either, but he got me so damn mad. Especially because the poor patient was the one who'd suffer if Thompson didn't do as I asked."

"Well, whatever you told them certainly seemed to resolve things," Frankie said. "Both corpsmen helped me all afternoon and I didn't even have to ask them to."

"Same with me."

THE FIRST THREE WEEKS AT THE AIRBASE PASSED quickly for Louise. She and the other nurses learned to salute, march, and count cadence, though never quite as crisply as the WAACs who were stationed there. On days off from the hospital, they did calisthenics and drills in the hot sun—and Louise felt proud she was able to keep up with the routines. They had dental appointments to ensure their teeth were in good condition. They received a series of vaccinations—often painful—to prevent diseases not common in the States, such as cholera, plague, typhus, and yellow fever. They became used to being called by their last names.

The day shifts at the hospital were busy enough to make time fly by for Louise, but she knew that the opposite was true for the patients; many were just kids far away from home. "I'm gonna ask my sister to write to a couple of them," she told Anna one day. "They get a boost every time they get mail."

"Don't we all?" her friend replied.

"That's true," Louise said. "And if I wrote more frequently myself, maybe I'd get a letter now and again."

Louise's social calendar left little time for correspondence. She'd gone out virtually every night with "her Dutchman." Though she'd acquiesced to a few dates with other fellows—mostly to convince herself she wasn't serious about Dutch—none compared to those with him.

He'd take her to the officers' club for dinner and dancing, often with Frankie and Alex or with Anna and her new beau, Tim, a pilot she'd known in Wisconsin and reconnected with at March Field. Sometimes they'd borrow a jeep and go off-post to a Mexican cantina in Riverside, with cheap drinks and a festive atmosphere.

The group dates were fun and nonthreatening, but Louise's favorite times were on the dance floor, when Dutch held her in his arms. "You and Dutch look so happy together," Frankie said to her in the ladies' room one evening.

"He's great," Louise replied, "but I'm not looking for a serious boyfriend."

Frankie raised an eyebrow. "You could've fooled me."

Though she wouldn't admit it aloud, Louise found the warmth of Dutch's touch intoxicating, an entirely new experience for her.

THE REALITY THAT THE WORLD WAS AT WAR OFTEN sabotaged Louise's elation at having escaped her provincial past and its harsh weather. After mail call one afternoon, Frankie found her sobbing in her room, an open letter in hand. Frankie sat next to her on the bed and gave her a hug. "What's wrong?"

Louise took several moments to catch her breath before

responding. "My aunt wrote to tell me that one of our neighbors' boys was killed in North Africa. He was such a cute kid...I used to babysit him and his little brother when I was thirteen and they were nine and seven."

"I'm sorry."

"It seems impossible that he was old enough to serve. But he enlisted before finishing high school. What a waste. And what a hateful war!"

Chapter Six

Assigned to work nights on the surgical ward, Louise's second three-week duty rotation felt like a prison sentence. She tried to look on the bright side: The work wasn't difficult since most of the patients slept during her shift. As the ward's ranking officer on duty, she was her own boss. And she also had two good corpsmen working with her—Quakers who, as conscientious objectors, had become medics rather than combat personnel.

But the downside to the schedule was huge: Louise and her Dutchman rarely found time to be together. The nights, which had always seemed to fly by while in his company, now dragged mercilessly.

Around two o'clock one morning, a patient went into convulsions with a high fever. Alarmed by the man's flailing and gray coloring, Louise felt certain his condition warranted summoning the on-call physician. Matthew, the older of her two orderlies, cautioned otherwise. "You know how the docs hate being disturbed for situations they think we can handle ourselves," he said. "My younger brother suffered from febrile seizures as a kid, and they usually passed relatively quickly. Let's try cooling him down first and see what happens."

"All right," Louise said. "You two make sure he doesn't fall out of bed. Dr. Connolly will be doing his rounds in about half an hour anyway, and hopefully things will be under control by then."

As she hurried to get a basin and some cold water, Louise couldn't help questioning her decision. *What if it's something other than a seizure? What am I doing listening to a medic who's had even less training than me? This kid could die.*

The patient stopped seizing after a few applications of cool cloths to his neck and brow. Louise, however, still felt uneasy when Captain Connolly arrived on the ward. "This man spiked a fever and went into convulsions about thirty minutes ago," she told him. "He seems stable now that we have him cooled down, but I'm not sure if there's something else we should be doing. Or if we should have called you right away?"

Connolly placed a hand on her shoulder and gave it a quick squeeze. "I know some of the doctors get annoyed when they're called to the wards for situations like this. I don't feel that way, and I'm happy to come running if you have questions. But on the other hand, I have confidence that you can handle things. This war will teach us to trust our own judgment sometimes, even if it's uncomfortable."

Louise looked down at her feet.

In the end, the doctor ordered more blood tests to see whether the patient had developed a post-surgical infection. And he recommended Louise and her orderlies take turns sitting at bedside to monitor his temperature and vitals.

The remainder of the shift was uneventful but nevertheless edgy. Bone-tired, Louise trudged away from the hospital looking forward to a few hours of restful solitude.

"Hey, gorgeous."

She startled as a man stood up from a bench in front of her barracks.

"Got time for a cup of coffee?"

"Dutch. What are you doing here?"

"Well, there are a few things I need to talk with you about," he said as he enveloped her in his arms. "So, I used my powers of persuasion and got someone to cover my shift for a bit."

"You know I always have time for you," she replied, despite her fatigue.

"Great, then let's head over to the club where we can have some privacy."

Once settled with coffee mugs in front of them, Louise finally noticed the sinking feeling in her stomach. "What did you need to talk to me about? I'm sensing it's not great news."

Dutch lowered his gaze. "Well, it's not. I got orders yesterday for six weeks of desert maneuvers in Palmdale—about eighty-five miles northwest of here. I leave in three days."

Louise's heart leaped into her throat, and she couldn't speak for a moment. "I won't see you for six whole weeks?"

"'Fraid not."

She blinked back tears. "And wouldn't you know I'm stuck on nights for five more days."

Dutch covered her hand in his and began stroking it with his thumb. "Well, I've made arrangements for a great farewell celebration, and we just need a few things to fall into place. Do you think you could get someone to cover your shift the day after tomorrow?"

"I'll sure as heck try."

With some fancy maneuvering, Louise managed to get someone to work for her. As instructed, at three o'clock in the afternoon two days later, she stood in front of the barracks wearing her best party dress...with her toothbrush and a nightgown tucked in her purse.

She gawked as a gleaming maroon convertible screeched to a

halt in front of her and Dutch hopped out. "Your chariot awaits, m'lady," he said as he extended his arm. "We've got plenty of gas ration stamps and the rental's good for twenty-four hours."

He helped her into the passenger seat and nodded to the back where a couple sat snuggled next to each other. "This is my partner, Lieutenant Dan Smith, and his lovely wife Martha."

"Very pleased to meet you," Louise said as she turned toward the pretty woman in a yellow silk scarf. *Maybe this was a mistake? These people are so sophisticated—she looks like something out of* Mademoiselle *and I'm something out of* Farm Journal.

"You too," Martha said, reaching over to clutch Louise's hand and immediately putting her at ease. "Trust me, these fellas are going to show us a grand time."

The sixty-five-mile trip to Los Angeles took longer than Louise would have expected. There were stops along the way for wildflower picking—"You gals can't walk into a restaurant without posies in your hair," Dutch insisted—and beers at a picturesque roadside cantina.

The foursome pulled up to the valet stand at Rodeo Drive's Romanoff Restaurant just in time for their six o'clock reservation.

"Oh, my gosh," Louise whispered to Martha as the maître d' led them to their booth, "I feel *so* underdressed."

"Relax," her new friend replied. "Everyone's so busy looking for movie stars that they wouldn't notice if we were wearing potato sacks."

When the waiter arrived with the cocktail menu and wine list, Dutch nonchalantly passed them off to Dan. "Lieutenant Smith is an East Coast blue blood," he told Louise. "If you girls don't mind, we'll let him order for us." The women bobbed their heads in unison.

"And we'll count on you to tell us which silverware to use when, dear," Martha added with a wink.

Never an adventurous eater, Louise took a deep breath and leaned back against the padded banquette. *Try everything and enjoy it,* she told herself. *Opportunities like this don't come every day.*

Dan ordered a round of martinis and three different appetizers to share: Oysters Rockefeller, shrimp cocktail, and fresh cracked crab. Next, he selected onion soup gratinee and a smooth white wine.

"I want you each to order your own salad and entree," he said when they'd finished, "but I'll choose a good wine to go with it."

"Good heavens," Martha said. "I'm not sure I can eat another bite."

"Me either," Louise echoed. "The soup was delicious but so rich."

Dutch chuckled. "You'll need plenty of nourishment for all the dancing we intend to do," he said.

"I'll tell the waiter to hold our dinners for a bit," Dan said. "We're in no hurry."

Louise and Dutch pored over the menu and finally selected Caesar salad and Chateaubriand for two.

"Excellent choices," Dan declared. "May I suggest the zucchini niçoise as your vegetable and a Cabernet to accompany them?"

"Whatever you say..." Dutch replied.

They finished the meal with coffee and peach flambe, ignited by their waiter at tableside, served with vanilla ice cream. "My sister will die of jealousy when I write to tell her about this meal," Louise said, dabbing the corner of her mouth and setting aside her napkin.

"She'll be even more jealous when you tell her who was just seated at the table in the corner," whispered Martha.

"Who?" her companions asked in unison as they turned to look.

"None other than Lana Turner," Martha replied, "but stop staring."

"Can this evening get any better?" Louise asked.

Dutch chuckled and put his arm around her. "I believe it can, my dear."

Martha turned toward Dan and raised an eyebrow. "I've been sworn to secrecy," he replied.

LOUISE—STILL SLIGHTLY TIPSY AND GIDDY FROM THE thrill of seeing a film star—became dumbstruck when she saw their next stop: the Hollywood Palladium. Even the more worldly Martha gaped in disbelief. The massive art deco ballroom that had opened two and a half years earlier on the original site of the Paramount studio lot was easily recognizable to any casual reader of movie magazines. And the marquee boasting Glen Gray and the Casa Loma Orchestra caused the women to squeal with delight.

"This is the best date imaginable," Louise told Dutch as he opened the car door to help her out.

He kissed her cheek. "Well, I hope so. I certainly don't want you to forget me when I'm up there flying over the desert."

"There's no chance of that," she said, feeling a flush move up her throat.

The electric atmosphere inside the ballroom—large enough to accommodate three thousand couples at a time—would revive even the near-dead. The foursome was immediately caught up in it.

"C'mon," Martha shouted, leading her husband to the floor.

Dutch watched in amusement while Louise stood still, savoring the scene. When she began swaying to the mellow strains of Gray's saxophone, he took her elbow. "Ready?" he mouthed.

"You bet."

Much to Louise's amazement and thrill, two of the orchestra's fifteen-minute sets were broadcast nationally over the radio. "Gee," she said wistfully to Dutch during the first one, "I sure hope Etta happens to be listening tonight. She'll be so excited when I write to tell her about it."

When the orchestra finished at one in the morning with the melancholy "Don't Get Around Much Anymore," almost all of the dancers continued swaying. Dutch pulled Louise close and nuzzled her neck. "I don't know about you, but I couldn't bear to head back to the base right now," he said. "Are you still all right with spending the night?"

THE SEVERAL WHITEWASHED COTTAGES IN THE TOURIST court, nestled among a grove of orange trees, gave off a charming air. Dutch squeezed Louise's hand as he parked in front of the VACANCY sign. She noticed his fingers trembling as he unlocked the door to the two-bedroom, one-bath unit.

"You two pick your room," Martha said to Louise and Dutch as she rushed ahead to use the bathroom.

Louise peeked in the doorways and realized both bedrooms looked identical—and each was appointed with only a double bed. Dutch extended his arm to lead her to the one on the left and gently closed the door behind them.

She nervously sat on the side of the bed, and he eased down beside her. "We can take turns in the bathroom when they're done. And if you weren't able to fit a nightie in your purse," he said with a half smile, "I'll be happy to lend you my shirt."

"I brought one." *Though Vivian looks like a goddess in the baby doll gown I borrowed from her, I'm gonna feel like a little girl playing dress-up in it. What on earth was I thinking?*

"Want to go first?" Dutch asked when Dan knocked on their door to say the bathroom was free.

"No...you go."

Five minutes later he returned to the room wearing an undershirt and shorts, his dress shirt and pants draped across his arm, and Louise stood on weak knees to take her turn.

Shivering, she washed up quickly, brushed her teeth, and donned the pink chiffon gown. Feeling naked, she practically ran the several steps from the bathroom to the bedroom but took a deep breath and opened the door slowly.

Dutch, lying with his back against the headboard, stared unabashedly when she walked in. "My stars, you are beautiful," he said.

Her nervousness—and all conscious thought—melted away when he took her in his arms.

Chapter Seven

THE TWO COUPLES STOPPED FOR A HUGE BREAKFAST AND a bit of souvenir shopping before hitting the road the next morning. Louise bought picture postcards of the Palladium and Romanoff's to send to her sister and aunt, while Dutch browsed in a different area of the shop. When they were seated in the car, he handed Louise a small gift bag.

"What's this?" she asked.

"Open it and find out."

Louise took out a tissue paper bundle and carefully unwrapped a bright orange headscarf with a map of Hollywood printed on it. Speechless, she held it up for their friends to see.

"Good heavens, man," Dan said from the back seat. "You couldn't find anything more garish?"

Louise felt her cheeks redden. Dutch looked crestfallen. Martha jabbed her husband in the ribs. "Hush, you ill-mannered snob," she said. "It's a souvenir, not a fashion statement. And I think it's sweet."

"I do, too," Louise said, leaning over to hug her date. "Thank you, Dutch. I intend to wear it the whole way back to the base and cherish it forever."

The awkward moment passed quickly, but so did the bitter-sweet drive back to March Field. Dutch dropped the Smiths off first, then held her hand as he took a circuitous route to the nurses' barracks. "Sorry we don't have time to get a coffee or a Coke," he said, glancing at his watch. "The car's due back in half an hour."

Louise looked at her lap. "That's okay. I need to get ready for my shift."

He got out, opened her car door, and gave her a lingering kiss. "Here's looking at you, kid," he said, then turned to go.

Louise couldn't help giggling. "You're *far* better looking than Humphrey Bogart," she replied.

"And probably a much better kisser."

"See you in six weeks," she said, beaming as she walked up the front steps.

TEN DAYS AFTER DUTCH'S DEPARTURE, FRANKIE, WHO'D just finished her first week on the night shift, and Louise, who had a day off, were in the mess hall for breakfast. "It's *awful* not being able to see Alex every night," Frankie wailed. Then, noticing the crestfallen expression Louise had been unable to hide, her friend added, "Oh, gosh...I'm sorry. It's got to be much worse with Dutch all the way up at Palmdale. At least Alex and I can sneak out and see one another every so often...."

"It's okay," Louise replied. "We write to each other every day. It feels like we're still connected—at least to me."

"He's crazy about you. Alex says all he ever talks about is you. And Lt. Smith's wife Martha told me she's sure he will ask you to marry him."

Louise beamed. "In one letter he asked me how I'd feel about being an aviator's wife."

Frankie squeezed her hand. "You see?"

.   .   .

AROUND TWO O'CLOCK THE NEXT AFTERNOON, WHILE Louise was checking a young man's blood pressure, Frankie came to her ward and stood in an aisle. Louise gestured she'd be done in a minute and hurriedly finished her task.

"What are you doing here? You look like you've seen a ghost."

"Alex just sent me a message that a bomber from Palmdale crashed and the whole crew was killed. We don't know the names yet—"

Louise's knees buckled, and her friend caught her before she could fall. "Oh, dear God! Please don't let it be Dutch."

"C'mon. Let's go sit in the office for a few minutes."

Louise meekly followed Frankie to the small but secluded office and collapsed onto a chair. "I'll go find the captain," Frankie said, moving toward the door.

"No," Louise replied, bolting from the chair. "I don't want her involved."

"Why on earth not?"

"I just don't. And we're likely to get news sooner here than at the barracks."

"Whatever you say, but let me know if you change your mind."

Louise finished her shift in a stupor, grateful to the ward man who gently corrected her when she went to change the dressing of an unconscious patient whose dressing she'd changed five minutes earlier, and even more grateful that no new patients were admitted.

Frankie met Louise outside the hospital and hugged her close. "There's nothing to report," she quickly announced. "I just didn't want you to walk back to the barracks alone."

Louise nodded her thanks.

When they'd gone a few steps, a man grabbed Frankie by the arm from behind, startling the women, and Frankie shrieked.

"Didn't mean to scare you," Alex said breathlessly, "but I couldn't wait to tell you that Dutch wasn't in the plane that crashed."

Louise threw her arms around him.

"That's the best news I've heard all day. And I don't mind that you scared the bejesus out of us." *That three hours' worth of panic felt like an eternity,* she thought. *How on earth do pilots' wives and girlfriends deal with it when they're actually in* combat?

The trio linked arms and skipped back toward the barracks, laughing uproariously. An M.P. jeep drove past them. "Hold it down, please," the driver said. "This is a hospital zone."

IN HER ROOM THAT NIGHT, LOUISE TRIED BUT COULDN'T sleep. She reluctantly got up, threw on her robe and slippers, and trudged to the lounge area, carrying her box of stationery and pen.

After several deep breaths and five or six silent pep talks, she began to write the letter she'd been postponing...to her fiancé, Joseph.

Through her tears, she scrawled, "I shouldn't have accepted the ring, because I don't love you enough to marry you. I didn't have the heart to turn down your proposal, and I convinced myself that it would be alright. I believed it for a while, too. I never meant to hurt you, but thought you should know before we both ship out overseas. I am so, so sorry..."

Louise didn't hear Vivian enter the lounge until the woman sat beside her on the couch.

"Hey, what's wrong, sweetie?" Vivian asked, putting her arm around Louise's trembling shoulder.

"I'm such a coward..."

"Well, I doubt that."

"No, seriously," Louise said, shaking her head furiously. "I never told you—in fact I never told *anyone* but Etta. But you remember my friend Joey? You met him when he visited me on campus that one day."

"Oh, sure..." Vivian said.

"Well, I'm writing him a gutless letter to break off our engagement."

"Wait a minute. When did you get engaged?"

"He asked me to marry him last Thanksgiving, just before he left for basic training."

"And you said yes?"

Louise sighed and hung her head. "Like the chicken liver I am, I didn't say *anything*. I just blushed and let him put the ring on my finger. I didn't want to hurt his feelings—especially with his whole family sitting in the next room. I thought maybe the idea would grow on me, especially because we'd been friends forever and I really do like him."

"But you don't love him?"

"Not enough to marry him—especially with him being Catholic and all. I know that shouldn't make any difference, but I can't help it that it does. I'd decided I would give him the ring back when he came home on leave for Christmas but never got up the nerve. Then after meeting Dutch..." She choked back a sob.

Vivian hugged her until her shoulders stopped heaving. "I heard about the plane crash. That had to bring all your feelings to the surface."

"Uh-huh." Louise sniffled. "Since he left, I've been absolutely lost. I haven't gone out once on a date and I have no desire to. I'd rather stay home and write to Dutch. It's a funny thing but it's wonderful...I always preached against getting married after only knowing someone for a short time, but I believe I'd do it if we could get enough time to be married. I never knew how it felt to be so crazy about a guy."

Vivian brushed an errant lock of hair from Louise's forehead. "Only another four weeks till he gets back, right?"

"Last I heard. It's kind of creepy how they move people around at the drop of a hat, though. I assume you heard about Anna Krause and Betsy Flannigan getting sent to Muroc for temporary duty?"

"No, where's Muroc?"

Louise sighed. "It's a small camp in the middle of the desert about one hundred twenty miles from here. Supposedly they needed a few nurses to help staff a new ward. They left right after breakfast this morning, and I sure hated to see them go."

"I'll bet Anna was furious."

"Yeah, and I don't blame her. It leaves an awfully empty feeling —we don't know when they'll be back or who will be shipped next."

"I guess we're going to have to get used to Uncle Sam's whims."

The friends sat shoulder to shoulder in silence for a while. "Viv?" Louise finally whispered.

"What?"

"Please don't tell anybody I was engaged, okay?"

"I won't."

Chapter Eight

June 30, 1943

NEWS SPREAD THROUGH THE NURSES' QUARTERS LIKE wildfire: the members of the 44th had gotten their orders to go to Fort Sill, Oklahoma, for overseas training. The thirty-four nurses were relieved of duty at the hospital and were told to get packed and ready to depart immediately.

Anna, who'd returned the day before from her temporary assignment at Camp Muroc, was infuriated. "They can't do this to us," she cried to the group of friends congregated in the lounge area. "Tim and I have five-day leaves scheduled to begin in two days."

During Anna's brief absence from March Field, Tim McNally had spoken of nothing but her, and he'd confided to Louise that they planned to be married and honeymoon while on leave.

"I didn't tell you, but we were gonna get married on Wednesday," Anna said, banging her fist on the table beside her. "It's just not fair."

Always pragmatic, Dot had little patience for Anna's moaning. "Have you gotten the license already?" she asked.

"Yes," Anna replied.

"Then why don't you get married today and ask to have your leaves moved up a couple of days?" Dot asked. "Captain Riley's always been decent about stuff like that, and McNally's got clout in his unit. The CO can wire Ft. Sill to say you'll be late."

Despite Anna's pessimistic certainty that their requests would be denied, everything went smoothly. By four o'clock that afternoon, the newlyweds were en route to Yosemite.

ANNA WASN'T THE ONLY ONE DISMAYED BY THE transfer orders. Surprised to find it closed, Louise knocked on Frankie's door after she left the confab in the lounge.

"Who is it?" came the muffled response.

"It's me. Louise. Can I come in?"

"Okay."

Curled up on her bed and hugging her pillow, her face blotchy and wet with tears, Frankie looked impossibly young and vulnerable.

"What's the matter?" asked Louise, sitting by her side.

"You heard we're shipping out, didn't you?" Frankie asked.

"Uh-huh. That's all anyone's talking about."

Frankie sat up and blotted her face with the corner of her sheet. "We knew it was coming, but I kept hoping it wouldn't be so soon," she said. "Now that Alex and I are married, I don't know how I'll be able to stand being away from him."

Louise's jaw dropped. "Married?"

Frankie nodded. "We got hitched six weeks ago but decided to keep it a secret. You know how quick the COs can be to transfer one of the couple out when they hear about a marriage."

"Well, first of all, congratulations," Louise said, hugging her friend. "Dutch and I just knew you two would be a match made in heaven."

Frankie managed a half smile. "We can't thank you guys

enough for introducing us. We're going to name our first son after Dutch and our first daughter Louise."

Louise's eyes began to sting. Dutch's six-week assignment at Palmdale had been extended for the second time and, worse yet, she hadn't received a letter from him in more than a week. She felt a vague foreboding—which had been growing since the time of the crash that had killed the Palmdale crew—that he had lost interest in her. She'd re-read his letters dozens of times, and it was obvious to her they'd gradually become shorter and less personal. "Speaking of Dutch," she said tentatively as she stood to leave, "has Alex heard from him lately?"

"He hasn't mentioned him. Why?"

"He hasn't written in over a week, which is so unlike him."

"There's probably a good explanation, like he's been assigned extra duty or something. I can ask Alex—"

"No," Louise said, surprised at her vehemence. "I don't need a go-between."

Frankie stood and began remaking her bed. "Whatever you say."

"Oh, geez, I'm sorry I barked at you. I suddenly felt like a high schooler or something—you know, asking your friend, 'Do you think so-and-so likes me?' I want to behave like a grown-up."

"It's okay."

"Do you want me to close the door?" Louise asked.

"No, thanks. I've got to head over to admin to make out my will. Cheery thought, huh?"

"I know. I'm scheduled to be there at two o'clock."

LOUISE RECEIVED A LETTER POSTMARKED AT PALMDALE during mid-day mail call the next day. Heedless of the group of people around her and with trembling fingers, she tore it open and began to read. With each word, tears pooled in her eyes, which quickly overflowed.

Dot noticed first. "Louise's got some bad news," she whispered to Shoe. "Let's get her out of here."

Without a word, Dot and Shoe each latched onto one of Louise's elbows and led her from the building. Louise didn't resist and followed them to a bench in the shade of some windmill palms. "Sit down," Shoe said, handing Louise her handkerchief. "Tell us what's wrong."

"How could I be so dumb?" Louise asked between sobs, the hankie clutched firmly in her fist.

"What do you mean?" Dot asked.

"I fell head over heels for him and would've married him if he'd asked," Louise said. "And come to find out he's got a gal back home..." She handed Dot the two-page letter, its ink now streaked with tears.

The trio sat in silence while Dot read and Shoe stroked Louise's back. Dot finally looked up, her face strained with anger.

"What?" Shoe asked.

"It's an 'I never meant to hurt you' letter from Dutch," Dot began, "complete with the 'I'll always cherish the time we spent together' line. He says his high school sweetheart broke up with him before he enlisted, that he came to March Field a free man, and that he honestly thought Louise was 'the one' for him. Then —after that flight crew was killed several weeks ago—his former girlfriend realized she'd made a horrible mistake and wanted him back. And he realized he'd never love anyone as much as he loved her. He's 'so sorry' and just knows Louise—being the great gal she is—will find someone who loves her too."

Shoe clenched her fists. "Louise, he's right that you'll find someone and all that. But he pulls this *after* your romantic getaway. It's just not right."

Dot drew a breath in sharply. "You're not in a family way, are you?" she asked.

Louise shuddered. "No...and I guess *that's* a blessing. And I think it'll be a blessing to get off this airbase. I'm afraid what I might do if another cocky pilot flirts with me."

Shoe burst out laughing. "Too bad most of them are also pretty handsome."

"Let's go have a beer before we finish packing," Dot said, "and if any pilots approach us we'll give them the cold shoulder."

"Pinky swear?" Louise asked.

Dot extended her little finger. "Pinky swear."

THE BEERS WITH FRIENDS—NOT TO MENTION THE rebuffing of several flirtatious airmen—buoyed Louise's spirits. When she finished packing, she sat in the nurses' quarters lounge, listening to the radio and writing a letter.

Frankie came in shortly after she began. "Sending Dutch a response?" she asked.

Louise chuckled. "No. I decided he doesn't deserve the postage —or even a free mailgram. It's a note to a young sailor I met on the bus when I left home. I promised him I'd write when I got my service number, and I've never gotten around to it. He was just returning to his base after his father's funeral."

"That's sweet of you."

More like penance for breaking Joey's heart, Louise thought but didn't say. *I'm no better than Dutch in that regard.*

Chapter Nine

Fort Sill, Oklahoma

After a royal send-off from March Field—including a midnight steak fry hosted by the enlisted men at the hospital, a party at the nurses' quarters thrown by the officers, and kisses at the station from the doctors they'd worked with—Louise and her cohorts boarded the train for the three-day trip to Oklahoma. Along the way, they received telegrams from the doctors wishing them well and plenty of attention from their fellow passengers, most of them soldiers, sailors, and marines.

Frankie and Louise sat and bunked together throughout the trip and commiserated some about their sadness. "I feel bad 'cause I don't want to join in partying with all the others," Frankie said as they were climbing into bed the first night. "I can't mope around for the rest of the war just because I'm not with Alex, but I guess I just need some time to get used to being apart."

"I know what you mean," Louise replied quietly. "I don't intend to dwell on how much Dutch hurt me, but like Aunt Margaret said when our parents died, you have to actually feel your feelings before moving on. Even if it takes longer than you'd like."

"She sounds like a smart lady."

"That she is, and I'm so thankful for her. My sister Etta too. I try to write them every couple of days, even if the censors don't allow us to say where we are or what's happening in the Army around us. I don't have a clue what I'd do without them."

THE NURSES COULDN'T HIDE THEIR AMAZEMENT AT ITS scale as they drove into Fort Sill, which occupied more than 100 square miles of land, much of it wooded, in Southwestern Oklahoma.

"This fort was built in 1869," their bus driver told them, "to house the soldiers who fought the Indian wars. After his surrender, Geronimo and about 400 other Apache were housed here. They were allowed to roam freely around the place, and he and some of the others were even granted permission to leave and participate in Buffalo Bill's Wild West Show. Geronimo's buried in the Apache POW cemetery near the northeast corner of the base, if you ever get over in that area."

The 44th General Hospital Unit, which would eventually consist of 500 enlisted men, sixty officers, and more than 100 nurses, was to be housed by itself in one corner of the base. The barracks—new tar paper frame buildings—were set among groves of trees, with plenty of chairs for outdoor seating.

Louise and several of her friends unpacked and went outside to enjoy the fresh air. Within the hour, a couple of officers parked their cars under the trees near the barracks next door and opened the trunks to reveal washtubs full of beer on ice. "Join us?" the taller of the two yelled to the group.

"Sure," Shoe called back. "C'mon, ladies. I don't know about you, but I'm parched, and a cold beer is just what the doctor ordered."

Louise and Frankie exchanged hesitant looks but nonetheless

followed Shoe and Anna. *We're gonna be working with these guys,* Louise thought. *Might as well get to know them.*

Before long, about twenty nurses and an equal number of officers had congregated. Calvin—the officer who had yelled the initial invitation—took charge, directing others to procure more beer, snacks, and chairs, then ran into the barracks for a portable record player and extension cord. His pal Tony brought a cardboard box piled with records and began to serve as disc jockey, striking up conversations with the women who asked him to play their favorite songs. It wasn't a dancing crowd, but plenty of people—Frankie and Louise included—sang along with the records.

One of the COs, Major Arthur Mason, showed up to introduce himself about an hour after the impromptu party began. With a distinct southern twang, he charmed his way into the nurses' hearts, calling them all "Sister" or "Sugar" and insisting he'd only answer to "Pops."

"Y'all realize you're not gonna be here long, don't you?" he asked. "A few weeks, or a few months at most—until your overseas orders come through. So enjoy this idyllic place and be happy you won't be staffing the hospital while you're here!"

WHEN LOUISE AND HER FRIENDS LEFT THE BARRACKS for breakfast at five o'clock the next morning, they were greeted with breezy sunshine. The aromas of coffee, ham and eggs, and fried potatoes greeted them as they approached the mess hall. "Smells great," Shoe declared. "This place seems pretty darned inviting."

Louise, Vivian, Shoe, and Frankie sat together at the end of a long table and ate with relish. "I think the food is better here than at March Field," Louise said after a few bites.

"Maybe it only seems that way because we haven't eaten since we got off the train yesterday," Frankie said, through a mouthful of scrambled eggs. She swallowed, took a sip of coffee, and wiped her mouth with a napkin. "Sorry for being rude—I didn't realize how hungry I was."

"I'm glad we got over here early," Louise said. "We'll have time to enjoy our coffee and eat more of this homemade bread and jam before our 0600 appointment at the training grounds."

"What do you suppose they'll have us doing?" Frankie asked.

"Probably more saluting and marching around the field," Vivian replied.

She couldn't have been more wrong.

The first hour of the first day's training consisted of calisthenics: jumping jacks, push-ups, sit-ups, squats, trunk twists, side bends, stork walks, and more. The drill instructor, WAC Sergeant Esther Dixon, was a tall, thin but muscular woman with short curly hair and a no-nonsense demeanor. She effortlessly demonstrated each exercise, then barked orders for the women to do twenty-five repetitions at a breathtaking pace. None of them were able to keep up. Several women, Frankie among them, lost their breakfasts, but returned to the ranks when they'd stopped heaving.

It felt like an eternity before Sgt. Dixon granted a fifteen-minute break. By then, either the breeze had died down or everyone was too hot to feel it. "I'm going to die out here," Shoe grumbled as they waited in line for water. "Or at the very least pass out."

Too short of breath to reply, Louise merely scowled.

After the brief rest period, the nurses were ordered to run around a marked course, much of it in the increasingly warm sun. Few escaped without blisters.

I'm not going to give this evil drill instructor the satisfaction of seeing me cry, Louise told herself as she stumbled and nearly fell. Propelled by anger, she rallied and completed the route in an hour.

Fifteen minutes later, when all the stragglers finished, Sgt. Dixon dismissed the group. "You've got thirty minutes to get some water, use the latrines, and assemble in Building Ten for further instruction."

"I sure don't need to use the latrine," Frankie moaned as they limped toward the barracks. "I threw up everything solid and sweated out every bit of liquid in my body."

"Well, I'm thinking of jumping in the shower," Vivian said.

"There isn't time," Anna said. "Building Ten is a quarter-mile away."

Shoe rolled her eyes, and Louise punched her in the arm before her friend could make a caustic comment.

Fortunately, the remainder of the day's activities consisted of instructional films, lectures, and the issuance of equipment—including helmets and gas masks. Though the gas masks, in particular, gave the women pause, they were too exhausted to complain.

MUCH TO THE NURSES' CHAGRIN, THE TRAINING sessions would become even more rigorous. There were obstacle courses and pull-up bars to master and ropes to climb. On the third day, they were required to crawl under low-to-the-ground barbed wire lattices with simulated bullets whizzing overhead.

The most disconcerting of the exercises was the gas mask drill. They were ordered to run around a supply shed four times until they were out of breath, then don their gas masks and slowly walk through the building, which was engulfed in a cloud of tear gas. Many of the women came away shaken—with watery eyes and runny noses—because the masks failed to fit properly.

"I'm glad we're done for the day," Vivian said when she and several others met to walk back to the barracks. "That drill was scary."

"The training officer said that our enemies haven't been using poison gas," Louise said, "...not like during the First World War."

"So far," Dot said, shaking her head, "but who knows what they'll do in the future. Believe me, I paid attention during the drill, and I'm glad my mask fits right."

"Mine didn't," Anna said, blotting her nose, "and I had it

pulled as tight as it would go. If we have to take the masks with us, I'm going to ask for a different one."

"And if not," Dot said, "whenever we get where we're going, we'd better make friends with the supply guys."

IT WAS NINETY DEGREES AT 1300 HOURS ON DAY SIX when the women gathered on the training field wearing fatigues, combat boots, wool socks, helmets, and long-faced looks, prepared for a ten-mile hike. They carried canteens, gas masks, and loaded backpacks.

"I can see why we need the canteens," Shoe complained as they set off, "but why couldn't we jettison the gas masks and backpacks?"

Louise shrugged.

Frankie strode up beside them. "Did you notice there's an ambulance following behind us? Probably in case somebody gets heatstroke."

"What are the symptoms again?" Shoe asked. "In about fifteen minutes I'm going to fake having it."

Louise and Frankie couldn't help but snicker.

The sun beat down mercilessly during the first three miles, and the women's stiff new fatigues chafed their arms and thighs. Having neither the energy nor the inclination for conversation, they stifled their complaints and hiked in silence. Fair-skinned Ruth Ziegler stopped to drink from her canteen and collapsed beside the road, scraping her cheekbone on a rock. "Sergeant!" her companion yelled. "We need help here."

The sergeant jogged to where Ruth lay like a rag doll on some scrub grass, dazed and disoriented. She waved the ambulance forward, took a cloth from her pack, and wet it with water from her canteen. With uncharacteristic tenderness, she wiped the blood from Ruth's cheek and then applied the cool rag to her forehead.

The ambulance attendants administered smelling salts, took

Ruth's pulse and blood pressure, and expertly loaded her onto the stretcher and into the vehicle. Sgt. Dixon's face was ashen as she conferred with them.

After the ambulance sped away, she used her whistle to get the attention of the women farther ahead. "Rejoin the group," she yelled. "We're heading back."

The nurses couldn't contain their relief and responded with whoops and hollers. "Praise the Lord," Vivian said, dousing her face with canteen water.

Half an hour later, the sky opened up with the most refreshing rain they'd felt in ages. The women laughed and sang all the way back to the barracks.

As they sat beneath the trees that evening, holding cool beer bottles to their sunburnt cheeks, Louise and her friends recounted the hike to the men from next door.

"I was pretty surprised when Sgt. Dixon cut it short," Vivian said. "She's usually so rigid."

"Hateful, you mean," Shoe said. "Always demanding more from us and never giving an ounce of encouragement."

"She could be worse," Louise said. "At least she never berates us if we can't keep up or make it to the top of the rope or obstacle course. I've had teachers who did that."

"Oh, Louise," Dot snorted, "you always see the best in people."

Louise blushed.

One of the doctors, Captain Connelly, smiled at her. "That's gonna be a good quality to have as this crazy war goes on. You'll see."

Chapter Ten

Less than two weeks after their arrival at Fort Sill, in anticipation of the unit's imminent departure to parts unknown, six-day leaves were granted to those who hadn't already received them.

Louise and Vivian made plans to travel together from Lawton, Oklahoma, to La Crosse, Wisconsin, where Vivian's father would pick them up. With multiple transfers, the trip would take them close to a day.

A woman on a mission, Vivian bucked the crowd when they boarded the train in Lawton and found them two seats close to each other. And within fifteen minutes she'd convinced her seatmate to switch places with Louise.

"Thanks," Louise said. "The guy next to me hadn't bathed in days, and I'm sure I would've vomited from the stench if I'd had to sit there much longer. I feel sorry for the soldier who switched with me, though."

"He'll be fine. Men have stronger stomachs."

They rode in silence for a while, both lost in thought. "Y'know," Louise finally said, "I'm a little nervous about going home. It seems like I'm a different person than the one who left four months ago."

"I know what you mean," Vivian said. "I'm jittery too. Do you think it might be because this could be the last time we see the people we love in a long, long time?"

"Maybe forever."

"Don't say that," Vivian replied with a shudder.

"You heard Sgt. Dixon yesterday," Louise said, then began mimicking her stern voice: "'You're not going to a *picnic*, ladies. You're headed to a war zone. And remember, the US of A's had seventy-seven nurses MIA from Corregidor for over a year now. You need to know how to defend yourselves.' How can we not be nervous?"

"Still, I think the odds are in our favor," Vivian insisted. "The army has to have learned something since then."

"I hope so."

THE FRIENDS SAID A QUICK GOODBYE TO ONE ANOTHER when Mr. Vogel dropped Louise off in front of Aunt Margaret's house in La Farge. Stiff from many hours of sitting—often cramped three to a seat—she hobbled up the front steps.

Margaret, wearing an apron covered in flour and smelling of Ivory soap, opened the door and gave her a sweaty hug. "Welcome home, dear. Etta is in the kitchen waiting for you. I've got cookies in the oven and coffee on the stove. I'd hoped to finish baking earlier to avoid the heat, but the man who promised Chuck his sugar ration coupons was late bringing them by."

Louise hugged her back. "It'll feel like the North Pole here compared with Oklahoma, even with the oven on."

She dropped her suitcase in the front hallway and hurried to the kitchen, her eyes pooling as she hugged her sister. "It's so great to see you," she said, sinking into an empty chair beside Etta. "How've you been? Did you decide whether to join up or not?"

Etta, always reticent, smiled. "I'm fine. I still haven't made up my mind, though."

"You don't have to rush into it," Louise said. "And if you want a change of scenery, you don't have to enlist. You can just move someplace new and find a job. California has so many job opportunities and great weather..."

"That's what I've been telling her," Margaret chimed in as she pulled a pan of cookies out to cool. "Your Uncle Chuck's got a good friend in Los Angeles who'd be happy to show her around."

Thankfully Margaret kept the conversation lively, filling Louise in on all the local news. Etta, on the other hand, became quieter as the visit progressed, answering questions with few words and many *I don't know*s.

"I'd really like to take a cool bath and nap for a bit," Louise finally said. "I'm covered in dust and feeling kinda cranky."

"Of course, dear," Margaret said. "There are clean towels laid out for you on the bed, and sleep 'til dinner if you want. We invited a few folks over for a cookout, but it'll be casual. Your cousin Bonnie's bringing Baby Annabell. Wait'll you see her. She's like a little china doll."

Languishing in the tub, Louise couldn't help comparing her life to her nineteen-year-old second cousin's. Bonnie, a petite blonde with a porcelain complexion, had been a popular, outstanding student in high school. Her English teacher had urged her to attend college to become a teacher or a writer, but Bonnie had more traditional ideas. Two months after graduation she married her high school sweetheart, the heir to a large dairy farm, and set about becoming the best housewife in the county. Nine months after the wedding, she'd given birth to Annabell.

Louise remembered receiving the birth announcement during the same mail call as a disappointingly short letter from Dutch at Palmdale. Bonnie had crafted the announcement out of pink paper with painstaking calligraphy and had included a snapshot of the baby.

Maybe I should've opted for life as a housewife, Louise mused. *No—a marriage with Joey wouldn't have made me happy.*

THE FOUR DAYS SHE SPENT IN LA FARGE FELT LIKE A blur. All the relatives and friends who weren't themselves serving in the military came by to visit Louise. The absence of young men hung over each gathering like a dark cloud, and much of the conversation and laughter seemed forced.

Though she cried saying goodbye again to Aunt Margaret, Uncle Chuck, and Etta, Louise felt a slight sense of relief when Vivian's father picked her up to begin the trip back to Oklahoma.

"Did you have a good time?" he asked Louise when she'd settled into the back seat of his 1940 Ford coupe, behind Vivian.

"Yes," she replied. "I got to see so many people, including my cousin's darling new baby."

Vivian turned around and rolled her eyes. Fortunately, the wind through the open windows made further conversation challenging, and they were able to ride most of the way to La Crosse in relative silence.

SEVERAL HOURS LATER, WHEN THEY FINALLY MANAGED to find seats together on the train, Vivian said, "Tell me the truth. Did you really enjoy your leave?"

Louise bit her lip. "I'm glad I went, but it was disappointing at the same time. I don't feel as close to everyone as I used to, and—to be honest—I was bored to tears half the time."

Vivian laughed. "Me, too. The people in our unit seem so much more *real* or something. I can't quite put my finger on it."

"They're a heck of a lot easier to talk to, that's for sure. Communicating with my sister was like pulling teeth or talking to a brick wall. She never told me how she feels about anything, and she's so uncertain about whether to join the WAVES."

"Maybe she's jealous of you."

"For what?"

"Seeing the world. Meeting new people. Dating gorgeous men."

"Getting dumped by a gorgeous man..." Louise added sarcastically.

Vivian nudged Louise with her shoulder. "There are plenty more where Dutch came from. You won't be single for long."

Their conversation was interrupted by a young soldier, looking bone-weary and dragging a duffel bag. "I hate to ask, but could I park myself on the edge of your seat for a while?"

"Sure," Louise replied, sliding over to make room for him to sit. "Are you hungry? My aunt made egg salad sandwiches and they'll go bad if we don't eat them soon." The women glanced at their laps when they noticed the soldier's eyes pooling.

"Yes, ma'am, I'm starving. 'Fraid I didn't bring enough money to last the whole trip." He took the proffered sandwich and devoured it in three bites, then gratefully accepted the cookies Vivian handed him.

"Where're you headed?" Vivian asked.

"Fort Leonard Wood, Missouri," he said, lowering his head. He didn't expound or inquire about their destination.

The friends exchanged questioning looks and chose not to try to engage him in further small talk. Within minutes he fell asleep, his head lolling toward Louise's shoulder. She scooted closer to Vivian, who leaned against the window. Their seatmate didn't awaken until the train pulled into Chicago's Union Station.

The trip grew increasingly uncomfortable on the last legs of their journey: the trains were stiflingly hot despite the open windows, with every surface covered in grime, and packed beyond capacity.

. . .

I can't wait to take a shower and get to my bunk," Louise told her friend that night as their transport pulled in front of the nurses' barracks at Fort Sill. "It feels like we've been on a journey through H-E-double-L."

They saw a group of about twenty men and women congregated under the trees near the next building. Laughing voices and the smell of beer and cigarettes wafted toward them when they got out of the bus.

"On the other hand, a cold beer would taste pretty good before that shower," Vivian said. "What d'ya think?"

"I think you're right," Louise said.

They left their suitcases near the front steps and walked over to join the party.

"Welcome back, you two," Frankie shouted. "How was the trip?"

"Grueling," Vivian said with a sly smile so that only Louise would know she was serious. "And we worked up a terrible thirst."

An officer sitting beside Frankie got up and fetched them two beers from a galvanized washtub filled with melting ice. Louise held her bottle to her forehead before taking a sip. "Thanks," she said, sinking into the chair he'd vacated. "This feels divine, and it'll taste even better."

"Don't get too comfortable," Shoe said. "We've got to get ready to go on a bivouac tomorrow."

"What's a bivouac?" Louise asked.

"A campout," Shoe replied, "where we learn how to act in the field. And this one starts at 0600 hours."

"You're kidding," Vivian said.

"I wish I was. The whole unit's going—all 700 of us—up near Medicine Park. Nurses will stay for the first three days."

"Maybe it'll be cooler there," Louise said.

"Don't count on it," Shoe replied. "It's bound to be a nightmare."

"It'll surely be a nightmare if we go into it with that kind of attitude," Louise said, too tired to filter her words. "Might as well make the best of it."

"Hear, hear," Frankie said, touching her beer bottle to Louise's. "I think it's gonna be fun."

Chapter Eleven

By six-thirty on the morning after Louise and Vivian returned to Fort Sill, the unit—wearing khaki attire, combat boots, and helmets—boarded a stream of jeeps and trucks for the thirteen-mile journey to the campsite. Thanks to a thick bank of clouds hiding the sun, the temperature was only in the eighties when the trip began. In high spirits—and perhaps still drunk from the previous night—the enlisted men in the lead truck began a rousing rendition of "I've Been Working on the Railroad," which passed through the convoy with increasingly bawdy lyrics.

When they arrived at the town of Medicine Park, established in the 1920s as a resort for the rich and famous, the nurses craned their necks to look at its cobblestone construction. "Look at the town hall," Louise said to Frankie who sat beside her in the cab of one truck. "It's like something from a quaint European village or something."

Their driver, an Oklahoma native, chimed in proudly, "The buildings, bridges, and decorative walls and balustrades are all made of cobblestones from the Wichita Mountains, just to the west. It's kind of like the town's trademark."

"I sure hope we have time to jump in that lake," Frankie said, pointing out the window. "It looks so-o-o inviting."

"I hate to be a killjoy, ma'am," the driver replied, "but the grassy areas alongside it are infested with chiggers, and rattlesnakes just love to sunbathe on the surrounding rocks."

Louise groaned.

"So much for trying to stay positive," Frankie mumbled.

DESPITE THE SERIOUSNESS OF THE TRAINING LESSONS, the bivouac provided lots to write home about. The point of the encampment was to replicate what would be their assigned duties while trying to avoid detection by planes flying overhead. Everyone pitched in to erect the medical and supply tents, under trees where possible and otherwise camouflaged with branches. Carrying a bundle of branches she'd collected, Frankie shrieked and dropped them in a panic when she heard a rattler to her right. Then she watched in awe as an eighteen-year-old enlisted man sauntered up to the snake and calmly shot it. "And, if you can believe it, he used only one bullet," she would later tell her friends.

For much of the day, the medical people simulated the operation of their multi-tented hospital, while listening closely for the planes armed with flour-sack bombs. When the aircraft came, everyone ran for cover and took to the ground. By mid-afternoon, they were hot, tired, and filthy.

Vivian, one of the few nurses who'd been besieged with flour, wore a serious expression when told the exercise was over for the day. "Why are we stopping? I could use a little more practice," she told Anna.

"Don't worry. I overheard the CO saying we're playing this game again tomorrow and maybe the next day, too."

"It's not a game," Vivian shot back. "The stuff we're learning could save our lives."

· · ·

Louise and her friends gratefully accepted the suggestion to bathe in a nearby stream fed by waters of the Wichita Mountain range. They took turns standing watch by the entrance to the area while others stripped and splashed in the ice-cold water to their hearts' content. Their raucous laughter muffled the sound of a low-flying plane—unarmed but perhaps bent on voyeurism. "Duck!" Anna yelled from the watch station, and they all covered their breasts and sunk beneath the water.

"I sure hope they didn't take any pictures," Frankie said when she emerged. "I'd hate to think my bare bottom might be adorning the lid of somebody's footlocker."

"Oh, c'mon," Shoe said. "Your cute little bottom might be a great morale booster for some lonely GI. You should do your part for the war effort."

During the daytime maneuvers the unit had lunched on sandwiches, fruit, and cookies that had been packed at Fort Sill. But dinner was another story. The medical personnel— doctors, nurses, and corpsmen—sat in convivial groups on the ground, leaning against their gear, as enlisted men passed out C rations. Each received two cans: a B portion and an M portion.

Anna expertly removed the metal key attached to the bottom of her B can and used it to wind off the top. "Candy and biscuits," she announced, then bit into one of the hard, dry cookies. "Tastes better than it looks."

"Good lord, what *is* this?" Shoe asked a few moments later when she managed to open her M can. "It smells hideous."

The enlisted man delivering rations to a nearby group responded with a hearty chuckle. "Meat stew with beans," he said. "It's usually better heated up."

"Are we going to have to eat this stuff wherever we're going?" Shoe asked.

Captain Riley chuckled. "Probably not. After all, the 44th is designated as a General Hospital rather than a Field Hospital. But it'll do you all good to see what the soldiers we'll be treating are dealing with. And we have been getting pretty spoiled by the great food at Fort Sill."

The nurses got ready to turn in for the night, assured by the perimeter guards that the rattlesnakes had no interest in bothering them. "Are you sure?" Louise asked. "One of the officers told me they'd killed three this afternoon alone."

"True, but you're safe now," said one of the watchmen. "We surveyed the whole area during daylight and made sure none were lurking in or around the tents. We'll be patrolling all night with flashlights. Believe me, they're leerier of us than we are of them."

"You from around here?" she asked.

"Yes, ma'am. Did my accent give it away?'

"Uh-huh. And it also made me believe you know something about rattlesnakes."

"I do. Now you ladies rest easy, okay?" he said, turning to go on about his way.

"Those tents are pretty stuffy," Vivian said. "Can we move our bedrolls and sleep outside?"

"Sure enough," the man replied.

When they were all situated, Louise climbed under her light blanket and looked up in amazement. "I don't ever remember seeing so many stars. And that's saying something, since I grew up in a house without electricity, in the country where it was totally dark at night."

"You didn't have electricity?" Frankie asked incredulously as she wiggled into her own bedroll.

"No. And no indoor bathroom either...that is until my sister and I went to stay in a rooming house during high school. That was the only way we could be sure we'd get to school in the winter."

"Gosh. And I thought we were backward in little ol' Janesville...No offense."

Louise laughed. "None taken."

The cooler night air, the sound of the breeze rustling through the trees, and the chirping of crickets in the distance put almost everyone at ease. Exhaustion gave way to sleep for all but the unfortunate folks on duty.

THE NURSES WERE SCHEDULED TO RETURN TO FORT SILL after dinner on the third day of the bivouac. Tired and aching from all the unusual activity, they stowed their gear and boarded the jeeps and transport trucks. Louise rode in a jeep with Anna, Vivian, and Dot.

"I'm sorry I made light of the exercises," Anna told Vivian. "The first day it all seemed kinda silly to me, but I have to say I learned a lot."

"I did too," Dot said, "but I was hoping we'd get some clues as to where they're planning to send us.

"We should find out soon," Louise said.

"I wouldn't hold my breath," Vivian said with a wry grin. "Judging from the fact they've issued us uniforms for all climates, I'm guessing nobody's actually decided."

"You're right about that," the jeep driver commented. "Hell of a way to run a war, huh?"

Chapter Twelve

THOUGH THE MEMBERS OF THE 44TH WERE CONFIDENT they'd receive their orders within days of returning from the bivouac, it wasn't to be. They managed to remain busy. Louise's sister abruptly decided to join the WAVES, and in late August Louise sent her a ticket to visit Ft. Sill before she enlisted. Anna was in seventh heaven when her husband was granted leave to spend several days with her. There were dinners and dances at the officers' club and more spontaneous parties under the shade trees in the evenings.

On September 8, 1943, the nurses and doctors gathered outside and listened with rapt attention to another of President Roosevelt's fireside chats, this one announcing the armistice with Italy. It was a "great victory," he intoned, but "(t)he time for celebration is not yet." He reminded the nation that the targets of Berlin and Tokyo were the ultimate objectives and would be costly to attain.

Roosevelt continued, "I know I speak for every man and woman throughout the Americas when I say that we Americans will not be satisfied to send our troops into the fire of the enemy with equipment inferior in any way."

"Hear, hear," Anna said, wiping a tear off her cheek.

FDR appealed to every American household to buy more war bonds. "Now it is your turn," he concluded. "Every dollar that you invest in the Third War Loan is your personal message of defiance to our common enemies—to the ruthless savages of Germany and Japan—and it is your personal message of faith and good cheer to our Allies and to all the men at the front. God bless them."

None of the nurses groused about their president's failure to mention the women in service. They felt proud about the part they'd volunteered to play in the war effort.

TEN DAYS LATER, THEY COULDN'T HELP GROUSING. "Five-minute break," Sgt. Dixon yelled to the nurses after an hour of calisthenics in the hot sun.

"Five whole minutes..." Shoe mumbled under her breath. "That doesn't even give us time to get to the water cooler."

"Drop and give me twenty push-ups, Shoemaker," the sergeant hollered. "And a bit of advice—if you're gonna complain, learn to do it more quietly."

Her friends couldn't help chuckling as Shoe threw herself on the ground and began her penance.

When she'd reached eighteen, though, Dixon yelled, "Attention, ladies. Your CO wants a word."

Shoe struggled to her feet and rejoined the others, who stood in reasonably straight lines with their shoulders back.

"I'm not particularly proud of what I've done with them," the sergeant muttered. "But they're all yours, Captain Riley." And she strode off the field.

"At ease," Riley said. "I've got something to report."

To a woman, the nurses all shuffled closer to hear—the captain's voice didn't project like their drill sergeant's.

"No," Riley said, shaking her head. "Our unit's orders haven't come through yet. But..." Here she paused as if trying to get up the nerve to share the news.

"Out with it," Shoe whispered so only Louise and Anna could hear.

"Unfortunately," Riley went on, "the Medical Corps has been reviewing and realigning its rosters, and they've determined the 44th has eight too many nurses."

Louise's stomach lurched, and she grabbed onto Shoe and Frankie's hands. The nurses were utterly silent.

After what felt like an eternity Riley continued. "The other COs and I will be meeting later this morning to determine who will be reassigned. The list will be posted on the bulletin board in the barracks by 1500 hours. If any of you would like to volunteer for reassignment, please see me now. The rest of you are dismissed."

The group dispersed slowly, walking toward the barracks in twos and threes. Occasionally they looked back over their shoulders: No one had gone forward to volunteer.

"What a dirty trick to pull on us at this late date," Anna muttered to Louise, Dot, Shoe, and Vivian, who had all gathered in Louise's room to commiserate. "And I'll bet you five bucks Frankie and I'll be on the list."

"Why do you say that?" Vivian asked.

"I've already been sent away once," Anna replied, "and Frankie and I just disappointed the powers that be by getting married."

Louise sat heavily on her bunk and felt her eyes filling with tears. "I couldn't bear that..."

"Couldn't bear what?" The group looked up to see Frankie standing in the doorway, having missed the first part of the conversation.

"Anna thinks you and she will be on the list for reassignment," Shoe said. "Because you're both married now."

Frankie's face went pale and she, too, started to cry. "That's not fair."

"Hang on, everybody," Vivian said. "None of this is fair—since we've just spent six months getting to know one another and learning to work as a unit. But we have no way of knowing what criteria they're going to use to make their decision. No sense getting more upset about it now than we have to."

THE DAY PASSED SLOWLY. AT 1300 HOURS ANNA AND Louise found themselves in line together in the admin building, waiting to fill out some new allotment forms. "I hope you're wrong about being reassigned," Louise whispered. "It just wasn't the same around here when you were at Muroc. I mean, we've come so far together."

"I hope so too. But I've been wrong before."

Louise raised an eyebrow.

"Remember when we first met Captain Riley and she made that comment about our being Krauts?"

"How could I forget?"

"And I said I thought you were overreacting?"

"Uh-huh."

"Well, when I was sitting behind a medical screen waiting for my typhus booster shot last week," Anna said, "I overheard Captain Riley talking with Captain O'Hara. She's that red-headed charge nurse who's stationed here—she looks like a taller version of Maureen O'Hara? Anyway, Riley said something like, 'You're lucky, Betsy, you get to stay here at this comfortable hospital and I'm getting sent heaven-knows-where with a unit full of bull-headed Kraut nurses.'"

"She said that?"

"Uh-huh. And when O'Hara asked her if she was joking, Riley tried to laugh and say she was. But she wasn't. You were right all along, Louise."

"Do you think that'll influence who she puts on the list for reassignment out of the unit?"

"My money's still on me and Frankie. And probably you and Shoemaker. And Albrecht and Ziegler."

Louise's shoulders sank. "Well, if we *do* get reassigned, it'd make sense for them to send us all to the same new unit."

"Since when has Uncle Sam ever made sense?" Anna asked bitterly.

"I don't know," Louise said. "They say there are only two ways to do a thing—the right way and the Army way. It burns me up sometimes—a person sure loses every bit of individuality in a place like this—their rights and feelings are never considered."

As expected, all of the 44th's nurses began waiting by the barracks bulletin board at 1450 hours. By 1500 hours, no one had come to post the promised reassignment list. Half an hour later, with tensions and speculation running high, and when most of the women had gone outside to have a cigarette or get some sunshine, a young corporal—his face still bearing angry teenage acne—came rushing up the sidewalk. He carried a fistful of papers and looked completely ill at ease as he approached the group.

"Is that the list?" Shoe asked.

The corporal handed her several onion-skin pages. "You can pass them out. Oh, and someone needs to put the original on the bulletin board and...um...I don't think I'm allowed inside."

"I'll do it," Anna said, taking the glaringly white page from him.

Louise walked into the barracks alongside Anna. "Who's on the list?" she asked.

"Anderson, Flannigan, Morelli, Murphy, Nelson, Olson, Roberts, and Terwilliger," Anna replied as she poked a thumbtack into the corkboard. "Guess I was wrong."

"Does it say where they're reassigned?"

Anna's face fell as she looked more closely at the list. "Seven different units—only Flannigan and Morelli get to stay together. Thank heaven for that 'cause they've been friends since grade school and Flannigan missed her terribly when we got sent to Muroc."

Louise leaned against the wall and wiped tears from her face with the back of her hand. "This is so unfair. It'll be like starting all over for those gals—especially the six that are going it alone. I don't know what I'd do without the rest of you."

Chapter Thirteen

At Sea

Struggling to untangle her legs from the bedsheet, Louise rolled onto her back and stared at the underside of the bunk above her. The stagnant air, heavy with moisture and the White Shoulders perfume that Anna had sprayed to mask the scent of vomit, felt suffocating. She tossed aside the no-longer-wet washcloth she'd used to cool her brow, put on her bathrobe and slippers, grabbed her life jacket, and padded to the doorway. The latch of the stateroom door opened quietly—as one would expect on a former luxury liner—enabling Louise to sneak out without waking her roommates.

She made her way to the promenade deck, holding tight to railings in the darkened stairwells, and breathed a sigh of relief when she saw the star-filled sky. Her eyes quickly adjusted to the ambient lighting, and she walked over to an alcove where she and other nurses often congregated in the daytime.

"Who goes there?" came the familiar voice of her friend Dot, huddled with her back against a corner wall.

"It's Louise," she replied. "I didn't even notice you weren't in your bunk when I left. How long have you been out here?"

"Long enough to cool off and wish I'd brought a blanket," Dot replied. "Sit next to me and warm me up, okay?"

Louise took off her robe, slid into a seated position beside Dot, and covered them both with the flannel garment. Her friend's gooseflesh disappeared within moments.

They gazed out over the blessedly calm ocean for a while. The two were among the 44th General Hospital Unit's ninety-plus nurses and eight thousand other passengers on the USS *West Point*, the navy's largest troopship, currently zigzagging across the Pacific at full speed to avoid Japanese torpedoes. They'd set sail on September 30, 1943.

"Couldn't sleep?" Louise asked Dot.

"I drifted off okay but woke up from a terrible dream—that we were bombed by the Japs and had to evacuate. There wasn't any way to go back to sleep after that." She gave a rueful laugh. "Then I figured I might as well come up here and be closer to the lifeboats in case my dream was prophetic."

Louise nudged her friend with her shoulder. "Have you ever had a prophetic dream before?"

"No," Dot replied. "But there's a first time for everything..."

"I'm guessing a whole lot of people live their whole lives without *ever* having one, and I'll bet you'll be one of them."

Dot sighed. "I wish I could be as optimistic as you. Nothing seems to rattle you."

"That's not exactly true. I get mighty grumpy with the two-hours-a-day water rationing, and I hate that they don't serve lunch on this boat. By 1300 hours I just want to sleep until supper."

"Still, you keep your discomfort to yourself, which is more than I can say for a lot of our fellow passengers. Especially the enlisted men."

"Believe me, I'd complain too, if I were them," Louise said. "Packed like sardines in every available space on the lower decks where the stench is unbearable. Do you realize they often have to wait in the mess line for an hour or more to be served?"

"Who told you that?"

"Lt. O'Malley, when I talked with him last night after the movie. He and his friend went down with a couple of the enlisted men from our unit and saw it firsthand."

"So, you're telling me our seven-to-a-room setup isn't bad?"

"Not by comparison. And don't forget we have a bathroom."

The two gasped simultaneously at a brilliant star shooting across the sky.

"Y'know, even though it seems like we've been at sea a lot longer than six days, I wouldn't miss this trip for the world," Louise said. "The ocean and the skies are simply gorgeous. We've met so many wonderful people. It's so pleasant to sit on deck in the evening and listen to the boys singing—and some of those harmonica players are amazing."

"Doesn't it bother you that we don't even know where we're going?"

Louise pursed her lips. "We're seeing parts of the world we'd never have had the opportunity to see otherwise, and we're getting paid to do it. Uncertainty and discomfort are just part of the deal."

Dot laughed. "See what I mean? You always look on the bright side. But I have to thank you because it's contagious."

"Shhhh," Louise whispered, standing quickly and pulling her friend to her feet. "I think I hear one of the patrol officers." Their slippers enabled them to tiptoe back to their quarters, their transgression undetected.

"Thank heaven," Dot said breathlessly with her hand on the stateroom door, "I'd like to avoid getting thrown in the brig."

"I'm pretty sure they don't throw nurses in the brig for curfew violations."

. . .

At 1100 hours the next day, Louise's sunny disposition failed her: Wrapped in her bathrobe and next in line for a shower—with water privileges ending in half an hour—she startled when the blaring alarm signaled an evacuation drill. "It's not *fair*. You know they're not gonna turn the water back on after the drill. I got the curse this morning, and I *really* need a shower."

"Then hop in and pretend you didn't hear the siren," Shoe suggested.

Though tempted, Louise knew it wouldn't work. Protocol required that all quarters be searched so no one would be left behind should the ship be abandoned. Mortified at the thought of heading to the lifeboats in only a robe, she hastily pulled on some clothes and trailed the others to the deck.

"Too slow, Dietrich," Captain Riley barked when she finally arrived at the appointed spot.

"Sorry...I was just getting into the shower..."

"Then you grab a towel, helmet, and lifejacket and hightail it to the deck. If the Japs attack, they're not going to do it at your convenience, and I'll be damned if I let anyone in my unit go down with the ship. What if this hadn't been a drill?"

"I...uh..."

"Exactly. You had no way of knowing the siren wasn't signaling a real attack." The captain stormed away, glaring at her stopwatch.

The tears Louise had managed to contain en route to the lifeboat began to flow. Shoe threw an arm around her shoulder. "Hey, don't take it so hard," she said. "Everybody gets chewed out once in a while."

Louise's face reddened. "It's not only that. I mean, it could just as easily have *been* an attack. This vessel is like a sitting duck out here, sailing without a convoy."

"Not really," Shoe replied. "It's a big ocean, and I heard some of the sailors explaining that the *West Point* can outrun even the fastest Japanese subs. We change course all the time and make sure no one throws even the smallest amount of trash overboard that spotters might see. Plus, we're serious about the total blackout at night too. Nobody would even consider lighting a cigarette on deck after dark."

"Okay, okay. So maybe they're reducing our risk, but we're at war," Louise said, her voice rising. "Look how unprepared we were for Pearl Harbor."

"What's going on?" asked Frankie, approaching the duo with alarm.

Shoe ignored the question, turned Louise around, and whispered into her ear, "Listen carefully. You know you can't dwell on the danger, and you certainly don't want to get everyone else all stirred up, especially Gladys Frankenburg."

Louise took a few deep breaths before facing Frankie. "I got dressed down by Captain Riley for being late to the lifeboat and got overly upset. Shoe was just talking sense into me."

"*Shoe* was talking sense into *you*. That's a new one," Frankie said.

"Attention, attention," came a voice through the public address system. "All polliwogs are to report immediately to the afterdeck. Repeat, all polliwogs to the afterdeck."

One of a group of the 44th's enlisted men standing at a nearby lifeboat yelled back, "What the heck's a polliwog?"

"If you don't know, then you definitely *are* one," said the Navy ensign manning the lifeboat. "Head to the afterdeck or face the consequences."

In truth, the non-naval passengers had been receiving ominous warnings for the past few days: Signs reading Polliwogs Beware! had been posted all over the ship, similar messages had been transmitted through the PA speakers, and almost every sailor they encountered had advised them, "The equator's getting closer and closer." The uninitiated knew to expect some sort of hazing, but its targets and methods had remained a mystery, adding to their unease.

"I'm guessing the order doesn't include nurses, does it?" Shoe asked the ensign with a taunting smirk.

"Then you guessed wrong, missy," he replied, "and I'm gonna recommend you for special treatment. Now move."

As Louise and her companions approached the afterdeck and saw a huge dunk tank, her trepidation became tinged with panic. *Why did I have to get my period* today?

"Hide behind Vivian," Shoe hissed at Louise, pushing her behind their tall redheaded friend. "That way they might not notice you."

"Thanks a lot," Vivian shot back, but she nevertheless stood shoulder to shoulder with Shoe, effectively blocking Louise from view.

As it happened, though nurses would be hazed on future voyages, they were spared on this journey of the U.S.S. *West Point*. They watched—with relief, amusement, and some horror—the initiation of the enlisted men, doctors, and other officers of the 44th who'd never crossed the equator.

Naval officers dressed as King Neptune and pirates Davey Jones and Peg Leg, along with their many "shellback" assistants, led the luckless polliwogs to barber chairs where their heads were shaved and rubbed with glue and raw eggs. They were smacked with wooden paddles and made to eat pies made of soap flakes and pepper. Finally, they were forced off a gangplank into the dunk tank full of seawater.

The festivities ended with a celebration. King Neptune presented each polliwog—including the nurses—with a certificate of initiation into the Solemn Mysteries of the Ancient Order of the Deep, signed "Neptunus Rex." They were now officially shellbacks.

THE NEXT DAY, MEMBERS OF THE 44TH WERE TOLD their destination: Australia.

.   .   .

TEN DAYS AFTER THEY'D SET SAIL, THE USS *WEST POINT* arrived in Sydney on a beautiful spring afternoon. The nurses breathed sighs of relief: no more seasickness, no more abandon ship drills, no more nightmares about being torpedoed.

They boarded a double-decker "omnibus," scrambling for seats on top—despite the occasional showers—for a better view. The houses had steep, red-tiled roofs, multiple gables, and elaborate ironwork. Even the shabbiest warehouses downtown had lush lawns and flower gardens. They saw every kind of tree imaginable, from apples to palms, all budding with new life.

"It smells fantastic here," Louise said to her seatmate Anna. "It reminds me of spring on the farm."

For once speechless, Anna nodded, looking over Louise's shoulder as they rode through rural areas with winding creeks, trees, and hills.

They arrived at their base at around four o'clock and were immediately led to the mess hall for a feast of chicken, dressing, chocolate sundaes—and coffee. "Well, since they've given us such a warm welcome," Shoe said between mouthfuls, "I guess we might as well stay."

Next stop was the barracks, which looked ten times more inviting than what had once been a luxury stateroom on the *West Point*. After indulging in a long hot bath—the first one in weeks—Louise joined Vivian and Dot in their "rec" hall: a room with two windows, a table and bench, and a squatty old-fashioned cookstove in the middle. "How cozy is this?" she asked her friends who were already seated at the table and writing letters home.

"Sometimes the stove feels too hot," Vivian replied, "but it feels great when you come in from outdoors. These Down Under seasons are going to take some getting used to." Little did they know that would be another understatement of their overseas tour.

Dot finished the letter she was writing, folded it with a flourish, and licked shut the envelope. "One down, four more to go," she reported. "Hey, Louise, do you want to go to the movie tonight? It's *Me and My Gal* with Gene Kelly and Judy Garland. I missed it when it played in Delavan last year."

Louise shrugged. "Why not? I've seen it and it's a little corny, but entertaining. Are you coming, Viv?"

"No thanks. Shoe and I are gonna try to find a ride into town to get a glass of Australian beer. They said it's seventeen percent here."

"Good luck with that," Louise replied.

A week after their arrival in Australia, the medical personnel of the 44th General Hospital were still not on duty. "All this taking it easy is getting hard on my nerves," Louise said to Frankie one afternoon while they played cribbage in the rec hall. "It's not like I'm hoping for battle casualties or anything, but it's hard to sit back and do nothing when there are units all over the world that are working their tails off."

Frankie nodded. "Fifteen-two, fifteen-four, and eight's a dozen," she said, moving her peg across the finish line, "and I've skunked you. Wanna try again?"

"Might as well."

Chapter Fourteen

Finally, orders were received for the unit to establish a hospital near the war zone in New Guinea. The doctors, officers, and enlisted men boarded a Liberty ship bound for Port Morseby, New Guinea, while on October 23 the nurses traveled by train to Brisbane to wait until the hospital was ready.

The 44th's Liberty ship was joined by six others and escorted through hostile waters by four Australian corvettes. On the second day at sea, the captain of one of the Liberty ships pulled out of the convoy because they were treading dangerously close to the Bougainville Reef. Under protest, he returned to the convoy as ordered by the Australian commander. That night, all seven Liberty ships ran aground the reef. A flurry of news reports about the incident, many of them erroneous, made their way back to the states.

While two of the Liberty ships were able to free themselves, the 44th General Hospital's was not. Their orders were changed, and the men were taken by smaller boats to Cairns, and later by train to Townsville, Australia.

Meanwhile, the 44th's nurses went to a new camp in the staging area about fifteen miles outside of Brisbane, which was decidedly more rustic than any of their previous posts. Their outhouses and showers were about half a block from their sleeping quarters, and the women would have to do their laundry in their helmets. Louise and Vivian were assigned to Tent #2 with twelve other women they didn't know well, ranging in age from twenty-eight to forty.

"Gosh, I feel like such a kid here," Louise whispered as she climbed under her musty-smelling mosquito netting the first night.

"Me too," her friend replied from the bunk beside her, "but they all seem nice."

The next morning the tentmates anxiously waited for mail call —only the second one since they'd left San Francisco. Louise got six letters, fewer than she'd hoped, and none from her sister. Mae Wentworth, the oldest of the group, noticed her disappointment. "Don't let it get you down," she said. "I've been in this army long enough to realize you can't let your happiness depend on the erratic nature of the mail. Some days you won't get anything, and on others there'll be a treasure trove."

"I guess you're right," Louise replied.

"Who were you hoping to hear from?" Mae asked.

"My sister Etta. She joined the women's naval reserves and got sent to basic training at Hunter College in New York. I worry about her 'cause she's just a small-town kid...and pretty shy."

"I'm sure she'll be fine. My little sister—" Mae began.

"What's *that*?" screamed Vivian, jumping up onto her cot.

"What?" several women shrieked back.

Vivian pointed to the corner of the tent. "That crawling thing."

A knock came on the doorframe of the tent. "Anything I can help with?" asked the Aussie soldier who'd been on patrol.

Mae tiptoed toward the foul creature. "It's a scorpion."

"They're quite common here," the soldier said through the screen. "Usually nocturnal, but because of all the rains"—this he pronounced *rines*—"they're out and about now. I'll gladly kill it for you."

Mae grabbed a nearby broom and turned to him with a cocky grin. "Save your energy to fight the enemy. We can handle this."

I can't, Louise thought, struggling to tamp down her panic. *That thing's disgusting!* Everyone watched in silence as Mae swatted the four-inch fellow to its death, then swept it out the door and under the tent platform.

"This place is like a zoo," Vivian said. "Yesterday a lizard, today a scorpion. What next?"

There would be more animals. A few weeks later, their campmates caught a baby parrot down near a river. Some of the men built a cage for the green and orange bird, and the nurses spent hours sitting around his cage, trying without success to teach him to talk. "I think he's too young," Anna said with some derision as she walked by the group one day. "You're all wasting your time."

"Thank you, Professor Krause," Shoe replied. "We'll be sure to take your advice and find better uses for our precious time."

Anna shrugged. "Suit yourself," she muttered and walked away.

"She'd be a lot less annoying if she took that stick out of her butt," Shoe said when Anna was out of earshot.

"You're awful, Shoe," Louise chided, but she couldn't stop snickering.

AND THEN THERE WERE THE HORSES. SIX OF THE NURSES in the unit purchased horses to ride through the outback in their abundant free time. "Why don't you buy the one you're riding?" Anna asked Louise from atop her newly acquired mount. "Vivian finally gave in yesterday."

"She told me," Louise replied. "And hers is a real beauty. But I can't see spending sixty dollars when I can just as easily rent when I want to ride. We may only be here a few weeks."

Anna laughed. "I'm betting we'll be counting our time here in months."

Not long after that conversation, during one of the many downpours requiring the nurses to pitch pup tents over their bunks to protect themselves from the leaks in the main tent, Louise listened with amusement as an alarm went up among her equestrian friends: their horses had gotten loose. She couldn't contain her laughter at the sounds of her friends swearing as they tramped through the mud, wailing when they lost their footing, and calling—mostly in vain—for the animals to come.

THE DAILY QUARTERS' INSPECTIONS, DRILLS, calisthenics, and menial jobs left many hours to fill. The nurses took up knitting, cross-stitching, and needlepoint. The camp had softball teams, and Louise—to her surprise—made the "scrub team." And there were weekly dances at the rec hall.

Louise was standing among a group of friends at one of the first dances when Frankie came rushing up with a man in tow. She pulled Louise aside. "I want to introduce you to someone," she said.

Louise turned to face the man—about five-ten, a little on the stocky side, with brown curly hair, and brown eyes—and thought fleetingly, *You took me away from an interesting conversation for him?*

"Lieutenant Dietrich, meet Lieutenant Dietrich," Frankie said, beside herself with laughter. "He's stationed at the quartermasters' camp down the road but originally from Milwaukee. Maybe you're related."

"Pleased to meet you, ma'am," he said, shaking Louise's hand.

She was surprised to find herself attracted to him: his dark eyes seemed warm and kind and lit up when he smiled. His voice was as deep and smooth as Bing Crosby's.

"Clearly, we won't be able to rely on formalities, Lieutenant," he said to her. "Please call me Richard."

"I will if you call me Louise."

"Perfect. May I buy you a drink, Louise?" he asked, extending an elbow to lead her to the bar.

"Why, yes. Thank you, Richard."

Louise ordered a beer and felt somewhat embarrassed when Richard asked for a Coke. "I'm not a drinker myself," he told her, anxious to put her at ease, "but I certainly don't have anything against it, and I always want my friends to enjoy themselves."

"Well...if you're sure—"

"Absolutely sure." He picked up the drinks and ferried them to a table for two, where they could talk more easily.

They quickly discussed their family histories and concluded that they were distant cousins many times removed, if they were related at all. "That's a relief," Richard said. "It'd be a shame to have to confine ourselves to being just friends."

That's a pretty bold statement to make to someone you just met, Louise thought but didn't say. And within half an hour, she realized she agreed with him: she wanted to be more than his friend.

"May I see you tomorrow night?" he asked when he walked her to the door of her tent.

"I'd like that."

"May I kiss you goodnight?"

Louise moved toward him and closed her eyes to enjoy his tender though brief kiss.

Vivian was already lying on her bunk when Louise went inside. "Looks like you and Richard hit it off," she whispered.

"We did, but how did you know about him?" Louise asked.

Vivian laughed. "I happened to spend the evening with his best friend, Jimmy Larson, and we were watching you. I told Jimmy a couple of times that we should go over and talk with you two, but he insisted we leave you alone. And now it turns out you didn't even notice us."

"I'm sorry," Louise said. "He's just such a nice guy and the time flew by. I'm seeing him again tomorrow night, so we'll be sure to meet up then."

RICHARD PICKED UP LOUISE TO TAKE HER TO HIS MESS hall for supper on Thanksgiving night, bearing a bouquet of tropical flowers and a foil-wrapped box.

"The flowers are beautiful," she said, kissing him on the cheek.

"Open the box," he said. "My mother sent it for you."

She raised an eyebrow. "Your mother?"

"I sent her a telegram the day after I met you and told her I'd found someone special. I guess she mailed this that very afternoon."

Louise ignored the little stitch of alarm she felt in her stomach and concentrated on opening the box. "Chocolates," she exclaimed. "Thank you."

"Look where they're from," he said.

Louise read the label: Barager-Webster Candy Company, Eau Claire, Wisconsin. "Oh, my goodness—my aunt used to buy these for us at Christmas time."

Richard beamed. "We knew you'd appreciate them."

The quartermasters' mess hall had roasted chicken and mashed potatoes to celebrate the holiday. But the pièce de résistance was dessert: warm pumpkin pie smothered in whipped cream. Richard watched as Louise ate her slice with abandon, and he tenderly wiped a dab of cream off her nose. "Would you like to finish my piece?" he asked. "Clearly you appreciate it more than I do."

She nodded gratefully and devoured what remained on his plate. "If I keep this up, I won't be able to fit into the uniforms they just issued."

"Then they'll just have to issue you new ones," he said with a grin.

· · ·

LOUISE RECEIVED SEVERAL LETTERS AT MAIL CALL THE following day and was reading one as she and Vivian walked back to their tent. "What's the matter?" Vivian asked.

"It's a letter from my father's cousin Donald—he and his wife have been managing the farm for my sister and me since our parents died. Donald says he can't enlist in the army because, as a farmer, he's considered essential, and he can't hire the help he needs to work the place. They're urging us to sell it."

"What do you think?"

"I'd hoped we could avoid that till I get stateside. I don't have any idea if the price they're suggesting—$3,500 for the farm and cattle—is fair."

"You don't trust them?" Vivian asked.

"Not entirely. We've been beholden to them for all these years because they stepped in when we needed them. But now..."

"Spit it out."

Louise sighed. "Something about it bothers me...I find it hard to believe Donald wants to join the military. I certainly can't see him taking orders from anyone; he drinks a lot and always acts like a big shot. Plus, our mother never trusted him."

"Hmm...you came up with those reasons pretty quickly," Vivian said with a gleam in her eye. "But seriously, why don't you talk with Richard about it? He was a banker in civilian life and might be able to say whether $3,500 is a fair price."

"Good idea."

As it happened Richard, though more than willing to help, had no expertise to give. "I'm sorry, kid," he said, "but since we don't have farms in downtown Milwaukee, I wouldn't know the first thing about deciding what yours is worth. And I'd sure hate to steer you wrong."

"That's okay," Louise replied. But she couldn't stop thinking about the looming decision.

. . .

Richard had said goodnight to Louise on the last day of November with a huge grin on his face. "My friends and I have a big 'Happy December' surprise planned for tomorrow evening," he'd said. "We think you gals are going to love it. Be sure and tell everyone to wear trousers, though."

Now the women were abuzz with excited speculation.

"What's so happy about December?" Anna grumbled.

"Richard told me we're celebrating another month of living," Louise said. "Corny—but I think it's kind of sweet."

Vivian, still dating Richard's friend Jimmy, was among those invited. A couple of weeks earlier, she'd received a letter saying that her twenty-five-year-old brother had been killed in a plane crash, and she sorely needed a pick-me-up. "Do you think it's disrespectful for me to be socializing so soon after Jack's death?" she asked Louise.

"Not at all, Viv," Louise replied, putting her arm around Vivian's shoulder. "He died in battle, for heaven's sake. He, more than anyone, would realize you have to seize every enjoyable moment you can. At least that's the way I feel."

"Well, we certainly haven't been under much duress here."

"True, but who knows what's to come?" Louise replied.

At precisely 1700 hours on the celebratory day, Richard pulled up in front of her tent driving an olive drab Army six-by-six truck. Dot's date, Marvin, a hulking former football player from Michigan State, sat in the front passenger seat, and four other guys were in back. All hopped out to help their girlfriends in. Dot and Louise were squeezed in between Marvin and Richard, and the other nurses were seated on crates and footlockers covered with army blankets in the bed of the truck.

"Where are we going?" Louise asked.

"Wait and see," Richard replied.

"What's that delightful smell back there?" Dot asked.

"Have patience, please," Marvin said, nudging her shoulder with his. "You'll find out soon enough."

The truck sped out of camp and for some five miles afterward. Then the winding road leading into some woods became increasingly more rutted, and the men in back gallantly put their arms around the women to brace them from falling. Richard apologized to Louise each time the gearshift hit her in the knee.

After about twenty minutes, they crested a hill and stopped in a grassy clearing. "Here we are, ladies," Richard called.

The men grabbed folding chairs from the truck and arranged them in a circle, then ceremoniously helped their dates to their seats. The nurses watched in awe as they quickly unloaded a table, mess kits, cases of beer, and firewood. Once the table was set, Richard revealed the entrees: each couple would share a roast chicken.

"Gosh, this is good," Louise said after her mouthwatering first bite.

"Mm-hmm," Dot added. "Did you guys *cook* these?"

Richard laughed. "No, we bought them at a market in town, already stuffed and roasted. The cooks in our mess hall let us keep them warm in the oven 'til we left."

"These muffins are pretty darn tasty, too," Shoe added. "Almost as buttery as my grandmother's. You need to give us directions to that market."

After dinner, Louise stood up to clear the table. Richard took her elbow and eased her back into the chair. "Not on your life, Lieutenant," he said. "You ladies are our guests tonight."

He turned to his friend. "Marv, why don't you get the campfire going and lay out some blankets? We'll be more comfortable on the ground than on these rickety chairs."

Once they were all situated around the fire with beers in hand, Jimmy went back to the truck and pulled out a suitcase.

"Is that a phonograph?" Vivian shrieked.

"It most certainly is," Richard replied. "And we've got a crate full of records that should last as long as the battery."

The terrain wasn't conducive to swing dancing, but that didn't stop the group from enjoying the livelier music. And when Jimmy put on the first slow number—Tommy Dorsey's "I'll Never Smile Again"—Dot stood and nudged Marvin to his feet. "We can't let this go to waste," she said. Soon all six couples were up and swaying to the song.

After darkness descended, Jimmy had to operate the phonograph by the dim light of a kerosene lantern.

Richard held his own as his friends became more boisterous from drink. Louise's heart ballooned with pride as she noticed how everyone hung on his every word and laughed a little louder at his jokes than at others'. She reveled in the warmth of his arm around her shoulder and couldn't help feeling blessed to be with him.

After checking his watch at ten-fifteen, Richard called to Jimmy, "We've only got time for one more song, mate, so make it good."

"Why so early?" Vivian asked.

"I only managed to get use of the truck 'til 2300 hours, and it'll take us a while to pack everything up."

Jimmy picked Bing Crosby's "White Christmas." The upcoming holiday would be the first anyone in the group had spent away from home, and they all listened silently, lost in thought and holding their dates' hands.

Richard cleared his throat. "Play it again, Jimmy, while we load up and douse the fire."

Silently the couples worked together to break camp. Louise helped Richard throw handfuls of dirt on the embers, then kissed his cheek, taken aback to find it wet.

"It's okay to cry, Richard," she said."

He wiped his face with one sleeve. "I just got a whiff of smoke in my eyes, that's all," he said, extending his other arm to lead her back to the truck.

· · ·

A COUPLE OF WEEKS LATER—JUST AFTER DARK—LOUISE was awakened from a deep sleep by Mae Wentworth. "Louise! Viv!" she bellowed. "You two are snoring like drunken eighty-year-old men. It's too early for bed and there's no way the rest of us can concentrate on our card games with you making such a racket."

Louise sat up and rubbed her eyes. Vivian turned over and covered her head with a pillow.

"Sorry," Louise mumbled. "We had an exhausting day."

"Doing what, pray tell," Mae replied.

"A bunch of us spent the day at the beach. I'd never been in the ocean before. I had no idea the waves that made us so sick on the ship would be so much fun to play in. I mean, they knock you down and you get up and let them knock you down again...It's more of a workout than any drill sergeant has ever given us."

Mae laughed. "Can you imagine what all our folks back home would think if they really knew what we were doing over here? Biking, horseback riding, swimming, picnicking, dancing..."

"Yeah," Louise said, "I feel pretty guilty every time I get a letter from somebody telling me what a hero I am for joining up..."

Chapter Fifteen

On December 20, Louise, Vivian, and Julia—another nurse from Tent #2— sat in their little rec hall writing letters and listening to rain peppering the roof. "Gosh," Julia said, "you'd think this rain would cool things off but all it does is make my hair frizz."

"And make the mud smell worse," Vivian added.

A few minutes later, Louise looked up from her paper. "It sure doesn't feel like it's almost Christmas," she said. "Maybe because it's a hundred and ten degrees and doesn't resemble in the slightest the holidays at home?"

"Probably so," Julia said. "You think it'd be a little more festive if we put up a tree?"

"Have you seen a single tree around here that looks anything like a Christmas tree?" Vivian asked, rolling her eyes.

"I remember some of the trees in the woods near where we had that picnic were kind of pine-like," Louise said. "We might be able to find one that'd do."

"How would we get there?" Julia asked.

"A kid in the motor pool told me he'd take some of us out for a ride in a jeep if we wanted," Vivian said, warming to the idea. "I'm willing to ask him."

"An enlisted man?" Julia asked. "We could get in trouble for that."

Vivian laughed. "We wouldn't be 'fraternizing,' we'd just be having him take us on a little errand."

The following day after their inspection and drills were finished, Vivian and Louise walked over to the motor pool to find Private Anderson. The freckled, moon-faced young man's eyes lit up when he saw them. "How y'all doin' today?" he asked with a thick southern accent.

"We're fine, thanks," Vivian replied. "The other day you mentioned you might be able to give us a ride somewhere."

"Well, yes, ma'am. I'd be happy to. Where you wantin' to go?"

"It sounds silly, but to a woods several miles from camp. We want to find a Christmas tree. And we'll cover for you if anyone stops us," Vivian added.

"Do you want to go now?"

The women hadn't expected he'd be free right away. "Well… sure…if that's okay," Louise replied.

Anderson pointed to a jeep sitting a few feet away with its hood up. "Hop in. I'll just go tell my partner I'm headed to test her out."

The women climbed in, Vivian in front and Louise in back, and waited for their chauffeur to return. "Remember, you agreed to do the talking if we get in a jam," Louise whispered.

Anderson came back a moment later carrying a saw and a khaki tarp, slammed down the hood, and got behind the wheel. The jeep sputtered to life, and they were off.

No one paid them any attention as they drove through the camp, but they had to wait at the narrow entrance/exit gate as another vehicle approached. *Oh no,* Louise thought, her heart racing in her chest, *it's Captain Miller. He's such a stickler for rules. Why did it have to be him?*

"Where are you off to, Lieutenants?" he asked as his jeep approached theirs.

The trio saluted, and Vivian leaned forward holding up a piece of paper. "Good morning, sir. We're headed over to the next camp. Captain Riley asked us to pick up an order of uniforms that were delivered there by mistake."

Captain Miller returned the salute without comment and sped away.

Louise leaned forward and asked Vivian, "What's that paper?"

"A letter from my grandmother, but he can think it's an invoice if he wants," she said with a smirk.

"What if he checks with Riley?"

"He won't."

"How do you *know*?"

"Because they dated a few times, he tried to dump her, and now she won't leave him alone."

"How do you know *that*?"

"I overheard him telling his friend about it when I was sitting at the bar at the officers' club. He'll do anything to avoid her, including ignoring our suspicious trip."

The corners of Private Anderson's mouth turned up a fraction of an inch, though his deadpan face suggested he hadn't been listening.

For fifteen minutes they drove through the woods, searching for anything vaguely resembling a pine tree. "How about that one?" Anderson asked, pointing to a four-foot green bush with a broad base and narrower top, situated among some thick underbrush about twenty yards from the road.

"That might do," Vivian said. "Let's go take a closer look."

Anderson jumped down and extended his hand to help the women from the jeep. "If y'all don't mind, I'll walk ahead," he said. "In case we encounter any critters." Then, using the saw to probe the brush, he led them toward the tree.

Four-legged or slithering critters weren't the problem: They'd gone only a few yards before mosquitoes swarmed around their heads. "It's not worth it," Vivian yelled, waving her hands frantically.

"You two go back to the jeep," Anderson said. "I'll get it."

Louise shot a questioning look at Vivian, who shrugged.

"Go ahead," Anderson called. "They don't seem to bother me. Guess I'm not sweet enough or somethin'."

Feeling more than a little guilty, the friends watched from the jeep as the young man struggled to saw through the tree trunk. "Maybe mosquitoes *don't* pester him," Louise said hopefully. "He's not swatting at them."

Finally, his face slick with sweat, Anderson returned, pulling the tree. "What do y'all think? Is it Christmassy enough?"

"It's great," Louise replied.

They laid it down on the floor of the jeep and covered it with the tarp, and Louise used it as a footstool for the ride back to camp.

After dark that evening, Private Anderson and a buddy delivered the tree, already situated in a makeshift stand they'd cobbled together, to Tent #2. The tentmates oohed and aahed over it and, to demonstrate their gratitude, insisted on sharing cookies and fruitcakes from their Christmas packages with the boys.

Decorated with pieces of cotton and pictures cut from Christmas cards, the tree was a bunya pine, according to an Aussie nurse who came by to see it. The nurses used some of the branches to craft wreaths to hang over the doors on each end of the tent.

THE NURSES IN TENT #2 DECIDED TO SKIP BREAKFAST IN the mess hall on Christmas morning. Instead, they bought food to have breakfast in their pajamas around their tree. Fortunately, the weather cooperated, and they didn't have to dodge leaks in the tent. They'd exchanged names and each purchased a six-shilling gift. Mae—wearing a Santa hat she'd secretly knit for the occasion —passed them out with a flourish.

The cooks outdid themselves to provide a turkey dinner with reasonably familiar trimmings in the mess hall at noon. They had pumpkin pie for dessert followed by a spontaneous round of Christmas carols. And before they could adjourn, Frankie—her eyes streaming with tears—stood up and began singing "God Bless America." Everyone joined in, tentatively at first, but ending in a resounding chorus.

There was a Christmas dance at the officers' club that night. Though the club was decorated with red and green streamers, the atmosphere was decidedly less festive than usual. During the swing numbers, only a few couples danced. And people seemed to shy away from requesting that the orchestra play the sentimental slower songs.

Louise and Dot sat at a corner table facing the dance floor while Richard and Marvin went to get drinks. "Y'know," Louise said, "it's hard work pretending to be festive when you don't feel it. Before I enlisted, I never thought I'd miss home this much."

The foursome finished the round of drinks, but the women declined when Marvin offered to get another. "I'm bushed," Louise said. "It's been a long day."

"We understand," Richard said softly. "There'll be other nights to celebrate."

Louise glanced at the bunks as she tiptoed into her tent: only Mae's was empty, and everyone appeared to be sleeping. She stripped to her bra and panties and climbed under the mosquito netting and her threadbare sheet—much cooler than the ones they'd recently been issued. Emotionally drained, she fell asleep.

Chapter Sixteen

On the last night of 1943, the Lieutenants Dietrich went to a huge party at his club. It's lovely," Louise said as they walked into the lavishly decorated hall. "Where on earth did you get silver streamers and all these little lights?"

"We're the quartermasters...It's our job to get things."

"I'd love to look at your supply catalogs."

"Sorry, they're classified." Richard winked. "C'mon, let's not let this music go to waste."

They danced—together, and occasionally with other partners from their gang—until Louise had blisters on her feet. "Why don't you take your shoes off?" Richard asked as he helped her walk toward their table.

"I don't want to ruin my stockings."

"If they get ruined, I'll get you another pair," he said.

"Do they have *those* in your supply catalogs too?" she asked.

He pantomimed locking his lips and throwing the key over his shoulder. In the end, Louise acquiesced, and she noticed many other women dancing in stocking feet.

Just before midnight, the lights dimmed, and the orchestra began playing "Auld Lang Syne." And at the stroke of the hour, everyone stopped to kiss. Content in the warmth of Richard's embrace with his lips on hers, Louise didn't want the moment to end.

"Hey, you two," Marvin called from the edge of the dance floor, "come back to the table—they're popping the champagne."

"Champagne?" Louise asked. "I've never had it before."

They watched Vivian's boyfriend Jimmy carefully twist the wire off the cork and all jumped back when the bubbly liquid exploded from the bottle. "I thought you knew what you were doing," Marvin said.

"Be quiet and hand me the glasses."

When everyone was served, Richard stood at the head of the table and lifted his glass. "May 1944 bring victory for the Allies and health and happiness for those who gather here. And may we all meet again soon back in the good ol' USA."

Richard took one sip, then handed his glass to Louise. "What do you think? Do you like it?"

"Mm-hmm, and I'll gladly drink your share."

"Slow down, though. It's reported to pack a wallop..."

I'll drink as fast as I want, she fleetingly thought. But the orchestra struck up a swing number and the champagne was forgotten.

Louise was tipsy but happy when Richard escorted her back to the tent.

There were changes in the wind, most more than rumors. Louise and Richard spent every evening together, especially since he'd gotten word that he'd be shipped out soon. The nurses, too, were being separated and sent to various places in Australia until the 44th could be established somewhere as a unit.

"When Richard leaves, I'd just as soon they pull my name out of the hat," Louise told Dot. "I can't imagine staying here without him."

"I know what you mean. I'll miss Marvin something terribly when he's gone."

"Has Marvin talked at all about marriage?"

"No. Has Richard?"

"Uh-huh. He wrote to tell his mother that he hoped to marry me. And last night he showed me a telegram he got from her. It read, 'New Year's Greetings and lasting happiness to you both.'"

Dot's eyes widened. "Did you say yes?"

"Not yet, but he's got me almost convinced. I mean, I've been in love before, but never like this. I adore his personality, and he always makes me feel so special."

THE SATURDAY NIGHT BEFORE THEIR RESPECTIVE departures, Louise and Richard, Dot and Marvin, and Vivian and Jimmy went on a picnic. The men had managed to get steaks and potatoes to cook on the campfire—to be complemented with the A.1. Sauce Marvin had received in a Christmas package from home. The women had ventured into town and found some rare pastries for dessert. Richard had contributed three bottles of sparkling burgundy from his alcohol rations.

The three couples crammed into one jeep and made their way to a nearby beach, where mosquitoes would be kept at bay by the ocean breezes. The women sat wiggling their toes in the sand while the men went to find firewood.

"Just look at this place," Dot said. "I can't imagine a more beautiful part of the world."

"At least when it's not raining," Vivian said with a laugh.

"I don't even mind the rain that much," Louise said. "We're a world away from home, with loads of interesting people—kind of like we're one big family. Sometimes I feel as though I should pay Uncle Sam for the privilege."

"I'm not sure I'd go *that* far," Vivian said. "Especially since the family's being broken up and we have no idea what to expect at our next duty stations."

Dot's eyes immediately pooled with tears. "I wish I'd gotten orders to go with you two."

Louise reached over and squeezed her hand. "We do, too. But remember they said it's temporary. The 44th will all be together soon."

"I hope you're right," Dot said, blotting the end of her nose with her shirttail.

"Here come the boys," Vivian said, her voice suffused with relief.

Thank God, Louise thought. *We so need for this to be an upbeat outing.*

The three men, dragging long driftwood logs and balancing armloads of branches, came whooping and hollering over a rise in the sand. "We found a whole bunch," Marvin called. "We'll get the fire started and then go back for more."

A true city boy, Richard wasn't much of a woodsman. But he put his weight to good use—as his buddies instructed—by jumping on the logs to break them into smaller pieces. And he'd had the wherewithal to bring some old newspapers to augment the kindling. Then off they went again for the rest of their cache.

The girls moved their blankets to avoid the smoke and laughed about their dates' antics until they returned with more wood.

The steaks—cooked over the coals in a huge cast-iron skillet—were a hit. "Don't smother it with sauce, Marv," Dot said, elbowing her date. "It's so juicy and tender. These Aussies know how to raise cattle."

"I'm going to put the A.1. on my potato," Jimmy announced. "It's a little dry without butter."

"Oh, good heavens," Vivian said. "Stop complaining or you don't get any dessert."

"And believe me, you don't want to miss it," Louise added.

The baked goods were worth every shilling the girls had spent on them.

The sun had set by the time they'd licked the pastry crumbs off their fingers. "Let's build up the fire," Marvin said. "It'll get a little chilly soon."

As usual, Richard led the conversation, telling personal stories and asking everyone about their lives, their experiences, their opinions. They sipped wine and talked until the wee hours of the morning, and only when the last of the firewood burned to embers did they struggle to their feet to leave.

"This was the best night I can remember," Louise said, and she walked arm in arm with Richard back to the jeep.

Chapter Seventeen

RICHARD LEFT TWO DAYS AFTER THE PICNIC, AS DID Dot. Louise hardly had time to adjust to her losses. Within a week, she and twenty other nurses from the 44th got orders to move out. This camp sat at the foot of some mountains, about thirty miles from the closest town.

Their mail had been sent on ahead for some inexplicable reason, so a big mail call awaited them, including a Christmas package from Louise's Aunt Margaret. She opened it eagerly and found candy, nuts, and gum and passed around the tin of nuts. "Have some, please," she said to her fellow travelers.

Anna took a few peanuts and whispered, "You're crazy to share."

Louise shrugged and went back to stand next to Vivian, Shoe, and Frankie.

"Ladies," their CO yelled. "You'll be four to a tent this time around. Unless there's a problem, you can pick who you want to bunk with."

The friends gratefully glanced at each other. Louise knew she and Vivian would miss some of the women from Tent #2, but it'd be good to be with Shoe and Frankie again. And it would be good to have a little more privacy.

"Can you believe these beds?" Frankie asked when they moved their belongings into their new quarters. She flopped on her back. "It's like heaven. And I don't see any holes in the tent."

"Hallelujah!" Shoe said.

The tents were situated around boardwalks with makeshift signs directing them to various camp locations. "We should name our boardwalk Wisconsin Avenue," Vivian declared as they headed for the mess tent. "You know, since we're all from the same state?"

"We get it," Frankie said. "I like the idea. Let's keep an eye out for a piece of wood for our sign."

The foursome waited at the door of the mess tent while their eyes adjusted to the semi-dark interior. "You're not going to believe how good the food is," Mae Wentworth yelled to them. "C'mon in."

Mae's assessment proved true. Dinner was a savory, piping-hot lamb stew with buttery biscuits and jam.

And while the nurses were eating, an army officer stood on his chair and cleared his throat. "I've got an announcement to make. At 1900 hours tonight, we're hosting a welcoming party at our club for the girls from the 44th General Hospital. There aren't many male officers in camp, so you may need to dance with each other. But never mind, wear your dancin' shoes!"

Cheers went up from the crowd and the tent buzzed with talk of the party. Louise and her tentmates—sitting together at the end of a long table—put their heads together. "Aw...I don't feel much like partying after our long day on the road," Frankie said.

"I don't either," Shoe said, "but it'd be rude not to go. We can stay for a little while and slip out quietly."

"Okay, but let's not jump into any more romances," Vivian warned. "In fact, why don't we make a pact that the first one to go out on a date has to pay a pound to treat the tent to a party?"

"Sounds good to me," Frankie said, "but—as a married woman—of course I'm less inclined to accept a date."

"Since no one *knows* you're married, it'll be hard to avoid," Louise pointed out. "Especially since we usually go in groups."

"True."

"Do we have a pact?" Vivian persisted and held out her hand.

They all shook on it.

As it turned out the party was a jovial affair, and the personnel who'd been in camp the longest made the newcomers feel right at home. The punch tasted fruity and benign but packed a wallop. Despite the dearth of male partners, within half an hour everyone was on the dance floor amid raucous laughter.

The men took turns acting as disc jockey, playing a host of swing records on their phonograph's highest volume. Occasionally someone would call for a slow tune, but the men pointedly refused. "We're trying to cheer you *up*, not make you miss your boys," one called back.

Feeling a little tipsy, Louise switched to soda after two cups of punch. "I can't enjoy dancing if my head's spinning," she told Frankie and Shoe, who both decided to follow her lead.

Vivian, on the other hand, kept right on drinking. When Frankie suggested she slow down, she replied, "This punch helps me forget how mush I miss Jimmy."

Frankie couldn't help giggling. "How *mush*?"

By 2200 hours, when the party finally broke up, Frankie and Shoe had to throw Vivian's arms around their necks to lead her back to the tent. Louise took pity on Anna and guided her home, stopping twice along the way so Anna could retch off the boardwalk.

"I feel as bad as you must've felt on that train to LA," Anna mumbled after one bout of vomiting.

"So far I've kept my promise never to get that drunk again," Louise said. "And I'll always be grateful to you for climbing onto that top bunk."

"S'okay. Thanks for walking with me."

FORTUNATELY, THE NURSES WEREN'T ON DUTY AT THIS camp either, as only a few of them would've been able to work the next morning. Their drill sergeant had been at the party, too, and quietly passed the word from tent to tent that they'd skip calisthenics until the following day.

"Thank God," Vivian said when she heard of their reprieve. "Wake me up for lunch, okay?" She covered her head with her pillow and began snoring within minutes.

Louise, Frankie, and Shoe walked to the latrine together, wondering aloud when more mail would catch up to them. "I can't wait to hear from Richard," Louise said. "It's only been a week, but it seems like forever since I've seen him."

As Frankie pulled on the door handle, a blood-curdling scream came from within the latrine and Mae Wentworth barreled past them. "There's a *huge snake* in there!" she yelled. "Somebody come kill it."

"Not me," Shoe said, leaning against the now-closed door. Louise echoed Shoe, and they all looked around for someone who might help.

"Hey, Captain," Shoe called to an Australian officer approaching a nearby tent. "Would you get rid of a snake for us?"

"How big?" he asked.

"We haven't seen it. Possibly 'huge.'"

"I'll just go grab a shovel."

"Wouldn't it be easier to shoot it?" Shoe asked.

The captain laughed. "It's frowned upon. Plus, I'm not a very good shot."

A few minutes later, carrying a flat-bladed shovel, he joined the women outside the latrine. He didn't need to tell them to stand back as he cautiously opened the door and peered inside.

"Crikey! He's got to be five feet long, but at least he's curled up in a corner."

"Be careful," Frankie said needlessly.

The women listened to the metal shovel blade striking the rocky ground several times in succession and to the officer swearing under his breath. "Okay," he finally said. "He's harmless now. Do you ladies want to wait down the walkway while I bring him out to bury him?"

"Yes," the women said in unison, and they hurried about eight feet away.

The officer carried the snake's body on the shovel and flung it to a clearing behind the latrine, then returned to get its head. As he set to work burying the remains, Shoe called to him, "Thanks a million. We hate being so helpless, but snakes are too much."

"You might 'ave to get used to it. They live in the mountains and wash down here in the rains and I'm told a fair number of them are poisonous. Most of the gals take sticks and brooms to the latrine to shoo them out."

The women shivered. "We should collect the longest sticks we can find to have at the ready," Louise said. "And maybe we can go in groups, though it looks like Mae—our fearless scorpion killer— won't be willing to lead the way."

"And I'm never gonna let her live that down," Shoe chuckled.

The captain's prediction was correct: a few days later a three-foot snake appeared in the tent next to theirs. Louise's tentmates joined the neighbors, all wielding their newfound weapons, and chased it out of the tent and up a tree.

The following night, another nurse heard shuffling around her bed. Using a flashlight to investigate, she witnessed a raccoon sitting on her shoe, munching an apple. When she shooed it, the raccoon snatched up her whole sack of apples, scurried from the tent, and ran up another tree. After eating each and every apple, the critter tossed the empty bag down.

The harrowing episodes made good stories to write home about. But the women took to sleeping with their sticks.

LOUISE AND HER SISTER, WHOSE LETTERS OFTEN crossed in the mail, still hadn't heard from their father's cousin about the proposed sale of their farmstead. Other members of her unit—some of them farm kids—had told Louise they shouldn't settle for less than five or six thousand dollars. The uncertainty nagged at her and was compounded by the loss of Richard, her best sounding board.

Chapter Eighteen

On January 30, the twenty-one nurses from the 44th moved yet again, some forty miles from their last posting to a camp on the northeastern coast of Queensland, Australia. "Quit grumbling," their new CO told them. "You're getting closer and closer to rejoining your unit. And you'll actually be *on duty* at this camp."

"I'm worried that I've forgotten everything we learned in nursing school," Louise told her tentmates—again Vivian, Shoe, and Frankie.

"What's it been? Seven months since we set foot in a hospital?" Frankie asked.

"Yep," Shoe answered. "Not since we left March Field. Boy, does that seem like ages ago."

Conditions at the new camp were worse than before: the heat persisted, but due to a severe water shortage, everyone was limited to one very short cold shower per day. "What I wouldn't give to feel cool and clean," Frankie said on their third day. "I'm kind of glad Alex *isn't* here, because I'd hate for him to see me like this."

The following day, the foursome went into town to check it out.

"This place is pitiful," Louise said. "All it needs is a few hitching posts and some gunmen, and it'd look like the scene in a John Wayne movie."

"I can't imagine the Wild West was this filthy," Vivian added.

The hotels and restaurants seemed shabby and covered in grime. "Certainly spoils the appetite, doesn't it?" Louise said as they walked out of one cafe without ordering. "Even though they had the only brand of ice cream we're allowed to eat, I couldn't stomach it in there."

"Can you believe only one dairy pasteurizes its milk?" Frankie asked. "It's a wonder the whole population isn't on death's door."

They walked several more blocks without finding a suitably inviting restaurant. "Let's go to the beach instead," Shoe suggested. "We can collect some shells and find the best place to swim when we come again."

The women stared with delight when they saw the aquamarine ocean, the waves beckoning them. Then they noticed that people were enjoying the sun and wading in the shallow water, but no one at this particular beach was swimming. "I wonder why?" Frankie mused.

"Excuse me," Louise said to a trio of teenage boys throwing rocks into the water, "is it safe to swim here?"

"No, ma'am," the tallest one replied. "Lots of sharks here. The next beach over has a seawall that keeps them out—it's safe there."

"Nowhere near as fun, though," one of his friends added.

Not a strong swimmer, Louise didn't find the news particularly disappointing. But Shoe, who loved riding the waves as they rushed into shore, grumbled. "What kind of godforsaken place is this? Can't *drink* what little water we have 'cause it tastes like chlorine and salt. Can't *drink* the milk 'cause we'll get the runs. Can't *swim* in the water 'cause we'll get eaten by sharks."

"I think we should head back to camp," Frankie said. "I overheard someone say our beer ration is coming in this afternoon. We know it's safe to drink *that*."

They picked up a few seashells and made their way to their newest home, happy to find the rumor had been true.

After finishing her second bottle of beer, Louise sat on her bunk to write some letters. "Since we're going to be working girls starting tomorrow morning," she said to Frankie, "I thought I'd better get a jump on these."

Frankie nodded. "Did you look at the assignment roster yet?"

"Uh-huh. I'm assigned to the officers' ward. How about you?"

"I'm a floater. I guess that means they'll send me to whatever ward is busiest, and I sure hope I'll remember what to do."

"I know," Louise said. "I feel like a kid before the first day of school—hoping the teacher won't call on me."

They read and wrote in silence for a while. "Is Richard writing on pink stationery these days, or is that from your little sis?" Frankie asked, nodding at the pages lying on Louise's bed.

"No, it's from Etta," Louise said with a chuckle. "She's all excited because she got orders to go to Oakland, California." Then she pointed to a stack of airmail envelopes. "*These* are from Richard. Four today alone, making eight since we left Brisbane."

Frankie's eyes sparkled as she glanced at her own letters. "You know, I wondered if I'd be able to write to Alex every day, but I never seem to run out of things to tell him."

"Same. I actually look forward to it—almost as much as I looked forward to going out with him. I believe we're meant to be together."

"Do you still want to wait till you get home to be married?"

"Well...if we were to be stationed together again, or if we could get leaves at the same time, I don't think I could wait."

After their shift at the hospital several days later, Louise and Frankie went to their rec hall to have a beer and open their mail. Louise tore the wrapping from a small package from her aunt—a set of hankies and a pair of stockings—then shuffled through several letters. "I got one from Richard's mother," she said, then ripped it open and began to read.

Engrossed in her smaller stack of V-mail from Alex, Frankie at first paid little attention to her. "Good heavens, what's wrong?" she asked when she finished and looked across the table.

"This letter...I should be happy she wrote it, but it scares the dickens out of me." She passed it to Frankie. "Tell me what you think." She absently scraped the label off her beer bottle with her fingernail and watched while Frankie read.

"I can see why you're scared," Frankie finally said. Then, quoting from the letter in a sing-song voice, "'I do hope you will write soon and that you will tell me all about your dear self and about the happy times you and *Richie* are having in the land Down Under. We would love to have you call us Mother and Father or Dad and Mom.' And to sign it, 'Your devoted Dad and Mother' before you even let her know if you're comfortable with it?"

"She and Richard are close, and I know she means well, but it seems so gushy and overdone. And even though my own mother and father are gone, why would I want to call these people Mom and Dad?"

"Is *Richie* her only child?"

Louise grimaced. "Please don't call him Richie. He had an older sister who died of scarlet fever when she was four, and it was understandably rough on their mom. I could see why she might be aching to have a daughter-in-law. Still, couldn't I just call them by their names?"

"That's what Alex and I do. And Alex's mom's pleasant to me but not crazy-sweet. Are you going to mention this to Richard?"

Louise took one final swallow from her beer. "I don't know. I'll think about it. But right now, I have to go take a shower and get ready for my date."

Frankie raised an eyebrow. "A date?"

"Uh-huh. Becky asked me to the dance in town tonight with

one of the fellows she knows. She's been bugging me to go out with them since we got here, and I finally gave in."

"I think you just waited because you didn't want to lose our bet," Frankie said.

"That may have crossed my mind, but don't you dare tell Shoe."

"I have to say, I'm surprised it took *her* until yesterday to go on a date. What'd she think of him? Lieutenant Bradley's his name, isn't it?"

"Uh-huh. She said he was okay but nothing to write home about. A little full of himself like so many of the officers."

Chapter Nineteen

THE NURSES FROM THE 44TH SETTLED INTO THEIR WORK at the temporary duty station. The army hospital—a series of twenty-bed "ward tents"—connected by outdoor boardwalks and wooden ramps, presented physical challenges: it took many steps to attend to their assigned patients, often in rainy conditions.

In early March, Louise began a three-week stint on the night shift, working from seven p.m. to seven a.m., seven days a week. The schedule had sounded daunting, especially since she'd be required to cover six tents on the surgical ramp, assisted only by two ward men. But by the second week, she'd become acclimated to the work and enjoyed being her own boss.

A monstrous thunderstorm hit at ten o'clock one night that week, with lightning strikes in the immediate vicinity of the camp. After one particularly large crack, the power abruptly went out—with none of the typical pre-outage flickering—leaving the hospital in total darkness. Louise was in the middle of changing the dressing for a patient at the time and heard piercing screams from the adjacent tent. "Keep your hand on this gauze, please," she told her patient. "I need to go see what's happened."

She cautiously felt her way to the door of the tent, grabbed the flashlight hanging beside it, threw on her rain slicker, and rushed next door. In the narrow beam of her light, she saw the patient in the second bed—a young Chinese soldier who could speak no English—wracked with sobs and shaking uncontrollably. Though no longer screaming, he'd begun uttering strings of words that clearly conveyed terror.

Tom, one of the two ward men, came running in with a kerosene lantern. "Is he hurt?" he asked.

"I'm guessing he's just really scared. Put the lantern on the floor and let's see if we can calm him down." Then, approaching the patient with her hands in front of her, palms up, she began murmuring, "I know you can't understand me, but Tom and I are here to help you. We need to examine you and make sure you're okay. Okay?"

"Okay."

Thank God there's apparently one universally understood word in this war.

She leaned over the bed and stroked the soldier's arm, and, to her surprise, he sat up and hugged her. She engulfed him in her arms and rocked him back and forth, as one would a panic-stricken child—and she realized he *was* a panic-stricken child. "He's probably no more than seventeen," she told Tom, "and I heard someone say he'd been a POW. No wonder he's afraid of the dark."

"What do you want me to do?" Tom asked.

Louise kept rocking. "Take my flashlight and get another couple of lanterns from our office. And find Joe and ask him to finish bandaging the appendectomy next door, please. He's in bed three."

As she comforted the soldier, she recalled the evening several days ago when he'd first arrived at the hospital. "Is that a Jap POW?" the surgeon on duty, a short man with uncommonly large ears and an equally big mouth, had asked.

"No, sir," the litter bearer replied. "He's on our side—Chinese not Japanese—he was a prisoner of the Japanese. Doesn't understand a lick of English. Several others are coming in behind me, but triage told me to bring this kid in first."

Louise had helped the corpsman get the new patient into his bed and glanced at the two-page "chart" that accompanied him. "He's got a serious infection on his right foot, Captain Howard. Here's hoping we can save it."

The doctor stepped up to the patient and spoke slowly, "I need to look at your wound." No response. Howard tried again, now slowly and loudly. "I need to look at your *wound*."

He's not hard of hearing, Louise wanted to yell. *He doesn't understand you.*

She pointed to the patient's foot and pantomimed lifting his blanket. He consented to the examination, which revealed the diseased tissue was beginning to heal. Captain Howard had affected a clown-like grin and had given the soldier a thumbs-up.

Now, Louise understood that the young man's foot injury might be the least of his problems: After being held captive by the "ruthless savages" of the Japanese Army—as FDR had termed them—he would likely be afraid for the rest of his life.

"Gee, I've missed you," Shoe said to her the next morning. "How's the night shift going?"

"Actually, I kind of like it," Louise responded. "Though last night during the monsoon when we lost power, it was crazy. There I was, plodding between the tents in a raincoat and galoshes and swinging an old-fashioned kerosene lantern. I felt like I was back at our farm...I think I told you we didn't have electricity?"

"Uh-huh."

"My ward men are great, and we have lots of fun. During the quieter hours—around two o'clock—we get together in the nurses' office and play cards to stay awake."

"I find it so hard to stay awake all night," Shoe said.

"We've gotten in good with the mess sergeant, and he brings us a fresh pot of coffee around three a.m. Sometimes some fresh pie or something he's just baked. Lucky I'm getting in a lot of walking, or I'd be gaining weight like crazy."

"I'm glad it has its good points. Still, I hope we get moved again before my turn on nights."

"The worst part of it is getting enough sleep during the day. I feel lots of pressure to sleep as soon as I get off work because by noon it's too hot to stay in bed. And my social life has certainly suffered, what with no days off. How's your social life? Are you still dating Lt. Bradley?"

"No," Shoe replied, shaking her head. "I've got my eyes on someone else, and maybe we can double-date when you get off nights."

"Gee, I don't know..."

"Are you still pining for Richard?"

"Uh-huh, and I'm a little worried. I got a letter from him yesterday saying he's in a combat area in New Guinea. Says they've had several air raids and he's spent a few nights in foxholes. And you know he's sparing me the worst details."

Shoe put her arm around Louise's shoulder and squeezed it. "I wouldn't fret too much about Richard. He's a force of nature and the kind of guy who'll make it home in one piece."

"He seemed like a force of nature here in the relative calm of Australia, but I wonder if a lot of that wasn't bluster. They're in the thick of it now, and this war has become way too real. His personality's not going to do much good against relentless enemies."

SHOE MANAGED TO STAY OFF THE NIGHT SHIFT, AND— despite having to deal with multiple levels of authority—Louise found herself happy to be back on days. Assigned to the officers' ward in the morning, she met plenty of men with whom she could dance at parties when they were on passes from the hospital.

But she preferred the afternoons when she treated the enlisted men—most quite young. Many suffered from malaria, dysentery, or deficiency diseases and would return to the front after convalescing.

"It's like having fifty younger brothers," Louise commented to Shoe after her second afternoon shift. "It's so rewarding here. Unlike the officers, these kids appreciate everything we do for them."

"And they're willing to do whatever they can for themselves."

The women strolled back toward their tent. "My new beau asked me if you'd be willing to go out with his friend," Shoe said. "Remember I mentioned that when you were on nights?"

"Who *is* your new beau? You've been pretty tight-lipped about him."

"His name's Jake Zimmerman and he's the swellest guy I've ever met," Shoe replied. "The thing is, he's off-limits."

Louise raised an eyebrow. "An enlisted man?"

"Uh-huh."

"Where do you see him?"

"I meet him outside the camp after dark, and we go different places to talk...sometimes down near the river. He introduced me to his friend Hutch, and I think you'd like him."

Louise thought for a moment. *Why shouldn't I?* "Sure, I'll go out with him."

"How 'bout tonight?"

"Sorry," Louise said. "Vivian and I are going bike riding."

"You two and your bikes," Shoe said, shaking her head.

"Hey, I paid over fifty dollars American for it—I intend to get my money's worth."

"Well, you don't ride after dark, do you?"

"No."

"Then we'll go meet the boys after you get back."

"What if our tentmates ask where we're going?"

"Frankie's covering Anna's shift tonight," Shoe said. "And you can tell Vivian if you want. Maybe she'll want to go some time, too. Jake's got lots of friends."

IT TURNED OUT TO BE A MAGICAL EVENING. AFTER AN early dinner, Louise and Vivian set off on their bicycles and followed one of the many small roads leading from the camp.

"I finally feel like I'm getting the hang of this," Louise said, beaming. "Remember that time back in Sydney when I ran into the tree?"

Vivian laughed. "I sure do, and I'm proud of you for keeping at it. I don't think I've ever met anyone who learned to ride a bike as an adult."

"Or to swim."

The road—just two tire tracks between worn grass—wound through the countryside, and the first fork they took led them to a clearing beside an equally winding river.

"It's so beautiful—let's stop and dip our feet," Vivian suggested.

They sat on some flat rocks on the riverbank, lazily soaking their feet and tossing pebbles into the water.

"We need to remember this route," Louise said. "This has got to be the most peaceful spot around."

"I think this might be where Shoe comes to meet her enlisted man," Vivian said.

"What? You *know* about that?"

"I overheard them behind the mess hall several days ago making plans for a rendezvous. By the way, she actually used the word *rendezvous*. Anyway, Shoe should learn to talk a little more quietly."

"Well, I agreed to go with her tonight to meet one of his buddies."

Vivian mimicked zipping her lips. "I promise I won't say a word. But we should probably be heading back so you have time to get ready."

At 1900 hours, Shoe and Louise nonchalantly walked past the latrine and out the gate behind it. They walked arm in arm to avoid stumbling in the dark and turned on their flashlights only when the camp's lights disappeared from view. "It feels like we're Nancy Drew and Bess Marvin searching for *The Message in the Hollow Oak*," Shoe whispered.

"Oh, I loved that book," Louise replied.

They knew Jake and Hutch would be waiting for them near the same fork in the road Louise and Vivian had taken earlier. Nevertheless, they jumped when they saw the men's shadows.

Jake gave Shoe a quick hug. "Didn't mean to scare you," he said, then turned. "You must be Louise—Shoe's told me so much about you. And this is my friend Hutch—Jim Hutchinson—the nicest man in the world. I know you two will hit it off."

Standing about six-feet, two-inches tall, Hutch towered over the group. In the flashlight beam, Louise could see a flush rising on his fair skin, and she liked him for it. "Pleased to meet you," he said with a slight lisp.

"You, too."

"How about we head to the river and sit awhile?" Jake asked. "We brought some root beers and a pocketful of cookie pieces, and Hutch has his harmonica."

"Sounds good," Shoe said, taking his arm. Hutch held out his arm for Louise, and the foursome made their way down the rutted path following Jake's light.

Near the riverbank they gathered twigs and branches to build a small fire, and the men threw on several scraps of lumber from a pile hidden in some underbrush. "We brought the wood out this afternoon with help from a friend in the motor pool," Hutch explained, then busied himself stoking the flames.

Jake and Shoe settled down together on a large rock, holding hands and kissing, while Louise sat alone feeling more than a little uncomfortable. Finally, Jake looked up. "For Cripe's sake, Hutch, the fire's fine," he said. "C'mon over and sit down."

Hutch blushed again but took a seat next to Louise.

"Thanks for the fire," she said. "It's so relaxing to watch."

"And it keeps the mosquitoes away," he replied.

"That, too. Tell me about yourself. Where are you from?"

"Minnesota. A town called Hutchinson—which wasn't named after my family, by the way. It's about an hour and a half west of Minneapolis."

"That's funny. I grew up in Wisconsin, about two and a half hours *east* of Minneapolis. What'd you do there?" she asked.

"My family's got a dairy farm."

"Oh, good heavens. My parents—they're dead now—had a dairy farm. In fact, my sister and I still technically own it, and a relative is trying to sell it for us..."

"Didn't you say something about refreshments?" Shoe asked Jake. With mock formality, he pulled four bottles of root beer and a tin of oatmeal raisin cookies from his knapsack and proceeded to pass them around.

"As you can see," he said, "the cookies didn't fare too well in the package from my granny. But I'm sure they'll still be yummy."

The root beer, though warm, tasted rich and sweet. And the broken cookies had retained their flavor if not their shape. "Break out that harmonica, Hutch," Jake said.

Louise, Jake, and Shoe sat mesmerized while he played several songs with nary a mistake: "Home on the Range," "Battle Hymn of the Republic," "Oh, Susanna," and "Rock of Ages."

"That's incredible," Louise said. "Where did you learn to play?"

"My grandpa played by ear and taught me. When I got into high school, I learned to read music and took some harmonica lessons."

"Do you know any songs from the Hit Parade?" Shoe asked.

"Well, my mother just sent me the sheet music for "Oh, What a

Beautiful Morning," from the show *Oklahoma!* I've learned the first half of it, but it's a little rough."

"Please play as much as you know," Louise said. "We've been dying to hear what it sounds like."

Though less polished than the other tunes Hutch had played, it sounded plenty good to his three rapt fans. Louise wiped a tear from her cheek and hugged him when he finished. "That was beautiful."

Hutch also proved to be an excellent conversationalist, and Louise stopped paying attention to his lisp as the evening wore on. They talked for two hours, pausing only when the fire needed more fuel, and reluctantly returned to the camp in time for curfew.

When Louise crawled into her bunk, she whispered to Shoe, "Thanks for inviting me. It was the best night I've had in ages. And I can't wait until we see them again Saturday."

AFTER DINNER ON SATURDAY EVENING, CAPTAIN RILEY approached Louise and her tentmates as they neared their quarters. "Ladies, mind if I come in for a bit? I wanted to share some scuttlebutt with you."

Louise and Shoe—who'd planned to meet Hutch and Jake in less than an hour— exchanged furtive looks. Frankie piped up, "Of *course*. We've even got beer if you want one."

"I'll pass on the beer," Riley said as she entered the tent. "But I'll have a smoke while we talk." She sat at the foot of the first bunk, which happened to be Louise's, and lit a cigarette.

Frankie fumbled inside a crate where they stored communal property and produced an ashtray. "Thanks," Riley said absently.

Louise sat beside Shoe on the next bunk. Frankie and Vivian sat on their own. "What's up?" Vivian asked.

As she exhaled a long puff of smoke, the captain's mouth formed a grin. "I've got it on good authority that the 44th will all be together again *very* soon. As in, we can probably count the days on our fingers."

It was what they'd all been waiting for: no more temporary attachments to other units with strangers for coworkers and COs; reunion with the other nurses and all the doctors they'd become close to at Fort Sill.

"I, for one, can't wait to rejoin our unit," Riley continued. "It's been difficult to take orders from commanding officers I don't know very well and to pass those orders along to my nurses. For some reason, this place has had me on pins and needles."

The tentmates, unused to hearing the captain's personal thoughts, weren't sure how to respond. Finally, Shoe leaned closer to Riley and said, "We appreciate your having had our backs while we've been here."

The captain nodded in thanks, then lit another cigarette. "Colonel Macalester is old-school army with little appreciation for how hospitals should operate. He gets hung up on army rules, rather than efficient medical treatment. His current preoccupation is what he suspects is 'rampant' fraternization. I can't tell you how many times he's lectured me about protecting our nurses from the likes of those—she lowered her voice by an octave—'sex-starved' enlisted men."

Louise's stomach lurched into her throat, and she noticed Shoe's face fall.

Riley stubbed out her cigarette and stood to leave. "Well, I'd better get moving and let my other tents know," she said. "Let's keep the news of our impending departure between our unit's nurses for now, though—until we get the official word."

The tentmates collectively held their breath until the captain was well out of earshot. "Do you think she knows about us?" Louise asked Shoe—openly, since they'd confessed their activities to Frankie and Vivian.

"I don't see how she could," Shoe replied.

"I told you I overheard you talking to your boyfriend," Vivian said. "What's to say other people didn't too?"

To this, Shoe remained silent.

"Well, I don't intend to stand up the boys tonight," Louise announced. "And I don't see how the army can make us stop being nice to them."

Vivian raised her eyebrows and stared at them. "They could court-martial you."

A light rain fell as Vivian and Frankie left for a party at the officers' club, joining another group of nurses headed in the same direction. A few moments later, Louise and Shoe—wearing their rain slickers—crept out of the tent, vigilant for watchful eyes. They stopped in the latrine, then drifted behind it to the pathway where Hutch and Jake waited.

"We were afraid you weren't coming," Jake said as they approached.

"Sorry to be late," Shoe said. "Our captain dropped by after dinner and told us Colonel Macalester's on the warpath about fraternization. We waited until we were further from camp to use our flashlights..."

"And, like a klutz, I fell twice," Louise added.

"Are you okay?" Hutch asked, hugging her.

She laughed. "Only my pride was injured. And I'm glad the rain stopped."

"Well, you gals will be really glad you came," Jake said. "We've got something special planned." He refused to tell them the nature of the plan, and both guys ignored all questions about the cardboard box Hutch carried.

When they arrived at the riverbank, the men went right to work on the fire. "Looks like your pile of scrap lumber's grown in size," Shoe teased.

"Yep," Jake said. "We decided to build a bigger fire so it won't go out if it rains a little. And we brought tarps to sit on." The couples got situated, opened bottles of root beer, and began to talk.

"What's new since we saw you last?" Hutch asked.

Shoe swallowed a swig of soda and began, "Looks like we'll be rejoining our unit very soon..."

Louise glared, but Shoe didn't notice.

"We're supposed to keep it on the hush-hush until the orders come through, so don't tell anyone," Shoe said.

Jake laughed. "Way to keep a secret, kiddo," he said, jostling her shoulder.

"Give her a break," Hutch said. "The news'll be all over the camp by tomorrow morning, even if we don't say anything." He turned to Louise. "I'll sure be sorry to see you gals go, though."

She bit her lip and blinked back a few tears, a little surprised she found herself sad to be leaving him. *You've only known him a few days.* "Me, too," she mumbled.

Jake and Shoe leaned closer together, touched foreheads, and began conversing quietly.

"Let's talk about something else," Hutch said to Louise. "Any news on the sale of your farm?"

"As a matter of fact, I got a letter from my sister today enclosing a letter from our father's cousin. He said he's pretty sure he's got a reputable buyer. They'll auction off the tools and equipment the new buyer doesn't want or need."

"That's good, isn't it?"

"Seems like it, but I don't know anything about the buyer— not even how much he agreed to pay."

"Couldn't you and your sister just nix the sale?"

"I suppose we could, but we'd feel pretty guilty doing that...after all they've done for us the past several years. And we don't have anyone else to keep up the property."

Hutch patted Louise's hand. "Maybe just give the cousin the okay to sell but for not less than $5,000."

"That's a great idea. We'll do that."

Louise tugged at her lower lip for a few moments. "Also, I'm a little nervous about our belongings. My sister moved almost everything to the farm for storage before she left for duty—we always assumed the place would still be ours when we got home. There's not much of value, but I'd want to make sure our keepsakes wouldn't get lost in the shuffle."

"I can imagine. I don't know what I'd do if my folks had to sell our farm…"

While they talked, he tended the fire, which kept blazing during periodic showers. Shoe and Jake got up once to "use the bathroom" in the nearby woods and were gone for half an hour. When they returned, Jake checked his watch. "It's midnight—time for the surprise."

Shoe opened the now-soggy cardboard box and extracted a cake, holding it in front of Louise. "The mess sergeant made it for us," Hutch said proudly. He took out his harmonica, blew a note, and Shoe and Jake began singing: "Happy birthday to you…happy birthday, dear Louise…happy birthday to you."

Louise's face flushed. "This may be the best surprise ever."

"How old are you?" Jake asked.

"Old," she replied. *An old maid.*

"Seriously, how old?"

"Twenty-three."

"Hey, I've got you beat by almost two years," Shoe said.

"Yeah," Jake replied, "you've got lots of good years in front of you."

Shoe cut slices of cake with Jake's field knife and dished them onto pieces of newspaper, brought for that very purpose. "We'll have to eat with our fingers," she said. "Somebody forgot to bring forks."

They finished their cake just before the downpour began. "Throw the rest and the box into the fire," Jake said, donning his raincoat. "This isn't going to pass soon."

They hiked back as quickly as they could—in pairs with tarps over their heads—the path now muddy and the flashlights less effective in the deluge. After turning off their lights to approach the camp, Shoe and Jake slipped and fell and began laughing out loud.

"Shhhh," Louise and Hutch whispered simultaneously.

But it was too late: An M.P. on perimeter patrol heard the commotion and came to investigate. The gangly policeman, who looked no more than nineteen, stood directly in front of them. "Stop. Identify yourselves," he said without preamble.

Jake stepped forward. "Staff Sergeants Zimmerman and Hutchinson, assigned to Supply," he said. "We're just returning to camp from an evening out. No need for alarm."

"Ladies?" the young man asked. There were no enlisted women in camp, so he was aware they were officers.

"I don't think we need to involve them, do you?" Jake asked.

"Your names, ladies," the patrolman responded.

Louise glanced at Shoe and could practically see the wheels turning: her friend was thinking about giving someone else's name. "Second Lieutenant Louise Dietrich," she said quickly.

Shoe sighed. "Second Lieutenant Bertha Shoemaker."

The M.P. removed a pad and pencil from his breast pocket. "Hold this, please," he said, handing his flashlight to Hutch. "I'll need the spellings."

"Is this necessary?" Jake asked. "You could let us off with a warning."

"That's up to the COs."

They complied with the instruction to spell their names. After brief handshakes with the women, the men stalked off toward their quarters. Much to their discomfort, the policeman insisted on escorting Louise and Shoe to their tent.

Reading with a flashlight under her mosquito netting, Vivian couldn't help noticing that both were crying when they entered. "What happened?" she asked.

"We got caught by the perimeter patrolman," Shoe said. "He took our names and is going to report us."

"After Captain Riley's warning..." Louise moaned.

When Frankie came in a few minutes later, they had to repeat the news. "They don't *have* to court-martial you," she said.

"But, like Vivian said before, they *might*," Shoe replied, stifling a sob.

Louise and Shoe spent a sleepless night and, thankfully, weren't on duty on Sunday. They went to a church service in the morning and fervently prayed they would be spared formal punishment. At lunchtime several other nurses from the 44th, bearing a cupcake with a candle, gathered around their table and sang "Happy Birthday." When she blew out the candle, Louise's unspoken wish was the same as her prayer.

It would be Monday afternoon before Captain Riley confronted the rule violation. Stone-faced, she came to the ward where Louise was dispensing oral medications. "Dietrich," she barked. "As soon as you're finished, come to the office." With trembling fingers, Louise passed out the remaining pills to her patients, carefully noting that she'd done so in the charts. The patients had overheard Riley's order and couldn't help giving her pitying looks with their thanks.

She breathed deeply as she made her way down the ramp, trying in vain to slow her heartbeat. *I feel like a sailor being forced to walk the plank over shark-infested waters.*

Shoe was already seated in the office when Louise arrived. Without speaking, she took the chair beside her. Exchanging worried looks, they glanced at their watches and waited for ten minutes before the captain returned. They both rose at attention when she entered.

Riley didn't tell them to sit, nor did she do so herself. "Over my objections, Major Mason insisted on keeping the two of you on our overseas roster," she began, her face red with fury. "'They're great nurses and I assure you they're trustworthy,' he told me. And now you're caught flagrantly fraternizing, after I specifically warned against it. I should've known better."

Louise thought her knees would buckle. Shoe swallowed audibly.

"When not on duty, you're confined to quarters for two weeks. Make no mistake, if anything like this happens again, you will be court-martialed. Now get back to work." Riley turned on her heel and left, letting the screen door slam behind her.

Louise sank into her chair and dropped her head into her hands. "I feel lower than a snake. Who knows what concessions she had to make with Colonel Macalester to get us off so lightly."

"And I wonder what happened to Jake and Hutch," Shoe added. "Enlisted men—'sex-crazed' as the colonel calls them—sometimes get in more trouble than officers."

It turned out Staff Sergeants Zimmerman and Hutchinson received a lesser punishment: they were assigned to quarters when off duty for only ten days. Frankie overheard their CO talking about it a few days later and reported the news to her tentmates.

"I guess you were right about Riley having it in for us," Shoe said.

"At least it's nice to know Major Mason's in our corner," Louise said.

"Small consolation since we're not even within shouting distance of him now."

Though Louise resigned herself to not being allowed to date Hutch, she felt happy whenever she saw him on the base, and they did manage to exchange service numbers so they could correspond in the future.

Chapter Twenty

On April 6, 1944, the long-awaited day arrived: Louise and the other nurses from her unit were transported to Black River, the newly constructed 44th General Hospital. Located fifteen miles outside Townsville, on the eastern coastline in Queensland, Australia, the base itself was very isolated.

"Barracks?" the nurses exclaimed with delight when shown their living quarters. While crude and unfinished, with only cardboard partitions to serve as walls, the barracks afforded some semblance of luxury.

"This feels like heaven," Louise said to Shoe as they flopped onto the bunks in their new room.

"Mm-hmm. And it will be heavenly when they get the electricity and telephones hooked up."

Louise jumped when Anna knocked on the edge of their partition and announced, "Captain says we're to report to the hospital at 1300 hours—wearing fatigues and our Li'l Abners—ready to work our tails off."

"That's ten minutes from now," Shoe said.

"Then you'd better get a move on."

"Her husband's sure lucky he doesn't have to live with her,"

Shoe muttered as Anna moved down the hallway to serve as messenger.

"Don't be mean," Louise replied.

"Dietrich. Shoemaker," Captain Connelly yelled when they walked into the hospital ward where he was directing traffic. "It's great to see you!"

They rushed over and he threw his arms around their shoulders. "I can't believe it's been six months. You gals look well."

"Thanks," Louise said, feeling heat rising in her cheeks.

"We've got a lot of hard work ahead of us," he said, "but where else would we get the chance to set up a brand-new hospital? And I can't think of any other unit as well-equipped to do it."

"We're so glad Captain Riley wasn't able to keep us off the roster when they reassigned the other gals," Shoe said.

Connelly looked at her in stunned silence—after all, how would they know about those private discussions? But before he could reply, Colonel Frank Weston appeared in the doorway. "At last," he said, "our nurses are here."

Dietrich and Shoemaker saluted. He returned the salutes, then strode over to hug them. "Glad to see you came prepared for dirty work," he said. "As soon as the carpenters finish each building, we've gotta go in and clean, then set up beds and bring in the equipment. Before you know it, this place will be like its own city. They're building us a PX, a chapel, a movie theater, barber and beauty shops. You name it, we'll have it."

"The best part will be having the 44th together again," Louise said.

"Amen to that," the colonel said, patting her on the shoulder.

At 5:15 the next morning, Louise, Vivian, and Shoe trudged bleary-eyed to the stockade in the next-door camp for an Easter service. As usual, Shoe grumbled about the hour and the distance, but even she was stunned by the beauty of the sun rising over a nearby hillock as music emanated from the bugler's brass instrument. The strains of "Christ the Lord is Risen Today" echoed joyfully off the walls of the former prison, which would serve as a chapel until the new one was built.

"Amen," shouted the forty or so attendees when the song ended. The chaplain, whose tattered and dusty olive drab cassock looked anything but celebratory, beamed with delight as he greeted them.

"Lord, we are so grateful for the opportunity to gather today," he began.

The service was brief: even the chaplain realized the importance of getting the hospital up and running. The nurses hurriedly went through the chow line and reported to duty for more cleaning, furniture assembly, and bedmaking.

"I finally feel like we're doing what we signed on to do when we enlisted," Louise said to Frankie that afternoon as they settled the first group of patients into the ward.

AMONG THE ITEMS WAITING FOR LOUISE AT MAIL CALL that afternoon were a box of cookies from her aunt Margaret, another box of candy—chocolate Easter bunnies—from Richard's mother, and six letters from Richard himself. She absently opened the candy and passed it around for her friends in the rec hall to share, then sat down to read.

My darling Louise, I'm worried sick because you haven't answered my recent letter. Are you well? Have I said something to offend you? Perhaps you think it's presumptuous of me to suggest where you get your wedding dress—

"Perhaps?" Louise said.

"Perhaps what?" Frankie asked from across the room.

Louise looked up, confused.

"You said 'perhaps.' Perhaps what?" Frankie repeated.

"Nothing. I was just thinking out loud."

"Something you want to talk about?" Frankie asked.

"Not really."

But the more she read, the more her blood boiled. *No*, she thought, *I don't want to set a wedding date. Or choose where to have the reception. And the fact is, I never actually accepted your proposal.*

She stood up, folded the remaining unread letters and stuffed them into her pants pocket, and headed for the door.

"Louise," Shoe said, "don't forget your candy."

"I don't want it."

THE NURSES OF THE 44TH QUICKLY BECAME acclimated to their new surroundings and mission: to treat the war-wounded who were stabilized and brought in from New Guinea for recovery. A separate navy hospital directly adjacent to theirs treated wounded personnel from battles in the Coral Sea.

After a couple of weeks Bertha Shoemaker's younger sister Helen joined the unit, and Shoe had decided to room with her.

"Would you mind very much, Louise?" Shoe asked. "Helen's pretty low right now. Her husband's stationed in England, and she worries about him constantly. I feel like I need to look after her, even though I'd rather be with you."

Louise agreed and asked Dot to move in with her instead. They spent much of their free time gathering items that could be used as furniture, painting their room, and decorating with whatever was on hand: dyed-blue cloth diapers hung as curtains, an old formal gown cut up to make a dressing table skirt, and old sheets dyed pink for bedspreads. They posted a sign on the door reading Ye Olde Coffee Shoppe and began inviting friends in for coffee.

"Your room is so homey," Shoe said when she came by on her next day off. "I wish Helen could get enthused about fixing ours up. She's just so glum all the time."

"I've forgotten, how long have she and her husband been married?" Louise asked.

"Only nine months, but they began dating in seventh grade. So I guess I can understand why she's a basket case...Hey, this coffee is great. How'd you manage to get a coffee pot?"

"Dot and I chipped in with Frankie and Vivian and bought it at the PX. We were lucky to get one of the last ones in stock."

"Is that a letter from Richard you were reading?" Shoe asked, pointing to the pages on her bed.

Louise swallowed a sip of coffee. "Uh-huh. It came in the mail yesterday."

"What's new with him?"

"He's getting sent back to the States for some three-month course. He doesn't write much anymore, which I guess is just as well."

Thankfully, Shoe didn't pry. *To think just a few months ago I practically agreed to marry Richard and now I'm more relieved when he doesn't write. His absence certainly hasn't made my heart grow fonder, and it's fine just to drift apart rather than have a messy breakup.*

They sat in comfortable silence for a few moments, both lost in thought.

Finally, Louise looked up. "Now that you broke down and got a bike, Shoe, you'll have to see the spot Dot and I found yesterday. We both had the day off, so after lunch we rode out in search of a quiet place to write letters. We went down that road near the mess hall and it led to this beautiful little stream. We took off our shoes and socks and sat on some rocks, dipping our feet in the water. It felt so much like home. Of course, we didn't get much letter-writing done."

"Sounds great. Are you free to go after dinner tonight?"

"Sure. It looks like it'd be a great place to watch the sunset."

"Then it's a date." Shoe got up to leave.

"You can ask your sister to come along," Louise added.

"She doesn't have a bike yet. Besides, I could use an evening away from her."

It soon became a ritual to ride to the stream after dinner and watch the sunset.

IN EARLY MAY, SOME OFFICERS STATIONED NEARBY invited Louise, Vivian, Dot, and Shoe to go on a Sunday afternoon picnic. They waited outside and saw the guys driving up in two beat-up jeeps, one of which sputtered and died in front of the barracks. Henry, Louise's date, stood up from behind the wheel of the other jeep and shouted, "Ladies, c'mon aboard. You are in for a treat."

The women glanced nervously at each other—not because the men looked untrustworthy—wondering whether the vehicles were safe enough. They had valid cause for concern.

The men hopped out and helped the women in, amid crates piled high with picnic paraphernalia. Henry, Mike, and Donnie waited while Del climbed into the driver's seat of the stalled vehicle. The trio pushed it, Del popped the clutch, and the jeep struggled to life. "Get in," Del yelled to Mike, who ran alongside and hopped in the back seat beside Vivian.

Henry and Donnie got into the other jeep with Louise and Dot. "We're gonna take it kind of slow," Henry said as Del pulled ahead, "since we don't have any brakes."

Louise grabbed onto the windshield frame and turned to Dot in panic. Henry patted her on the back. "Don't worry, the roads won't let us go over fifteen miles per hour."

Their long journey to the ocean took them through woods, creeks, and ditches. Henry's jeep got stuck, and Louise had to take the wheel while he, Donnie, and Dot pushed. "I'm glad I learned to drive on the farm," she said when the others got back in. "And my father had to push me out of a snowdrift a time or two."

Later, the jeep became mired in a creek bed and they had to repeat the process.

"Maybe *I* should drive the rest of the way," she said, and Henry laughed but nonetheless slid into the driver's seat.

The women watched with amusement at the beach as the men scurried around like mother hens herding their chicks. From the jam-packed vehicles, they unloaded blankets, a portable radio, a case of reasonably cold Australian beer, and three wooden crates.

"Relax and make yourselves comfortable," Henry told the group. When the blankets were spread and everyone was seated, he produced a huge carton of fried chicken from one of the crates and they all dug in.

"I don't believe it," Vivian said, "but this might just be the best fried chicken I've ever tasted. Where did you guys get it?"

Del laughed. "The less you know, the better."

Louise leaned in and whispered to Henry, "Is it stolen?"

He winked. "Just enjoy it, okay?"

The group laughed and talked and sang along to songs on the radio, and the time seemed to fly by. When Henry handed Louise a third beer, she pushed it away. "This Aussie stuff tastes great but makes my head spin," she said.

"Mine too," Dot said. "You guys can have the last ones."

"Okay," Henry said, "but you gals might have to drive back to the camp."

As the sun sank lower in the sky, the group got up off their blankets and huddled under them instead. "We'd better head back before dark," Donnie said. Though somewhat reluctant to leave the beach, the others knew he was right.

There were no mishaps on the ride home, but everyone was chilled to the bone. While Vivian went in to brew a pot of coffee, the rest gathered on the sidewalk in front of the barracks, wrapped themselves in blankets, and turned on the radio. As they sat under the stars, sipping piping hot coffee and listening to Harry James and his orchestra play "Sleepy Lagoon," Louise felt as though she'd died and gone to heaven.

"Why don't we all go over to our club?" Shoe asked when the song ended.

"Heck, yes," Del replied.

Fortunately, the club was within walking distance and well supplied with more beer. "I haven't laughed this hard in ages," Louise said when it was time to go.

"Me neither," Henry said, looking around at the group. "Are you all up for doing it again on Thursday?"

They were.

ON MAY 12, LOUISE, SHOE, VIVIAN, AND DOT WALKED into Frankie's room and presented her with a card and a bouquet of paper flowers they'd made for her. "It's not much," Louise said, "but happy first anniversary."

Frankie's eyes pooled with tears. "You gals are so sweet," she said. "I was just sitting here feeling sorry for myself and worrying about Alex. He's flying bombers right in the thick of it now, and I can't seem to stop thinking about it."

"What you need is a change of scenery," Vivian declared. "We're taking you over to the club."

Their friend looked dubious but uncrossed her legs, got up off her bed, and went to run a brush through her hair.

"Put on a little lipstick, too," Dot suggested. "That'll make you feel more festive."

They linked arms and—five abreast—strode purposefully toward the club. It was Friday night, and the place was crowded and smoky. Vivian surveyed the room and pointed to a rear corner. "There's a table back there," she yelled over the upbeat music blaring from the jukebox. "I'll grab us some beers and be over in a jiffy."

As usual at their club, the beer was strong and cold. But the women could hardly hear themselves talk, and Frankie looked uncomfortable rather than consoled. "It's too noisy here," Shoe said. "Let's go back to the barracks and make coffee royals."

"What are they?" Frankie asked.

"You'll see."

Louise brewed the coffee while the others went to get their cups. Shoe came in a few minutes later bearing her secret ingredient. "A coffee royal," she said proudly, "is coffee laced with brandy, and is it yummy."

The others were skeptical, but gamely poured brandy into their cups and tasted the concoction. "I wouldn't say 'yummy,'" Frankie said after her first sip, "but it goes down pretty smoothly."

An hour later, Anna appeared in the doorway and stared at the five friends, now giddy from the effects of their newfound concoction. None of them noticed her.

"Ahem," Anna finally said, "can I come in?"

Frankie looked up from the middle of the group. "Of *course*. But go get your coffee cup first. Have we got a treat for you?"

Anna shrugged and went away, then returned a few moments later carrying her cup and a stack of printed pages. Louise scooted over and made room for her while Shoe prepared another royal.

"What've you got there?" Dot asked, nodding toward the papers.

Anna swallowed a sip of her drink, wrinkled her nose, and set the cup down before she began passing out copies. "It's called *Adventures of the Amazing 44th*, written by a press reporter to counteract all the misinformation that's going around about us at home. The colonel wants us to send them to our families to set the record straight."

"The record about what?" Shoe asked, clearly peeved to have their merriment disrupted by someone bearing orders from above.

"About the Bougainville Reef episode, when the ship carrying all our doctors, officers, and enlisted men ran aground," Anna replied. "You must've seen that article from the Sheboygan paper. The one saying that we'd been torpedoed, that hundreds of our men were killed, and that many of us nurses were now Jap prisoners."

"That all happened six months ago, *nobody* was killed, and there weren't any nurses anywhere near that reef," Shoe shot back. "None of the people we know believed a word of that article."

"Well, we weren't allowed to write about it specifically until now," Anna went on, "and he wants folks at home to know the truth."

"Where'd the Sheboygan paper get that phony story anyway?" Frankie asked.

"Had to have been from some Japanese leaflet," Dot said. "They'll do anything they can to demoralize us."

Anna nodded sagely and stood to leave. "So you'll send them home?"

Her friends—except Shoe—nodded and went back to their party.

"She can be such a know-it-all," Shoe muttered when Anna was out of earshot.

Chapter Twenty-One

In late May, when the number of casualties coming to the 44th from New Guinea for convalescence temporarily slowed, the nurses began getting a day and a half off each week. On one such occasion, Louise, Shoe, and Dot went downtown to stay at the Red Cross nurses' club.

They had planned to spend the picture-perfect sunny day at the beach, but the weather had other ideas. Arranging the beach blankets had been the first task, and each time they spread one out, a gust of wind captured an edge and sent the whole thing billowing into the air.

"Okay, we'll bury all four corners in mounds of sand and lay down in the middle," Shoe declared.

When they finally got the blankets anchored and laid down to sunbathe, wind-driven sand found its way into their hair and eyebrows and stuck to their lipstick. "This is crazy," Dot said.

"I know," Louise echoed, "and it's not the least bit relaxing. Let's go back to the club. Later, maybe we can go shopping or out for lunch instead."

They'd closed their eyes and shaken out the blankets, taken

turns brushing sand from one another's backs, and had run from the beach to the relatively wind-sheltered Townsville streets.

"You gals look like you've been through a tornado," Sarah, the club manager, said with a chuckle when they collapsed onto a sofa in the sitting area.

"We feel like it, too," Shoe said. "It was a battle just to get off the beach."

"I don't think our patients would appreciate you using the word 'battle' so loosely," Dot said, wagging her finger at Shoe.

Shoe's face fell. "You're right. Sorry."

"I was halfway kidding," Dot replied.

"But it's true," Shoe said. "We're not getting the most serious battle casualties—but even the relatively minor injuries are no picnic to handle."

"All the more reason for you to relax and enjoy yourselves during your rare time off," Sarah said. A heavyset woman of about forty, with cherubic cheeks and an ever-present smile, she exuded good sense. "The winds on the beach typically die down in the late afternoon or evening. We can pack you a picnic supper—you can even invite some mates to join you. Make a little campfire."

"That sounds good," Louise replied, then turned to her friends. "Who do you think we should call?"

"How about those three boys we discharged from orthopedics yesterday?" Shoe asked. "They're just hanging out waiting to get sent back to the front."

"Great idea," Louise said. "I remember the taller handsome one is Tom Morrison. Do you know the other two fellows' names?"

"No," Shoe said, heading out to make the call. "But I'll ring their barracks and ask for Tom. "He'll work out the rest."

"Sounds like a capital plan," Sarah said. "I'll go let the kitchen staff know. Feel free to rummage through the cupboards and closets around here and find something entertaining to do in the interim. There are plenty of puzzles and board games and heaven knows what else.”

“Thanks, we will,” Dot replied.

“We will what?” Shoe asked, returning to the sitting room.

Dot repeated Sarah’s invitation to use anything they could find around the club. “Now tell us what Tom Morrison said.”

“He said he and his pals John and Art will meet us at the beach at six, and they’ll bring some beer.”

“Did he know which nurses we were?” Dot asked, and Louise cringed inwardly at her needy tone.

A hint of embarrassment crossed Shoe’s face. “He definitely remembered Louise, and he remembered you when I told him you look like Doris Day,” she replied. “Truth is, he said they’ve been bored out of their minds, and my guess is they would’ve jumped at the chance to go on a picnic if it was the bride of Frankenstein calling.

An hour later, the three friends sat on the floor of a ten-foot by ten-foot storage closet surrounded by cardboard boxes and mounds of clothing—apparently costumes from various stage performances. “Look at this,” Dot shrieked as she pulled two tangled grass skirts from one of the boxes. “There must be a dozen of them, and they look like the skirts worn by natives in New Guinea.”

Louise stood up, grabbed another skirt, and held it up in front of herself. “These’ll fit us,” she said. “We *have* to have a picture of us wearing them.”

“Yeah,” Shoe said. “Posing in front of palm trees.”

“We can take my camera and go to the beach a little bit before meeting the boys,” Louise said. “We’ll wear our bathing suits under our clothes, and we can stuff the grass skirts in our rucksacks when we’re done.”

. . .

AFTER THE TITTERING TRIO GOT TO THE BEACH, PEELED off their outer clothing, and donned the skirts, they each took a turn with the camera.

They jumped when their former patient Tom appeared from behind a tree. "Well, look what we have here," he said with a sneer. "I'll be happy to take a snapshot of all of you."

Louise blushed as she and Dot hugged themselves to cover their bare midriffs.

Shoe handed Tom the camera. "Take three," she said, apparently nonplussed as Tom's two friends, John and Art, arrived.

As soon as the shutter clicked for the third time, the women hurried to a grove of trees where they dressed and stowed away the skirts. By the time they'd collected themselves, the men had three blankets situated around a small fire. Tom made introductions and, with none-too-subtle maneuvering, he ushered Shoe to his side and paired John to Dot and Art to Louise.

"Would you gals care for a beer?" Art asked when they were all situated. Without waiting for their reply, he reached into a brown paper bag and pulled out three bottles of Toohey's. "It's Aussie beer—a little stronger than you're probably used to, but the bottles are small."

"Don't worry," Shoe said, sitting a bit taller and throwing back her shoulders, "we're all from Wisconsin and learned how to handle our beer when we were just kids."

Dot and Louise exchanged subtle glances but accepted the proffered bottles and joined the other four in a toast. "To a pleasant evening," Art said.

After she finished her first beer and when Shoe was halfway through her second, Louise opened the lid of the picnic basket and began passing out sandwiches.

"What's the hurry?" Tom asked.

"Oh...I...uh...I'm just famished, and I assumed everybody else was too," Louise said.

"I am," Art said. "I vote we eat. And it looks like they packed enough food to feed a battalion..."

The three boys—including Tom—devoured two tuna salad sandwiches in under five minutes. Shoe nibbled on hers, focusing more on her beer. Setting the sandwich aside, she leaned on Tom's shoulder and got to her feet. "I need to use the little girls' room," she said. "I'll go over behind those bougainvillea bushes, and don't you boys dare peek."

Louise stood and inclined her head toward Dot, who also rose. "Hold up a minute—we'll go with you." They grabbed Shoe's arms and led her to a secluded spot.

"You need to slow down with the beer, Shoe," Louise hissed. "And make sure you get some food in your stomach."

"Yes, Mom," Shoe said.

The three women helped each other hold their skirts up to relieve themselves without too much difficulty. "Oh, ick," Dot exclaimed as she finished, "I still got some on my shoe."

"Kick some sand on it," Shoe muttered and wobbled off toward the campfire ahead of her friends. "You boys have it *so* much easier," she called to the guys.

"We can't leave her alone with them," Louise whispered to Dot.

The evening took a quick turn for the better: Shoe finished a whole sandwich, a tin of peaches, and two sugar cookies, and she accepted a bottle of soda from Louise rather than the third beer offered by Tom.

The men declined to talk about how they'd been injured in the fighting but willingly told stories about their hometowns and sporting victories. And they all took turns telling ghost stories. Eventually the couples laid back on their respective blankets, looking at the stars.

Louise and Dot forgot to keep an eye on their friend's beer consumption. They didn't notice when Tom pulled Shoe to her feet and asked her to help him collect more driftwood for the fire.

As Art leaned over to kiss Louise, she heard a muffled cry from the direction of the water's edge. She bounded to her feet. "Where's Shoe?" she asked.

"They went to get firewood," John mumbled.

"C'mon, Dot," Louise yelled. "We gotta find her!"

The two women ran toward the ocean with Art trailing several steps behind. Louise stumbled over a rock and fell to her knees; Dot helped her up and they began calling, "Shoe! We're coming...hang on."

Just beyond a mound of sand, they saw their friend, pinned to the ground under Tom's weight, struggling and biting at the hand he held over her mouth. Louise and Dot were on him in a minute, pummeling his back with their fists. "Get off of her," Louise shrieked. "Help us, Art."

Her date hastily moved to the scene. "Stop it, all of you," he said and pulled Tom away from the women. "It's over now."

Shoe sobbed in her friends' arms, tears and snot streaming down her face. Dot noticed her bathing suit bottom in the sand by her side and snatched it up. "Did he...?"

"No," Shoe said, shaking her head. "You...you got here in time."

Tom, pacing as he shoved his shirttail into his pants, muttered, "You know you wanted it."

Art grabbed him by the elbow. "Be quiet, for Chrissake," he said, then turned to Louise. "I'll help you get her back to the club."

"We can manage on our own," Louise said as she and Dot each threw one of Shoe's arms around their shoulders and trudged back toward the fire.

Tom stumbled away.

"You can expect a visit from the M.P.s, Sergeant," Louise yelled.

"I'd advise against calling them," Art said, walking alongside the three women.

"Why?" Dot asked.

"Three female officers fraternizing with enlisted men—and former patients, at that. Signing out of the barracks for wholesome R&R at the Red Cross, but instead cavorting around the streets of Townsville in bathing suits and hula skirts and drinking to excess. Definitely 'conduct unbecoming.'"

"You bastards..."

"Well, this particular bastard will follow you back to the club and carry your picnic basket so you can see to your friend," Art said as they neared the campfire and saw John asleep on his blanket. "I'll collect my friends when the dust settles, and I'm sure I can convince them not to file a complaint against you. With any luck, you'll never hear of us again."

BACK IN THEIR ROOM AT THE CLUB, DOT AND LOUISE eased Shoe onto her bed and gently examined her. Dark bruises encircled her upper arms, and her legs were covered in scratches. Her lower lip had begun to swell, and one of her fingernails was broken and jagged. "Let's get you into the bathtub," Louise said, "and then we'll decide who to report this to."

Shoe shook her head. "The M.P.s might believe us if we reported it," she said, "but they'd also believe I was asking for it. We would get in trouble for fraternizing and probably be cited for conduct unbecoming an officer. I'm not throwing away my military career and benefits for one night of stupidity. And I won't let you throw away yours."

"But..." Louise began.

"And nothing really happened," Shoe whispered. She grabbed a towel and her toiletry bag and hobbled into the hallway. "I can get myself in and out of the tub alone, thanks."

Dot and Louise watched warily as Shoe turned toward them again. "And one more thing," she said, "if you *ever* breathe a word of this to *anyone*—including my sister—I'll never speak to either of you again. Understood?"

They nodded.

"Do you believe her? That nothing happened, I mean," Louise asked Dot when the door closed behind their friend.

"I honestly don't know."

"Me either. But not reporting it..."

Dot shrugged. "Is it our choice to make?"

Now it was Louise's turn to shrug. But the episode would haunt her for weeks.

When the trio returned to camp the following morning, Shoe's physical injuries were visible only if one looked closely. The swelling in her lip had receded to the point that "an insect bit me" was a believable story.

After a particularly grueling shift about ten days later, Louise and Shoe gathered their toiletries and headed toward the shower. "The sun's already setting, and I'm too tired for this," Shoe groused, "but I've got to wash off the blood and guts."

"I'll bet there's no hot water left," Louise said, wrapping the towel around her shoulders against the evening chill.

"I can't remember the last time I had a hot shower," Shoe said. "Or even a warm one for that matter. But I guess we don't have much choice."

Louise stood at the edge of her partition—out of the shower head's reach—and turned the handle. She cautiously put a foot in the spray but jerked it back. "It's freezing!"

"You're torturing yourself trying to get in slowly," Shoe said from the adjacent stall. "I'm going to jump in and get it over with."

Louise followed suit, frantically rubbing the grime and goose-flesh on her arms and legs with soap and her washcloth. She ducked her head under the spray, added a dollop of shampoo, and washed and rinsed her hair as fast as she could. Shoe finished a few seconds before her.

"I think we've set a world record," Shoe said as they toweled off and put on their robes.

"I'm sure you're right," Louise replied. "How can it be so beautiful during the day and so cold at night?"

"I don't know, but I'm told it gets worse."

They hurried back to the barracks, dressed, and wrapped themselves in wool army blankets. A few minutes later, Shoe appeared at Louise and Dot's door carrying a coffee mug. "Can I bum a cup?" she asked.

"Of course," Dot said, "but you'd better enjoy it while you can. The guy at the PX says coffee's getting scarce."

"What next?" Shoe moaned. "I'm not sure I can handle this war without coffee." She settled down on Louise's bunk, holding her mug with both hands, savoring the warmth. "Hey," she added, "did you hear the news? They've decided to allow us to date enlisted men?"

"Really?" Louise asked.

"Uh-huh. There was scuttlebutt about it at lunch, but no one knew for sure. Then Anna confirmed it with Captain Riley this afternoon."

Dot laughed. "It probably won't be as much fun as when we had to sneak—" She threw an apologetic look at Shoe.

"You might be right," Louise said. *And wouldn't you know it? After I've finally met a nice Air Corps officer.*

The friends sipped their coffee, seemingly lost in thought for a few moments.

"What's new at home?" Shoe finally asked.

Dot's eyes lit up. "My mom sent me some newspaper articles about the Allies' invasion in France and all the celebrations they had on June 6th."

"But there were so many casualties," Louise said. "My aunt wrote to tell me another one of the kids from my high school was killed."

"There'd be more casualties if we didn't fight back against the Nazis now," Shoe said. "I just hope it's over quickly."

"And I hear the B-29s are doing a pretty good job over Japan," Louise said. "Maybe we'll all get to go home soon."

"Hopefully before the coffee runs out," Dot teased.

"No," came a voice from the doorway. They looked up as Vivian walked in. "Don't tell me there's a coffee shortage."

"The guy at the PX says we should be prepared," Dot replied. "We didn't see you at dinner. Where've you been?"

"At a party planning committee meeting, for the anniversary soiree on the twenty-fourth," Vivian said. "I sure could use somebody else to help with refreshments."

"I'll do it," Louise replied. "I don't have much of a social life with my flyboy in New Guinea."

"I sure hope everything's okay there," Vivian said. "I don't hear from Jimmy as much as I'd like, and I can't help but worry. You're lucky your Captain can fly back here now and then. At least you can occasionally see with your own eyes that he's okay."

"I'm afraid I'm getting pretty attached to him," Louise said with a sigh.

"And it's no wonder," Vivian said, "what with him taking you on moonlit sightseeing tours in a C-47."

Louise blushed. "We weren't up there that long. Just flew around the 44th a few times to see it from the air."

HER AIR CORPS CAPTAIN—WILLIAM ROGERS JOHNSTON but nicknamed Will Rogers, after the famous cowboy actor— showed up again five days later and came by the hospital while Louise was on duty. First Lieutenant Davis, her head nurse and a stickler for discipline, saw them talking in the doorway and tapped her wristwatch sternly. "Back to work, Dietrich."

"I've got to go," Louise said.

He brushed her cheek with a quick kiss. "I understand. Pick you up at six for dinner at my club?"

Louise's eyes sparkled with happiness as she went back to

work. Will, a handsome dark-haired guy with a charming Oklahoma accent, always turned heads. His sparkling blue eyes and dimpled chin gave him a playful air, and his laugh was infectious. Louise walked confidently as they entered the crowded, smoky club that evening.

He'd reserved a table for two and shook off several couples' offers to join them, leading Louise purposefully to the corner of the dining room. "Hope you don't mind, but I want you all to myself tonight," he said with uncharacteristic seriousness.

Louise met his gaze. "I don't mind at all."

He ordered a bottle of wine and poured her a generous glass. After the first sips, he began telling her about his recent missions. "We brought in a load of Japanese prisoners today for you to take care of," he said, then paused a moment to choose his words. "I have to say the medics used more restraint than I would've in their positions. They treated them like human beings rather than the way they treat Allied prisoners."

"Do we really know how they're treating our boys?"

Will nodded gravely. "There's a group of missionaries at our base in New Guinea who've been prisoners of the Japs for two years—we'll be bringing them here in the next few days and you'll get to meet them yourself. They've told horror stories about their captivity. I'm sure they'll fill you in, but what little I heard turned my stomach."

Louise reached over and stroked his hand. "It's hard, isn't it? What we're seeing? I wish we were allowed to keep diaries so we could get it off our chests. We can't even write home about the battles nearby or the horrific injuries we're treating because our letters are censored."

"It helps me to talk to you. You're such a good listener." He picked up her hand, brought it to his lips, and kissed it gently.

The simple gesture brought tears to her eyes but, determined to keep the evening pleasant, she blinked them back.

Will must've read her mind. "Hey, let's order our dinner, and maybe we'll be done in time to see the movie. How does steak sound?"

"Great. And I've been dying to see *Going My Way*. I love Bing Crosby."

They exchanged light-hearted stories over dinner: how Louise and her friends had posed in grass skirts on the beach, how the party plans were going, how Will and his friend had played a joke on their navigator. When the jukebox began playing Rudy Vallee's "As Time Goes By," Will pulled Louise to her feet. "This song's too good to pass up," he said, leading her to the dance floor.

He held her closer than usual and she rested her head on his shoulder, reveling in the feel of his freshly shaven skin and the scent of Palmolive. As the song ended, he kissed her neck and whispered, "We'd better go if we want seats."

Will kept his arm around her waist and hugged her closely to ward off the cold on their walk to the movie theater. As expected, there were only a few remaining seats, on a bench in the front row. Louise felt proud to move through the crowd with her flyboy and happily held his hand as they settled in to watch.

"Bing plays a priest in this picture," she whispered to Will as the title screen appeared. "It'll be different to see him in a non-comedic role."

She loved every minute of the movie and cried unabashedly when Crosby sang "Ave Maria" and "Silent Night." She loved that Will pulled her closer and gave her his soft white handkerchief.

As they stood to leave, Will asked, "Do you want to go back to the club for a nightcap?"

I want to go snuggle up with you by a fire in a cabin someplace, but the club is better than going back to the barracks and climbing under three blankets and *my mosquito netting.* "Sure," she said.

This time, they could not avoid his friends who, like Louise, wanted some of Will's attention. After one drink, she touched his arm. "I need to get some sleep so I can be on my toes tomorrow," she said. "We're short-staffed because a few nurses are down with dengue fever."

He gave her a warm and lingering kiss at the front door of the barracks—men weren't allowed inside—then said, "I'll do everything I can to make it back for the party on Saturday night."

Chapter Twenty-Two

Louise and Vivian ate breakfast together the following morning. "What are you so happy about, Viv?" she asked as they carried their trays to a table. "You look positively radiant."

"There were two letters from Jimmy waiting for me when I got off work yesterday. His words blow me over—he's such a good writer. He keeps telling me how much he loves me and wants to spend his life with me."

"Do you feel the same?" Louise asked, chiding herself for the twinge of jealousy she felt.

"Absolutely," Vivian replied. "We'll probably wait 'til we get home to get married though. I want my family to be there with us when we do."

"Gee, I'll be the only old maid around here pretty soon. Did you hear that Shoe's engaged?"

"What?"

"Bertha Shoemaker is engaged."

"To who?"

"Del—the guy she's been paired with for several group dates."

"It seems awfully quick," Vivian said. "I had no idea it was that serious."

"I guess it is kind of quick," Louise replied. "Anyway, he's having his own ring—the one with the diamond in it—made over into an engagement ring."

"Well, if Shoe's happy I'm happy. And speaking of romance..." Vivian said sotto voce, "how was your date with Will last night?"

Louise smiled shyly. "Pretty great."

"It just so happens that I was with a group of people at the club too, and we saw you over in the corner eating dinner. He sure looks smitten."

"He hasn't told me how he feels," Louise replied. "It doesn't seem like we know each other with him being gone so much."

"Well, I'm betting things'll heat up soon."

When Louise and Vivian got to work, the hospital was abuzz. "There's a bunch of Japanese POWs in the empty south ward," Lieutenant Davis told them before they'd even removed their coats. "They're heavily guarded and only the medics are taking care of them. Just thought you should know."

It was all anyone could talk about. Anna came by Louise's ward mid-morning. "You should go by and see them on your break," she said. "The guards'll let you in. I even took a few pictures."

Louise raised an eyebrow. "I don't know. Maybe tomorrow.

But her curiosity got the better of her. The Japanese had been vilified since Pearl Harbor and she'd treated so many casualties of their viciousness, she realized she wanted to see the enemy. When her break rolled around, she told Samuel, her ward man, "I'm headed over to the south ward."

"Can't resist, can you?"

She approached the guard at the ward's entrance somewhat timidly. "I hear I might be allowed in to see the prisoners?"

"Hell yes," the six-foot two-inch, two-hundred-pound Sergeant told her, "though I can't let you go in unescorted. My partner's showing a doc around right now, but he should be back in a minute or two."

Louise waited nervously, staring at her feet. A moment later the doctor emerged with another large guard—wearing the name tag WILSON—who glanced at her knowingly and said, "Next."

She saw at least eight other armed men stationed throughout the tent, watching about twenty prisoners. Sergeant Wilson, apparently noticing her surprise, chuckled and said, "Little, aren't they?"

"Yes, and I wasn't expecting that."

"They're pretty friendly—I'm guessing because they've never had it so good as they have it here. They're happy to pose for photos if you want to come by again and take a few shots. The higher-ups tell us it'll be about a week before they're moved."

Louise glanced toward the closest prisoners, who'd pulled their bunks next to one another and were playing some type of card game. They grinned and waved at her.

"Thanks, Sergeant," she said as she hurried toward the door.

"What'd you think?" Samuel asked when she returned to duty.

"They're so much smaller than us—it seems like maybe it's not fair to fight them," she replied.

"Well, just look at the injuries they've caused our boys, who *are* just boys." Samuel, a twenty-eight-year-old medic, had seen a lot during his ten years in the Army.

"You're right about that," Louise said. "I feel like a grandmother in here some days. And I sure wish they would treat our prisoners as well as we're treating theirs."

"Not likely, from what I hear," he muttered.

THE SUBJECT OF THE JAPANESE'S TREATMENT OF prisoners came to the forefront again several days later when the group of missionaries Will had spoken of were brought to the 44th for treatment and rehabilitation.

The men, malnourished and bewhiskered, were housed in another empty ward, awaiting transportation south. Over 100 missionaries, including forty nuns, had been rescued by American soldiers after the Japanese army fled Hollandia, New Guinea. The group included Germans, Poles, Czechs, and Dutch. Two Australian Lutheran lay workers were among those hospitalized at the 44th.

Most of the men were eager to share their stories with the medical personnel, and several talked with the doctors, Louise, and three of her fellow nurses after their shift one afternoon. When the Australians became exhausted in the recounting, others chimed in using broken English.

"You won't believe it," Louise told Dot when she returned to the barracks that evening. "The mission had been operating in New Guinea since 1910. When they took Hollandia, the Japanese captured all of the people there, including the nuns, and held them prisoner for close to two years.

"They said the Japs didn't show any partiality to the missionaries who were German, which you might have thought they would because they're allies and all. One of the Australians said he thought the Japs treated the Germans even more harshly."

Wrapped in a blanket as usual, Louise pulled it tighter around herself.

"How did they treat the nuns?" Dot asked.

"Awful. And they certainly weren't given any special treatment because of their age or medical conditions. The women were often slapped in the face, and one nun was beaten when she asked for flour to mix with their rice.

"None of the prisoners had enough to eat, and they're all just skin and bones. I looked at one man's chart—he's five-feet ten-inches tall and weighs only ninety pounds. And even though they were malnourished, the men were forced at bayonet-point to do manual labor like road construction. Can you imagine?"

"It's just plain hateful," Dot said. "Though I have to say the

POWs that are here right now don't seem capable of acting so barbarically."

"The missionaries said that after successful military actions by the Allies they were all punished—men and women alike. Sometimes they'd be ordered to stand up for long periods of time until their legs would give out. These are middle-aged people, not strong young soldiers. It makes me just sick."

"Are they doing okay medically?" Dot asked.

"Mostly, though, it'll take a long time for them to recover. They're all so grateful for their treatment since being rescued. Even the Germans were anxious to shake our hands and say thank you."

"Well, that's one good thing about this place, I've never had an ungrateful patient," Dot said.

Louise nodded and swatted at the mosquito buzzing around her head. "How cold does it have to get before these damn things die off?"

"Beats the hell out of me."

Still clothed, Louise climbed under her mosquito net and pulled on another blanket. "I refuse to get malaria or dengue fever."

In mid-July, Louise returned to the barracks from mail call one day carrying a somewhat battered, brown paper-wrapped box.

"A package," Dot said as Louise walked into the room. "Who from?"

"My sister," Louise replied, shaking the box gently. "She's stationed in Oakland, California, now and wrote to tell me she was sending cookies and a surprise."

Dot got up off her bunk and gave the box another shake. "It's not very heavy. Hurry up and open it."

Louise grabbed the scissors from their dressing table and began cutting away the paper.

"Oh, c'mon," Dot said. "Doc Connelly could take out an appendix quicker than that."

Louise stopped entirely. "I like to savor the suspense. As a matter of fact, maybe we should crack open some of the American liquor we got yesterday and make this a real celebration. Which would you rather have—champagne, whiskey, or rum?"

"None of them goes well with cookies. Now open the box."

Louise resumed cutting and pulled out a cookie tin and a tissue-wrapped bundle. "Oh my gosh, it's a housecoat. I'm going to feel like a civilian again wearing something so gorgeous."

She shook out the pink garment with ruffles adorning the closure, collar, and cuffs and put it on over her uniform, twirling around the room.

"It's beautiful," Dot said quietly. "Etta is the best."

Louise sniffed back a few tears and nodded. "I sure do miss her."

In silence they nibbled on crumbly but delicious cookies from a bakery in San Francisco and startled when someone knocked on the door. "Dietrich," the duty officer announced, "you've got a phone call."

Still wearing the unfastened pink housecoat, Louise rushed down the hall toward the telephone, her stomach flip-flopping along the way. *Will isn't due back from his seven-day leave in Sydney till tomorrow. I hope nothing's happened to him.*

"Hello," she said tentatively.

"And hello to you, my little chick," Will said.

Louise let out the breath she didn't realize she'd been holding. "Oh, I'm glad you're okay. Are you still in Sydney?"

"No, ma'am. I came back early 'cause I got wind of orders for another mission starting at 0600 tomorrow, and I couldn't bear to leave again without seeing you. Are you free this evening? They haven't put you back on night duty yet, have they?"

Louise laughed. "Next week, and, yes, I'm free this evening."

"Whew. I was worried that someone else had won your affection. How 'bout I pick you up at six for dinner at the club?"

"Sounds great. See you soon."

Louise practically floated back to the room, her ruffles flowing in a cheerful pink wake behind her.

"Good news, I take it?" Dot asked, looking up from a crossword puzzle book.

"Uh-huh. Will came back a day early from his leave and we're going out tonight."

"I'm glad for you."

Louise flopped down on her bunk and selected a piece of cookie from the tin. "The only trouble is he has to leave early tomorrow for another mission."

"Did he say where to?"

"You know he's not allowed to say until he gets there."

"I know, but sometimes Dwayne gives me little hints."

Louise raised an eyebrow. "Will doesn't. The last time it was New Guinea. The time before that Guadalcanal and, gosh, he was really shook up after that one."

"It's so hard dating an aviator, never knowing when he'll be around. They're always dreaming up last-minute missions for them...and ones that are always in the thick of things. It's awful to say this, but it's been a godsend to me that Dwayne's been grounded for a month with jaundice."

Louise pulled off the housecoat. "It's not awful—after all, his medical condition isn't life-threatening or anything. Will's been good to me, always calls the minute he lands, and always leaves me a message when he flies away again. And really, I'm surprised he's still here at all. After two and a half years, his stateside orders could come any day."

Dot hung her head. "Dwayne's too."

. . .

Several days later, Louise came back to the barracks after her second night shift. She tiptoed into the room, hoping to avoid waking Dot, and crawled into her bunk topped with three wool blankets. Ten minutes later—her teeth still chattering—she reached underneath the bed to grab an open bottle of whiskey, the remains of the last liquor ration. The first generous swallow sent a rush of warmth through her body—the second set off waves of coughing.

"You okay?" Dot mumbled as she rolled over to look at her.

"S-s-sorry…I didn't mean to wake you. The whiskey just went down the wrong pipe."

"You're drinking in the morning?" Dot asked, sitting up.

"I can't shake these chills," Louise said, then took a smaller sip from the bottle. "It gets so desperately cold in the hospital at night. I don't think we'd be warm in those screen buildings even if we had heaters."

"Is that long-handled underwear under your uniform?"

"Uh-huh. And I never dreamed we'd need them in the tropics. The doctors are loaning us some extras they received."

"Guess you should've asked your sister to send you some instead of telling her you needed a new housecoat."

"Believe me," Louise said, "I'm gonna write her about it as soon as I stop shivering."

Chapter Twenty-Three

WHEN LOUISE GOT OFF NIGHT SHIFT IN EARLY AUGUST, she was transferred to the general medicine ward. "I'm a little sorry to be leaving surgical," she told Dot. "I can't imagine it'll be very challenging. Probably just a bunch of stomach aches and dengue fever cases."

Her first day proved her wrong. One of the doctors—Captain Connelly—caught her attention the minute she walked onto the ward. "Dietrich," he said, standing beside the second bed, "meet me in the office, please. I'll be there as soon as I finish this exam."

Puzzled, she turned around and headed to the office. Thankfully, there was still coffee left in the pot, so she filled a cup. It was bitter but piping hot—in fact she burned her tongue on the first sip—and it took away her chill. She finished the cup just as Connelly walked in.

"I wanted to fill you in so you wouldn't be alarmed when you saw our new patient, the one in bed two," he said, grabbing his own half-filled mug of coffee, probably stone-cold by now. He took a swig, apparently unconcerned.

"What's to be alarmed about?" Louise asked.

"He's a Philippine kid, about fifteen years old, who looks

awful. He's got skin lesions and nodules covering his right arm. He lost feeling in the arm, and it's very weak. We scraped some cells from one of the lesions and Captain Harold is studying them. He thinks it may be leprosy."

"Leprosy?" *They didn't cover that in nursing school.*

"I've forgotten anything I might have learned about it in med school," the doctor said, "but our Merck Manual seems to indicate Harold's right. And it says leprosy isn't very contagious, which is good news."

Louise breathed a silent sigh of relief.

"Trouble is," Connelly went on, "to be prudent, we decided to have him wear a mask, and now the other patients are afraid they'll get whatever he's got."

"What do you need me to do?"

"Presume he's got leprosy, which isn't transmitted by casual contact, and treat him like any other patient."

"And if he's got something other than leprosy that *is* more contagious?"

Connelly shook his head. "We'll cross that bridge if we come to it. Harold should be done with his tests in a few days."

Louise stood up to go.

"By the way," Connelly said, "the kid doesn't speak English, but his older sister sits with him almost every day and speaks pretty well."

Louise went to work with some trepidation. But she recognized the ward man—Sergeant Joe Scarpetti—who was bathing the patient in bed one. She'd worked with him many times and liked the guy. "Hi, Joe. Good to see you."

"Same to you, Lieutenant. I'm guessing this is your first day on this ward?"

"You guessed right."

"We've got a good group of patients, and they've calmed down since I made the announcement that Ramil here"—he pointed toward bed two—"isn't contagious."

She raised an eyebrow. "When did you make the announcement?"

"When you and Doc Connelly were in the office just now."

"Did he tell you to announce it?"

Joe laughed. "Heck, no. But you and I both know that the docs don't always use common sense."

Louise glanced around the ward. The twenty patients all looked relaxed. Some dozed. A couple were writing letters. Others were playing cards. "Good call, I'd say," she said. "Anything else I should know before I make my rounds?"

Joe thought a moment. "Oh, yeah. The kid in bed seven has gone deaf from meningitis. If you need to ask or tell him anything, you need to write a note."

Half an hour later, Louise approached bed seven and picked up the patient's chart. *Dale Swaggart, age 19, diagnosis: bacterial meningitis resulting in bilateral, total deafness.* A pad of paper and pencil sat on the bedside table. She picked it up and wrote: *Hi, Dale. I'm Lt. Dietrich. I'm going to take your vitals and give you your meds. How are you feeling this morning?*

"Good mornin', ma'am," he replied.

Louise dropped the pad and paper.

"I am sorry," Dale drawled, at a slightly lower volume, "I didn't mean to scare you. Since I cain't hear anymore, I guess I talk louder than I should. I'm feeling better today than yesterday."

Louise stooped to retrieve the pad of paper. The pencil had rolled under the adjacent bed, where Joe was collecting a urine sample. "Let me get it," he said, stifling a laugh. "I didn't think to warn you about the volume."

She took Dale's temperature and blood pressure, noting the results in the chart. She mimicked breathing deeply, and he followed suit so she could listen to his heart and lungs. She handed him water and some pills, which he dutifully swallowed, then wrote: *Your temp and blood pressure are still a little high. I'll be back in a few minutes with an aspirin.*

"Thank you, ma'am."

Dale smiled when she returned with the aspirin. "This should help my headache, too. At least that's what my mama always gave me for headaches."

She was right, Louise wrote. *Where are you from?*

"Cain't you tell?" he asked, laughing.

She shook her head.

"The great state of Alabama," he said. "Birmingham, to be exact."

Are your folks still alive?

"Yes, ma'am. My daddy joined up again after Pearl Harbor and is stationed in California. Doesn't look like he'll get sent overseas—thank the Lord. Mama's holdin' down the fort at home and workin' in a factory that makes parts for ships."

Well, it looks like you'll be heading back to Alabama soon. I'm sure your mom will be glad of that.

"I'm tryin' to stay in the Army," Dale replied. "Just 'cause I cain't hear don't mean I cain't be useful. My CO says he'll see what he can do."

Good luck with that.

"Thank you, ma'am. And have a good shift."

Louise couldn't help humming as she walked away.

SEVERAL DAYS LATER, LOUISE RETURNED FROM A BIKE ride with Vivian to find Dot sitting on her bed with her hair in curlers and painting her nails. "How was your ride?" she asked.

"Good. You should've come with us."

"I wanted to save my energy for the party tonight at Dwayne's club. There's going to be a live band and I know he'll want to dance to every song. He's a heavenly dancer."

Louise plopped down on her own bed. "Did Dwayne tell you that his pal Will is due back any day now? This past month, while he's been in New Guinea, has sure dragged for me."

"He did tell me, and we've got loads of plans for the four of us when he gets back."

"I just hope he can stay awhile this time," Louise said. "I hate to get my hopes up." She took off her shoes and rubbed her feet. "Speaking of which, have we had a mail call yet?"

"No," Dot replied, "and they might just as well not bother. The mail's been so sparse—I haven't gotten a single letter in a week."

"Me neither. Well, I could use a cup of coffee. Do you want some?"

"Sure."

Louise set about brewing a pot, and just as the coffee finished perking, someone came down the hall calling, "Mail's in."

Louise and Dot hopped up and put on their shoes. Dot put a hat on and stuffed her curlers under it, and they went to stand in line.

"Albrecht," the clerk called, and Dot beamed to see him holding a letter.

Louise's face broke into a smile when she heard the clerk call her name, and she pushed through the remaining nurses to collect her mail: a letter from her sister and one from her Aunt Margaret. Tearing open the one from Etta, she began reading as she walked toward the barracks.

Dot looked up when she entered the room, and Louise noticed tears in her eyes. Louise's breath caught in her throat. "Bad news?"

"No, it's a letter from my sister. It just makes me homesick."

"I got one from my sister, too, and I miss her like the dickens." She poured herself a cup of coffee and sat down to finish reading.

They sniffled as they read and reread their mail.

Louise finally set the precious pages aside. "Can I ask you something?"

"Of course."

"You're three years older than me and at least three years wiser. Do you think I've changed since we've been in the Army?"

"I think we all have, but what exactly do you mean by change?"

Louise sighed. "Everyone here tells me I look and act like a little kid. I think some of them mean it in a positive way, but I'm twenty-three years old and would like people to see me as a grown, competent woman."

"Oh, good heavens," Dot said with a laugh. "People love your youthful exuberance and your sweetness. When they say you act like a kid, they're envious. Everyone knows you're a competent grown-up, and they respect your nursing skills and value your opinion. Does that answer your question?"

"I guess so. I do feel like I have more confidence than I did before I left home. I just wish I could quit blushing at the wrong times—it's so embarrassing."

Dot opened her bottle of nail polish and began applying a second coat. "We all have little embarrassing quirks. My left eyelid twitches when I get nervous—I have to cover half my face to keep people from noticing."

"Well, it must work because I never knew about it. And even twitchy eyes couldn't change Dwayne's opinion. He's obviously taken with you.

"I am too."

THE NEXT MORNING WHEN SHE REPORTED FOR DUTY, JOE Scarpetti was already on the ward. "What's new?" she asked him.

Joe wrung out a wet cloth that he'd been using to wipe a patient's brow. "A load of patients back from the front," he said. "The battle wounds went to the surgical ward. We got six—all of them feverish. Docs think the one in bed ten has malaria and the others probably dengue fever."

"I was hoping for some positive news," Louise said.

"Ramil's tests came back. He *does* have leprosy."

"It's good for us that he's not contagious but not so good for

Ramil." She'd taken a look at the Merck Manual on her break the day before and knew leprosy could have more than just cosmetic consequences.

"Doc Connelly told me they're flying in some new meds that have been found to be pretty effective," Joe replied. "Hopefully they'll ward off permanent nerve damage."

"I'll say a few prayers that it does." She moved on to do her rounds.

LATER THAT AFTERNOON, LOUISE HAD TIME TO VISIT with one of the new patients, Private Benjamin Walters from Freeport, Maine. He'd been diagnosed with dengue fever or "break-bone fever"— often painful but less lingering than malaria —and was alert and talkative. "Do you mind?" she asked, indicating the foot of his bed.

"I'd be happy if you would," he replied, and she sat. "You're the first girl I've seen in about a month."

Louise took no offense at the word "girl" and, in fact, it took her a few minutes to realize exactly what he'd said—his thick Maine accent was difficult for her to understand. She asked him several questions about his home, his family, and what he'd done before enlisting, then about his experiences in combat.

Walters got a faraway look in his eyes and took a few breaths before responding. "It was so goddamned uncomfortable. We didn't have baths for days or even weeks, and the rations they gave us turned our stomachs. The Japs kept shelling us, even at night. We had to sleep two to a foxhole so one guy could keep watch while the other tried to get some rest. It was hell to be scared shit-less *all* the time...pardon my language."

Louise reached over and handed him a cup of water. "Take a few sips—we need to get you rehydrated. And you don't need to tell me any more if it's too difficult."

He dutifully drank and then shook his head as if to exorcise demons. "I need to talk about it...We hardly ever saw any Jap soldiers even though we were constantly under fire. When we saw one that appeared to be dead, we were told to shoot him again—they're skilled at lying motionless for days and then attacking.

"The second day of my fever was the worst day of my life." He paused to blink back tears and took another sip of water. "We'd been in a foxhole all night, and I'd never felt such pain. I couldn't stop shaking, even when my buddy put his arms around me and tried to warm me up. At least there wasn't any shelling. At dawn our lieutenant gave the order to move out and comb the area.

"I was delirious, and everything looked hazy and yellow. My buddy and I came upon two Jap soldiers who had to have been dead for days, but he said we needed to shoot 'em to be sure. He shot one and I shot the other, and then we searched them. We took their knapsacks and rejoined the other guys, then got the heck out of there.

"I passed out when we got back to the base. The medic tried to get my fever down and gave me some morphine for the pain. I guess I refused to let go of the knapsack when they put me into the ambulance for evac. I've still got it with me."

"Have you looked in it?" Louise asked.

"Yeah," Walters said. "Do you want to see?"

Do I want to see? she thought. *I honestly don't know.* After a moment she said, "Sure."

Walters reached under his bed and produced the satchel. He undid the buckles carefully and pulled out a wad of Japanese currency and a stack of leaflets.

"What are those?" Louise asked.

"Propaganda. They leave them all over the place. Stories and pictures showing American girls back home laughing on the arms of handsome men—saying none of the girls wait for their soldiers, that they all find other guys to date. I mean, we all *know* it's phony, but it still gets you wondering, especially when you're stuck in a foxhole. Here—you can look." He handed her a couple of leaflets and a few pieces of currency.

She quickly handed them back. "It makes me feel creepy just to touch this stuff."

Walters nodded. "It made me feel creepy to take it from him. I can't figure out why I wanted to keep it."

She patted his hand. "Who knows why we do what we do? You'll figure it out someday."

"I hope so."

"You'd better get some rest now."

She left the ward, went into the office—which was thankfully vacant—and sobbed.

Will these boys ever be able to forget the horrors and fears they lived through? she wondered. *And will we nurses be able to forget their stories or the awful wounds we've seen?*

Chapter Twenty-Four

THE REMAINDER OF AUGUST WAS A WHIRLWIND OF activity for Louise and Dot and their other three friends who dated pilots in Will's unit. There were dinners and dancing and picnics filled with plenty of hugs, kisses, and laughter.

After one evening's festivities, Dot and Louise wobbled to their room and readied themselves for bed. "It sure is cute how Will calls you 'Chick' in that Southern drawl of his," Dot said.

Louise's eyes sparkled. "And tonight, when he called me his 'beloved little chick,' I thought my knees would buckle. There's nothing I'd rather be."

Dot sat before their makeshift dressing table and applied cold cream to her face, wiping off her makeup with a tissue. "Has he told you how he feels about you?" she asked sheepishly. "Dwayne hasn't."

"Well, he's never made any promises, and he's never handed me a line," Louise replied quietly. "We never talk about romance and sentiment, but I believe we do have sort of an unspoken understanding about how we feel about each other."

Dot turned toward her friend. "If he asked, would you marry him?"

"He's the finest, funniest, sweetest guy I've ever known. If he asked me to wait a hundred years for him, I believe I'd do it. Only he won't ask me because he's going home and I'm not for a long time yet. Even though it can't last, at least I've had the pleasure of knowing that there are still people like him in the world."

"I wish I could feel the same way you do. I just know I will be devastated if Dwayne leaves without asking me to marry him. There's a little time yet, so I'm hoping and praying."

THE FIVE PILOTS CALLED FOR THEIR DATES AT THE nurses' barracks on the evening of August 29 for the informal farewell party being held at their club—they'd all gotten their stateside orders. Already moody, Dot clung to Dwayne's arm a tad too tightly. Louise wanted to whisper to her to ease up a little, but the opportunity didn't arise—Will never left her side or took his eyes off her.

He bought champagne for their table and toasted his chick and her friends. He made sure plenty of slow songs were played on the jukebox and danced every dance with her—talking all the while about the fun times they'd had and how much he'd miss her.

He kissed her slowly and deeply at the barracks door, then—choked up—wordlessly waved his goodbye. He and his four buddies, including Dwayne, would be flying out of Townsville at 0600 the following day.

Louise climbed into bed and buried her face in the pillow, crying silently. Dot came in a short while later sobbing. "He...he...he didn't ask me..."

Sighing, Louise rose and went to hug her friend. "I'm sorry," she said, pulling her tight and stroking her hair.

"Do...do you think maybe...maybe he'll write to ask me?"

"Shhhh. Try not to think like that."

Suddenly Dot pulled back. "Did Will ask you?"

"No."

. . .

LATE IN THE AFTERNOON THREE DAYS LATER, LOUISE and her friend Abby received word that they had visitors. They walked down the hallway together, speculating about who the visitors might be. "Maybe boys we met at Fort Sill or in Sydney," Louise suggested.

"Could be," Abby said, "but I would think they would've written to say they were headed this way."

Louise opened the front door to find Will Rogers and Abby's boyfriend Pudge Booker standing there grinning. The men engulfed the women in their arms and swung them around wildly.

"Surprise!" Will said. "There was a flight scheduled to come here to bring a load back tomorrow, and we volunteered. We have to head out again at 0600 tomorrow, but we've got tonight free. How 'bout you gals?"

Louise's eyes lit up. "I'm free."

"Me too," Abby said. "And there's a dance at our club—should be fun."

"It's a date then," Will said. "Pick you up at seven?"

Louise went back to her room, hesitant to tell Dot the news. But, of course, Dot asked, "Who are your visitors?"

"Will and Pudge. They flew a transport plane down to take back a load tomorrow."

Dot's face fell. "I wonder why Dwayne didn't come."

"My guess is it was only a two-man job. Say, want to head over to the dining hall for an early dinner?"

"Thanks, but I'm not hungry."

"Well, you're still coming to the dance tonight, aren't you?"

"Not without a date," Dot replied sullenly.

"We *all* planned to go without dates before Will and Pudge came. There'll be plenty of boys to dance with."

"Quit pestering me about it, okay?" she said and flung herself face down on the bed.

Pestering? Louise thought. "Suit yourself."

THE TWO PILOTS MADE FOUR SIMILAR TRIPS TO VISIT Louise and Abby—sometimes flying up and back from New Guinea in the same day. "We're just taking advantage of the fact that operations in Townsville are winding down and people and equipment need to be moved north," Will told them.

"And who better to do it than us?" Pudge added.

"This must be some sort of record," Abby said. "Flying eighteen hundred miles in a day for a few hours of courting nurses."

"You gals are worth it," Will said.

The men planned a picnic for one of the evenings. "Wait'll you see what we brought," Will said when he helped Louise into the front seat of the jeep they'd procured.

"What is it?" she asked.

He kissed her cheek. "Patience, my little chick. We don't want to spoil the surprise."

She snuggled up next to him and leaned her head on his shoulder as they drove toward the river. Abby and Pudge huddled under a blanket in the back seat, laughing and kissing.

When they got to the river the guys jumped down, then gallantly lifted the girls from the vehicle. "Oh, you boys are spoiling us," Louise said.

She and Abby stood beside the jeep as instructed and watched while Will and Pudge spread several blankets on the ground. "Close your eyes and count to 100," Will told them.

At ninety-nine, the men led them to the blankets. "Okay, you can look now," Pudge said.

They opened their eyes to see a case of American beer displayed prominently in the middle of the blankets.

They shrieked in unison, "American beer!"

"How did you ever get it?" Louise asked incredulously, giving Will a playful punch to the arm.

"We're beginning to get it with our rations in New Guinea now, though I doubt you will here," he replied. He ceremoniously swept a towel off the top of a box sitting beside the beer and said, "What goes better with Schlitz than roast chickens? Let's all sit down and dig in."

There were reasonably fresh biscuits to accompany the chicken, which was tender and delicious. And the beer reminded everyone of home. The girls polished off two each and the guys three before dinner was even over.

"I don't think anything ever tasted so good," Louise said, standing up to stretch after the meal. "Now I need to find a spot to...powder my nose. Want to join me, Abby?"

"I most certainly do."

Pudge helped Abby to her feet, then headed off in the opposite direction.

As Abby and Louise walked back toward the picnic site they overheard Will say, "I'm betting she will."

Louise stopped in her tracks and began to tremble. *He's going to ask me to marry him and he's betting I'll say yes!*

"Betting who will what?" Abby asked.

Will didn't miss a beat. "I was just telling Pudge here that I'm betting our plane—we call her Sadie—will make it back to New Guinea in record time tomorrow since the guys are tuning her up tonight."

"*Good one, Will*," Louise thought, rolling her eyes.

"Say, honey," Pudge said to Abby, "why don't we take a little walk?"

"Sure."

Pudge bent down and gathered a few blankets, throwing them casually over his arm, and extended his other arm to escort her from the picnic area. After a few steps, he returned and pulled two beers out of the case, putting them in his pockets. "And now, we're all set," he said.

Will offered Louise another beer, then took one for himself.

They sat cross-legged on the remaining blankets, shoulder to shoulder and clinked their bottles in a toast. "To a most pleasant evening," he said, then stared off in the distance.

Louise waited in silence. But as the lull went on, she realized the error in her thinking.

"Pudge's going to propose, isn't he?" she asked.

"Why on earth would you think that?"

Louise forced a laugh. "I didn't believe a word of your cocka-mamie story about your plane named Sadie and how fast she'll fly."

"You're one smart chick." He paused to take a swig from his bottle. "So, what do you think? Will she say yes?"

"In a heartbeat," she said in a whisper.

"That's what I told him." He took the beer from her hand and set it next to his alongside the blankets. Then he leaned over and kissed her—more passionately than he had the night of their orig-inal farewell.

She melted into his arms, and they rolled back onto the blan-kets, still kissing. Louise was certain nothing could feel more magi-cal. *If he wants to go further, I won't say no.*

But after several minutes, Will gently pulled away and lay on his back. He reached for her hand, kissed it, and intertwined their fingers. "Just look at those stars," he said, gazing up at the sky. "I swear they're even brighter here than in Oklahoma, and that's saying something."

She collected her breath and waited for a moment to be sure her voice wouldn't crack. "They *are* beautiful," she said. "And having once slept under the stars when I was at Fort Sill, I have to agree they're brighter."

Will began pointing out various constellations. "My grandpa taught me all about astronomy and even bought me a telescope. We'd spend hours out on his ranch studying the stars. He's the one who got me interested in flying, too. He'd take me up in his little crop duster and let me hold the controls..."

"He sounds like a special man."

"I was devastated when he died."

"How old were you?"

"Eleven. And he was only fifty-six. Had a massive heart attack."

Louise squeezed his hand. They'd never spoken much about their families. "I'm sorry. I know what it's like to lose loved ones."

Their beers forgotten, they talked for two hours: about their families, their hometowns, their schooling, their hopes for the future. Though they didn't talk about their feelings for each other, Louise felt closer to Will that night than she ever had before.

They heard Pudge and Abby coming well before they reached the picnic site. "Aw, shucks," Will muttered. "I'm not ready to share you."

"Me either," Louise said with a sigh.

But they sat up expectantly when their friends came to announce the big news. "We're engaged!" Pudge said, unable to contain himself.

"Congratulations," Will and Louise said in unison, then stood to hug the couple. Abby, whose mussed-up hair and mis-buttoned clothing suggested they'd already consummated the marriage, beamed.

"I'm happy for you," Louise said.

They drank another beer—thankfully not as strong as the Aussie brews—and reluctantly packed up to leave. Will pulled the jeep to a stop in front of the nurses' barracks just shy of their curfew. "'Fraid we'll have to give you gals tomorrow night off," he said. "We've got to get some sleep. But you know we'll be back as soon as we can arrange it."

Will gave Louise a quick kiss. "Goodnight, my little chick," he said. "Sleep well." She felt his eyes on her as she walked to the door and turned to see him standing still, watching her intently—as though he was trying to memorize her. She blew him a kiss before going inside.

Will's orders came through and he left the New Guinea airbase four days later, never having been able to arrange another flight to Townsville.

SEVERAL DAYS AFTER WILL'S DEPARTURE, LOUISE WENT to a dance with his former roommate, a young pilot named Brandon. "It'll just be as friends," he'd said when he invited her. "I'm guessing your heart still belongs to Will."

They sat at a table for two during one of the orchestra's breaks.

"How are you holding up?" Brandon asked her.

"I miss him like crazy," she replied, surprised at her candor.

"I'm sure he misses you too. He admitted to me that he's flummoxed about what to do. He has strong feelings for you, but his gal back in Oklahoma writes to him every day, and he kinda thinks he owes it to her to wait till he gets home to sort things out..."

Louise's jaw dropped open. *What gal back in Oklahoma?*

"...Just between you and me, he speaks way more highly of you than of her."

That explains a lot, Louise thought, speechlessly blinking back tears. *But it doesn't matter if he thinks highly of me, he's going back where she is.*

Brandon changed the subject and she forced herself to make small talk. But when the orchestra began the next set with "As Time Goes By," she bolted through the crowd of dancers and ran to the barracks.

Chapter Twenty-Five

The 44th was abuzz with rumors about moving out, and the nurses began preparing for their departure from Townsville.

On the morning of Tuesday, October 2nd, Vivian came bounding into Louise's room to find her friend still asleep. "Wake up. Time's a-wasting. Is Dot on duty today?"

Louise groaned and pulled the pillow over her head. "Yes, Dot's on duty," she muttered, "which is why I planned to sleep in."

Vivian grabbed the pillow and tossed it to the foot of the bed. "C'mon. I got us a ride into town, and we're leaving in half an hour. We need to spend our Aussie money before we ship out."

"Okay, okay," Louise said, dragging herself to a seated position with her feet on the floor. "But I need a quick shower."

Since the water was cold, the shower was indeed quick. Within twenty-five minutes she and Vivian were standing in front of the barracks, dressed and ready, their purses full of Australian currency.

In the last six months they'd gotten to know the shops in

Townsville. "Where to first?" Louise asked when they were dropped off.

"I want to get some more yarn," Vivian said. "I promised Jimmy I'd knit him a scarf, and if I get going on it maybe I can get it to him by Christmas."

Louise laughed. "You're a fast knitter, but I wouldn't count on Uncle Sam to deliver it by then."

"He's in New Guinea, for heaven's sake. Maybe we'll be sent there too, and I'll be able to deliver it in person."

"I guess that's as good a possibility as anywhere. I can't see them sending us stateside—not while Japan's still putting up a fight," Louise mused.

"At least things are going our way in Europe—liberating Paris was a real victory."

Louise linked her arm with Vivian's. "Okay, enough war talk. Let's head to the knitting shop."

The two women oohed and aahed over the vast supply of wool yarns, fingering many skeins and occasionally bringing them up to their cheeks to feel the softness. The shopkeeper, a stout woman with the sweetest accent, suggested which yarn would be best for a scarf and told Vivian how much to buy.

"I just can't decide whether to get some or not," Louise said after her friend made her purchase. "I finished knitting the sweater I started last month, but I wonder if we'll have time to knit at our next stop."

"Well, it's not heavy so it wouldn't cost much to ship it home if we don't," Vivian said, then noticed the stricken look on her face. "What's wrong, kid?"

Louise swallowed the lump in her throat. "It's kind of a long story."

"There's a tea shop next door. Why don't we go have a cup and you can tell me?"

Sitting at a window table with cups of tea and a plate of

cookies in front of them, Louise finally began her story. "Your mention of sending yarn 'home' struck a nerve…"

"I'm sorry."

"No, you shouldn't feel sorry. It's just that I don't really *have* a home. You know Etta and I inherited our parents' farm when my father died, but we were only fifteen and sixteen at the time. By then, my father's cousin and his family had moved in to take care of us and the farm. During the winter months we stayed at a rooming house in town so we could be sure to get to school. And we often stayed at Aunt Margaret and Uncle Chuck's so we could remain in touch with our mom's family. Then I went off to nursing school and the Army, and Dad's cousin and his family stayed with the farm." Louise paused to nibble on a cookie and take a sip of tea.

"Didn't you tell me the farm was recently sold?" Vivian asked.

"Uh-huh. We still haven't gotten the accounting from the sale. Aunt Margaret heard that a few of our belongings were sold at the equipment auction instead of going to storage like they were supposed to. And I'm hearing that some of my dad's other relatives are going through the boxes and taking what they want."

"How dare they?"

Louise shrugged her shoulders. "I guess they justify it by thinking they're owed some inheritance. I just hope the things we really care about will still be there when we get back. The only person I completely trust is my Aunt Margaret—but her house is fairly small, and I certainly can't send her my excess stuff from over here."

Vivian put her hand over Louise's. "If you need to send anything home, you can always send it to my parents. They've got plenty of room in their attic, and I promise it'd be safe. And you know they're only about twenty miles from Margaret and Chuck."

Louise blinked back tears. "Thanks. I just might take you up on it."

Vivian washed a bite of cookie down with the last of her tea.

"You don't suspect that your dad's cousin took some of the proceeds, do you?" she asked.

"No, not really," Louise said, picking at her lip. "But I'm not sure he tried very hard to get the most they could for it."

"You, my friend, are a saint for being so calm about all this."

"Or maybe just too trusting," Louise said wryly. "I've always been willing to give people the benefit of the doubt, sometimes to my own detriment. I can't seem to decipher who to trust and who not to."

"Maybe that fortune-teller in the back room can help," Vivian said, nodding toward the sign which read Tea Leaves Read - 1 shilling. "Let's go do it."

"Only if we can do it together."

Vivian approached the counter. "Can we both have our tea leaves read at the same time?" she asked.

"Yes, ma'am," the clerk replied, "but you each have to pay a shilling. I'll check if she's free to see you now." She disappeared through a curtained doorway and returned a moment later. "This way, please."

Louise and Vivian giggled nervously as they entered the back room. Louise fully expected to see a large Gypsy woman adorned with scarves and ornate gold jewelry in a room illuminated only with candles. Instead, the occupant of the brightly lit room, sitting in a chintz upholstered chair, was a frail elderly woman wearing a blue cardigan over a flowered dress. She rose with some difficulty and extended her hand.

"Hello, girls," she said pleasantly. "I'm Mrs. Southworth. Please take whichever seats you'd like." She motioned them to four chairs situated at a round table.

The women sat beside each other and watched as Mrs. Southworth went to a sideboard and selected two cups and saucers. Her hands shook, causing a delicate clinking as she carried them to the table. Next, she poured water from an electric kettle into a china teapot and brought it to the table. Finally, she brought over a wooden box.

"The clerk tells me you've already had tea in the front of the shop," she said with a twinkle in her eye. "I hope you can manage another half cup."

Louise and Vivian nodded.

"Good," she said, spooning fragrant tea leaves from the wooden box into the cups. She poured water from the pot onto the leaves. "Make a wish before you drink, and as you sip, I want you to contemplate your wish."

The women exchanged bemused glances, then began to drink.

"Leave about a tablespoon in the bottom of your cups, please."

It took several sips before the requisite amount was left. "There," Mrs. Southworth said. "Now hold the cup in your left hand and swirl it three times clockwise."

Neither of them was left-handed and they awkwardly performed the swirls.

"Next, use your left hand to invert the cup over your saucer. We'll leave it there for about a minute," she said, then consulted her watch as Louise and Vivian fidgeted in their chairs. "Good, now rotate the cup three times...And finally, turn the cup upright with the handle pointing toward the front door—that's due south."

The women saw tea leaves stuck to the cups in unusual clusters.

"Let's have a look." Mrs. Southworth stared first into Louise's cup. "Oh, my dear. I see you have a very deep affection for someone and you're wondering if that affection will be returned. I can tell you it will and that you and your gentlemen will both return home safely. You have a very, very happy future to look forward to."

Though skeptical of the whole process, Louise couldn't help feeling hopeful. Vivian's leaves foretold similar happiness, and Mrs. Southworth ventured to add that she saw several children in her future. She gave them a few more benign predictions, collected their shillings, and sent them on their way.

"Several children?" Vivian shrieked as they left the shop. "I'm not sure I want *any*."

"Well, I'm just glad I'll be *very, very* happy."

SINCE THE FIGHTING HAD MOVED SO MUCH FARTHER north, the 44th received no more battle casualties in Townsville. The nurses worked only five-hour shifts, which were generally stress-free.

It was now early summer in Australia, the temperatures creeping up again, bringing bugs, lizards, and more mosquitoes. But the flowers and blossoming trees made up for them. "I'm guessing we can't expect the next place we find ourselves to be as beautiful," Louise told Dot one afternoon when they headed out to the drill field.

"I'm also guessing we won't have to march around in the sun and do calisthenics for two hours a day," her friend replied. "My muscles are so sore it hurts to get out of bed."

"Mine too. But you know there'll be a trade-off for not having to drill, don't you?"

Dot nodded solemnly. "Battle casualties will keep us hopping."

"And as we get closer to the front," Louise added, "this physical training may just save our lives."

"Let's hope it doesn't come to that."

ON OCTOBER 10, THE TRANSPORTATION OFFICER offered Louise a ride into town to sell her beloved Oscar—her bicycle. "I'll be happy to meet the prospective buyer with you," he told her. "I'd hate to see you get taken."

Louise had mixed emotions about the offer. After all, she'd like to be able to look out for herself. But she knew other nurses had been swindled during similar transactions. "Thanks," she told him. "I'd appreciate it."

As it happened, she could've handled the sale alone: the buyer answering her posted ad was a skinny gentleman of about seventy who wanted the bike so his daughter wouldn't have to walk to and from work. They agreed on seven and a half pounds, very near her asking price.

Afterward, the transportation officer drove to the ordnance depot to pick up some repaired equipment. While they were waiting, he and Louise wandered around, looking at all the army vehicles: tanks, scout cars, ambulances, and heavy trucks among them.

"This is amazing," Louise said when they stood in front of a tank. "I've never seen one this close before."

"Do you want to go inside?"

"Can we?"

"Sure. I'll climb up first and give you a hand."

As she awkwardly searched for footholds, she momentarily regretted her decision. "C'mon," her companion said, "you can do it."

Once inside, Louise ran her hands over the control panel and the heavy sidewalls and stared out the porthole. "On the one hand you'd feel invincible in this thing, but on the other hand you'd be kind of a sitting duck. And I'd sure be claustrophobic with the hatch closed."

Her escort laughed. "I couldn't agree more."

Back in their jeep, as they circled the depot heading back to camp, Louise couldn't help shuddering. *So much equipment in only one little area. There must be thousands of similar depots all over the world—no wonder this war's going on forever.*

Chapter Twenty-Six

IT TURNED OUT THAT LOUISE HAD SOLD HER BIKE JUST in time. The following day, a Tuesday, the members of the 44th got twenty-four hours' notice of their impending move to undisclosed destinations. The doctors, male officers, and enlisted men would again travel separately from the nurses.

There was a flurry of activity as everyone packed their gear and disposed of what they couldn't take along. People said goodbye to their friends from nearby units. Others said tearful farewells to the pets they'd adopted while at Townsville. Frankie's grief was palpable as she hugged the cat she had named Smokey—one among many who roamed the camp—who'd shared her room and her tears since soon after they'd arrived. "I'll miss him almost as much as I miss Alex," she moaned.

A few hours before the scheduled departure, though, the orders were canceled, and everyone was told to report to work at the hospital on Thursday. "Isn't this just like the Army?" Shoe said, pulling toiletries out of her musette bag. "I worked up a sweat packing and now we've gotta unpack. I'm heading for the shower." Of course, only cold water awaited her.

After their five-hour shift on Thursday, Louise and Dot went back to their room to dress for calisthenics and joined the other nurses on the drill field. They were surprised to see Captain Riley stride onto the field in place of the drill instructor. They all saluted.

"At ease," Riley called out. "Once again, we've received orders." A buzz went up among the group, and even Riley couldn't stifle a grin. "I have it on good authority that these orders will stand. Our departure is set for 0600 tomorrow. Be packed and waiting in front of the barracks. Dismissed."

"Wouldn't you know it?" Shoe grumbled. "Now we'll be leaving on Friday the thirteenth."

"You don't believe in omens like that, do you?" Vivian asked.

"Says the gal who went and had her tea leaves read," Shoe shot back, albeit with a smile.

"Ladies, ladies," Louise said, "let's make the most of the time we would've spent doing calisthenics and sweating in the sun."

"The club in half an hour?" Vivian suggested.

Everyone nodded and went to change.

ON FRIDAY, OCTOBER 13, 1944, THE NURSES BOARDED AN Australian troop train in Townsville bound for Sydney, some 1,300 miles south. Louise, Dot, Frankie, and Vivian shared a compartment with two other women—one of them, Esther Schultz, six-foot-one—and all of their luggage. Seated three to a seat, facing one another with the luggage piled in between, it was impossible for any of them to get comfortable, especially Esther.

Three times a day, the train stopped for meals at towns along the way. It was a mixed blessing: everyone was happy to stretch their legs, but the troops had to stand in line with their mess kits and canteens to wait for their chow. Worse yet, by the second day it became clear the menu would always be the same: boiled mutton and cabbage for breakfast, creamed lamb on raisin bread for dinner, and sheep stew for supper—all served with sweetened tea.

"I'm not eating one more bite of this so-called food," Vivian declared. "Let's see what else we can find."

At most of the stops they found pie wagons and other vendors selling food. "This is a darn sight better than soggy mutton," Louise exclaimed after biting into a small chicken and vegetable pie. "And I'm going to top off my meal with cookies from that cart across the street."

"Why don't we chip in and get a bag of them to take on the train?" Frankie asked. "They'll make a good midnight snack."

"I'll treat," Louise said. "I'm flush with the proceeds from the sale of Oscar."

AFTER FOUR DAYS, THE TRAIN PULLED INTO THE SYDNEY harbor and the women gratefully disembarked. "You realize we traveled nearly the length of Australia," Louise said to Frankie, "and even though it was awfully uncomfortable, I still enjoyed the scenery."

"Most people would say we're nuts, but I have to agree with you."

The nurses were taken directly from the train to the AHS *Maetsuycker*, a Dutch hospital ship bound for New Guinea—though they didn't know it at the time—on its way to pick up a load of patients. They were the only passengers aboard.

Gathered on deck, they listened intently as an English-speaking crew member—Captain Hans Van Dijk—told them the rules for the trip. He seemed pleasant enough but deadly serious about the instructions.

"He looks a little like *your* Dutch from March Field," Vivian whispered to Louise. "What was his name?"

Louise felt her cheeks flush at the memory. "Lieutenant Jesse van der Berg," she replied sotto voce. "Now hush and listen. We don't want to get in trouble on our first day."

"You'll sleep in the patients' beds, just below the top deck,"

Van Dijk went on. "You'll wear a life preserver and a canteen at all times, including while you sleep, and there will be frequent 'abandon ship' drills. Please take them seriously. We'll be crossing the Coral Sea, which can often be very rough. And though we travel under both Dutch and Red Cross flags, remember that the Japanese torpedoed an Australian hospital ship last year."

Frankie grabbed Louise's hand.

"My crew will be happy to assist you in any way they can," Van Dijk concluded. "Now, your Captain Riley will brief you on other expectations for you during the voyage. God willing, we should reach our destination in about ten days."

"*Ten days?*" Vivian moaned. "In rough seas?" She was not the only member of the group grumbling, but everyone quieted down when Riley began to speak.

"Inspection will occur every morning at 0930," she said. "I know I can count on you to maintain the 44th's high standards. Now I'm told the chow on this vessel is top-notch, but the crew is stretched thin. You'll be doing part of the KP—serving meals and doing dishes afterward. I'll post a schedule for each meal."

Riley nodded toward a young officer standing beside her.

"Take your gear and follow Lieutenant Bakke to quarters. You're free to select your own bunks."

Louise took a top bunk because, as she had learned on their trans-Pacific voyage, she was less likely than her friends to become seasick. Then, donning their life vests and canteens, they headed to the mess hall.

"If they serve mutton, I'm going to mutiny," Shoe said.

"It doesn't smell like mutton," Frankie said. "It smells pretty good."

The hearty chicken stew, served piping hot, surprised everyone. "This is delicious," Louise said. "Tastes like something my mother used to make, though there's not as much chicken."

"Try the bread," Frankie exclaimed, closing her eyes to savor it. "It's heavenly."

It would be the last meal they ate with relish on the whole journey. By the following day, almost everyone became seasick. Even Louise ate sparingly, finding it easier to settle her stomach with less in it. The waves were so high they often washed over the upper deck, and absolutely no one bucked the order to wear life jackets.

The constant rocking made sleep, playing cards, and writing letters difficult. One afternoon's attempts at letter-writing were interrupted by the second "abandon ship" drill of the day. "Oh, for heaven's sake," Louise said after the drill concluded, "I might as well go take a shower. I can't think of anything new to write my sister about anyway."

"I think I'll join you," Frankie said with a sigh. They made their way back to quarters and nodded to a couple of friends who'd returned to their bunks in hopes of catching some sleep.

Frankie had just lathered up her hair when the ship began to roll precipitously. She lost her footing and slid on her bottom from one wall of the shower to the other. "Are we going down?" she shrieked as she slid back toward the other wall.

"I doubt it," Louise said, seizing onto a towel hook to keep from joining her friend on the floor. She reached out a hand to Frankie.

They clung to the towel hook, praying it wouldn't become detached from the wall. Several minutes later the sea calmed a bit, and they were able to rinse off and retrieve their soggy towels from the floor.

They made their way cautiously to their quarters only to find chaos: a couple of portholes had been left open and two nurses—Esther Schultz and Kitty Zimmerman—had been washed from their top bunks. "Are you okay?" Louise asked them.

"I think so," Esther replied. "I'm pretty sure I didn't hit my head, and nothing feels broken."

"I'm fine," Kitty added. "I'm just flummoxed and soaking wet."

Louise and Frankie had just helped them to their feet when

Anna walked in and surveyed the wet bunks and floor. "What on earth?" she asked.

Frankie rolled her eyes.

"Would you mind getting a mop and bucket from the kitchen, Anna?" Louise asked.

Returning a few moments later, Anna ran her hands through her hair. "If you think it looks bad in here, you should see the galley," she said. "A whole platter of spaghetti with red sauce flew off the counter and hit the wall."

The group took turns mopping the floor and managed to find dry bedding. "I think we've had enough excitement for one day," Louise declared.

But around 2300 hours, after the nurses had just gotten to sleep, the ship hit more rough water. Loose furniture skidded across the floor, cupboard doors popped open causing dishes to fly out, and several women fell out of bed. Everyone woke up.

It soon became clear that while the ship wasn't sinking there'd be no more sleep for the night. "Anybody got anything to eat?" Vivian asked.

Frankie brought out some candy. Louise found a hunk of cheese. Shoe contributed a package of crackers. And they ate—not enough to cause nausea, but just enough to settle the nerves—while hanging on to their bunks for dear life.

A FEW DAYS LATER WHEN THEY'D PASSED THE WORST OF the rough seas, Dot, Shoe, Vivian, Frankie, and Louise sat in the dining room writing letters. Shoe finished the soda she was drinking and stood up to throw away the empty bottle.

"Wait a minute, Shoe," Vivian said. "We should put a letter in that bottle and throw it overboard."

"That's a great idea," Louise said.

"Yes, let's do," Frankie echoed.

Louise pulled a blank sheet from her stationery box and held up her pen. "You all tell me what to say and I'll write it."

"Here we are on a boat in the Coral Sea," Vivian began dictating, "headed only God knows where..."

"Correction," Frankie said. "Uncle Sam knows too."

"Okay, God and Uncle Sam," Louise said, rolling her eyes. "What next?"

"We're five nurses from the 44th General Hospital Unit, presumably heading closer to the fighting to treat battle casualties. It's been a rough journey, but we should be on land soon. We hope whoever finds this bottle is a friend rather than a foe. Write to us, please," Vivian added. "Then we should all sign our names and put our APO addresses."

Each of the women added a little greeting and signed the letter. Vivian rolled it up and placed it inside the bottle. "I'll go seal this with candle wax and meet you on the afterdeck in a few minutes," she said.

When they were all assembled, Vivian presented the sealed bottle. "You throw it, Shoe," she said. "You've got the best arm."

"It'll probably have a better chance if you toss it as gently as possible," Shoe said. "...just far enough so it doesn't hit the side of the ship."

"Okay," Vivian said. "Here goes."

"Godspeed, bottle!" Frankie said.

Chapter Twenty-Seven

On October 24, the hospital ship landed in Hollandia, New Guinea. The nurses spent the first night on the ship in the harbor, disappointed they couldn't immediately go ashore but relieved to be able to see land and hold down their dinner.

The next morning they were loaded onto landing barges for the trip to shore. "What do they think we are?" Shoe grumbled. "They've packed us in here like sardines."

"And we're going to be crispy sardines with this glaring sun," Dot added.

After an hour, they'd progressed only about halfway. Louise, not usually a complainer, began to feel panicky. "Can't this thing move faster than a slow crawl?" she moaned. "Even I could swim quicker."

"You'd better cover your nose with a hankie or something," Dot told her. "It's beginning to blister."

When their barge finally landed, two nurses had to be carried off on stretchers and hospitalized for heatstroke.

Wide-eyed, the nurses boarded troop trucks that took them up several hills into the thick of the jungle. Frankie grabbed Louise's hand when their truck halted in front of a stockade-like, high-fenced enclosure. "This can't be our camp…" she said, stumbling to her feet.

Captain Riley strode up beside the truck. "'Fraid so, Frankenberg," she said. Then, nodding toward a red muddy rectangle of land perhaps the size of a baseball diamond, she called, "Everyone through the gate and gather in that clearing. I've got important announcements."

Two armed M.P.'s held the gate open for the women to enter, while several others walked the perimeter.

"None of this was here two weeks ago," Captain Riley began once they'd all assembled. "It's a staging area—housing hundreds of people from lots of different units, all waiting for orders. It's a wild jungle under the best of circumstances but even more dangerous because there are still Japanese hiding in the hills. None of you is to leave the camp after 1800 hours without an armed escort.

"If you want to go on a date," she continued, "you need permission from your chief nurse, who will need to know where you're going and confirm the man is armed. No exceptions."

Louise stared at her own feet, convinced that Riley was looking directly at her.

"This is malaria country," Riley said. "I know it's oppressively hot, but you *will* wear trousers and long-sleeved shirts at all times. Further, you'll be receiving Atabrine pills which you *will* take every day to prevent the disease. Your skin'll turn yellow from it, but I don't care—you'll take it as instructed without complaint.

"Four-man tents. No furniture except your cot and a suitcase. Any questions?" She didn't pause to check if they had any, but merely barked, "Dismissed."

Dot, Vivian, Frankie, and Louise nodded to one another and walked toward an empty tent at one end of a makeshift road. "When Riley said 'cot,' she wasn't kidding," Vivian said as she stepped inside. "There aren't any springs or mattresses."

"Or pillows," Louise said.

A bare light bulb hung from the ceiling of the tent. Vivian pulled the chain to turn it on. "Twenty-five watts, I'm guessing," she said.

"At least the electricity's on," Dot said.

"Mail call," someone hollered from outside.

Like lemmings, they hustled outside and followed the crowd to what turned out to be the mess tent. "I doubt we'll have anything here yet," Frankie said, "but it doesn't hurt to check."

Frankie and Vivian each got a letter from a relative, but Dot's and Louise's shoulders sank when the last of the names was called and they were empty-handed.

Walking arm in arm with Dot on the way back to the tent, struggling to find the least mucky footfalls to tread, Louise couldn't help shedding a few tears. "My head tells me the thing with Will Rogers was just a fling," she said, "but my heart knows it was so much more. I fell for him. Hard."

Dot squeezed her arm. "I know."

THE WORKING CONDITIONS THE 44TH'S NURSES experienced for the next ten weeks in Hollandia would be the most difficult they'd encountered. They weren't informed where their male colleagues had been sent and, while awaiting orders to join them, the nurses were placed on detached service to other hospital units in the massive staging area. Some traveled by ambulance to and from their assignments at the 27th General Hospital about a half mile down the road.

Vivian, Dot, and Louise were all placed at the same hospital treating battle casualties from the Philippine invasion—a grueling and frustrating job. The smell of disinfectant couldn't cover up the ever-present odors of blood and oozing wounds. New patients streamed in before the staff could get to know the ones they were already treating. And duty rosters changed so frequently that the friends often worked with unfamiliar staff. On the tenth day after their arrival, Louise and Vivian were pleased to learn they'd been assigned on a ward together.

"You two," the charge nurse barked before they'd even introduced themselves, "change the dressings for beds ten through twenty. And make sure they all use a urinal or bedpan, whether they need it or not."

They had quickly learned they'd be relegated to tasks that had formerly been handled by their ward men, since most of them—medics by training—had been transferred to the front lines. But they hadn't been prepared to be ordered around so rudely. "Please tell me I never treated our ward men like she's treating us," Louise whispered to Vivian as they lifted a heavyset patient to change his soiled sheets.

"Believe me, you didn't," her friend replied. "And you should know better than to ask. Remember how Joe Scarpetti choked up when he said goodbye to us? We were all on the same team."

The patient nodded at them conspiratorially. "That woman's a bitch, plain and simple," he said. "Pardon my language."

Later, after Louise changed the dressings of a soldier with two angry-looking gunshot wounds to his thigh, she accepted his "no, thank you" at her offer of a portable urinal. Unfortunately, the charge nurse noticed. "Dietrich," she yelled. "I told you to make them use it whether they want to or not. I expect you to follow basic orders."

Louise and the soldier turned the same shade of crimson. "I'm sorry, ma'am," he said to her, reaching out for the wide-mouthed jug. "I didn't mean to get you in trouble. I can make it to the latrine by myself for heaven's sake, but I'll pee in the bottle just to get the Wicked Witch of the West off your back."

The sailor in the bed next to him, whose right leg had been shot off during an airstrike, immediately pulled himself to a seated position and grabbed his crutches. "I'm not going in that stinkin' piss bottle," he said, laughing. "Watch this."

With that, he settled onto his crutches and walked to the lavatory—meandering through the aisles to be sure he caught the head nurse's eye.

"What do you think you're doing, Seaman Holtz?" the charge nurse asked.

"Hitting the head, Lieutenant. And if I feel like it, I may walk over to the PX and buy a six-pack of American beer—I heard they got a supply in last night."

Louise and Vivian stifled smiles and silently went about their duties.

By the time the ten-hour shift ended, every muscle in their bodies ached. They'd done every bit of grunt work the head nurse had assigned them along with a fair amount of the other nurses' as well. To add insult to injury, they'd stopped to check for mail before returning to the tent, and neither had received any.

ON THE BOAT TO HOLLANDIA, FRANKIE AND TWO OTHER nurses had contracted dengue fever and had been hospitalized soon after arrival. Frankie had been the first of the three to be discharged, but she was still confined to the tent for another few weeks.

She lifted her head off the pillow she'd been issued—by virtue of the painful medical condition—when Louise and Vivian dragged themselves into the tent. "How was your day?" Frankie asked.

"You don't want to know," Vivian responded.

"Yes, I do. I'm bored to tears and anxious to hear how it's going."

Louise put the back of her hand on Frankie's brow, then sat on the end of the cot. "Hard to tell in this heat, but you don't feel feverish. That's good."

"I'm well enough to hear about your day," Frankie insisted.

Louise sighed. "We've done enough detached service assignments since we've been in the army to realize how hard it is to work under someone else and do things their way. We expected to get the dirty end of everything. But we've never gotten a deal as raw as this."

Frankie's eyes grew wide. "Really?"

"Really," Vivian said. "We've been assigned to a poor excuse for a hospital, and the people we have to take orders from are even poorer excuses for nurses."

"I've never seen such a disinterested, indifferent, filthy, dumb bunch of people," Louise added. "It breaks my heart because so many of these boys are seriously injured and they can't count on getting their dressings changed regularly or their meds issued on time. The nurses are rough and rude and never take the time to say a kind word to any of the patients."

Vivian flopped back on her cot and covered her eyes with her forearm. "We can't even describe some of the stuff we saw today."

Louise nodded. "Remember how proud we were of our hospital and how we worked to make it the best in the country? Our COs would've told these ignoramuses to shape up or ship out."

"The orders for us to rejoin the 44th can't come quickly enough," Vivian said.

"You can say that again," Dot said, pushing through the door of the tent.

"Are you just getting off work now?" Frankie asked her.

Dot sniffled and blotted her nose with her shirtsleeve. "No. I ran into Shoe and her sister. They got a letter today saying their brother was killed in France last month."

"Oh, no," Frankie cried. "How're they handling it?"

"Shoe's pretty stoic about it," Dot replied. "But Helen is hysterical. She was very close to him, married to his best friend and all. He was only twenty-three years old. Handsome as the dickens."

"Can this day get any worse?" Louise asked.

"I hate to say it, but it probably could," Vivian said. "We might as well have a few bottles of our warm Schlitz so we'll be good and snockered if some Kamikaze pilot decides to dive-bomb this hellhole."

"I thought you hated warm beer," Louise said. "Why'd you sell me half your ration if you're willing to drink it now?"

Vivian shrugged. "Today it's better than staying sober."

The tentmates—except for Frankie whose medications didn't sit well with alcohol—drank in silence.

Vivian was the most pensive. "You know that soldier who got his leg blown off?" she asked Louise. "The one who defied orders and got up to use the head?"

"Uh-huh."

"I heard him cracking jokes this afternoon. Telling the other guys how lucky he is because now it'll only cost him a nickel to have his shoes shined, rather than a dime."

Louise brushed a few errant curls from her forehead and blinked back tears. "That doesn't surprise me," she said. "Just goes to show that attitude is everything."

FOR THE NEXT TWO DAYS, LOUISE AND DOT WERE scheduled to work on a ward treating Filipino women and children who'd been injured in air raids. "I'm not sure I can handle this," Dot said, staring at the muddy floor when they walked into the tent.

"You most certainly can," Louise replied, leading her friend by the elbow toward the desk where the charge nurse sat writing intently on a chart.

"Excuse me," Louise said. "Dietrich and Albrecht from the 44th General Hospital, reporting for duty."

The nurse, a stout graying woman, peered over her reading glasses at them. "I'm Captain Wilkes," she said. "As you can see, we've got a full house here. Eight orphaned babies. No—make that seven—one died early this morning. There's a pregnant girl in bed ten who had part of her hip shot off. Half of the women are missing at least one limb. Most of them were injured by American shells simply because they were caught between us and the enemy. But believe it or not, they're *grateful* to us for coming to free them."

Dot swayed on her feet and grabbed hold of the desk.

"Are you Dietrich or Albrecht?" Wilkes asked.

"Albrecht, ma'am."

"I assume, Lieutenant Albrecht, that you've treated battle casualties before?"

Dot nodded.

"The only difference between these patients and the others you've dealt with is that they're women and children," she said, not unkindly. "First Lieutenant Parks will be back on the ward in a few minutes. She'll give you your assignments. In the meantime, see if you can corral Hopalong Cassidy over there"—she pointed to a boy who looked to be about four years old, laughing and running in the aisle—"and change his dressing. They found him and his mother under a pile of rubble and he's got a nasty gash on his back."

So enthralled were they with charming little Hopalong that they didn't even notice Lieutenant Parks' arrival. "Albrecht and Dietrich, if you can tear yourselves away from the little devil," she said caustically, "the patients along the far wall need to be toileted and bathed. Don't bother changing their sheets, though—we can't spare clean ones. And ignore the wailing baby in the first crib."

Though Lieutenant Parks ran her ward similarly to the Wicked Witch of the West, Louise found the Filipino women and children a refreshing change from the male patients. All the nurses seemed to rally around the pregnant girl, now about seven months along, excited at the prospect of welcoming a new life into the world. They brought baby presents: tiny hand-knit booties and sweaters, carved rattles purchased from some of the natives, and a supply of new diapers procured from heaven knew where.

"I'd be happy to be assigned to this ward all the time," Louise said to Dot after their first shift ended.

"Me, too," Dot replied.

"Let's head over and see if the mail's been sorted," Louise said, though they'd come away empty-handed too many times to count.

Today was no different, but the absence of any letters sent Dot into a tailspin. "I can't understand why Dwayne hasn't written," she moaned. "Why didn't I press him for a commitment before he went stateside?"

"First of all, you don't *know* he hasn't written, Louise said. "You're not the only one who isn't getting any mail—"

"But Shoe and Helen got the letter about their brother..."

"Oh, for heaven's sake, Dot," Louise said, unable to hide her exasperation, "you're not saying you're jealous of them getting mail?"

"No. No, I didn't mean that," Dot sputtered.

"Frankie and Anna haven't even gotten letters from their *husbands*, and you can't get much more committed than that. Everyone's morale is low, but we've gotta do our best to keep our spirits up."

"That's easy for you to say," Dot replied. "Always having some new guy chasing after you."

Louise recalled the last of her recent dates: he'd taken her to the firing range where they practiced shooting carbines and pistols, and she'd actually hit the target one time. "They're a good diversion," she admitted. "But the truth is, I compare everyone I meet to Will. And so far, no one's measured up."

Dot nodded. "Don't you regret not asking Will for a commitment?"

"Not for a minute, I don't. He needs to sort things out on his own, and if it's not meant to be, so be it."

When they returned to the tent, they found Frankie sitting cross-legged on her cot, knitting. "Did you hear the good news?" she asked, beaming.

"Oh, is the war over?" Louise said.

"No, silly."

"Have they irradicated all the rats in camp so we don't have to keep shooing the awful things out of the latrine and our tents?" Dot asked.

"That'd sure be something to celebrate," Louise said.

Frankie sighed in exasperation. "Just *listen*. Vivian's lieutenant is here—in the hospital! He was wounded in the Philippines but fortunately, not seriously. She's over visiting him right now. I'm so excited for her. They've always been the cutest couple."

Dot stalked over to her cot and flung herself facedown onto it.

Frankie looked at Louise, who mouthed, "Don't ask."

"I got some good news today, too," Frankie said, shrugging. "The doc said I can start taking my meals in the mess hall."

"Great. Want to head over after I shower? I can't bear to eat in these sweaty clothes."

"It's a date."

Neither of them bothered to ask Dot.

On the way back from dinner, the women heard a friendly voice calling from a nearby row of tents. "Hey, Louise. Is that really you?"

"Walter Kuhn," Louise said and strode over to accept his bear hug. "You left Townsville so long ago, I was sure you'd be back in Milwaukee with your fiancée by now."

"I thought I would, too, pal," he replied. "And yet here I am in this swampy staging area waiting for orders like hundreds of other people."

"Well, it's great to see you again," Louise said, then nodded toward Frankie. "You remember my friend Gladys Frankenburg?"

Walter took Frankie's hand between his. "How could I forget this cherubic face?"

Frankie looked down at her feet. "You're sweet," she said. "I'm gonna head back to the tent, Louise. My first outing has tuckered me out."

"Okay," Louise said. "I'll be back soon."

"Remember, our electricity's out," Frankie said. "I'll keep a candle burning till my eyes get heavy."

"We've got light in our tent," Walter told Louise. "And beer. And a cribbage board."

"And I don't have any plans for the evening." She took his arm and followed him to the tent.

"Fellas," Walter said to his two tentmates, "meet my 'kid sister' Louise Dietrich. She's a fellow Wisconsinite who I met back in Townsville, and she plays a mean game of cribbage. Either of you guys want to play three-handed?"

"I've got a date," the younger one said, getting up to leave.

"Not me," said the other, nodding toward a radio. "I want to listen to the next program."

"You've got a radio?" Louise asked. "What can you get?"

"Only one station," Walter replied. "It's called Jungle Network and it's just for entertaining us Yanks. Reprograms of stuff that's already played back home. Sometimes just records but never any commercials."

"Mind if we listen a bit?" Louise asked, sitting on the edge of Walter's cot.

"Not at all. Want a beer?"

Taken in by the introduction to *The Fred Waring Show*, she nodded absently, and she was quickly absorbed in the musical variety show. Bemused, Walter watched her laughing at Waring's banter and tapping her foot along with the songs.

When the show ended, Louise looked up at Walter. "Gee, I can't remember when I've enjoyed a program so much."

He laughed. "I don't think you even tasted your beer."

Louise glanced at the empty bottle in her hand and felt her face flush. "You're right, and I'm sure I forgot to thank you for it."

"Don't give it another thought," he said. "And you're welcome here any time. Since there aren't any clubs, or movies, or even any towns in this godforsaken place, we've gotta devise our own entertainment."

Since she was again unattached, Louise spent many an evening at Walter's place, talking, playing cribbage, or listening to the radio. He often managed to procure a speedboat and, on free afternoons, took Louise and her friends for rides on a nearby lake. He insisted she learn how to swim…"Contrary to your beliefs, the dog paddle isn't a recognized swimming stroke," he'd say.

"Seems like you're getting awfully fond of your friend Walter," Dot said when she returned to the tent after dark one night.

"I am," Louise replied with an edge to her voice. "He's like the big brother I always wished I had. For your information, he's engaged to a gal back in Wisconsin who he loves dearly and would *never* cheat on. We're friends, plain and simple, and I'm grateful to have him." Illuminated by candlelight, she noticed Dot's lower lip trembling but couldn't bring herself to care.

This gal's gotta stop her selfish moping or nobody's going to want to spend time with her.

Chapter Twenty-Eight

Nearly all the nurses from the 44th suffered from low morale: the mud, the heat, the lack of mail, and—most of all—the working conditions undermined their efforts to stay positive.

In early December, Louise returned to the tent after a grueling twelve-hour night shift to find Frankie writing a letter.

"You've got the day off?" Louise asked.

"Uh-huh. And I'm finally getting around to sending some Christmas notes. Since we can't buy any actual cards, I'm trying to make them festive with some little drawings," she said, holding up a folded piece of paper. "Do you like it?"

Louise collapsed on her own cot. "I should warn you I'm pretty grumpy. You sure you want to know?"

"Of course."

"The card is cute. But it's hard to even think about Christmas when it's 110 degrees and there's not a town or a store in New Guinea to shop at. I think we should just skip it this year and have three or four in a row when and if we ever get stateside."

"What'll you do to celebrate?"

"Behave like a perfect maniac!" Louise said, then thought for a while. "For starters, I'll spend six months' pay on Christmas presents for everyone I know—maybe even for people I only sorta know. Then, I'll eat a dinner four times bigger than I can actually hold. And afterward, I'll take off my shoes and socks and jump into the biggest snow pile I can find. Then, on New Year's Eve I intend to get rip-roaring drunk!"

"Sounds like a great idea."

Picturing the scenes in her mind, Louise couldn't help but smile.

"So," Frankie said, "tell me what you're grumpy about."

"I've only finished four of these night shifts and I can't imagine making it through eleven more. I plod through gooey, sticky mud all night long and have to cover five whole wards. Most of the patients are good eggs, but there are a few professional goldbricks that stretch my patience—they do nothing but complain.

"And it's so hot that three hours' sleep is the most I can seem to get. If Walter didn't take me swimming most every afternoon, I don't think I'd ever cool off."

"I'm sorry," Frankie said. "I feel guilty because I haven't been assigned any night shifts."

"That's not the only thing making me cross. Dot still hasn't heard from Dwayne and she's taking it so hard—always sniveling and acting like a martyr. Sometimes I want to shake her and say, 'Quit acting like a high school adolescent!' She gets all jealous when anybody does anything fun. She's even jealous when Vivian goes to the *hospital* to visit Jimmy. I don't know how you can always be so pleasant to her."

Frankie shrugged. "We're all different, I guess."

A FEW DAYS BEFORE CHRISTMAS, LOUISE, DOT, AND Vivian had a day off—the first in two and a half months. "This feels heavenly," Louise said as she sat on her cot and opened a bottle of beer. "My laundry is done, the tent's clean, and they gave us each a whole case of beer instead of the usual twelve bottles."

Vivian looked at her watch. "Drinking already?" she asked. "It's only nine-thirty!"

"It's a toast to my sister," Louise replied. "I told you she got promoted to be in charge of an accounting office, didn't I?"

"Maybe you did," Vivian said, "though I think I was too busy enjoying the Christmas cookies she sent for the news to register. But...since it's a special occasion, I'll have one too. Want one, Dot?"

"Why not?" Dot replied, accepting the bottle Vivian handed her.

"How's Jimmy doing this morning?" Louise asked. Her boyfriend had suffered a setback in his recovery.

Vivian took a long pull on her beer before replying, "His fever is down and his incision is looking better, so we're assuming the infection is under control."

"That's good news," Louise said.

Her friend picked at the label on the beer bottle, clearly lost in thought. "I guess it is good news," she finally said. "I mean, I'm certainly glad the complications seem to be relatively minor. And it's awful for me to say this, but the longer his recovery takes, the longer he gets to stay here."

"Any chance they'll send him home?" Dot asked.

"Not unless the infection becomes life-threatening," Vivian replied. "And we sure as hell don't want that."

"Stupid war," Louise said.

They all nodded and enjoyed a few moments of companionable silence.

"By the way," Vivian finally said, "I saw Shoe over at the hospital this morning visiting her sister. The docs told Helen they'll send her back to the States if she wants, but she hasn't decided yet. Shoe's exasperated...she was yelling at Helen when I left, 'You're an idiot if you don't go home!'"

"I can just hear it," Dot said.

"Me too," Louise said. "Say, I'm going swimming with Walter and a couple of his friends after lunch. Why don't you two come along?"

"Thanks for asking, but I promised I'd go play cribbage with Jimmy," Vivian said.

Louise couldn't help but notice the indecision on Dot's face. "You should come, Dot. It'll be fun. The guys are all attached, so it's not a date or anything."

"Where're you going?"

"This beautiful clear water lake a few miles from here. Walter's teaching me to swim, you know, and we often go to the harbor. But he says I'm getting too reliant on the saltwater and wants me to practice where I'm not so buoyant."

"He sounds like quite a taskmaster," Vivian teased.

Louise laughed. "He is. It's as though he thinks I can be the next Esther Williams or something." She turned to Dot. "So you'll come?"

Her friend actually smiled. "Sure."

Louise wore the new bathing suit her sister had sent and lent Dot her old one, which was still far more stylish than the one Dot owned. "I sure wish *my* sister was as resourceful as yours," Dot said. "The only suit she could find makes me look like my grandmother."

Louise laughed. "I think it helps that Etta is in California—she *does* seem to send pretty fashionable things."

Louise and Dot were waiting near the mess tent when Walter drove up with four friends already in the jeep. Ever the gentleman, Walter noticed the panic-stricken look on Dot's face. "Don't worry, ladies," he said. "You two'll sit up front with me and these clowns can squeeze together in back. It'll only take us ten minutes to get to the lake."

Ten minutes turned into thirty when the jeep got stuck in a quagmire on the road outside camp. All five guys jumped out to push. "You drive," Walter told Dot with a laugh, lifting Louise to the relatively dry terrain next to the road. "I don't trust this gal to steer us out—she practically ran our boat aground the other day."

The wheels spun impotently as Dot gave the vehicle gas, spraying all the guys as they pushed. Louise pulled out her camera and took a few funny pictures.

"Hold it," Walter finally yelled. "We're gonna need to find something to give us traction."

The men spent ten minutes scavenging pieces of palm bark and large fronds of leaves to jam under the wheels. Louise and Dot fanned themselves with their towels to ward off mosquitoes and create a breeze.

"Too bad you guys aren't in the Army Corps of Engineers," Louise said as they argued about where to strategically place what they'd gathered.

"Whitey here tried to join," Walter said, "but they wouldn't have him."

"At least *I* didn't flunk high school physics," his friend shot back.

"That's probably because your high school didn't even *offer* high school physics," Walter said. "Okay, let's give it another try. Ready, Dot?"

"Uh-huh." This time the wheels found purchase and Dot pulled the vehicle onto solid ground.

When they got to the lake, everyone stripped down to their bathing suits and ran into the water, leaving towels, drinks, and snacks for later. "I've never felt anything so refreshing," Dot said, floating on her back.

Louise floated in shallower water, occasionally using her toe to touch bottom. "No cheating," Walter called to her.

"Killjoy!" she yelled back.

The group rinsed their muddy clothes in the lake and laid

them to dry on rocks in the sun. "We should've brought buckets to take some of this water back to camp," Whitey said. "I don't know about you all, but having water only two days a week is getting pretty old."

Walter nodded. "The post up the hill from us is better off in that regard. I met an Aussie from there who said we can come take showers if we want."

"Come to think of it," Whitey said, "you haven't been complaining like the rest of us. How long ago did you meet this guy?"

Walter didn't reply.

"I can't thank you enough for inviting me along," Dot said to Louise when they returned to their tent. "It was just what the doctor ordered."

"You're welcome. It was worth it to see you happy for an afternoon."

Dot hugged her tightly. "I'd almost forgotten how it felt."

Chapter Twenty-Nine

Despite missing the easy camaraderie of the 44th and being away from her sister, Louise's second Christmas overseas turned out more pleasant than she had expected.

On Saturday evening, December 23, Walter picked her up for a Christmas dance at the Quartermaster Corps officers' club in a jeep festooned with red crepe paper and several jingle bells. "How on earth did you manage to find decorations?" she asked with delight.

"You'd be surprised at the various supplies the Quartermaster Corps has on hand," he said. "And wait'll you see the club."

The decorations at the club took her breath away. "It's beautiful," she said. Silver stars and twinkling lights hung from the ceiling. Colorful floral arrangements—while not exactly Christmassy —sat atop linen-clothed tables and smelled heavenly. The bar held a huge crystal punch bowl flanked by dozens of candles and plates of finger sandwiches.

A fifteen-piece band played instrumental songs, most conducive to slow-dancing but with the occasional swing number thrown in. Louise felt relaxed and graceful in Walter's arms. *Prob-*

ably because we aren't trying to court each other, she thought. *It's so much easier to just be friends.*

He must've read her mind. "I never realized you were such a good dancer," he said. "Back in Townsville your flyboy wouldn't let any of us near you—even for a quick spin around the floor."

Louise flushed and decided to ignore his comment about Will. "You're a pretty good dancer yourself."

When the orchestra took a break, Louise and Walter joined his roommates Whitey and Mack and their dates Catherine and Betty for cups of tropical punch and sandwiches. "Careful with the punch, gals," Whitey said. "It's stronger than it tastes."

Catherine smiled up at him. "Thanks for the warning—I vowed not to drink too much tonight. I've got the early shift tomorrow and the charge nurse is hard enough to deal with without a hangover."

"Me, too," Louise said.

"So, you girls are all off tomorrow evening?" Mack asked.

They nodded.

"Well then, you should come to our place for Christmas Eve dinner," he said. "The QM club's catering it, and it sounds damn tasty."

"Great!" Walter said. "I was hoping it'd all come together."

The orchestra's next set included "White Christmas" and "Jingle Bells." All the partygoers stood around the dance floor swaying and humming or singing along. Then someone turned off the lights and the band began softly playing "Silent Night." The crowd remained hushed.

Louise's eyes filled with tears, and she stifled a sob. Walter put his arm around her, and she rested her head on his shoulder. *Dear God*, she prayed, *may we all be safe at home this time next year.*

At 0950 on Christmas Day, the difficult charge nurse—now officially nicknamed "W3," short for Wicked Witch of the West—called Louise and Catherine to her desk. They exchanged wary glances as they went to stand before her.

"The Catholic chaplain's holding mass in the hospital chapel at ten o'clock," W3 said. "I'll tend the patients if you want to go."

Catherine did a double-take. "That'd be nice—thanks so much," she said.

"I'd like that," Louise added.

"It's a Christmas miracle," Louise whispered as the two walked toward the chapel.

The Latin mass was brief and largely lost on Louise, but she couldn't help noticing that Catherine, a devout Catholic, loved every second of it.

"Thanks again, Lieutenant," Louise told the charge nurse when they returned to the unit. "That meant a lot."

"You're welcome. I wanted you ladies to know that even 'W3' has a heart..." the nurse replied with half a smile. "One that breaks every day for what we have to witness here."

"Um...a..." Louise began, frantically trying to formulate an apology.

"Not another word, Dietrich. Get back to work, you two. Beds six and seven need to be bathed, and all of the patients need to be toileted before you leave at noon."

After their two o'clock dinner, Louise, Shoe, and Abby stayed for the service the Lutheran chaplain was holding in the dining hall. "I need to say an extra prayer for forgiveness," Louise said, "for calling the charge nurse a nasty name."

"Oh, go easy on yourself," Shoe said. "You have to admit she usually deserves it."

"Maybe. But she gave Catherine Murray a big dose of Christmas cheer today by covering for us while we went to Mass, and that has to count for something."

The women helped move the benches so everyone could face

the chaplain, a bespectacled man of about fifty whose uniform hung on his thin frame. He passed out battered hymnals and began the service in a strong yet calming voice. "Blessings to you all this last Sunday of Advent and as we prepare to celebrate Christ's birth tomorrow. Let us begin by singing "Joy to the World," on page eighty-seven for those who might not know all the verses."

He led the way, in a vocal range almost everyone could sing loudly, and the dining hall was immediately transformed into a place of gladness.

"Let us pray," the chaplain said when they finished singing. "Heavenly Father, we ask that You instill within us the wonder of this holy season. Please give us faith and hope as we deal with the difficulties we encounter here on a daily basis and comfort us as we ache for our loved ones so far away—or perhaps those gone from this world..."

After another hymn—"While Shepherds Watched Their Flocks by Night"—and a prayer of confession, which Louise prayed fervently, the chaplain began his sermon.

"How many of you are spending your first Christmas overseas?" A few people raised their hands. "And the second?" The majority raised theirs—though some slowly. The pastor chuckled. "I sense several of you are hesitant to admit how long you've been away from home," he said. "And how horrific, exhausting, and thankless your work here is. But in my experience, reluctance to admit the adversity you face doesn't make it any easier to face. This is an awful war, despite the noble reasons for which we fight. And it sure doesn't look like Christmas here in the jungle."

The nurses all nodded gravely.

"We've become accustomed to the snow and the fir trees," the chaplain continued, "the trimmings, the colored lights, the turkey dinners, and the gloriously wrapped presents. So accustomed, in fact, that we sometimes forget why we celebrate. Let's take a moment to think of those shepherds we just sang about—the ones watching their flocks. They had no decorations or presents and probably very little food. But the angel brought them something more important. A message of hope. The glorious news of the birth of Christ—*the son of God.* What could be better? God sent His son to be with us, to teach us, to save us. He is with us even now, in this muddy jungle.

"Many of you will celebrate tonight and tomorrow, perhaps with more turkey, perhaps with some of your liquor rations"—at this Louise and her friends laughed nervously—"and probably by exchanging presents with some folks who've become like family to you. Enjoy your celebrations. But I ask you to please, please remember *why* we celebrate. God has given us the greatest gift of all.

"Now, let us conclude with "Hark, the Herald Angels Sing!" and sing with all your hearts."

As Louise and the others filed out, the chaplain hugged each one, murmuring, "God bless and keep you."

ONE OF THE NURSES WHO'D GONE OUT THE DOOR before them had gathered a group in front of the dining hall. Louise approached warily...This particular nurse, Barbara Roberts, had treated her rudely on more than one occasion.

"Want to go with us to sing carols at the hospital?" Barbara asked.

"Uh...well, sure," Louise stammered, then looked toward Abby and Shoe.

"Why not?" Shoe said.

Barbara linked elbows with Louise as the group made their way toward the hospital. "I know we haven't been as welcoming to you gals on detached service as we should have been. Like the chaplain just said, we're all so sick and tired of this place and this horrible work. I'm afraid we've forgotten how to behave, and we shouldn't take it out on you or the patients."

Louise squeezed Barbara's hand. "Thanks for saying so."

Without the chaplain leading them, the nurses sang a tad off-key. But the patients—even the Filipinos who spoke little or no English—beamed with pleasure.

THAT EVENING, BETTY OLSON, CATHERINE MURRAY, and Louise went to the guys' shack for the promised Christmas feast. The men had pushed their cots to the edge of the tent to make room for chairs and a folding table covered with an only slightly soiled linen tablecloth borrowed from the club.

When the women arrived, the guys doused the single bulb hanging from the ceiling and lit candles for the table. "Take your seats, please," Walter said, then began serving individual shrimp cocktails while Mack poured wine.

"I can't remember when I last ate shrimp," Catherine said, popping one in her mouth and closing her eyes. "And I don't ever remember it tasting this wonderful."

"The tropics are good for something," Whitey said.

Walter cleared away the shrimp cups and opened another bottle of wine. "The steward from the club's bringing dinner in a few minutes."

"What's on the menu?" Louise asked.

"Turkey, of course," he said. "Dressing, gravy, mashed potatoes—no doubt dehydrated, so don't get your hopes up too high—cranberry sauce, and olives."

"Olives?" Betty asked.

Walter shrugged. "The cook asked if we wanted them and I said, 'Why not?' Oh, and there's chocolate layer cake for dessert."

"Good lord," Louise said with a sigh, "we won't be able to fit through the door when we're done."

"We can walk down to the harbor between dinner and dessert to let things settle a bit," Walter said. "I hear the ships are gonna put on some fireworks after dark."

With the exception of the potatoes, which were in fact dehydrated, the dinner was a hit. It was dark when they finished, so they hurried out the door.

The couples could hear the commotion in the harbor as they walked toward the water. By now, Louise was used to being one of a platonic couple while others in the group were romantically involved. So as not to fall on the unlit pathway, she took the arm Walter offered her. And she hardly even noticed that Betty and Mack and Whitey and Catherine held hands and occasionally stopped to kiss along the way.

Ablaze with lights, the ships in the Hollandia harbor sent up flare after flare and sounded their horns to the wild cheering of the sailors and onlookers. "It's awfully festive," Louise said, "though it seems more like New Year's Eve than Christmas Eve."

Walter nodded. "Better to celebrate now. Who knows where we'll be a week from now?"

After the fireworks the couples began the walk up the hill. "It didn't seem this long coming down," Betty complained, laughing. "We'll be famished and ready for that cake by the time we get there."

Mack laughed, picked her up, and threw her over his shoulder. "We wouldn't want you to get *famished* now, would we?"

Whitey, standing six inches shorter and weighing thirty pounds less than Mack, groaned. "Thanks for making me look like a boor and a weakling, Mack," he said. "And Catherine, even though you're light as a feather, I can barely make it myself." Catherine snorted, took his arm, and pretended to drag him up the hill.

Louise glanced at Walter. "Don't you even *think* about carrying me," she said. "We've got enough patients in the hospital as it is."

The hijinks lasted only a few minutes. And after a half hour of huffing and puffing, all six made it to the shack on their own feet. "Cake and beer anyone?" Walter asked when he'd caught his breath. Everyone nodded.

They drank and talked and listened to the Christmas programs on the Jungle Network until one-thirty in the morning—the extended holiday curfew. "Thanks for a wonderful evening," Louise told Walter when he walked her back to her tent. "I wasn't expecting to have such fun."

"You're welcome," he said and kissed her on top of her head. "We'll celebrate again if you're still here next week."

As it happened, they were still in Hollandia on December 31st. Walter took Louise to a New Year's Eve dance at the officers' club associated with the several battalions of Filipino Americans in the area.

"What does 'Bahalama' mean?" Louise asked, referring to the sign outside the club.

Walter laughed. "I've heard two versions. 'Come what may, we are ready' or 'We don't give a damn.' For all I know, neither one is accurate. But they sure know how to put on one a heck of a party."

Louise's jaw dropped when she saw the inside of the club. Long strands of several varieties of berries practically covered the ceiling, and there were lush and fragrant tropical flowers everywhere she looked. "And they sure know how to decorate."

The Filipino band members all wore leis and played a sweet brand of dance music that was both romantic and fun. Walter and Louise danced several numbers before someone tapped him on the shoulder. "It's up to the lady," Walter told him.

Louise's cheeks reddened, but she nodded in assent. At least ten other men cut in, each of them as charming as could be.

As the evening wound down, Walter stepped in. "I've shared her long enough," he said. "The last dance is for me."

They twirled and dipped and laughed as though there might be no tomorrow. *I sometimes wish he wasn't attached,* Louise thought.

. . .

On the second day of 1945, Louise planned to skip mail call. "Why bother?" she asked Dot as they finished their hospital shift. "I heard everything's being sent on ahead to wherever we're going."

"That's not exactly true. Shoe got a letter yesterday, so at least some is coming through."

"Alright. It's only a few steps out our way."

And to their surprise, they each had mail: Dot got a letter from her mom and one from her sister, and Louise got one from none other than Will Rogers. They rushed back to their tent to read.

"I think this calls for a beer," Louise said, opening a bottle before even opening the thin airmail envelope. "I need to be prepared for any eventuality—bad or good."

"You're grinning like a Cheshire cat," Dot said a few minutes later, looking up from her mother's letter. "I'm guessing good news?"

Without taking her eyes off the pages, Louise held up a finger. She finished reading, put the three pages back in order, folded them, and replaced them in the envelope.

"It's just *so* Will Rogers," she finally said. "A funny, newsy letter about what it's like to be back in the States. About eating all his favorite foods and listening to songs we couldn't hear over here. He makes me laugh and feel all good inside."

Dot gaped. "Did he...did he say anything about a future with you?"

Louise took another sip of beer and smiled. "He said so far, no woman would have him and wanted to know if the 44th could use another slightly used captain!"

"Well, that sounds promising."

"No. It sounds like a swell guy writing to say he's thinking about me and the good times we had. And that'll have to be enough for me—at least for now."

. . .

ON JANUARY 3, 1945, THE NURSES FROM THE 44TH WERE relieved of duty and told to pack for departure. Louise accepted Walter's invitation to spend one last evening at the shack. They listened to the radio, drank a couple of beers, and played cribbage. "You look kind of down," he said to her after one game, "which is odd since you just skunked me."

She lowered her head. *You can't cry,* she told herself. *You've been champing at the bit to get out of this place for two months—this is a good* move.

"Tell me what's on your mind, kid," Walter insisted.

Louise sighed. "This camp is the absolute worst and our duties here have been awful," she said. "But you've been a great friend to me and made our time off so much fun. I'm going to miss you..."

"I'm gonna miss you too, sis," he said, his voice cracking.

Chapter Thirty

On January 5th, the nurses were back aboard the AHS *Maetsuycker*, the same Dutch hospital ship they'd traveled on to Hollandia, this time bound for somewhere in the Philippines. It would be a shorter and less eventful journey than their last. Because their quarters were stiflingly hot, they spent many hours on deck enjoying the breezes and re-reading the few books they'd managed to scrounge up in New Guinea. When the sea was calm enough, they played cards and wrote letters.

"I'm so glad to be done with that god-awful detached service," Shoe said while waiting for Louise to deal their next rummy hand one day. "I sometimes felt like I was walking on eggshells having to answer to those nincompoops—then I'd look down and see it was mud."

"I bit my tongue so many times to avoid saying something insubordinate that it bled," Vivian added.

Frankie picked up her cards and began to sort them. "And even though we're heading closer to the battlefields, I'll feel a heck of a lot more confident with the men of the 44th by our sides."

"We need to give those docs and nurses some slack," Louise said. "They've been uncomfortable, overworked, and bone-tired for months with no end in sight—it's no wonder they're bad-tempered. Now, no more shop talk...we need to focus on winning this game. Remember, future beer rations are riding on it!"

THE *MAETSUYCKER* ARRIVED ON THE ISLAND OF LEYTE on January 10, 1945. In pouring rain, the nurses were taken in open G.I. trucks to an area about forty miles away.

"This is the muddiest mud I've ever seen," Louise said to Shoe as they caromed against one another. "And I can't see the road we're driving on through the downpour."

"You're assuming there *is* a road," her friend replied. "Looks like this island is just one big lake surrounded by mud."

During the three-hour trip, the nurses' optimism about the new duty station faded. But after taking showers and donning dry clothing, they went to the mess hall to join the men of the 44th, who'd prepared a welcoming dinner of sauerkraut and wieners. There were hugs and laughter, and the men couldn't stop talking about how glad they were to see them.

"So, where the heck are we?" Shoe asked one of the doctors as they stood at the plank tables to eat—there was no room for benches or seats.

"Burauen," Captain Connelly replied. "About four miles west of where General MacArthur had his headquarters. We moved here and began taking patients a week after we landed. And boy, has it been eventful!"

"Eventful?" Louise asked, and she and her friends leaned in to listen.

"When the Americans took over Leyte, we inherited the airfield a few miles from here—it'd been one of the enemy's best fields. It became the base for the Fifth Air Force, used for our P-51s, P-38s, and C-47 cargo planes. A real asset for the Allies. At least until December 6, when two Jap planes dropped about sixty paratroopers to try to recapture it. They came close to succeeding

—killed all the American personnel manning the field and destroyed all the fighter planes."

The women gasped.

"But by the next morning," Captain Connelly said, "the perimeter guard and local infantry managed to kill all but two of the paratroopers. They were taken prisoner and brought to the hospital."

"It must've been difficult for you to treat them," Shoe said. "I know we had POWs at Townsville, but we didn't know specifically what they'd done. With these guys, you *knew*."

The doctor shook his head. "It wasn't that hard. Remember, we took the Hippocratic oath and, unlike the Japanese who'll shoot at a hospital without batting an eye, we pride ourselves on following the rules. These guys seemed pretty pathetic—they were in a lot of pain from their injuries."

He paused to take a bite of his dinner, then brushed a dribble of sauerkraut off his chin with the back of his hand. "But the story gets worse. We got word through Filipino informants that the Japs planned to send additional paratroopers to rescue the two guys from our hospital. The Army armed all of us so we could defend ourselves."

"Did you have to?" Louise asked. "Defend yourselves, I mean?"

Dr. Connelly nodded. "We sure did. On the night of December 10, they attacked the west perimeter of the hospital and unfortunately overran the machine gun crew. For the next nine hours we—and I mean docs, medics, all of us—fought 'em off. One American paratrooper died and two of our docs, Birge and Bingham, were shot but not badly injured. The next day, the bodies of twenty-three Japanese soldiers were found dead in the area—some only a few feet from our tents. We consider ourselves damn lucky, and as difficult as it's been for us to run a hospital without you gals, I'm glad they waited to send you."

Louise clutched onto her dog tags to steady herself. Frankie's face turned ashen, and all the women were temporarily speechless.

"Actually, we were pretty lucky from the get-go," the doctor continued. "When we first arrived, Japanese snipers positioned themselves in trees around the hospital and they'd take potshots at us in the morning. So the machine gunners routinely sprayed the trees to make sure they were gone."

"Are there still any in the area?" Louise asked, afraid to hear his response.

"Yeah, but they're pretty whipped and not doing much harm. Colonel Weston says all you nurses will be issued revolvers just in case, and you'll have to stay within the hospital perimeter."

"Not again," Shoe grumbled.

"It's not so bad," Connelly replied. "There's an officers' club already, and we should be getting some USO shows and first-run movies."

THE HOUSING ACCOMMODATIONS WERE PRIMITIVE: four-person tents with mud floors and cots. The tents leaked like sieves, and there was no electricity. Nevertheless, the nurses were happy to be reunited with the 44th and quickly pushed the presence of Japanese snipers to the back of their minds.

There were dozens of Filipino women willing to do their laundry in exchange for just about anything. They washed the clothes in a nearby river, beating them with rocks, and turning them white and clean as could be. The Filipino women, who themselves lived in dilapidated grass huts in the middle of rice paddies, also braided palm leaves into strips of rope to fashion a fence around the area.

The rumors that the nurses' mail had been sent ahead to Leyte turned out to be accurate, though it was reported that there were still stockpiles of mail waiting to be sorted at every American base. Louise received fourteen letters in the first mail call alone.

Not recognizing the return address, she puzzled over one of them and decided to open it while waiting with her friends. "You're not going to believe this," she said. "It's from a twenty-two-year-old Aussie soldier on Morata's Island. He and his buddies found our bottle—the one we sent from the ship three months ago on the way to Hollandia!"

Dot and Shoe, standing nearby, searched their mail. "I got one too," Dot said.

"Me, too," Shoe added. "Who woulda thunk?"

"I thought that only happened in movies or books," Louise said. "And he wrote the sweetest letter."

As it turned out, Frankie and Vivian had also received letters from soldiers on the island. The hospital buzzed with the news of the miraculous connection.

WITHIN A FEW DAYS OF THEIR ARRIVAL, THE NURSES were hard at work tending to wounded soldiers, hindered alternately by rain and lack of water. The only available water was whatever they caught during the rainstorms and supplies often ran out before the next rain came.

"Today I treated a soldier who has a broken arm, four gunshot wounds, and a bayonet wound in his other arm," Louise told her friends. "I told him I was sorry I couldn't offer him any water. You know what he said?"

"What?" Shoe asked.

"He said they're so used to sleeping in dirty, wet foxholes and not washing for days or weeks at a time that a few days without water is nothing to them."

"Maybe so," Dot replied, "but I'm having trouble getting used to it."

"The thing I'm having trouble getting used to is those air raids," Shoe said. "I thought Doc Connelly said the Japanese aren't very threatening anymore. But, to me, one or two planes flying over and dropping a few bombs is more than a nuisance. The movie last night was interrupted by another one, and having to scatter, drop to the ground, and cover your head scares the hell out of me. It surely isn't my idea of entertainment."

"I heard that one was actually about twenty miles away," Louise said, trying to tamp down her own concern.

"Still, some are a lot closer," Shoe insisted.

Vivian, who still had nightmares about being hit with flour bombs during their bivouac in Oklahoma, remained conspicuously silent.

THE NURSES WORKED TEN- TO TWELVE-HOUR DAYS AND were typically so tired at night that they went to bed early and slept till their next shifts. One Sunday evening though, Louise, her friend Joyce, escorted by two of the medics, Joe and David, strolled into the Filipino village situated next to the hospital.

"I've never seen so many little kids running around such a small town," Joe said. "It's clear what the favorite pastime of the locals is..."

Louise poked him with her elbow.

They walked about half a block farther and came to a roped-off area surrounded by what seemed like a crowd worthy of a major league baseball game. "Wonder what's going on?" Joyce asked.

Joe nudged partway through the throng and—being several inches taller than the Filipinos—was able to see. "They're getting ready for a cock fight," he reported to his companions. "This seems to be the betting phase. There's some room under the trees to our right. C'mon up." He reached around and grabbed Louise's hand, and the other two followed.

The women shrank back, intimidated by the frenetic shouting, as most of the spectators gave their instructions and currency to the odds-makers. After about forty-five minutes, two large roosters were led forward, each with a razor-sharp knife blade tied to the spur of its leg. Upon spying the weapons and finally realizing what was about to occur, Louise and Joyce covered their eyes. The actual fight—amid excited cheers—lasted less than ten seconds and ended when the champion rooster slashed the other to death.

"Keep your eyes closed," Joe said as he and David led Louise and Joyce away from the bloody scene.

"I could've lived forever without witnessing a spectacle like that," Joyce exclaimed when the coast was clear.

"For the record," David said, "you *didn't* witness it."

"Oh, you know what I mean!" she replied. "The *idea* of it is so barbaric."

"Not my cup of tea, either," Joe said, "but cockfighting is popular in lots of places around the world."

"I suppose we should try not to judge," Louise said, "but I, for one, am never going near one of those things again."

One of the 44th's enlisted men Louise was delighted to be back in contact with on Leyte was Bob Weber, their supply sergeant. Six-foot-two with vivid blue eyes, curly brown hair, and irresistible dimples, he had always flirted unabashedly with her whenever they'd met. The attention made her a little giddy, and she gladly offered to take requisition orders from the hospital to the supply depot whenever the situation arose.

During one such visit, Bob was alone in the office. "I sure was sorry the ban on nurses dating enlisted men has been reinstated here," he said to her. "I heard you're unattached now and was hoping we could go out sometime—maybe a double date with your friend Shoemaker and my buddy Quinn."

Louise felt her heart flutter but thought back to the trouble she and Shoe had gotten into for fraternizing with Hutch and Jake close to a year earlier. "I don't know," she replied. "We already got called on the carpet for that once."

"I remember," he said with his dimpled grin, "but it's been so long ago and the rules were relaxed between then and now. If you get caught, you can always claim you didn't know it'd been banned again."

You remember me getting caught fraternizing with another man?

"I'll talk to Shoe and see what she says," she replied.

"Thanks, kid. Let me know."

Shoe was on duty when she got back to the hospital and Louise pulled her aside. "Bob Weber just asked me on a date," she said breathlessly, "and he wants us to double with you and Sergeant Quinn. You know which one he is, don't you?"

"Of course, I do—he's the cutie in supply who's been toying with me ever since we got here. He never came right out and asked me on a date though."

"What do you think? Should we go?"

"Why the heck not?"

"Well, for one thing you haven't dated since you got engaged to Del."

"Del and I agreed we could go out on casual dates with other people," Shoe replied, "and a double date surely fits the bill."

"My main reluctance is because it's against the rules—*again.*"

"Didn't you and Joyce go over to the village with the two medics the other night?"

"That wasn't a date—we just happened to run into them while we were out for a walk. And they're both married, for heaven's sake."

"It's still fraternizing," Shoe said peevishly. "I say we go out with Weber and Quinn and just make sure we don't get caught."

THE FOURSOME'S FIRST FEW DATES—PICNICS BY THE river—turned out to be fun and casual, though Bob Weber tended to make more physical contact with Louise than his friend did with Shoe. He often patted her arm to make a point, brushed a stray lock of hair away from her face, and squeezed her hand. She didn't mind. In fact, she loved the little thrill she felt when he touched her.

"You gals want to go to the movie together tonight?" he asked one day when she stopped by the supply depot.

"Isn't that a little too public?"

Weber shook his head and smiled his perfectly straight white-toothed smile at her. "I hear nobody's paying too much attention to the rule right now. Our CO caught Jackson with one of the nurses last night and just winked at them."

"Okay. I'm sure Shoe will say yes, but I'll get word to you if she's got other plans.

The movie was *Arsenic and Old Lace*, starring Cary Grant, which everyone thoroughly enjoyed. "What a hoot!" Louise said, holding onto Bob's arm as they walked from the theater.

"It was much better than I expected," Shoe added.

Engrossed in conversation about the actors' performances, the foursome didn't notice the chief nurse watching them. "Dietrich. Shoemaker," she barked. "See me in my office at 0800 tomorrow."

"Yes, ma'am," they said and slunk away from the guys.

"Damn, damn, damn," Louise said on the way to their tent. "Do you think we'll get court-martialed this time?"

"I doubt it," Shoe replied, though Louise detected a hint of concern in her voice.

As punishment, the nurses were restricted to their tent and required to work two extra hours per day for a week. "I told you they wouldn't court-martial us," Shoe whispered as they left the chief's office at 0805. "And other than saying we'd be watched like hawks from now on, she didn't even lecture us."

"Thank heaven for small favors," Louise replied. "But I sure am going to miss those two goofballs."

When they returned to their tent after their fourteen-hour shift that evening, they found bouquets of flowers and four bottles of beer along with a note reading, "To help pass your evening—From your not-so-secret admirers."

"How sweet," Louise said.

There were additional gifts the following nights: paperback books, crossword puzzle books, a deck of cards, and more flowers and beer.

"I think they're trying to convince us to go out with them again," Shoe said one evening.

"I sure wish we could. They are about the best guys in this camp."

The threat of being closely watched, however, kept them in line.

For a while at least.

Chapter Thirty-One

UNDER INCREASINGLY HORRIFIC CONDITIONS, THE seventy-seven American nurses captured by the Japanese when Corregidor fell in May 1942 had been imprisoned at the former University of Santo Tomas in Manila. On February 3, 1945, when the United States Army liberated the camp, they found that all had survived. They'd lost an average of thirty percent of their body weight and required hospitalization but for close to three years, had managed to minister to the thousands of internees detained along with them.

The evacuees were flown to the 126th Army General Hospital, also on the island of Leyte, for medical examinations and treatment before their transport home several days later.

The news of the Corregidor nurses' rescue was met with relief and joy by the members of the 44th. "Thank the Lord they're finally safe," Colonel Weston said to Louise and a few other personnel who were talking about it during their shift that day. "I can't imagine how I'd cope with the knowledge that my nurses were in Japanese hands."

"I know," said Captain Connelly. "And it had to have caused

General MacArthur a boatload of anguish back in '42 when he, his family, and his staff were ordered to evacuate without them."

"Do you think President Roosevelt was right to order the evacuation?" Louise asked.

"Yeah," Connelly said. "Unfortunately, FDR didn't have the resources to fully back the war in the Pacific with the more pressing priorities at the time."

"Well, I'm sure thankful MacArthur's got his support now," Louise said. "Maybe we can all go home before too long."

IN MID-FEBRUARY, LOUISE GOT HER FIRST CHRISTMAS package. She was pleased to see it arrived relatively unscathed when many of her colleagues' packages came through water-soaked and moldy. They also got their first beer ration since Christmas. "Wow! Twelve whole cans," Louise commented to Shoe.

"It's supposed to last two weeks," Shoe replied.

"Mine'll never last that long," Louise lamented. "Hey, did I tell you about the Filipino dance Mary Davy and I went to a couple nights ago?"

"No. How was it?"

"We were the only two American girls there and they treated us so nice. They even played one American song for us to dance to. Guess what it was."

"I just finished a fourteen-hour shift," Shoe said. "I'm too tired to guess."

"Beer Barrel Polka."

Shoe burst out laughing. "Sounds like your reputation precedes you!"

"I'm getting another reputation too: The boys on the orthopedic ward think I give the best penicillin shots. They've named me Miss Penicillin 1945."

"Congratulations," Shoe said, then suddenly fell silent before adding, "Have you ever thought how many lives we could've saved if penicillin had been available earlier in the war?"

"I can't even imagine. I'm just grateful we have it now."

Within the next five days, Louise received four additional Christmas packages, including two more from her sister. She still hadn't heard from Will Rogers.

In late February, after a long workday that had brought Frankie and Louise near to tears with exhaustion, they nevertheless trudged over to see if they'd received any mail. Their moods immediately lifted: Frankie had received a package from her husband, Alex, and Louise had finally received a letter from Will.

"Let's open 'em when we get back to the tent," Frankie said excitedly. "Vivian and Dot are on night duty, and we can read in peace."

Thank heaven, Louise thought. *We're all so tired we're grouchy as bears with gout—I'm afraid the four of us will come to blows one of these days.*

Frankie's package contained a beautiful clock, a huge bottle of cologne, and a five-page letter. "You know," she said wistfully when she finished reading, "we've been married for nearly two years, and I only got to spend four months with him before I left the States."

"I can't imagine how hard it's been, kid," Louise said. "Any chance he'll be sent over here?"

Frankie shrugged. "He's in Los Angeles waiting for his overseas orders. He says it looks promising..."

"I'll say some prayers for you two."

"Thanks. Now tell me what Will had to say."

"His old outfit is moving here within the next month," Louise said. "He's trying to get the okay for another overseas hitch so he can join them."

"That'd be wonderful. I can't help thinking he'd ask you to marry him if he just had time to get to know you better."

"Maybe..." she said pensively. "Dating here is nothing like back home. You know I went to that dance at the 77th Division on Monday?"

Frankie nodded. "You said they served steak and ice cream and beer."

Louise began swinging her foot. "The orchestra played some of my favorites—"I'll Get By," "Long Ago and Far Away," and "My Heart Tells Me"—and my date was such a good dancer. But the men so outnumbered the women that we couldn't go more than a couple steps before someone cut in. There I was, the belle of the ball in my slacks and Army brogans with sun-bleached hair and yellow skin. I can't imagine what it'll be like when we get home and have competition for the men."

Frankie reached over and squeezed her friend's hand. "You're pretty and sweet, and everyone loves you. Will would be a ninny to let you get away, but even if he does, there'll be plenty more guys who'll want you."

"You're a honey to say that, but in the back of my mind, I can't help thinking that my best chance to find a husband is in the service."

"I don't know about that. With these hellish shifts, there's not much time or energy left for socializing. At least in the civilian world nurses get actual days off."

Louise nodded. "That's true. I keep hoping and praying these waves of casualties will stop, but they never end. Keeping men on stretchers until we can set up another ward is no way to practice medicine."

"At least we can do it in an hour's time. That's impressive."

"And we can be proud of the great care we give—even treating 1,500 men in our '1,000-bed' hospital. Things never ran this smoothly in Hollandia."

Chapter Thirty-Two

In mid-March, Louise got another letter from Will. She laughed when a Schlitz beer bottle label fell from between the folded pages. Vivian, standing next to her at mail call, raised an eyebrow.

"Will says he wishes he could drink a few of these with me again," she said in response. "Then he says he might have some real news for me soon."

"Maybe he'll get to rejoin his old unit over here? I heard they've moved from Biak to Leyte—and only about thirty miles from us."

"I don't dare hope for that. My luck just doesn't seem to run that way."

"Stop it, Louise," Vivian chided. "You don't want to turn into a pessimist like Dot. And don't forget that against the odds, Frankie and Alex got a chance to be together here for a couple weeks."

"Actually, Dot's pretty upbeat since we started hanging out with the group of Air Corpsmen we just met. They're a bunch of screwballs and lots of fun to be around. Since I've been working nights, they sometimes come visit me on the ward."

"What's the guy's name that you go with?"

"Ed Winter. His birthday is three days before mine, so when I go off night duty, they're planning a big party to celebrate."

"Is it serious—the thing between you and Ed, I mean?"

Louise shrugged. "Just like I say when Frankie asks if I think she might be pregnant—it's way too soon to tell."

PURELY THROUGH HAPPENSTANCE—BECAUSE THE ARMY wasn't known for its sentimentality—Louise got off night duty the day before her twenty-fourth birthday and had three days off in a row. The gang of aviators and nurses spent a glorious afternoon at the beach, splashing in the vivid blue water, sunning themselves on the sand, and drinking American beer.

At one point, Ed came up behind her and put his hands around her waist. "You know I can't think of anyone else I'd rather share a birthday with," he whispered. "And do you realize your eyes are the exact color of the water?"

She felt her cheeks flush as she turned toward him. "You sure are one sweet guy."

He bent down and gave her a quick kiss. Then he shouted to the group, "Shoulder wars, anyone?"

"I am *not* getting up on your shoulders," Louise giggled. "I probably gained five pounds working the night shift."

"Don't be silly," he said and ducked under to lift her up.

Dot and Michael were their first opponents, and Dot fell off his shoulders without putting up much of a fight. Feeling more than a little self-conscious, Louise squirmed down. "I've had enough war for one day and one lifetime," she said. "Plus, I want to live to see twenty-five."

"Okay, okay. And God willing, you won't be celebrating in the South Pacific next year," Ed said.

The group, plus a few others who'd been on duty during the afternoon, went to the guys' club for dinner. The meal itself was nothing special, but the cook wheeled out a cart bearing their dessert: a large cake decorated with flowers that read "Happy birthday, Ed and Louise."

The cook stuck one large candle in the center. "Sorry, gang—I couldn't drum up fifty little ones," he said.

"Not fifty," Ed said. "She's twenty-four and I'm only twenty-five, which last I heard makes a total of forty-nine. But now I can see why you flunked out of pilots' school."

The cook lit the candle. "Be quiet and let the lady make a wish."

Ed glanced at Louise, who nodded, then they both blew out the candle.

Half an hour later, when everyone began moving toward the dance floor, Dot whispered to Louise, "So what'd you wish for?"

"Can't tell or it won't come true," she said with a Mona Lisa smile. *If you only knew,* she thought, *that I couldn't decide* who *to wish for—Will Rogers or Ed Winter...*

Before they left the club, Ed took Louise aside and handed her a paper-wrapped present. "I got you a little something," he said.

"Oh...but I didn't get you a gift."

"Never mind that. Go ahead—open it."

She took out a delicate silk pouch containing a travel-sized manicure set. "It's beautiful!" she said, leaning in to hug him. "Thank you."

"You're welcome. By the way, will you be my date for the Air Corps dance on Friday night?"

LOUISE SLEPT LATE THE NEXT MORNING AND WOKE UP to relative quiet. Her tentmates—except Shoe who was hospitalized with jaundice—were all on duty. She showered and dressed, then munched on some nuts and candy Etta had sent for her birthday. *This feels so odd,* she thought, *a day off with nothing to do and nobody to do it with.*

She reached under her bed and found the Armed Services edition of *A Tree Grows in Brooklyn* that she'd received several weeks earlier but hadn't had time to open. Completely engrossed, she startled when Joe Scarpetti called to her from outside the tent shortly before noon. "Hey, Dietrich. You're needed on the ward ASAP!"

"What for? It's my day off."

"I don't question Captain Riley's orders, Lieutenant. She said to come get you and that's what I'm doing."

"Okay. I'll be right there."

On the way to the hospital, she wracked her brain to think what she might have done to warrant a reprimand.

She opened the door to the ward warily and heard everyone—doctors, nurses, ward men, and patients—yell, "Surprise! Happy birthday, Dietrich!"

"So? Were you surprised?" Joe asked.

"Look at my cheeks," she said, punching him in the arm. "I can feel that they're beet red. So, yes, I was surprised. Plus, my birthday was yesterday."

"We know," her friend Ruth replied, "but that aviator had other plans for you."

Louise looked at the table they'd set up with sandwiches, pretzels, candy, and plates of cookies. Everyone who was able stood around it. "This is so sweet of you all," she said, blinking back tears.

After lunch Joe presented her with a hand-painted card made by one of the Red Cross volunteers and signed by everyone on the ward. She read their heartfelt notes with tears flowing freely now. "Thank you all! I have to say I don't mind growing old this way."

"Old," scoffed Captain Riley. "Why you're just a kid."

On Friday evening, Louise and Ruth were surprised when Ed and Ruth's date, Pete Carpenter, came to pick them up for the Air Corps party in a C-46 transport plane. "We thought you'd enjoy traveling in style," Ed said. "And we'll have time for a spin over the harbor before the party starts. You can each have a window seat—you'll be amazed at how far you can see."

As Louise gazed over the Leyte Gulf, she couldn't help marveling at how peaceful the water looked. *How different from the rough seas we sailed on to get here. I'd love to come back and enjoy the beaches when this war is over.*

The party was anticlimactic compared to the plane ride to it. But Louise felt confident and happy in Ed's arms as they danced almost every song—and especially when he refused to let other men cut in. "Who knows how long before one or the other of us gets ordered to go somewhere else," he said after rebuffing one of his friends. "I'm going to enjoy every minute I have with you."

That's the closest he's ever come to telling me how he feels about me, Louise thought. *What is it about these flyboys?*

THE HOSPITAL CONTINUED RECEIVING MORE BATTLE casualties, and it grew to twice its capacity. "We're borrowing cots from the Navy for this last wave of patients," Captain Connelly told Louise one day. "The Japs gotta know they can't win this thing, but they're still putting up a heck of a fight."

Chapter Thirty-Three

FEELING SUDDENLY DIZZY DURING AN AFTERNOON SHIFT in early April, Louise stopped to get her bearings and stood still for a moment. "What's the matter?" Joe called from across the tent. "You look feverish."

"No, just worn out, I think," she replied. "With all these new patients, I haven't been off my feet for a minute all day."

"Go sit in the office for a bit. Grab a Coke or something to raise your blood sugar."

Louise nodded and began walking away. But a second later she and the tray of instruments she was carrying dropped to the floor. Stunned, she raised her hand and felt a trickle of blood on her temple.

Joe rushed to her side. "Don't try to stand up," he said, touching her forehead. "You're burning up.

"I must've tripped on something."

"All I know is you fell and it looks like you smacked your head on the way down," Joe said as he felt her pulse. "David, run and get more help, please," he yelled to his fellow corpsman. "Her heart's racing and we need to cool her down."

David and another orderly returned a few minutes later

carrying a stretcher, with Captains Riley and Connelly in tow. "Get back to your beds," Riley barked to the patients who'd gathered around. "We need room to move!"

"She's feverish, Doc," Joe said. "And I think she hit her head pretty hard."

Connelly took a flashlight from his coat pocket and lifted one of Louise's eyelids to check her pupil's reaction. "Possible concussion on top of whatever's causing her fever," he said. "Let's get her to the infirmary."

The nurses' infirmary, a large tent within the stockade, already housed thirteen patients, including Bertha Shoemaker.

Joe and David carried Louise to a screened-off area of the tent and set the litter on an examining table. "Thanks, gentlemen," the doctor said. "Head back to the ward, David, and let the patients know she'll be okay—Dietrich's one of their favorites."

Realizing in an instant that several of Louise's friends were mere feet away, the doctor lowered his voice. "Joe, see if you can rustle up some ice."

As the ward men left the exam area, Shoe sat upright against her several pillows. "Did I hear Louise's name?" she called to them. "What's happened?"

Joe went to the bedside. "She fainted on the unit and hit her head. Relax—she'll be fine."

As it happened, Louise insisted she hadn't lost consciousness, her head wound was superficial in nature, and concerns of a concussion were quickly dispelled. Nevertheless, her temperature hovered between 101 and 103 degrees for a solid week, during which time she was rarely awake. The diagnosis: infectious hepatitis—probably caused by contaminated water.

Three friends, including Shoe, were in beds close to her. They kept close watch over her and promised they'd play card games whenever she was able.

. . .

LOUISE WAS NOWHERE NEAR WELL ENOUGH TO PLAY cards on the evening of April 13, 1945, when Anna stopped by to visit her and Shoe.

"Have you heard the news?" Anna said before any of the patients had even mumbled a hello.

"What news?" Shoe asked.

Anna sat heavily on the end of Louise's bed. "What's the matter?" Louise asked, glancing at her, "you're shaking and you look like you've seen a ghost."

"FDR's dead."

"What?" Shoe gasped. "What happened?"

Unable to hold back her tears, Anna mumbled, "He collapsed while posing for a portrait at the Little White House in Warm Springs. Probably a massive stroke."

Louise began crying, too. "I can't believe it," she said. "It felt like we knew him, being able to listen to his fireside chats and all. And he was such a great leader."

"And now we've got Harry Truman," Shoe moaned. "Nobody knows a thing about him...at least I don't. Can we trust him to get us out of this war?"

Louise moved her head from side to side, unable to lift it from the pillow. "He's got mighty big shoes to fill. We'd better pray hard for him."

WHEN LOUISE'S FEVER FINALLY BROKE A COUPLE OF days later, she was convinced she'd soon be released, but the doctors thought otherwise. She was still hospitalized on the red-letter day when all the patients were given "honest-to-god" baked potatoes for supper.

"Mail call for Lieutenant Louise Dietrich," Vivian chirped when she came by to visit as the orderlies were picking up the supper trays. "You got two letters."

"Did you get baked potatoes in the mess hall this evening?"

Louise asked her.

"Heck no! Do you mean to tell me you all did?"

Louise nodded. "First time in ten months, we figured," she said. "And boy, was it delicious. They probably had a limited supply and decided to give them to us invalids."

"I'm happy for you," Vivian said, "but right now my skin is green from jealousy, not from Atabrine."

"What's new?" Louise asked. "I'm feeling well enough now to be bored."

Vivian scratched her head. "Let's see...Frankie is pretty sure now that she's in a family way."

"I've kept my fingers crossed, even during the height of my fever. What else?"

"Gee, I can't think of anything," Vivian replied. "Why don't you read your mail while I visit a gal I know from the 27th—she's over on the north end. I'll be back in a few minutes."

Louise felt her blood pressure rising as she read the first letter —four pages in tiny script from her sister. And the three-page one from her Aunt Margaret didn't do anything to calm her down.

"Not bad news, I hope?" Vivian said when she returned.

"Not exactly bad," Louise replied. "More like annoying. Etta wrote to say that our Aunt Mabel—our father's sister—is complaining to everyone she knows about items at our farm that should rightfully have gone to her. A set of dishes. A couple of quilts. An antique dresser. It's all so childish. And now our sweet Aunt Margaret is caught in the middle of it."

Vivian patted her hand. "I'm sorry."

"It's okay. After our dad died, the probate judge put the deed to the farm in Etta's and my name. But instead of trusting our relatives to look out for us, we should've had the verbal agreement about all the other stuff put into writing."

"But you were just kids then."

Louise brushed a tear off her cheek. "I know."

They didn't talk for a few moments.

"Has Ed been by lately?" Vivian finally asked.

"He was supposed to come yesterday but had to fly. He left a message that he'll be out tomorrow night and for me to ask the doctors if I can have a pass to go to the movies. That'll cheer me up."

"Good. I hope it all works out."

ED VISITED LOUISE FAIRLY OFTEN AND MANAGED TO help her fend off boredom. "Your eyes are still as yellow as the muddy Mississippi," he said one day a couple of weeks into her stay. "Are you feeling *any* better?"

"I feel much too well to be here, but the truth is I still get awfully tired when I'm up for very long."

"What's new since I saw you last?"

"I learned to play Pinochle. It's fascinating and it turns out I'm pretty good at it. Yesterday Shoe and I beat Esther and Abby five games out of seven. After the third win, we tried to bet some of our future beer rations on the next game, but they said no..."

"Funny you should mention cards. Pete and Ruth are planning to come by this evening so Pete and I can teach you gals how to play bridge. I remember you saying you didn't know how and neither does Ruth."

"I'm warning you that my Aunt Margaret and Uncle Chuck tried to teach me and Etta one time and they got plenty frustrated."

"Maybe you just need better teachers."

"I'll be sure and rest up before tonight, so my brain is fully functioning."

"You do that," he said, stood to leave, and planted a kiss on her head. "See you later, kid."

When Ed, Ruth, and Pete arrived after supper, though, they wore long faces. "Why are you all looking so glum?" Louise asked.

Ed sat on the end of her bed. "We just heard about Ernie Pyle

—he was covering the Okinawa campaign and was killed by Japanese machine-gun fire on the island of Ie Shima."

Louise's breath caught in her throat. "How horrible. He was my favorite correspondent. He covered all the major campaigns in this godforsaken war and really connected with the troops...It feels like a personal friend has died."

Ruth nodded, brushing away tears. "First Roosevelt and now him."

"You know the movie *G.I. Joe*—the story about Ernie Pyle's life—is supposed to come out in a few months," Ed said.

"I'd forgotten that," Louise said, "but there's no way I'll miss it now."

The group sat lost in thought for a while. Louise said a silent prayer that Joey, her former fiancé now serving in Okinawa, would survive what everyone knew was a fierce campaign.

"Do you still want to learn bridge?" Ed asked the girls.

They nodded. "Might as well," Louise said.

Ed carefully described the object and rules of the game, while Pete kept saying, "Deal a hand face up—that's the only way to learn."

Even using that approach, the lesson went poorly. After her second flub, Ruth threw her cards on the table. "I'm sorry I'm a rotten partner," she said to Pete. "I just can't remember all these details."

"Me neither," Louise said. "Maybe we're just dunces."

Ed laughed. "I know that's not true, but we can give it a rest and try another time. When we're not feeling so blue."

"That'd be good," Louise said. "I am getting tuckered out."

Pete and Ruth took this as their cue to leave. "Let's go to your club," he said to her, then turned to Ed. "Join us later if you want."

Ed and Louise held hands. He watched while she downed her fourth quart of water for the day and gallantly walked her toward the latrine afterward. "I swear I'd regain my energy a lot quicker if they didn't make me drink so much water," she said. "I'm exhausted from all the trips to the bathroom."

The doctors granted Louise and Shoe passes to see comedian Joe E. Brown perform at the camp, and they sat next to each other during the show. "I can't laugh anymore or I'm afraid I'll wet my pants," Shoe said at one point. The laughter continued, though.

"That was great," Louise said as they walked back to the infirmary. "He's so modest, too. He didn't even mention that this is already his second tour of the Pacific theater."

"I heard that since his son was killed, he's spent practically all his time overseas entertaining the GIs."

One morning, the patients were each served an orange for breakfast. Louise picked hers up and smelled it. "Does this mean the war is over?" she asked the ward man.

He laughed.

Chapter Thirty-Four

May 8, 1945

THOUGH THE NURSES OF THE 44TH GENERAL HOSPITAL were happy to hear the war in Europe was over, to those fighting the brutal war in the Pacific and treating its casualties, V-E Day was much like any other day. Except Louise and her friends had two other causes for celebration: Louise's release from the hospital and Frankie's having been boarded to return to the States.

"Welcome home," Dot said to Louise when she got back to the tent. "How're you feeling?"

"Pretty good. I still tire easily and I'll only work four-hour shifts for a while when I start back to work next Monday. But I gotta tell you, four weeks in the hospital felt like six years—and I was lucky enough to get passes near the end. I'm going to have a lot more sympathy for our patients from now on."

"Did you hear Frankie is packing to head home?"

Louise turned to Frankie, who was fully engrossed in sorting items. "So, the army finally recognizes you're in a family way?

Frankie's eyes sparkled. "And I can't believe I collected so much stuff since we last moved—and you're welcome to anything

I've laid out on Shoe's bunk. Anna already came and took a couple of books and my bathing suit—it won't fit me when I get home."

"This feels kind of like we're vultures—circling around for the good pickings," Louise teased.

"Don't be silly," Frankie said. "I couldn't care less about this stuff. Today's our second wedding anniversary and the best present I could ever get was to be boarded home. I'm so excited I can barely see straight!"

Louise strode over and hugged her. "I couldn't be happier for you two...I mean you *three*."

"Alex and I haven't forgotten our promise to name our baby after you or Dutch—we're so thankful you introduced us."

Oh goodness, Louise thought. *It seems like forever ago that I was head-over-heels for Dutch. And it was half a world away.* "Well, I'll hope for a boy—no baby girl should be stuck with my name."

Louise glanced through the discard pile and selected a half-full bottle of Prince Matchabelli cologne and two bottles of nail polish. "Any idea when you'll be leaving?"

"As soon as transport can be arranged."

"For your sake, I hope it's soon, but we're sure gonna miss you."

LOUISE'S FIRST ASSIGNMENT AFTER SHE WENT BACK ON full-time duty was a specialized care shift, where she took care of only one patient—one who was likely to die. Though this was her fourth such shift, it was particularly difficult for her.

Captain Riley briefed her before she went to meet the patient. "His name is Private Richard Phillips. Eighteen years old. Hit by a shell in his foxhole a week ago. Massive internal injuries with two surgeries to try to repair the damage. One lung is still collapsed. In and out of consciousness. Looks like a systemic infection may be shutting down his organs, but we'll continue the penicillin in hopes he'll turn around. Doc's guessing less than eight hours."

Louise nodded and went to sit by the young man's bedside. The oxygen mask seemed to swallow his face. When she took his hand in hers and gently squeezed it, his eyes fluttered open.

"Good morning, Richard. I'm Louise, and I'd like to help make you more comfortable. Blink once if you can understand me."

He did.

"Good. I'm going to put a cool cloth on your forehead and then go get your medications."

He nodded.

Save your energy to fight that infection, she wanted to tell him but realized it didn't matter whether he blinked or nodded—the chances of his beating organ failure were slim.

All day she mopped his feverish brow, administered penicillin and morphine, and spoke reassuringly to him. She'd finished the two o'clock penicillin injection and was preparing the pain medication when Phillips pawed at her arm. "What is it?" she asked, then removed his oxygen mask so he could try to speak.

"Want...to...stay...awake...a bit."

Louise replaced the mask. "You're telling me you'd like me to hold off on the morphine for a while? Because it makes you sleep?"

He nodded.

"Okay, we'll try it...for a bit. May I hold your hand?"

Another nod.

Louise fought back tears as she watched his labored breathing and periodic grimaces. "Squeeze my hand if you want the morphine," she whispered. He shook his head.

Perhaps an hour later, he used his free hand to move the oxygen aside. "Want to sit up..."

Louise knew moving him would cause him great pain, but she wasn't about to deny what might be his last wish. She signaled the ward man who was working across the aisle, and together they placed three pillows under Phillips's torso to move him to a seated position.

"Okay?" she asked.

Though his face contorted with pain, he again nodded and eventually adopted a more peaceful look. He lifted his hand as if to reach for the mask. "Let me get it," she said and removed the oxygen.

"In my pack...letter..."

"You want me to get a letter out of your bag?"

"Uh-huh."

She reached for the musette bag underneath his bed, set it beside him, and unbuckled the clasps. Lying on top of the items inside the pack was a crumpled, muddy envelope. She pulled it out and showed it to him. "This letter?"

He nodded.

"Would you like me to read it to you?"

He inclined his head a quarter of an inch.

With trembling fingers Louise took out the single-page letter. She began to read, "March 12, 1945 - Dearest Buddy, Just a short note to give you the wonderful news. Your father should be home by the time you receive this letter! He had the cast removed from his leg two days ago but would need further rehabilitation before being fit for duty, so instead they issued a medical discharge."

Louise paused to readjust his pillow and oxygen mask. "Your family calls you Buddy. May I call you that too?" He nodded.

"Because of the good news in the European theater," she continued to read, "we've been able to convince Danny to wait until he graduates to enlist. God willing, the war will be over on both fronts by then and he won't enlist at all. I don't think I could bear having both my children in the service. We continue to pray for your safe return. Be as careful as you can, dearest boy. Love, Mom."

Louise swallowed the lump in her throat. "I'm so glad your parents and brother are safe. It must be some comfort to you."

She noticed a tear trickling onto his pillow. He raised his hand

and pantomimed writing. "Do you want me to help you write them a letter?"

Another barely discernible nod.

"I've got paper and pen you can use," said Artie, the boy in the next bed. His leg in a cast and suspended in an elevated position, he nodded toward the bedside table. "I can't reach it, but it's right there, and you can write on my book."

"Thanks." Louise took the writing materials and sat on the edge of Buddy's bed.

Artie must have sensed her indecision about how to begin. "Why don't we give him suggestions so he doesn't have to wear himself out by talking?" he asked. "Buddy can blink once if he agrees or twice if he wants a different suggestion."

"That's a great idea. Blink once if that's okay with you, Buddy."

One blink.

"How 'bout we start with Dear Mom, Dad, and Danny?" Artie asked.

Buddy blinked and Louise began writing.

Artie continued, "I was so happy to get your letter about Dad's discharge and Danny's decision to finish high school."

Another blink.

Artie turned to Buddy. "I assume you want us to say goodbye to your family in case you don't make it."

Buddy blinked once.

"Okay," Artie said. "Let's try this…We ran into a difficult fight with the Japs here in the Philippines, and I was hurt pretty badly."

One blink.

"They moved me to a great hospital here on the island of Leyte," Artie continued, "where the doctors and nurses are doing all they can for me. I am comfortable and with people who care about me."

One blink. Louise wrote what Artie had dictated.

While Artie paused to consider the following words, Buddy

moved his hand to his face and pushed his mask aside with more force than Louise would have thought possible. "Want...to say...the rest 'self..." he said in a barely audible voice.

"Okay," Louise said. "Take your time."

She held her breath and waited with pen poised, leaning in to hear more easily. Finally, Buddy began, "I'm not...'fraid. I saw... Grammy...she's waiting. Love...y'all so...much. Budd..."

Louise reached over to replace the oxygen, but he shook her off.

"Don't...send...unless..."

Artie interrupted. "Don't worry, she won't send it if you make it. And I've seen plenty of guys in worse shape than you pull through. Now take the morphine and get some rest."

Louise repositioned the mask. "Artie's right," she said, "I promise to hold onto the letter, but you need some pain-free sleep."

A few minutes after the injection, Buddy's eyes closed and his face relaxed. She signaled the ward man to help move the pillows so he'd be flat on his back and could breathe more easily.

She copied the return address from Buddy's mother's letter onto an envelope Artie supplied, folded the letter they'd just created, and put it inside. She slipped the envelope into her pocket and said a silent prayer that she wouldn't need to send it.

"Thanks, Artie," she said. "I couldn't have done that without you."

"It was nothin'. Us guys look out for each other."

"And we nurses appreciate it more than you can imagine."

The relief nurse came on duty a short while later, and Louise went back to her tent feeling emotionally and physically exhausted.

"Hi, Louise," Shoe said while unwrapping Abby's hair from home permanent curlers. "How was your specialized care day?"

Louise pulled a beer from the box beneath her bunk and opened it. "Hard," she said, then took a sizable swig. "With the help of the kid in the bed next to him, we composed a goodbye letter to his parents and younger brother. I'm praying I won't have to mail it..."

"I'm sorry."

"Does it look like he might survive?" Abby asked.

Louise shrugged. "Yesterday his kidneys weren't putting out any urine, but there was a little in the bag when I left today. Maybe the penicillin is doing its job?"

"Let's hope," Shoe replied. "Hey, we've got half a bottle of Charm Curl solution left you can use if you want. I'm getting pretty good at putting in these curlers if I do say so myself."

"That'd be great. I plan to spend as much time as I can swimming, and my hair could use a lift. After dinner?"

"Okay. It'd be best if you left them in overnight if you can stand it."

Louise tossed and turned until midnight, unable to get comfortable with a head full of tight curlers and unable to get her mind off Buddy Phillips. *I don't care if the Charm Curl doesn't turn out as well as it might—I'm taking these things out.*

She met Shoe in the latrine the next morning. "Your hair looks pretty good," Shoe said, "considering you didn't follow directions."

"I was trying to be quiet but couldn't sleep—I just can't get my patient off my mind. I'm going over to the ward before my shift and see how's he's doing."

The bed next to Artie was empty when she got there. "Where's Phillips?" she asked the ward man, hoping to hear they'd taken him back into surgery.

"He died about midnight."

"Oh, no!" she gasped, causing Artie to awaken.

"I'm sorry, Lieutenant," Artie said. "It's probably for the best... I mean, even with the morphine he was moaning in his sleep."

"Did he regain consciousness after I left?"

"No, ma'am."

Frankie left a few days later. Though happy for her, Louise would sorely miss her bubbly personality.

"Is it just me, or does Dot seem moodier since Frankie left?" Shoe asked Louise one day when they waited in the chow line for lunch. "She's been getting on my nerves."

"Mine too," Louise admitted. "Sometimes I think she's going psycho or something. But I suppose we're just as hard to get along with, and she's jealous about not going out in our crowd. At least when Frankie was here, Dot had somebody to sit home with."

"We spend most of the time at the beach—she could come along," Shoe replied.

"But we're all paired off with the guys from Ed's outfit. I can see why she'd feel left out."

"You're probably right," Shoe said, then stopped in her tracks. "Hey! Are those apples I see?"

The people in front of them were oohing and aahing and taking their time choosing from a large fruit bowl filled with shiny, red apples.

"Oh, my gosh!" Louise said. "I can't believe it."

"Believe it," said one of the servers. "We got a food shipment with them this morning. There were also fresh carrots and toma- toes and honest-to-God butter."

"It's like we're in heaven," Louise said.

"I wouldn't go *that* far," Shoe replied.

"Say, I wonder if the shipment also had rice," Louise mused. "I've been packing my extra film in rice and cotton because I heard it keeps the heat from ruining it, and I'm running a little low. I've been taking lots of pictures of our gang and I really want to get some good ones.

"We're in the Philippines, for heaven's sake—we should be able to get rice."

IN MAY AND EARLY JUNE, THE 44TH MADE PREPARATIONS to move the hospital to General MacArthur's former headquarters on the beach near Tacloban. Louise made the twenty-five-mile trip several times ahead of the move to help with the planning.

"How is it?" Shoe asked the first time she returned.

"You're not going to believe how amazing it is. The ocean is right at our doorsteps and there are these huge coconut palms shading the tents."

"Tents again?" Dot grumbled.

"Yes, tents," Louise said, trying hard to hide her exasperation. "But they're right on the beach and have actual wooden floors and frames. There are several administrative buildings and actual concrete sidewalks, not to mention water towers and wonderful showers. There's a real officers' club for dances and gatherings, and there's even a reading room with an ample supply of paperback books."

"Sounds incredible," Shoe said. "Did the colonel tell you when we'd be going?"

"Not exactly—*maybe* in a couple weeks," Louise replied. "Probably just about the time I finish my night-duty rotation which, by the way, always seems to last an eternity."

"When do you go on nights?" Dot asked.

"Tomorrow. I hate it because it will make it so much harder to see Ed. We've been cramming in as much time together as possible the last few weeks…"

Shoe gave Louise a quick hug before heading out the door. "Aw, don't worry. He's crazy about you and will find a way to get together during your off-hours, night shift be damned."

Chapter Thirty-Five

Louise got a reprieve from night duty when she was assigned as part of the advance echelon to move to and organize the new hospital. She had apprehension about the assignment when she learned Captain Riley would also be among the four nurses sent ahead. Sure, there'd be male officers and enlisted men in the group, but she worried she might have to share sleeping quarters with Riley.

The group worked twelve-hour shifts for four days preparing for the patients' arrival, cleaning, sorting supplies and equipment, and setting up beds.

After the third day—a particularly exhausting one—Captain Riley put her hand on Louise's shoulder and said, "I knew I'd be glad to have chosen you for the advance team, Dietrich. I can always count on you to smile through tough tasks."

Flustered by the unexpected praise, Louise felt her cheeks redden. "Um...thanks...but I never thought you thought very highly of me."

Now Riley looked flustered. "I had hoped you'd never noticed, but that was pretty naive on my part," she said. "How 'bout we head over to the club so I can buy you a beer and give you the explanation I owe you?"

Louise wanted nothing more than to go back to her tent, strip off her sweaty work clothes, and dip her feet into the ocean, but she knew she couldn't turn down this invitation. "Uh...sure...if you want."

Once inside the club, the captain nodded toward two stools at the end of the bar. "I think we'll be left alone over there."

When the bartender delivered their beers, Louise immediately held her chilled bottle against her forehead. "This feels as heavenly as I believe it'll taste right now," she said. "Thanks."

Riley took a long pull from her own bottle, then lit a cigarette and inhaled deeply. Louise followed suit. "Simple pleasures," Riley said. "But I guess I didn't realize you smoked."

Louise nodded. "It's a recently acquired habit I picked up from an aviator I'm going with."

"Gotta watch out for those flyboys," Riley said with a wink.

The two women sipped and smoked in silence.

"I don't know whether you know this or not," Riley finally began, "but the nurses of the 44th were my first command. I'd been a first lieutenant like yourself only two months before I met you all at March Field, and I was greener than green."

Louise inclined her head a quarter of an inch.

"And even though I was raised in Chicago, I was pretty sheltered," Riley went on. "I grew up in an Irish neighborhood. Attended an Irish Catholic school from kindergarten through grade twelve and took my nurses' training at an Irish Catholic hospital. It wasn't until I joined the Army that I met people from other ethnic groups and realized how different I could be from others. I put up walls to hide my insecurities and harbored a lot of resentment when people didn't seem very welcoming."

"That must've been hard," Louise said.

Riley nodded and signaled to the bartender for two more beers. "Instead of socializing very much, I threw myself into work, vowing to become the best nurse I could. I volunteered for all types of assignments and training and got promoted in record time. Trouble is, I didn't really grow up along the way."

Louise lit another cigarette to hide her discomfort, thinking *You aren't going to catch me commenting on all this.*

"I also failed to realize how my parents hated German Americans," Riley continued, "and how they'd instilled that in me."

Louise couldn't help but raise an eyebrow, though she did manage to hold her tongue.

"When did you first suspect I had something against you?" Riley asked.

Louise choked on the sip of beer she'd just taken and coughed for several moments.

Riley patted her on the back. "You okay?"

Louise nodded.

"You don't have to answer," Riley said. "That was an unfair question. The thing is, I didn't realize it until we got to Fort Sill and the other COs and I were meeting to decide who the 44th would leave off our overseas roster."

"Oh?"

"Uh-huh," Riley said, staring at the bottles lined up behind the bar. "At Colonel Weston's request," she finally admitted, "I'd made a list of the eight nurses I recommended we transfer out of the unit. Major Mason looked at it first and said something like, 'You can't be serious. These are some of our most skilled staff.' And I shot back, '*All* of our nurses are highly skilled.' Then Mason handed the list to the colonel, and we all sat while he studied it."

Riley paused again, obviously replaying the scene in her mind. "The colonel looked at Mason and the other officers and said, 'I'd like a few private words with Captain Riley,' and they all stood up and left his office. I couldn't figure out what was going on. He passed my list back to me and asked, 'What do they all have in common?' I looked at it and recognized that every single one of the nurses I'd selected was German. There was no hiding it, but I couldn't bring myself to say it."

She wiped a tear from the corner of her eye.

"Fortunately," she went on, "Colonel Weston didn't press it. In a very gentle voice, he said, 'Sheila, I know you grew up in an ethnic neighborhood in Chicago, where I know there are underlying animosities toward people of different backgrounds. You're probably unaware of some of your prejudices because they're often formed when we're so young, but as an adult and an officer, you have a responsibility to rise above them.'" She looked down at her feet. "I felt like I was two feet tall."

Louise cleared her throat but couldn't find words to speak.

"And then I remembered a few times when my dad came home from the plant, raging about the 'Krauts'—and he used other words that weren't as nice—who'd gotten the promotions over him or his pals. And I realized he talked that way about Germans *all the time*. I told Colonel Weston about a few of those incidents and said I thought he was right. I apologized about twenty times and promised to watch myself if he'd just give me another chance. Thankfully he did, and I've sure tried to keep my promise."

Louise nodded and thought about her exchanges with Captain Riley since they left Fort Sill. "I guess Lieutenant Shoemaker and I didn't make it very easy for you," she said, "what with our fraternizing and all."

Riley burst out laughing. "No," she said, "but by then I had the sense to realize that had nothing to do with your heritage."

They finished their beers in companionable silence.

"I meant what I said, Dietrich," Riley said when they got up to leave, "I've appreciated your positive outlook these past several days—we've worked our hind ends off and you've never complained."

"Thank you, Captain," she replied. "But it's easier to stay upbeat in a place like this—when you realize you can take a relaxing swim in that gorgeous ocean the minute you get off duty."

"True, but the water's not always calm enough for me to unwind in it."

Louise raised an eyebrow. *I would've thought you'd be an accomplished swimmer. Even I—a relative novice—love playing in the breakers when the wind is up.*

"There are some things I'm not very tough about. We didn't have an ocean in Chicago, and my neighborhood was pretty far from Lake Michigan."

THE HOSPITAL WAS CHAOTIC WHEN ALL THE STAFF AND patients were finally transferred to Tacloban, but everyone, including Dot, was in high spirits. Dot, Shoe, and Louise plunged happily into decorating their tent. Within days they'd covered the floor with straw mats and a homemade table and stool with red and white checked fabric to serve as their dressing table. White netting remnants from their days at Townsville served as curtains.

There was also more activity at Tacloban than there'd been at Burauen. "What're you and Ed doing tonight?" Shoe asked Louise shortly after their arrival.

"Hitchhiking over to the Navy base to see a first-run movie he heard about. *The Picture of Dorian Gray.*"

It took only ten minutes to catch a ride, though Louise had to sit on Ed's lap. He grinned and hugged her tightly as the jeep rounded the first curve. "Don't worry, I won't let you fall out."

She leaned her head back on his shoulder, as happy as she'd felt in months.

"This is amazing," she said when they walked into the theater. "Actual seats."

"Let's sit in the first row," Ed suggested. "We don't want to have to crane our necks if some tall sailor-boys plant themselves in front of us."

As the movie—a black and white horror drama—progressed,

Louise grabbed Ed's hand. "I'm not sure I can stand the suspense," she whispered.

He chuckled and kissed her neck.

They and most of the other moviegoers watched mesmerized until the credits finished. "That's the best damn film I've seen in ages," said a sailor in the row behind them.

Louise nodded in agreement. "Fascinating and so different from the usual stuff we see."

The couple met up with their ride outside the theater and were back at the camp in time to meet their friends for drinks at the officers' club. "How 'bout we dance?" Ed asked Louise when someone put "My Dreams Are Getting Better All the Time" on the jukebox.

"I'd be delighted."

As they glided around the dance floor, Ed ignored the several guys who approached to cut in.

"Thanks for a wonderful evening," she told him at the door to her tent.

"It *was* wonderful, wasn't it?" he said before kissing her good night—a long, slow kiss that she'd remember clearly for a long time to come.

MIDWAY THROUGH LOUISE'S SHIFT TWO DAYS LATER, Joe Scarpetti came to find her. "Your flyboy's on the phone."

It wasn't particularly unusual for him to call her at the hospital —he'd often telephoned to tell her he had some outing planned for the evening. *I wonder what he's got up his sleeve for tonight?* she thought as she scurried to the desk to pick up the call.

"Hi, Ed—"

"I got my orders this morning," he said without preamble. "They're sending me on rotation back to the States."

Louise sank onto the edge of the desk chair. "When?"

"Two hours from now." He cleared his throat. "And, uh, I

won't have time to stop over to say goodbye in person…I've got to finish some records and pack up my gear."

"So…so soon?"

"I know. You usually get at least twenty-four hours' notice. My CO couldn't give me a good reason—just that the transport would be leaving, and I'd be on it."

Louise couldn't speak.

"Maybe it's better this way," he said. "Like pulling off a Band-Aid—"

She didn't respond.

"Take care of yourself. I promise to write from Manila before I leave for the States."

He hung up before she could say goodbye.

Determined not to break down in front of the patients or ward men, Louise kept the news to herself until she left the hospital. She burst into tears the moment she entered the tent.

Shoe looked up from the book she was reading. "What's wrong?"

"Ed left this afternoon."

"What d'ya mean he left?"

"He got his stateside orders."

"When?"

"This morning."

"And he's gone *already*?"

Louise nodded, her shoulders heaving with sobs.

Shoe came over to hug her. "Oh man, I'm so sorry."

When she finally collected herself, Louise broke from her friend's embrace and mopped her face with her sleeve. "I told myself I'd never fall for anyone as hard as I did for Will," she said, "but this is worse. I feel like a hole has been blasted in my life—a life that had been filled with fun and laughter. Ed and I never wasted a minute of the time we were together. We enjoyed every bit of it."

Shoe nodded.

"I just wish I could go home too. If we don't get a leave or if this war doesn't end pretty soon, I'm going to be psycho material."

"Well, I heard something today that might cheer you up."

"What's that?"

"One of the doctors said they're going to start sending nurses home after twenty-four months overseas. You and I are getting close to that."

"Not close enough," Louise mused.

They sat in silence for several minutes.

"You mentioned Will," Shoe finally said. "I take it nothing ever came of his request to come back here?"

"I guess I never mentioned it, what with being swept off my feet by my newest flyboy," Louise said in a sardonic tone. "He wrote to tell me it'd been denied. He's out of the Air Corps now and is flying for United Airlines."

"That's too bad for you I guess, but it's good to hear there is life after war."

Louise's intrinsic optimism helped her through the following weeks. "The sunrises here are spectacular, aren't they?" she asked Dot when they climbed from their tent at six o'clock one morning.

"Mm-hmm," Dot replied. "But I'm partial to the moonrises over the water at night."

"They both send chills up my spine. I've been trying to take pictures of this place to show my sister."

"Too bad they don't have color film at the PX."

"I sent some money to the Eastman Company," Louise said. "Supposedly they'll send two rolls of Kodachrome film per month to anyone overseas. If true, I intend to take full advantage of it."

"Remind me to order some too. I've been trying to describe this place in letters to my family and can't do it justice. I mean, even the hospital looks like some picturesque college campus in the tropics."

Louise laughed. "Uh-huh. Wards made of woven palm leaves are a heck of a lot better looking than muddy tents."

"Have you noticed that even the patients seem happier here?"

"Yes. And I have to say that you do, too," Louise said, then immediately regretted her comment. After all, neither she nor Shoe had ever directly spoken with Dot about her moodiness in Burauen.

Dot paused for a moment. "You're right, I *am* happier here. Maybe it's because we're right in the center of so many big camps and I've already been on several dates. I felt pretty low when you, Shoe, Ruth, and Esther all went out with the same group of fellows, and I sat home."

"I'm sorry, Dot. Shoe and I weren't very good tentmates for you back there."

Dot nodded. "Are you ready to date again, Louise? After Ed, I mean?"

Louise felt her cheeks flush. "I'm going to take in a couple of parties next week with guys who've asked me. I can't imagine having as much fun as I used to have with him, but I guess it'll be good for me to get out."

A week later, Louise came home after work and mail call to find Ruth and Shoe sitting on the beach with heads bowed, tears streaming down their faces. "What happened?" she cried.

Shoe raised her head to answer. "Ruth just got word that Pete Carpenter was killed when his plane was shot down a couple days ago."

Louise sat beside Ruth and put her arm around her. "How awful. I am so sorry."

Ruth laid her head on Louise's shoulder. "He was the best guy.

I can't believe he's gone...He'd planned to fly down here for a dance next week..."

Louise shuddered. Pete Carpenter had not only been Ed Winter's best friend, but they'd flown multiple missions together. *If Ed hadn't gotten sent home, he might have been on the same plane.*

Ruth's tentmate came by several minutes later. "C'mon, sweetie," she said, pulling her to her feet. "Let's get you a cup of coffee or a beer."

Louise and Shoe sat in stunned silence as they watched the women walk toward their quarters, Ruth leaning on her friend. "And to think that just a few weeks ago we were all having such a good time," Shoe said.

Louise glanced at the sand and noticed the stack of mail she'd placed there when she sat down. "I just got prints of the film I sent to be developed—I'd planned to open them in the tent so they didn't get dirty. There should be some of our gang."

Shoe stood up. "What are you waiting for?"

Louise scrambled to her feet and up the steps to the tent, then tore open one of the envelopes. Her face fell as she leafed through the photographs.

"I could just cry," Louise said, sitting heavily on the bed. "At least half of this roll's been ruined by heat. Several of Ed are so blurry you can't tell it's him." She handed the first batch to Shoe and began looking through the second envelope.

"What about those?"

Louise passed her two snapshots with large blank spots in the middle. "These were of Ruth and Pete."

"Damn it."

Louise threw the pictures on her end table and reached for her pack of cigarettes. "Do you have any of your beer ration left? I sure could use one."

Shoe nodded and pulled two bottles from under her bed. She

opened one and gave it to Louise. "Why are you still smoking now that Ed left?"

"I don't know, I guess it helps me remember him. And I sure as heck don't have any photos to do that."

"I wish for your sake he'd never taught you how."

Louise sighed. "To be honest, it was more fun when I first started because it made me light-headed and dizzy as a loon. Don't worry—I'm sure I'll never become a habitual smoker. I just like 'em when I drink."

After they'd each finished their second beer, Shoe turned to Louise and asked, "Are you going to stay in the army after the war?"

"*Heck* no! How about you?"

"Not a minute longer than I have to. I thought it might be fun to stay in San Francisco for a while when we hit the States. What we saw from the harbor looked pretty interesting."

"I'd join you if you'd have me—especially if my sister's still in Oakland. Neither of us wants to go back to La Farge."

"Of course, and Dot might want to stay, too. What about after that?"

"If my prospects for marriage are as slim as they are now, I was thinking I'd like to take advantage of the G.I. Bill of Rights and go to college for a year or two."

Shoe looked incredulous. "To study what?"

Louise laughed. "Something as far away from nursing as possible...maybe languages, art, or philosophy. Nothing to make a career out of or anything. Maybe it's just a pipe dream, but I'm having fun thinking about it."

A few weeks later, Shoe and Louise were in their tent writing letters when Vivian stopped by. "Did you hear the news about Ruth Ziegler?" she asked.

They shook their heads.

"She got boarded to go home because she can't shake that sinus infection that's kept her in the hospital for the past ten days," Vivian replied.

"Well, good for her," Shoe said. "She's been so down since Pete died, it's no wonder she hasn't been able to get healthy."

Vivian nodded. "Yes, but she told me she's got mixed emotions about going home. You know, since all her close friends are here, and everybody's been so kind to her."

"I can understand what she means," Louise said. "Even though I'm anxious to get out of the army, I can't imagine what life'll be like without all of you."

Shoe laughed. "Yeah, misery loves company."

Chapter Thirty-Six

In mid-July, Louise, Shoe, and Dot were sitting in their tent one evening when a speedboat drifted by. "Hey, ladies," yelled the driver. "Put on your bathing suits and my friends and I'll take you for a ride!"

The women exchanged questioning looks, then nodded in unison. "Give us five minutes," Shoe called back.

The boat pulled up on the beach next to their tent a few moments later. "Lieutenant Jacob Kowalski, at your service," the driver said. "But you can call me Butch. My friends are Hugo and Tucker."

"I'm Lieutenant Louise Dietrich, but you can call me Louise," she said as Butch helped her aboard. "And my friends are Shoe and Dot."

"We were thinking of heading out to the coral reef and dropping anchor for a while," Butch said. "The water's crystal clear and smooth as glass out there—great for swimming. Are you gals game?"

"Sure," Shoe replied for the tentmates. "We didn't have anything on our busy social calendars for tonight."

The roar of the motor precluded conversation. Tucker took

three beers out of a cooler and offered them to the guests. Wide-eyed at the rare specter of the cold bottles, they gratefully nodded.

"This tastes *so* good," Louise mouthed after her first sip.

"It sure does," Shoe yelled. "Warm beer tastes like swill by comparison."

Butch killed the engine near the reef and Tucker heaved the anchor over the stern.

The ocean was indeed beautiful and inviting. Shoe and Dot wasted no time getting into the water, and Hugo and Tucker pulled off their shirts and jumped in after them.

Still somewhat nervous in deep water, Louise gamely sat on the edge of the boat, planning to ease herself in.

"You can swim, can't you?" Butch asked.

Louise nodded.

"Well then," he said, leaning over and picking her up, "no sense postponing the enjoyment." He tossed her into the water, then stood on the boat's stern and dove in himself.

"See what I mean?" he asked when he swam up beside her.

Louise pretended to sputter in anger, but his infectious smile got the better of her.

The group swam in lazy circles, floated on their backs, and treaded water while getting acquainted. Butch, a curly-haired Polish guy from New York, had been a P-47 pilot until three months earlier when he'd injured his eye in a crash. Now a ground crewman, he and his buddies had purchased the boat when they'd arrived in Tacloban.

Tucker focused his attentions on Dot, whose melodic laughter carried across the placid water. Hugo and Shoe seemed to hit it off as well.

After about an hour, Butch sighed. "We'd better head back."

"How on earth will we get back into the boat?" Dot asked.

"Never fear," Tucker said. The most muscular of the guys, he pulled himself up over the rear gunwale and hooked on a rope ladder. "C'mon, I'll help you climb up."

It'd been a while since the nurses had had time for calisthenics, so this task put their upper body strength to the test. Dot went first, faltering only slightly and taking Tucker's hand at the last minute. Louise took a deep breath and followed her, surprised and proud that she climbed the ladder with relative ease and without help from anyone.

Shoe had—or pretended to have—the hardest time. "I don't think I'm strong enough to do this," she groaned.

"Out of the way," Hugo said as he grabbed onto the ladder. "Put your arms around my neck and I'll give you a ride."

Shoe grinned as she rode him piggyback up and into the boat, then turned to Louise and gave a sly wink.

Louise rolled her eyes.

ONE NIGHT AFTER DINNER, DOT AND LOUISE WENT TO take a swim together. "It seems awfully dirty tonight, doesn't it?" Dot asked as they waded in.

Louise nodded as she peered into the water. "Butch told me it's 'cause the ships in the harbor dump all their garbage overboard and when the currents flow a certain way, it comes drifting in toward us."

"*Ick*—should we skip it tonight?"

"Let's."

Back in the tent, Louise opened her beer ration box. "Can you believe we got a whole case each this time?"

Dot gave a catlike stretch. "Too bad they couldn't give it to us in coolers with ice. Those boys sure have spoiled us with cold beer."

"Yeah, and with all the boat rides and riding the surfboard behind it."

"I'm looking forward to the beach party tomorrow night. Tucker says they're bringing sandwiches to go with the beer—and a phonograph. You're coming, aren't you?"

Louise sighed. "I wouldn't miss it…"

"But?"

"Butch is so sweet and funny, and I've had fun with him. But he's not Ed. We went swimming last night around ten o'clock and all the phosphorus in the water made it look like millions of diamonds. I think Butch meant for it to be a romantic evening, but I kept wishing it was Ed with me instead."

"Have you told him how you feel?"

"You mean Butch?"

"Yes, Butch."

"Uh-huh," Louise said. "I told him I was hung up on a guy who just got sent stateside and I'm not going to get involved with anyone else until I know where I stand."

"Ed left, what, five weeks ago?"

A nod.

"Have you heard from him since he left?"

A tear trickled down Louise's cheek. "Not a word," she mumbled. "He didn't even follow through on his promise to write from Manila. I keep telling myself this can't be happening. That he couldn't just go home and forget all the good fun we had. But I know it happens all the time. That's just life, I guess."

"Did you hear that Jimmy hasn't written to Vivian since he left either?" Dot asked.

"Yes. Shoe and I sat and cried with her after the movie last night. She hasn't heard from him at all since he left to go stateside three weeks ago. But she's most worried that something's happened to him, though. I mean, unlike Ed, he's been pretty open about his intentions for her."

"True, but things change when the scenery changes. Remember how much in love Anna was when she got married two years ago? Now we never see her because she's been running around with the mess officer for a year."

"I think Anna is a little ashamed of her husband," Louise said with a twinge of guilt—she'd been somewhat ashamed of her fiancé Joey when she'd first enlisted in the Army and hadn't even told people about her engagement to him.

"Well, I think *she* should be ashamed of cheating on him."

"I think we should probably quit gossiping about her. None of us is perfect." She opened another beer and lit a cigarette.

"Can I have one of those?" Dot asked, nodding toward the cigarette.

Louise handed her the pack. "Help yourself. When I finish the carton, I'm going to quit."

Dot began coughing after her second puff. "Silly," she said, stubbing out the lengthy butt in her friend's ashtray. "What was the movie, by the way?"

"Movie?"

"The one you saw with Shoe and Vivian last night."

"Oh, yeah. *Without Love,* with Spencer Tracy and Katharine Hepburn. Kind of fitting, isn't it?"

Chapter Thirty-Seven

The first week of August passed pleasantly in Tacloban. The nurses of the 44th were placed on shifts of only six hours per day, giving them more time to go swimming and boating and to enjoy their beachfront officers' club. The beer ration was increased to two cases per person. Big band leader Kay Kyser and comedian Ish Kabibble came to the island for a USO show that everyone enjoyed.

"We're living like kings," Louise wrote to Etta. "Must be a catch somewhere. Maybe they're trying to make us like it in the Army so we'll sign up for thirty years."

Incongruously, the Pacific war was at the same time in full crescendo. Having ignored the ultimatum of July's Potsdam Conference to "surrender unconditionally or face utter destruction," Japan was being pressed from all directions and all allied countries. Japan persisted, but the threat to destroy them was delayed by bad weather until August 6, when the United States dropped an atomic bomb on the city of Hiroshima. Three days later, another atomic bomb was dropped on Nagasaki.

In the early morning hours of August 10, the Japanese Cabinet and Supreme Council voted to accept the Potsdam offer. The news reached Tacloban at nine o'clock that night when Louise and Butch were at a dance.

Everyone on the dance floor looked bewildered—and more than a little irritated—when the manager of the officers' club stopped the orchestra from playing and grabbed the microphone. "The Japanese government just accepted the Potsdam offer!" he announced.

The dancers hugged one another while the orchestra resumed playing, this time soft renditions of "I'm Dreaming of a White Christmas," "When the Lights Go on Again," and "California, Here I Come!"

"I don't know whether to laugh or cry," Louise whispered to Butch. "And my elbows and knees feel like they've turned into Knox gelatin!"

"Don't worry," he replied, hugging her tightly, "I won't let you fall."

Soon, pandemonium began to set in. Men popped the corks on champagne bottles, heedless of whether bystanders were sprayed. Countless toasts were offered. And everyone kissed everyone, regardless of familiarity or rank.

Outside, air raid sirens and vehicle horns sounded. People screamed with delight. Word traveled quickly: the harbor was in full celebration mode.

"Let's go!" Butch cried, grabbing Louise's hand.

When she saw the harbor, Louise couldn't hold back her tears. "It's the most beautiful thing I've ever seen!" she said. Every ship in the harbor had its lights blazing, and rockets, flares, and guns were shot from the decks. The Air Corps searchlights flooded the sky.

In the hospital, patients stood on crutches and leaned on one another to crowd around radios.

Virtually no one in the whole staging area slept a wink.

· · ·

"WHAT DO YOU MEAN, THE WAR'S NOT OVER?" LOUISE said when she got to work the next morning and reality set in.

Even Captain Connelly, always steady as a rock, looked drawn and exhausted. "Japan did surrender but with the stipulation that the emperor remain the sovereign ruler of the country," he told her. "The Allies haven't accepted that stipulation yet."

"Well, I sure hope we accept the offer," Louise said. "I wouldn't quibble over letting them keep their emperor—after all, he's just a religious figure to them and has no government powers. Kind of like the king of England. And it'd mean so much to these fellows over here to get this war over with."

Connelly nodded. "I agree, but I suspect it'll take a few days to get the final verdict."

"Meanwhile, we're all on pins and needles," Louise said with a sigh. "I guess it would only take one or two more atomic bombs to bring the Japanese to their knees anyway, but those horrible things scare me. All I can say is I hope they never get into the wrong hands."

"You can say that again."

"I FEEL LIKE WE'RE ALL IN A TRANCE," LOUISE SAID TO Shoe two days later. "Why is it taking so long for the Allies to decide?"

"The morning news said the Allies agreed to allow the emperor to stay but with the understanding that the Supreme Allied Commander will govern Japan. They're still waiting for Japan's reply," Shoe said, her voice quivering. "I just want this to be *over* so I can get home to comfort my mom. She's been a basket case since my brother was killed in France, and Helen's no help."

Louise hugged her friend. "I know it's hard."

Shoe sniffled and dabbed the end of her nose with her sleeve. "The news also said we're dropping leaflets from bombers to let the Japanese people know what's happening. Maybe that'll force the issue."

"Let's hope."

ON AUGUST 14, 1945, EMPEROR HIROHITO surrendered. The news was met at Tacloban with happiness, of course, but far fewer raucous celebrations than on August 10.

"I felt more like kneeling down and saying 'thank you' than I did jumping and shouting," Louise later wrote to her sister.

On August 15, a special worship service was held in the hospital chapel and everyone sent their thanks to the heavens.

Chapter Thirty-Eight

Speculation as to when they'd be sent home became rampant. "Have you heard anything?" Louise asked Colonel Weston when he was making rounds one day.

He shook his head. "Nothing definite, but everybody believes we'll return to the States as a unit—men and women at the same time—and maybe set up a new hospital there."

Hmm, maybe I would *stay in the Army if we could all work together,* she thought. *Though I guess it'd depend on where.*

"I expected that waiting around to see when and where we're going would be pretty tedious and would make the days drag," Dot said to Louise after her shift in late August. "But it was so busy today I didn't even have a moment to think about it."

"Captain Riley says they're closing down most of the hospitals around here and sending the patients who can handle it to Japan. So even though we're shipping our own patients home as quickly as we can, we're still going to be getting new ones. And some of them in pretty bad shape."

"Worse than the ones we've got now?"

Louise nodded. "That's what she told me. I'm glad Shoe, Vivian, and I put our names on the list to be temporarily assigned as nurses with the occupational army in Japan. It'd be an interesting change to see another country."

"One where two cities have been destroyed by our atomic bombs?"

"Colonel Weston says we'd be stationed a safe distance away from Hiroshima and Nagasaki. And he says they really need experienced nurses."

"I'm still not sure it was such a good idea."

"I'm not sure either, but who knows if we'll get picked. One thing I do know is this place isn't like it used to be. All the new GI rules and the list of prohibitions are getting ridiculous. I can handle the formal inspections and saluting everybody every time we turn around but standing six-thirty reveille every morning is going way too far."

Dot laughed. "And how 'bout memorizing the ten general orders in case the guards walking by decide they want to quiz us?"

"Right! What are they going to do if we don't know them? Lock us up?"

"That'd be something to write home about."

"I was just telling my sister about being able to wear 'girl clothes' again when we go on dates. And how Butch almost fainted when I appeared in a skirt last night."

"Same with Tucker and me. I thought it was kinda fun."

"In a way," Louise said. "But now it's going to take us more time to get ready and we'll have to remember to keep our knees together. Dressing like tomboys for the last year had its advantages."

On August 30, Louise got a call from the head nurse. "Sorry to do this to you, Dietrich, but I need you to come in tonight for a 'special.'"

Louise groaned. She'd barely gotten over Buddy Phillips's death three months earlier, and she found facing that prospect again more than daunting. *I'm not going to get personally involved this time,* she told herself. *Really—I'm not.*

Seaman David Summers—a twenty-year-old sailor injured in the attack on his supply boat by a kamikaze pilot ten days before Japan's surrender—had undergone multiple surgeries but was now bleeding steadily from his intestines, apparently reinjured during transport to Tacloban. The doctors didn't believe he could withstand another operation.

Captain Riley briefed Louise. "Check his pulse and BP every half hour, temp every hour. He had a transfusion an hour ago but he'll need more. The last nurse had to change his sheets about every two hours or else he'd have been lying in a pool of blood. Penicillin every four hours, and either oral or hypodermic pain meds as indicated."

"Is he conscious?"

Riley nodded. "Cooperative as all get out and very thankful. But he's delirious and all he does is talk, so it's hard to know if what he's saying is something you need to pay attention to. Doc Connelly stops by to check on him pretty often, and he's on duty so you can call him if it's urgent."

Louise dragged herself to Summers's bedside and introduced herself.

Summers grinned a loopy grin. "Sorry, I'm kind of a lot of trouble...I seem to keep bleeding."

"Don't worry. We'll deal with whatever comes up," she said with more confidence than she felt.

By three o'clock in the morning, she'd given him two transfusions and changed his sheets four times. When Captain Connelly made his rounds at four o'clock, Summers had finally fallen asleep. Connelly looked at the chart. "His BP's getting way too low. I'm going to wake Tom Constantine. We need to open this boy up again and see what's going on."

"I thought he was too weak to undergo another operation."

"That's Captain Emerson's opinion but thankfully he's not on duty tonight, and Tom will back me up. Seaman Summers is a great kid who's got a fighting chance to go home, and I intend to give it a try."

Louise beamed at him. She'd been wondering why they hadn't operated again earlier. "Can I help?" she asked.

Connelly shook his head. "We've got a pretty well-oiled team and don't have the time to show you what to do. I just hope Tom didn't stay at the club too long last evening."

Louise said a quick prayer for the sailor as she watched Connelly head out to get his colleague and added a prayer that he'd find Constantine sober.

Summers was still in surgery when she went off duty at 0700.

Back at the tent she found Shoe in bed—feverish with a damp cloth across her forehead.

"I thought you were feeling better yesterday. Another setback?"

Shoe groaned. "Uh-huh. Doc Emerson still thinks it's gall stones or kidney stones but can't decide which. Right now, all he can say is 'Wait and see.' I'd like *him* to feel this pain—he sure as heck wouldn't give me such a flippant response if he did."

"Anything I can do?"

"No, thanks."

Louise peeled off her sweaty socks and shoes and began massaging her feet.

"How's your special doing?" Shoe asked.

"Losing blood as fast as we could get it into him. Doc Connelly took him back into surgery around four-thirty and wasn't done when I left. I have to give him credit for trying. Your buddy Doc Emerson gave the old 'he's too weak for surgery' line yesterday morning."

"I wish they would've sent Emerson back to the States when his hospital closed instead of sticking the 44th with him," Shoe said. "I'd rather we were shorthanded than have a lazy son of a gun like him on our staff."

Louise laughed. "Doc Connelly seems to agree with you, though he wasn't quite as forthright." She grabbed a beer and her package of cigarettes and went to the door. "I'm going to soak my feet in the ocean and drown my sorrows for a bit. Try to get some sleep."

She, herself, had a difficult time sleeping that day. The mosquito netting kept the bugs from biting but didn't silence their annoying buzzing, and there was no breeze off the ocean to hold the temperature down. The most significant deterrent to rest, though, was what she saw in her mind when she closed her eyes: the bloody sheets she'd changed so frequently for Seaman David Summers the night before.

Butch and Tucker met Louise and Dot outside the mess tent after lunch.

"Bad news, ladies," Butch said. "There's been a shark scare and there are guards on the beach to keep everyone out of the water."

"We can't even go for a ride in the boat?" Dot asked, unable to mask her disappointment.

Tucker laughed and put his arm around her. "You can call me a chicken if you want," he said, "but in my humble opinion that boat's not big enough to tangle with a shark."

"I agree," Louise said.

"How about going over to the club for a few games of pinochle instead?" Butch asked.

"Sure," Louise said, then turned to Dot and Tucker. "That is if you're ready for us to beat you again."

"Oh, I think we're up to the challenge," Tucker replied.

There were several empty card tables when they arrived at the club. "I'll buy the first round," Butch said. "What'll it be?"

Tucker and Dot asked for beers. "A Coca-Cola for me, please,"

Louise said since she had to be on duty at seven that night. She looked up a few minutes later to see Butch balancing two beers and two Cokes. "Good heavens. Just because I can't drink this afternoon doesn't mean you shouldn't."

He patted her on the shoulder. "We'll make an even more formidable team if we're both sober."

In fact, the opposite was true. Louise made several glaring mistakes during the first game. "I'm sorry I'm being such a dunce today," she said to Butch. "I don't know what's gotten into me."

"It's to be expected. You're worried about your 'special,'" Dot replied, reeling in a trick from the table.

"What's a 'special'?" Tucker asked.

As Dot explained the term and what she'd been told about Seaman Summers, Butch looked at Louise with unabashed concern. "I'm sorry," he said. "You still don't know whether he pulled through or not?"

"I thought about going over to the hospital this afternoon but —in case the news was bad—I didn't want to ruin my time off," she said ruefully. "As it turns out, I kind of ruined it anyway."

He abruptly stood up from the table, then pulled her to her feet. "Let's go find out. If he didn't make it, I'll be your shoulder to cry on."

She followed him and approached the head nurse's desk warily. "Excuse me, Captain," she began. "Seaman Summers was my patient last night and—"

The nurse—a woman who Louise knew only slightly—looked up from her paperwork. "He's in the post-op ward. Bed seven, I think."

"He survived the surgery?"

The nurse nodded. "Yes, and I understand he's doing well."

"Thank you!"

Louise turned and hugged Butch. "And thank *you*!"

. . .

THE NEXT DAY, LOUISE AND VIVIAN RECEIVED WORD they'd be going with Colonel Weston to Japan. If it hadn't been for her illness, Shoe would've gone instead of Vivian.

"We've got twenty-four hours to pack and say our goodbyes," Louise said tearfully to still-feverish Shoe. "Which is hard, since we don't know how long we'll be on detached service."

Her friend moaned. "I'll never forgive you if you don't get back here before our orders to go home come through."

Louise squeezed her hand. "The colonel said the priority is getting all the POWs in Japan repatriated, treated, and evacuated, and it's supposed to happen 'post haste.' He's pretty sure we'll be assigned to assist in the processing. Estimates we might be there a month...and my guess is the 44th will be here at least that long."

Chapter Thirty-Nine

Tokyo
September 2, 1945

WHEN A POCKET OF TURBULENCE ROCKED THE C-46, Louise's breath caught in her throat. She grabbed the armrest and closed her eyes. Sitting beside her, Vivian casually leaned forward and looked out the window to watch as the plane banked for a steep descent.

"They say the wind currents here are tricky," Vivian said, "which is why the bombsight that guy Norden invented never worked right. The water looks gorgeous, though, doesn't it?"

Opening her eyes, Louise replied, "Everyplace in the South Pacific looks gorgeous 'til you get up close. And how in heaven's name can you stay so calm as we bounce around?"

Vivian shrugged.

The passengers listened as a garbled announcement came over the intercom. Seated across the aisle from the two nurses, Colonel Frank Weston yelled out, "Say again! We couldn't understand you."

"I don't think the flyboys up front can hear us, sir," Vivian said, "but I'm pretty sure he told us we'd be landing soon."

While the plane circled the Tokyo airstrip, the passengers all stared in disbelief at the devastation on the ground. Dubbed "Operation Meetinghouse," the massive Allied firebombing attack on the city, using an estimated 1,500 tons of napalm, had occurred on March 9th and 10th—nearly six months earlier. Yet rubble and dust still covered the ground between the remaining brick buildings and the buildings themselves.

The passengers stepped onto the tarmac just after the sun had set. "It's like we've left Technicolor Oz and returned to Kansas," Louise said to Colonel Weston, who offered her a steadying arm. "Everything here is sepia-toned."

"I'm told the Japanese refer to the attack as the Night of the Black Snow, and we can still see the evidence and smell the smoke. About a million people lost their homes, and a hundred thousand civilians were killed."

"Yet they didn't surrender."

"They believe there's no honor in surrender," the colonel said. "One is expected to fight to the death."

Louise's eyes tightened. "I just don't understand..."

When they arrived at their waiting jeep, their driver confirmed that General Douglas MacArthur and Foreign Minister Mamoru Shigemitsu, representing the Emperor of Japan, had signed the Instrument of Surrender aboard the USS *Missouri* in Tokyo Harbor that very morning.

Colonel Weston, Louise, and Vivian rode to the building now housing the 42nd General Hospital and were directed to staff quarters. The rooms, though spartan, had been cleaned and stocked with linens and toiletries.

The trio then proceeded to the administrative office. "Colonel Frank Weston and First Lieutenants Louise Dietrich and Vivian Vogel, of the 44th General Hospital, reporting for duty," Weston said, stepping into the office and offering a casual salute toward the desk. "The rest of our contingent will be along shortly."

The man seated behind the desk, wearing soiled surgical garb, rose and extended a hand. "Colonel Bob Brundage, here," he said in a booming voice that matched his girth. "Pleased to meet you all. Care for a beer while I shower and change?"

Brundage summoned an aide to get the refreshments and motioned for his visitors to sit on the couch.

Colonel Weston sat between the two women, put his arms around their shoulders, and pulled them into a fatherly hug. "I want to thank the two of you for volunteering for this assignment. I'll be glad to have some experienced people around—heaven only knows what awaits us."

Vivian laughed. "If Shoe hadn't gotten sick, you'd be putting up with her smart mouth instead of my sunny demeanor."

"Which I would have tolerated with equanimity."

Both women grinned knowingly.

Twenty minutes later, over ice-cold bottles of Schlitz beer—brewed in Louise and Vivian's home state of Wisconsin—Brundage told them what to expect. "'Fraid we can only put you up here for tonight. We're all heading to Yokohama tomorrow morning to begin receiving and processing prisoners of war liberated from camps throughout Japan. It's one of twelve embarkation points that have been selected. We've set up hospital facilities in warehouses in the dock area, and there are also hospital ships in the ports waiting to evacuate the critically ill."

"Sounds daunting," Colonel Weston replied.

Daunting turned out to be an understatement. Louise would remember only snippets of the ensuing eighteen days: the First Cavalry division band playing popular music to welcome the thousands of befuddled evacuees arriving at Yokohama Central Station. The readily apparent camaraderie and love between prisoners who helped one another walk toward the hospital, while officers and nurses distributed candy and cigarettes to them along the way. The tears of gratitude on the faces of the prisoners as they ate their first warm meal. The individuals taking showers while their clothing and personal effects were sprayed with DDT. The sunken eyes, the broken bones visible beneath the patients' emaciated skins. The endless vital statistics—heights, alarmingly low weights, temperatures, and pulse and respiration rates—she recorded along with the prisoners' names and personal data. Their downcast eyes as they recounted how they'd received their various injuries.

More than seventeen thousand prisoners and internees were processed through the 42nd General Hospital before its assignment ended on September 21.

"Thank heaven we're done with that," Louise said as they boarded the train to head back to Tokyo. "I'm exhausted and not sure how much more I could've witnessed."

"Amen," Vivian replied.

THE NEXT DAY, LOUISE AND VIVIAN REPORTED TO THE hospital and were assigned to work on a general medicine ward, treating Japanese civilians.

The first patient Louise encountered, an impossibly small ten-year-old girl, lay moaning on the bed. She'd sustained napalm burns over eighty percent of her body during the Night of the Black Snow, and she was finally succumbing to the injuries. The shot of morphine Louise administered restored the girl to blessed unconsciousness, though the exposed portion of her forehead remained furrowed with indelible pain.

"It can't be long now," said the young medic sitting by the bedside holding the girl's hand. "She's been struggling to breathe."

Louise sat speechless on the opposite side of the bed. A few moments later, the patient took her last breath.

"I've been praying for God to let her go," the medic said, wiping tears with the back of his free hand. "Everyone talks about the horror of the atomic bombs we dropped on Hiroshima and Nagasaki. But, in my opinion, the firebombing of Tokyo was every bit as bad—there were thousands of other victims just like this poor kid, suffering every minute until they died."

Louise nodded and, through her own tears, stumbled to the head nurse's desk to receive her next assignment.

The nurse glanced over to see the medic covering the dead child's face with a sheet. "Thankfully that little one can finally rest in peace," she said, "and we can ready ourselves for the next tragedy."

Louise didn't reply.

"I've prepared a sodium amytal injection," the nurse continued. "Please give it to the young woman in bed twenty. They just brought her in, and she's hysterical."

"What happened to her?" Louise asked.

"Gang-raped by four American GIs. She'll live but she's in rough shape."

Louise flinched. *Gang-raped? By Americans?*

Vivian was already at the patient's side, gently cleaning her facial injuries. The woman—no more than twenty years old—sobbed and tried to pull away. "Please help us hold her steady so we can give her the sedative," Vivian said to the M.P. standing at the foot of the bed.

Within seconds of the shot, the patient relaxed, and Louise and Vivian began to examine her. Her legs were covered in blood, and gravel stuck to several raw wounds on her knees, shins, and buttocks.

Everyone looked up when a second M.P. arrived. "Did you catch the sons of bitches?" the first policeman asked.

"Yeah," he said, shaking his head with disgust. "They were wandering down the street laughing about it. Said she had it coming because she ignored their advances."

"TASFUIA…" the first M.P. muttered.

It was the last thing Louise heard before she blacked out.

Disoriented in all respects, Louise awoke to find sun filtering through the paper partitions that surrounded her. She reached over the edge of the thin futon she lay on and felt a soft straw mat below it. The quiet room smelled pleasant. *Where am I and how did I get here?* she wondered, then drifted back to sleep.

A while later, perhaps a half hour or so, Louise heard the familiar voices of Vivian and Colonel Weston.

"Are you awake?" Vivian asked, sliding aside a partition and entering the room.

"Silly question," Weston said with a chuckle. "Her eyes are open."

"What's happened to me?" Louise mumbled.

Vivian pulled her to a seated position and placed a small bowl of tea into her hands. "Drink this," she said. She and the CO sat cross-legged on the *tatami*—the rice straw mat—though Weston looked anything but comfortable.

Louise took a tentative sip and then another. "Tell me."

"Do you remember coming back from Yokohama?" Vivian asked.

Louise nodded. "We were assigned to work at the hospital. I remember a little girl dying…"

"Anything else?" Weston asked.

Louise sipped her tea and paused before replying, "We were treating a rape victim."

"Yes," Weston said quietly. "Two awful things to witness, especially after spending two and a half weeks treating POWs who'd been starved and abused for years…" He hesitated a moment, and the women saw him blink away tears.

"You had a breakdown," Vivian continued. "It looked like you lost consciousness for a few minutes, and then you became hysterical. We got you back to staff quarters and called Dr. Weston."

"I decided to give you sodium amytal and keep you sedated until we could decide what to do," Weston added.

"Is this a psychiatric ward?" Louise asked, with a tinge of panic in her voice.

Weston shook his head. "No. Dr. Yamazaki, one of the Japanese psychiatrists on staff here, thought that would be counterproductive—too chaotic and noisy. He said you needed a quiet place to rest and volunteered a room in his home. His wife, Azumi, who is a nurse, has been tending to you and administering the drug for the past several days."

Louise looked incredulous. "Days?" she asked.

"Uh-huh," Vivian replied. "Today's Wednesday, September 26th."

"How, how…"

"Whenever the sedative lightened, Azumi would feed you and take you to the bathroom, then give you another injection."

"You may remember bits and pieces of the past few days as you wake more fully," Weston said. "Right now we want you up and about to see if you're fit to travel tomorrow," Weston said.

"Travel where?"

"Back to the 44th," he replied.

"I'll be ready to travel tomorrow," Louise said more confidently than she felt.

"We think so, too," Vivian said.

Louise closed her eyes, apparently trying to formulate her next question, "Will this…uh…will this 'breakdown' mean a psychiatric discharge?"

"That depends on how you're feeling when you land," Weston said. "I spoke with Captain Connelly and told him you must've come down with a little bug in Yokohama. He'll check you out and make sure you're up to returning to duty."

Louise nodded. "Thanks."

"I've got to head back to the hospital," he said, struggling to disentangle his extremities and get to his feet. "Vivian will stay here with you tonight, and I'll have a driver pick you both up at 0900 tomorrow."

"Okay…"

"By the way, Dr. Yamazaki gave Azumi some barbiturate tablets that you should take if the agitation returns. He says the main thing is to remain calm and keep talking about what upset you. Azumi is a good listener—especially since she understands very little English," Weston said with a wink. "But Vivian assures me she can handle whatever you need to talk about."

He gave a little wave and was gone.

"Do you think we'll see him again?" Louise asked, crying softly now.

Vivian shrugged. "I don't have a clue."

THE YAMAZAKIS' NEIGHBORHOOD HAD BEEN SPARED from the Allies' firebombing, and the two friends spent the day sitting and talking in their out-of-this-world backyard garden. When Louise tried to steer the conversation away from the painful episodes that had precipitated her breakdown, Vivian gently brought up the memories. And—after only one barbiturate tablet—they were able to share their feelings.

"You know," Louise said with a sigh, "it was easier just to hate the Japanese and keep telling ourselves this was a 'good war.'"

Vivian nodded. "We can believe it was a justifiable war but still see how awful it was, on both sides," she said. "At least that's what I think."

Louise took a sip of tea and gazed into the water fountain, which wept slowly from its upper tier to the pool below. "I think so, too," she whispered.

Chapter Forty

When Louise and Vivian's plane from Japan landed on Leyte, Captains Connelly and Riley were waiting for them in a jeep. Connelly got out of the vehicle and ran to give them hugs. He whispered into Louise's ear, "How are you feeling?"

"Fine, now that we're someplace familiar," she replied cautiously.

"Ready to go back on duty?"

She nodded.

"That's great. Captain Riley hasn't been told about your little R & R, and I don't see why she needs to know."

Louise and Vivian returned to their tents and found Dot and Shoe sunbathing on the beach. Shoe jumped up and engulfed them in a group hug. "Thank heaven you made it back before our orders came through," she said. "Otherwise, I would've had to track you down and strangle you!"

"No news yet?" Vivian asked.

"Nope. So how was Tokyo?"

Vivian and Louise exchanged a glance. "It was pretty awful and we'll tell you about it eventually," Vivian replied. "Louise and I are just glad they didn't need all of us anymore. Colonel Weston and the other six nurses are still there, who knows for how long."

Louise nodded. "We've been dying to hear what's new here."

"And I hope you haven't gotten into our beer rations," Vivian said. "I'm really thirsty right about now."

They threw their duffle bags into their tents and rejoined Shoe and Dot on the beach. The gentle waves rhythmically lapping against their bare feet felt, to Louise, far more relaxing than the barbiturate she'd taken the day before. She didn't touch her beer.

"The big news is that the officers of the 77th Division hosted a festival in Cebu for all the nurses on Leyte who wanted to come," Shoe replied. "Dot and I were among a group of thirty that flew up there on the 18th. They treated us like royalty—put on this amazing steak dinner, cocktail parties, and a dance. We stayed overnight at the Red Cross and came back the next day."

"Wow!" Louise said.

"Because of heavy rain, the flight there took longer than the thirty minutes they'd promised us," Dot said. "And when we landed and looked out the windows to see more than a hundred officers on the tarmac jockeying for the best spots to greet us, I didn't want to get off the plane."

Shoe started snickering. "One of the pilots overheard us talking about being embarrassed and said, 'I hate to tell you this, ladies, but the plane's staying right here 'til 1000 hours tomorrow and it'll be plenty stuffy in here by then. So...I suggest you come to the party!' And I said, 'C'mon, then. Might as well enjoy ourselves.'"

"Shoe, Allie, Anna, and I got paired with four boys who turned out to be lots of fun," Dot said. "We stayed together for all of the festivities the first night. Then they took us out for breakfast and back to the plane the next morning."

"Hey, before we forget," Shoe said when she finished her beer, "a bunch of us are having a party at our club tonight to celebrate our second anniversary overseas. It's great you made it back here in time."

After dinner, about two dozen nurses from the 44th's original group met at the club. Major Mason—who they'd first met at Fort Sill—came over to have a few drinks with them. "I sure am sorry to leave the 44th," he moaned. "The hospital they've assigned me to here just isn't the same."

Louise nodded. "You probably feel like we all felt when we had to do detached service in New Guinea," she said. "We hated it."

They spent a couple of hours telling stories about the funny and sad and scary things they'd been through. "They never told us nurses when we signed up that we'd be earning battle stars," Shoe said, "and come to find out, we get one for the Hollandia campaign and one for Leyte."

"Well, we deserve them after putting up with the air raid scares and all the sky fireworks we saw," Anna said. "We didn't have to fight, but we were pretty close to it. And it's clear the Japanese didn't respect the hospital's noncombatant status."

"Anyway, it's good we got the stars and the points that go with them," Louise said. "Now we'll all have enough points for discharge when we get home, even if they change the formula yet again."

"All these rumors and policy changes are making my head spin," Shoe said.

"I think the cocktails might be contributing to that," Major Mason said with a laugh, nodding toward the three empty glasses in front of her.

"Point taken," Shoe replied.

"Well, the rumor about flying all medical personnel back to the States wherever possible *is* true," the major said. "I saw the order today. But—given the 'wherever possible' clause—I doubt it carries much weight. I'm still betting you gals will be on a slow boat."

"As long as it's headed in the right direction, it's better than sitting here," Louise said.

As had been typical since V-J Day, there were lulls in the evening's conversations when everyone wore dazed, faraway expressions on their faces.

"It's sad that there's so few of us left," Dot said, glancing around the room. "I miss Frankie and Helen."

"Ruth too," Louise added, her eyes shiny with tears. "We've made such good friends since we joined up..."

Shoe got to her feet—a tad unsteadily. "This party's getting too maudlin for me," she said. "I'm going to hit the sack."

"I'll walk you back to the tent," Louise said.

"What's that?" Shoe asked her when they'd settled in.

"A letter from Will."

"So, what'd he have to say?"

"He's a co-pilot for Eastern Airlines now, flying cargo planes from Miami to D.C. He and his roommate have a little house in Miami they call Sleepy Hollow. Look—he's got stationery printed with Sleepy Hollow—Home of the Near Great." She waved the paper at Shoe, who groaned.

"He invited me to come visit him when I get home," Louise continued, "and I think I'd like that."

"Oh, no—you're not gonna get all hung up on him again, are you?"

"It's just that I realize he was the most on-the-level, regular guy I've encountered since I joined the army. No lines. No pulling the wool over my eyes." She lit a cigarette and blew the smoke away from Shoe.

"That's true," her friend said. "And unlike that S-O-B Ed Winter, he didn't leave you with a nasty smoking habit."

"The carton's almost gone."

. . .

ALL BUT LOUISE NURSING HANGOVER HEADACHES, THE tentmates struggled to get up for reveille the next morning and reported for duty only to receive bad news: their days off had been taken away. They'd be working eight hours a day, seven days a week.

As usual, Shoe grumbled the loudest. "Explain to me why, again," she said to Captain Riley who, fortunately, took the complaining in stride.

"Because—counting the nurses who've been sent home with illnesses, the six who are in Japan, and those who were transferred to other hospitals—we're down to a complement of only thirty-nine," she replied and turned to go. "And we've got over 1,100 patients."

"And none of them battle casualties," Shoe muttered under her breath. "Instead, we've got whiners with ingrown toenails, cut fingers, and—occasionally—appendicitis."

That wasn't exactly accurate. The patients suffered many different ailments, including dengue fever, infectious hepatitis, and amoebic dysentery. And, as Louise and her friends all knew from personal experience, patients diagnosed with those diseases were well and truly sick.

LOUISE WAS FURTHER DISHEARTENED AT MAIL CALL that afternoon. Shoe watched the color drain from her friend's face. "What's wrong?" she asked.

"Sean Murphy..." Louise mumbled.

"Who?"

"A sailor I met on the train the day I left home two years ago. Just an eighteen-year-old kid returning from a furlough after his father's funeral. He was sweet. Maybe I told you about him."

Shoe shrugged. "If you did, I don't remember."

"Anyway, he looked so forlorn I suggested we write to each other. And we did, every so often—like big sister to little brother,"

Louise said, holding out an envelope. "This is the last letter I sent to him two months ago. It's been returned, marked deceased."

Shoe took the envelope and stared at it. "Where was he?"

"Last I knew he was somewhere in the South Pacific, but of course he couldn't say exactly," she said, hanging her head.

Shoe put her arm around her shoulder. "I think you could use a beer."

They greeted a few people they knew at the club, but Shoe led Louise purposefully to a corner table, giving everyone a look that clearly said *Leave us alone.* She went to the bar and returned a moment later with two bottles of reasonably cold beer.

"Thanks," Louise said, took a long pull, and then reached into her pocket for her cigarettes. Shoe didn't chastise her.

They sipped in silence for a while. "We see patients die pretty often," Louise finally said. "It's never easy, but usually I'm able to handle it. The ones we hear about by mail—like your brother, and Vivian's brother, and my neighbor kid, and now Sean Murphy— seem harder somehow."

"Yes," Shoe replied.

"Y'know," Louise said, then lit a cigarette and took a drag, "so many of the boys we've fixed up were headed directly back into action. I wonder how many of them didn't make it home."

"Probably a lot, but we'll end up in the loony bin if we keep thinking about it."

Louise managed a half smile, then raised her beer. "You're right, but at least let's toast those boys."

Shoe raised her bottle. "To the lost boys. May they rest in peace."

Maybe it was the long hours and seven-day workweeks or perhaps the uncertainty about when or how they'd be sent home. For whatever reasons, Louise and Shoe threw caution to the wind and were again persuaded to go out with Bob

Weber and Steve Quinn, the two supply sergeants with whom they'd been caught fraternizing in January. And the sergeants' friend Matthew Miller convinced Dot to come along.

Fortunately, the women were all assigned the day shift, and the sixsome began spending nearly every evening together.

"I'm so glad we decided to see these goofballs again," Louise said to Shoe and Dot when they made their way to the tents after one of the first dates. "Bob says the sweetest things to me, and he's so down-to-earth and funny. We'd be missing out on some swell times if we'd said no."

A little tipsy, Shoe nodded vigorously then grabbed Louise's elbow to steady herself. "That's for sure," she said. "And I think sneaking around to avoid the M.P.s adds a little excitement to the whole thing."

"I don't know about *that*," Dot said, "but Matthew makes me laugh harder than I've laughed in months. And he's one great kisser..."

"Bob is too," Louise said quietly, feeling her cheeks flush. "But I refuse to fall for him."

"Why?" Shoe asked.

"In case you've forgotten, I've fallen for a few too many men already."

"Well, there sure as heck are a lot of them around here," Dot said. "I doubt that'll be true when we get home."

IN EARLY OCTOBER, THE NURSES HAD BEEN TOLD THEY could expect their orders within two days. That news, coupled with the reports that a ship leaving on the 18th would have room for 300 women, gave them high hopes. But the orders hadn't come as promised, and the story about the ship had apparently been fiction.

Louise tried to console her tentmates. "At least we get to stay here rather than in the overflowing replacement depots waiting for transport," she said. "I heard there are thousands of people in each depot—some of whom have been there for over two months."

Dot nodded. "They're sleeping on cots so close together you can't walk between them, with no floors and no electricity. And can you imagine the chow lines? One of my patients told me there was a riot at the 28th Replacement Depot a couple days ago and a general had to come down and settle it."

"This isn't any way to treat American citizens," Shoe said. "And the shipyard and coal strikes back home are idling the troopships. It's criminal."

The orders finally arrived on October 19, and on the following Monday they went to the crowded replacement depot for processing. Their Philippine money was exchanged for U.S. currency, and they turned in all their military equipment. A huge poster at the depot gate bore a picture of the Golden Gate bridge and the words: Soldier, You are Going Home!

Best of all, they were relieved of duty and were sent back to the beach to wait.

Chapter Forty-One

Sadly, Colonel Weston was still on duty in Tokyo on November 13, 1945, when the 44th's nurses were taken to White Beach by truck to meet their ship, the USS *Admiral Hugh Rodman*. Unlike the USS *West Point,* that brought them to the South Pacific, the *Rodman* was built specifically as a transport ship and had been in operation less than a year. They boarded and moved out of the harbor the following day.

The nurses were delighted to find plentiful hot water in their cabins and good food. The "abandon ship" drills, while annoying, were routine rather than frightening.

The celebration ritual when the ship crossed the 180th Meridian on November 21—the Domain of the Golden Dragon —was much less raucous than the one held when traveling *to* the South Pacific. The nurses were included in the initiation into the "Silent Mysteries of the Far East" and weathered the dunking and shaving-cream-pie-in-the-face hijinks with little apprehension.

One of the crew members had a portable phonograph and stacks of records. Dancing was dicey on the decks, but everyone gathered most nights to listen to music. For obvious reasons, Doris Day's "Sentimental Journey" was a favorite. One doctor from the

44th had taught himself to play ukulele and played "Show Me the Way to Go Home"—rather badly, Louise thought—so frequently that people finally refused to sing along.

Thirteen days and many conversations and card games after they'd embarked, the ship passed under the Golden Gate Bridge and into the San Francisco harbor. From there, the passengers were transported to Fort Stoneman, the massive army staging area on the eastern peninsula of San Francisco Bay.

LOUISE HAD SENT A LETTER TO ETTA THE DAY BEFORE they departed Leyte, urging her to request a leave so they could meet in San Francisco when she landed. At Fort Stoneman, she sent a telegram confirming their arrival.

Etta managed to get a two-day leave and made the short trip from Oakland to the fort on November 30. Louise cried when her sister got off the train. "Oh, kid, it's so great to see you!" she said, hugging her tightly. "Let's promise never to be apart for so long again."

The two days passed before they'd had much chance to talk privately. The barracks were crowded and noisy, and Louise's friends all wanted to meet Etta, whom they'd heard so much about.

"You two look and act exactly the same," Dot said when their group of friends went out for drinks the first night.

"Yeah, except Etta doesn't make as much noise as our pal Louise," Shoe said.

Louise blushed. "She doesn't have a chance to say much with all of you jabbering all the time."

When she saw Etta off again at the station, Louise said, "Gee, this was nice. But it's going to be *way* better when we can really chat. There's so much I want to tell you about and so much I want to hear about."

Etta nodded. "Me too."

"Promise me you'll see about getting a longer leave to come back to Wisconsin?"

"I will."

"Keep me posted on the news about your discharge."

"Will do."

"And don't you *dare* sign on for another hitch. Uncle Sam has had his way with us for entirely too long."

At this, Etta laughed. "I promise."

A FEW DAYS LATER, LOUISE BOARDED A TRAIN WITH about 300 women—all nurses with the exception of twenty WACs —bound for Fort Des Moines, Iowa. Only the troop commander, three enlisted men, and the train crew members were men. The women were each assigned to do KP for one meal, but no one complained.

They slept in Pullman cars, four women per compartment, and had a relaxing time. Louise, Dot, Shoe, and Vivian shared a compartment.

Vivian was beside herself with excitement: her fiancé Jimmy had arranged a fifteen-day furlough when he'd received her first telegram saying they were leaving and was already waiting for her at Fort Des Moines.

During one half hour stop, Louise and Dot went to look for postcards at a local Woolworth's store. Louise spotted a brown leather-bound diary, complete with a brass lock and key, displayed on a shelf in the stationery department. "Look at this," she said, nudging her friend. "Now that we're civilians again we can keep diaries! I'm going to splurge on this one."

"How much is it?"

"A dollar-fifty."

Despite the bumpy ride, once they were underway, Louise immediately began writing in it.

. . .

THE NURSES ARRIVED IN DES MOINES ON DECEMBER 7, 1945. "It seems like way more than four years ago that Pearl Harbor was attacked," Louise said to Vivian as they walked toward the door of the train car.

Vivian didn't hear her—she was frantically looking out each window they passed to find Jimmy. When she saw him, she pushed ahead. Everyone in the aisle eyed her tolerantly. "Excuse me, please," she said. "Thank you..."

Louise choked up as she watched Jimmy embrace Vivian, pick her up off the ground, and swing her around before planting her firmly on the platform.

"You look great, Jimmy," Louise said to him when she approached the couple.

"I've put on a pound or two since I left the hospital in New Guinea," he said, patting his stomach. "Plus, I've been eating pretty well since I got here seven days ago."

"THIS PLACE LOOKS LIKE SOME RICH KIDS' COLLEGE campus," Louise said to her friends as their bus pulled into the fort. "Look at those pillared mansions..."

The driver, a WAC, laughed. "We call them 'barracks' here."

"You're kidding, aren't you?" Shoe asked. "Have we died and gone to heaven?"

"You won't have much time to get used to all this opulence," the driver said. "It's our mission to get everyone processed and on their way home as soon as possible. I'm guessing a few days at most."

The WAC post was operated essentially by women, and Louise and her friends were amazed at its efficiency. Spotless buildings and grounds. Clear, friendly, and concise communications. Impeccable military deportment.

The 44th's nurses—virtually all now first lieutenants—were met with crisp salutes by the enlisted WACs wherever they went. "I feel silly returning their salutes," Louise said. "They must wonder how an old lady like me can return them like such a rookie."

"Who cares what they think?" Shoe asked. "We just need to wait till our names come up on the processing roster, go do our paperwork and get our physicals, and we'll be civvies before you know it."

Louise nodded. "I can't wait," she said, but in truth she felt some uneasiness about returning to civilian life. *Where will I fit in?*

"There's one thing that's got me nervous," Dot said. "What if our physicals turn up something that causes them not to let us out? Have you heard that some of the gals were hospitalized because they found albumen in their urine—that chemical that can signal kidney problems? That could happen to us."

"Oh, I hadn't heard that," Louise said, shaking her head. "I'd better not flunk out or they'll have to put me in the psychiatric ward!"

Around two a.m. Louise bolted upright in her bunk, her nightgown drenched in sweat, the phrase *psychiatric ward* echoing through her head. *What if Colonel Weston was compelled to put something in my medical record about my breakdown in Tokyo? What if they refuse to discharge me without further evaluation? Can I trust Captain Connelly's word that no one knew about my—what was his wording?—"little R&R"?*

There was no going back to sleep.

Her eyes rimmed with dark circles, Louise cornered Vivian in the chow line at 0630 that morning. "Do you think my episode in Tokyo might keep me from getting discharged?" she whispered, then watched in fear as the color drained from her friend's face.

"Uh...I hadn't thought of that possibility," Vivian stammered. "But I think if there was a chance of that, the colonel would've said something to us. Don't you?"

Louise bit her lip to hold back tears. "I just don't know."

Shoe came up behind them. "You don't know what?" she asked.

"Nothing," Vivian muttered. "I was just asking Louise here what she was going to buy with her muster-out pay."

"Well, I'm gonna buy that blue silk dress from the cover of January's *Vogue* magazine," Shoe said.

"You're not mustering out as a general, you know," Vivian retorted. "I'm betting that dress is way over your budget."

"Maybe so..." Shoe moaned. "And we'd better eat quick or they'll dock our pay for being late for our physicals."

LOUISE WIPED HER DAMP PALMS ON HER SKIRT AS SHE walked into the base hospital. Giddy with excitement, Dot and Shoe chatted like schoolgirls as they waited their turn to be examined. Vivian sat silently beside Louise, occasionally nudging her shoulder for encouragement.

When called into the exam room, Louise surreptitiously looked at her chart to see if she could spot any unusual notations. She felt her anxiety ease when she didn't see any, but she still watched like a hawk as the nurse recorded her vitals—all normal. *I don't want to be denied discharge for some clerical error*, she thought.

"When will the results of our urine and blood tests be done?" Louise asked the laboratory nurse in charge of collecting and labeling all the samples.

"You're on the roster for processing in two days," the nurse replied after checking her clipboard. "The tests will be done by then."

THE FOUR FRIENDS REPORTED TO THE ADMIN BUILDING at 0700 hours on December 10, all in high spirits though Louise had spent a restless night worrying about a possible hidden file notation and the dreaded albumen.

She was also the last one called in for the lab results. Sitting alone on the hallway bench—the only person not taken in alphabetical order—she began to sweat. After fifteen minutes, she began to pace. Ten minutes later, she got up the nerve to approach a passing clerk.

"Excuse me," she said, "I'm Lieutenant Dietrich, and I've been waiting quite a while to get the results of my physical. I'm...I'm the only one left."

"Hmm...That seems odd," the clerk replied. "I'll go check for you." She disappeared behind a wooden door and Louise returned to the bench.

A moment later, a heavyset nurse burst through the door, bearing a clipboard. "I am *so* sorry, Lieutenant Dietrich," she said. "It seems your test results were mistakenly stapled to someone else's. Your friends got worried and came to ask me about you."

"Did I pass?"

"Yes, dear," she said. "Now let me take you to where your friends are waiting—in another line, I'm afraid."

THEY'D ALL PASSED THEIR PHYSICALS. EVENTUALLY, they signed on the dotted lines and began making arrangements to leave the following day. Shoe and Dot would take the train through Chicago to their homes in Walworth County, Wisconsin. Vivian and Jimmy—who still had eight days left on his furlough— would be traveling with Louise and several other nurses on the midnight Rock Island Rocket to St. Paul. The couple would stay at a hotel in St. Paul for two nights before heading to Wisconsin so Jimmy could meet the Vogel family.

Because gas shortages were still prevalent, Louise and her friend Allie had to take another train from St. Paul to La Crosse. They waited eight excruciatingly long hours for it to arrive, growing more impatient by the minute as delays in the schedule were announced. "Do you think we're jinxed or something?" Louise asked Allie after the fourth such announcement.

"I don't know," Allie said as she fished through her purse to find change to call her parents yet again. "But I'm sure glad my father has the patience of a saint. I can just hear him telling my mother, 'Relax, Martha, she's coming home for good now and you'll have all the time in the world to catch up.'"

When Allie's parents met the train, Martha insisted on sitting in the back seat so she could hold hands with her daughter. Louise sat in front and focused on the scenery—enjoying familiar sights— during the forty-five-mile ride to La Farge, where they dropped her off at her Aunt Margaret and Uncle Chuck's home.

Her aunt had been keeping watch at the front window and rushed outside when the car pulled up, her uncle trailing a few steps behind. They thanked Allie's parents profusely, and Chuck passed her father a two-dollar bill as a contribution for the gas. They grabbed her luggage and refused to allow Louise to carry anything into the house. "You've had a long trip," Margaret said. "This is the least we can do."

"You two look wonderful," Louise told them after they ushered her into the living room.

"You do, too, dear," Margaret replied. "You're so tan and fit!"

"Would you like a beer?" Chuck asked.

"I'd love one," Louise replied.

Chuck returned and offered Louise an ice-cold bottle of Heileman's Old Style lager along with an empty glass.

"I've been thirsty for an Old Style for so long, this seems like a mirage!" she said, accepting the bottle. "You can save the glass, though. We learned not to stand on formality in the army."

He handed the glass to Margaret. "I wouldn't call my wife formal, but she still refuses to drink from the bottle," he replied. He returned a moment later with two more beers and settled next to Margaret on the couch.

Margaret expertly poured her beer, sipped off a bit of foam, and raised her glass. "Here's to having my dear sister's eldest daughter home at last! We are *so* happy to have you."

They talked into the wee hours of the morning.

"I know it's your first day home," Margaret said as they bid each other goodnight, "but are you worried about something? You've bitten your nails to the quick."

Louise glanced at her hands. "I guess I'm just worried about what comes next. Etta and I are counting on proceeds from the farm sale to get ourselves set up as civilians, and Donald's been curiously silent about the whole deal."

"Chuck can get a ride to work tomorrow, and I'll take you to the bank to see what's what."

"That'd be great."

In bed, Louise felt the Wisconsin wind leaking through the windows. And though comforted by the warm welcome from two people she truly loved, she couldn't shake her sense of foreboding.

Chapter Forty-Two

Louise wrote in her diary the following evening:

A Terrible Day. My plans are smashed to pieces.

Margaret and I went to the La Farge Savings & Loan this morning. We waited twenty minutes until Mr. Albertson—the bank president with his weak chin and florid complexion—could see us. My anxiety didn't increase during the wait because, though I'd never met him before, Etta had described him as honest. But I should've known something was amiss when he hesitated to show us the records of Etta's and my account.

It turns out our balance is less than $500! I asked him how this could be when we'd instructed Cousin Donald not to accept anything less than $5,000 for the sale of the farm. Albertson showed me the bill of sale: it did sell for $5,000.

But then he pulled out several notarized liens that had been filed against the deed to the property. Since Etta and I enlisted, Donald had mortgaged most of the farm equipment and the cattle to "raise money to cover necessary expenses," all but one of the notes held by the crook who bought the farm. There were also judgments, from places like the feed store, the implement mechanic, and a roofer, for goods and services Donald had purchased in Etta's and my names. And

Albertson said that even though he was hesitant to turn over the funds to pay off the obligations, the bank's lawyer told him he had no choice. Our account contains all that was left of the proceeds.

I couldn't even speak, but Aunt Margaret was apoplectic. She insisted on talking to the bank's lawyer, who was no help at all. Then we went to the sheriff's office to file charges against Donald, who was clearly in cahoots with the buyer. The Sheriff was friendly, but he said we didn't have a case. It seems everyone in town is on Donald's side—they believe he and his wife were owed something for taking such good care of Etta and me for all those years.

It makes me so damn mad I could scream.

I'm going to finish the beer I just opened and call it a night. Maybe I'll wake in the morning to find it was all a bad dream. I'm going to wait to tell Etta for now. No sense in both of us being upset.

LOUISE SLEPT LATE THE NEXT MORNING, AND AUNT Margaret knocked softly on the door around eleven o'clock.

"Come in."

"Good morning, dear," she said, sitting on the edge of the bed. "I'm heading next door soon to help Greta with her sewing project but wanted to see how you were doing before I left."

Louise leaned up on one elbow and caught a glimpse of herself in the vanity mirror: puffy face and red-rimmed eyes. "As I guess you can see, not so hot."

"I know you're hurt and upset. Do you want to talk some more about it?"

"Not really. I just want to forget the whole thing as soon as possible," Louise said.

As Margaret hugged her, Louise inhaled a whiff of Halo shampoo—a product Margaret had always sworn by. "It's *much* less harsh on your hair than soap," she would often chirp to anyone who'd listen. For some reason, smelling the shampoo felt more comforting to Louise than any words her aunt might say.

"Okay, dear. I'll be back around two, and maybe we can go downtown and do a little shopping?"

"That sounds good," Louise replied and sank back onto the pillow.

AFTER A FEW DAYS AT MARGARET AND CHUCK'S, LOUISE went to stay with her mother's friend Toots and her son Ernie in nearby Viroqua. "I'll feel like an imposition if I stay anywhere too long," she told Margaret.

"I'm fine with you going to Toots's for a while," Margaret replied, "but I want you with us for Christmas. And you wouldn't be an imposition even if you lived with us permanently."

Toots took her shopping, and Louise found a red corduroy dress and a green camel hair coat. "Those box-style coats are the newest thing," Toots said after they perused the relatively bare department store racks.

Maybe in Viroqua, Louise thought, turning to look at the back of the coat in the three-way mirror. *I'm not so sure about St. Paul, Minneapolis, or Chicago.*

"It *is* cute," she said. "I think I'll get it. Maybe if I find a bright yellow hat and some purple shoes to go with the dress and coat, they'll put me on the cover of *Vogue.*"

"You've always been so funny!"

That evening, Louise and Ernie stopped for a beer at a little roadhouse on their way downtown to buy a Christmas tree. "Go get the tree, then come to the dance over at the Pines," one of Ernie's friends told them. "A bunch of us are heading over, and everyone'll want to see Louise."

Ernie gave her a questioning look.

"I guess that'd be fun," she replied.

An hour later, she found herself in the throes of regret: regret that she'd agreed to come *and* regret that she'd left the Army. The

Pines was a madhouse: people pushing and yelling and some even fighting. *Who* are *these people?*

Worse yet, she found herself embarrassed at her inability to remember the names of numerous people who came to say hello. *Have I completely lost my mind? Sure, some of these folks have changed, but certainly not so much that I shouldn't know them.*

SEVERAL DAYS BEFORE CHRISTMAS, LOUISE GOT together with her friend Ruth Ziegler, who was also in Viroqua, visiting with her parents while on a furlough from Brook Army Hospital at Fort Sam Houston, Texas. "Let's meet for lunch at the coffee shop on Main Street," Louise had suggested when Ruth called.

"Great. See you at noon tomorrow."

Ruth stood up and the women hugged each other tearfully when Louise walked in. "It's great to see you, Louise."

"You, too. How are things at Brook? Are you glad you stayed in?"

"It's too early to say for sure," Ruth replied, signaling the waitress for a cup of coffee. "I was granted leave before I'd even worked a full month. But I liked the other nurses and the hospital itself. It seems like battle casualties are still trickling in from the war and that most of them will be long-term patients."

"Why *did* you re-up? I never got a chance to ask you about it."

The waitress came to take their order. "We need a minute," Ruth said and began to peruse the menu.

"Okay," Ruth said after the waitress had returned and written down their choices. "Why did I re-up...? When I got boarded home because of the sinus trouble, I was completely lost. You know, Pete and I were really in love. Before he got killed, we'd talked about marriage, where we'd live, how many kids we'd have and all. Then there I was back in the States—not legally a widow but grieving like one, nonetheless. All my close friends were still overseas. My family couldn't understand what I was going through and kept telling me to just get over it. And, frankly, they were driving me crazy."

She paused to stir more sugar into her coffee. "It's funny... before the war, I never drank sugar in my coffee. But somehow all the time we couldn't get it, I grew to crave it. I'm going to weigh a ton if I keep this up."

Louise chuckled. "I wouldn't worry if I were you. All those patients are going to keep you hopping."

"That's what I keep telling myself. Anyway, signing up for another three-year hitch seemed right to me at the time. So far, I haven't regretted it, and San Antonio sure beats rural Wisconsin."

Louise stared over Ruth's shoulder to look out the window at the sidewalk. Covered with ice mixed with sand and lined with piles of dirty gray snow, it made her ache for sunshine and warm weather. She felt tension in her neck and shoulders. *If only Donald hadn't cheated us...*

She took a deep breath and continued. "I've been thinking of re-enlisting myself, but I need to wait until my little sister comes back—either on furlough or when she's discharged—so we can make some decisions together. Aside from my maternal aunt and uncle, she's all the family I've got."

"I remember how close you and your sis have always been."

They ate their lunch—club sandwiches with potato chips and dill pickles—and chatted about their mutual friends and experiences.

"I got a birth announcement from Frankie yesterday," Louise said. "They had a baby boy, and she seems so happy. I have to admit I'm envious."

"Weren't they going to name him after Alex's friend Dutch? Or you, if it was a girl?"

Louise dabbed mayonnaise from the corner of her mouth. "Uh-huh, and luckily the baby was a boy—I've never been fond of *my* name. They named him Jesse."

"That's sweet."

They finished their sandwiches and put their napkins aside. "So, what's next for you—till Etta gets home, I mean?" Ruth asked.

"After the New Year, I'm going down to Walworth to visit Dot and Shoe," Louise said, lighting a cigarette. "They're going on a trip to Florida, and I might go along."

"You should. Believe me, it's great to be back with people who know what it was like over there. And who know how much you can grow to love a man you've only known for a couple of months."

Louise slowly exhaled a puff of smoke. "I've been doing a lot of thinking about the relationships I had when I was in the service, and they all feel a little unreal to me now. But while they were going on—and the serious ones each lasted about three months— they were very, very real."

Ruth let the waitress refill her coffee cup and stirred in more sugar. "I've decided Pete and I—and probably everyone over there —fell in love fast and hard because of all the uncertainty we faced every day," she said. "I mean, when you don't know what tomorrow might bring, you'd better enjoy today. And enjoy it, we did."

"True. And even though some fellows hurt me pretty badly, I wouldn't have traded the good times I had with them for anything."

"No regrets?" her friend asked.

"One, I guess," Louise said, stubbing out her cigarette in the ashtray. "I probably shouldn't have let Ed Winter talk me into taking up smoking."

"Probably not. But do you regret getting involved with him after how he left you? Flying off without a personal goodbye and never writing you like he promised to?"

Louise shrugged.

"I mean, if you'd known he was a lout from the beginning, would you still have gone with him?"

"I'm not sure," Louise replied tentatively. "But I sense there's something you're not telling me."

Ruth hung her head. "So...you know Ed and Pete were pretty close? After Ed left, Pete told me he had another gal on the string, and when he got his orders, he spent the day with her instead of you. Pete asked me not to tell you..."

Louise's face fell. "Well...I hate being taken for a fool. But the truth is, even if you or Pete had warned me Ed was a liar, I probably still would have fallen for him. And we did have some great times together..."

Chapter Forty-Three

As promised, Louise went back to spend Christmas with Margaret and Chuck. Though Margaret and Louise had talked daily while she'd been at Toots's, Margaret still greeted her with unabashed affection, and Louise was surprised when tears sprang to her own eyes and spilled down her cheeks. She brushed them away with a mitten-clad hand. "I don't know why I get so emotional over everything, but I sure do feel welcome here."

"You are," Margaret replied. "And you remind me so much of your mom it sometimes takes my breath away. I know she'd be so proud of you."

They opened their presents on Christmas Eve. Louise's eyes teared up yet again when she saw the gifts from her sister: a Parker fountain pen set, a leather portfolio, a lacy white slip, and a box of candy. "I don't know how she does it," Louise said to her aunt and uncle. "She knows exactly what I like and need—I don't think she's *ever* given me a bad gift. I feel just punk about the presents I've picked out for everyone this year."

"You're just a little out of practice," Chuck said.

Margaret shot him a withering look. "Your uncle's wrong,

dear," she said, patting her hand. "We love the centerpiece you got for us. The florist did a grand job."

Chuck nodded. "We really do like it."

Louise couldn't help smiling at his well-intended but disingenuous comment—she knew her uncle couldn't care less about the centerpiece. *I should've gotten him his own gift—maybe a bottle of brandy or something.*

"Open your gift from us," Margaret said.

Louise pulled off the ribbon and carefully removed the wrapping paper, setting them aside. The package contained a bottle of Dorothy Perkins cologne, an embroidered handkerchief, and another slip.

"Since Etta already gave you a slip," Margaret said, "we can take that back and exchange it for something else."

"Good heavens, no!" Louise replied. "After wearing trousers for so long, I'm going to wear skirts and dresses *all* the time and this will come in handy. Thank you both."

The snow started falling about midnight, and by Christmas morning La Farge was snowbound. Louise woke up early and could hardly see out the window.

Gee, back in New Guinea when we were singing "I'm dreaming of a white Christmas" *last year, I wasn't anticipating* this. *And I so wanted to go to church this morning.*

"I sure hope Leon and Jane can make it here for dinner," Margaret said as she bustled around the kitchen that afternoon. "Chuck, give them a call, please, and see what things look like in their neighborhood."

Chuck rolled his eyes. "They live two miles away. It's bound to look the same as it does here."

"Still. Call them." She turned to Louise. "Would you mind peeling the potatoes? I need to focus on getting this pie in the oven."

"Leon has the driveway cleared," Chuck reported when he

hung up the wall phone in the kitchen. "The streets look passable, so they're planning to come."

"That's good," Margaret said. "There's no way the three of us can eat all this food by ourselves."

The house smelled heavenly by four o'clock with the aromas of roasting chicken, freshly made apple sauce with cinnamon, and pecan pie cooling on the rack. "My mouth is watering in anticipation," Louise said when she emerged from her bedroom wearing her new red dress.

At five o'clock, Leon arrived, stomping his snow-covered feet on the entryway rug. "Come in, come in," Margaret called, rising from the sofa in the living room and rounding the corner to greet him. She pulled up short. "Where's Jane?"

"In the car. We got stuck three times on the way over here, but she kept insisting we come. Now we find there's no place to park except in the middle of the street."

Margaret's shoulders sank. "Did you go around the block?"

"I drove around three blocks without any luck. We can't abandon the car—someone will surely need to get past it. I'm afraid we can't stay."

Margaret started to protest, but the sound of a horn—honking for Leon to move the car—brought the reality of the situation into clear view. "I understand," she said. "Give Jane a hug for us."

Margaret, Chuck, and Louise tried to keep the conversation light as they ate the special dinner, which truly was delicious. Afterward, they drank a little wine and played a few games of three-handed cribbage.

Louise went to her room at nine o'clock to write in her diary:

Aunt Margaret is so darned swell and everyone's done so much to make this a good Christmas.

I just wish I could stop feeling empty and lonesome all the time. From her last letter, it's clear that Dot has felt the same way since she's been home. We never dreamed it would be like this.

Maybe it would help if there were some young people here that I could do things with. Playing cards or even going out with Aunt Margaret and Uncle Chuck just isn't the same as being with people my own age.

I'm looking forward to visiting Dot and Shoe in January.

Chapter Forty-Four

AT ELEVEN P.M. ON JANUARY 1, 1946, LOUISE BOARDED A bus for Walworth, Wisconsin, and arrived at ten o'clock the following morning, in time to celebrate Dot's twenty-eighth birthday.

Dot met her bus and drove her to her older sister Donna's house where she was then living. Donna, her husband, and their fourteen-year-old son were all home.

Donna hugged Louise warmly. "We're happy to finally meet you. Dot's told us so much about you—all good, of course!"

I'm glad she didn't mention how insensitive Shoe and I were to exclude her when we were in Burauen. We were acting like junior-high schoolers or something.

The phone rang as they settled in over cups of coffee. "It's Bertha," Donna told Dot. "She says she'll be over in ten minutes."

Dot and Louise giggled. "In the army, no one ever called Shoe by her first name, including her many boyfriends!" Dot said.

Louise took a sip of coffee, then poured in a bit more cream. "It sure is swell that you two live so close to each other," she said, unable to mask her jealousy.

"You could move down here, too," Dot replied.

Louise shrugged. "I'm waiting for Etta to get home. Wherever we go, it'll be together."

Within the first hour after Shoe's arrival, she and Dot began trying to convince Louise to go to Florida with them. "I want to be home when Etta gets out," Louise said. "And I'd need to let Aunt Margaret know the plans and get my bathing suit—"

"We're only going for two weeks, and it'll be at least several weeks before Etta's discharged," Dot countered. "I'll take the bus back up to La Farge with you so you can set your aunt's mind at ease and collect your bathing suit and warm weather clothing."

"Well—"

"Great! It's a deal," Shoe said triumphantly.

On Friday night, January 4, Donna dropped Dot and Louise off at the bus station in Walworth. They made it some twenty-six miles to Janesville before the buses stopped running due to hazardous conditions: rain, fog, and ice-covered roads.

"What are we supposed to do now?" Dot asked the ticket clerk.

"I've been calling all the hotels in town," the clerk replied. "The Monterey Hotel—which is about three blocks from here— has one room left if you want it."

Dot and Louise looked at each other and shrugged. "We'll take it," Louise replied.

"I'm glad we only brought overnight bags," Dot said as they inched their way, arm-in-arm, over the slippery sidewalks. "It would've been hard to stay upright if we were carrying big suitcases."

"But if we had suitcases, we could sit on them and slide ourselves along," Louise said. "You know, this is exciting—I've never stayed in a hotel before."

"Me neither, which is funny if you think about it. We've been all over the world, on trains, planes, buses, and ships, but we've never stayed in a hotel."

The Monterey didn't disappoint. The six-story Art Deco hotel, built in 1930, boasted many famous visitors. Its only drawback at one-thirty a.m. was the lack of round-the-clock housekeeping services. "I apologize, ladies," the desk clerk told Dot and Louise when they checked in. "I have plenty of clean sheets and towels, but there's no one available to make up your room."

"We were nurses in the war," Dot replied. "We've had plenty of experience making beds."

"Oh, my," the clerk started to reply, but Louise handed the room key to Dot, picked up the stack of linens, and turned toward the elevator.

"Thank you," she said over her shoulder. "We don't want to spend all night talking to him," she whispered to Dot.

In the room, they hung up their damp outerwear and took turns taking hot showers to get warm. When Louise came out of the bathroom, she found Dot seated at the desk, eating one of the several sandwiches Donna had sent along and writing a letter. "Look at the elegant stationery I found in the drawer! I'm writing a congratulatory letter to Frankie and Alex."

Louise looked over her shoulder. "Is there an extra piece so I can write to Etta?"

Their letters and snacks finished, the two friends settled down in the most comfortable beds they'd ever slept in. "I'm so glad our bus was delayed," Louise said.

A week later they were in Sarasota, Florida. Dot, her sister Donna, Donna's friend Marge, Shoe, and Louise drove down in Marge's car. Dot's parents were already there, staying in a travel trailer they'd towed down a few weeks earlier. The new arrivals rented two cabins in the same campground; Dot, Shoe, and Louise shared one, and Donna and Marge had the other.

"It feels glorious to be warm again," Shoe said as the three veterans sat on the front porch of their cabin sipping beers late the following afternoon. "Back in Leyte I never imagined I'd be complaining about cold, but Wisconsin winters sure are disheartening."

"I'm not sure it's just the weather that's disheartening," Louise said. "It's also boring..."

"And sometimes lonely," Dot added, nodding thoughtfully.

"But at least you two can get together pretty often," Louise said.

"It *is* nice," Shoe said. "The thing is, there were people around us *all* the time in the Army, not just a couple times a week. If I wanted to do something my tentmates didn't, I'd just find someone else to do it with. We were all pretty much the same age. We'd been through the same experiences..."

Louise nodded her head vigorously. "Like sitting with dying patients, or doing air-raid or abandon-ship drills, or dealing with monsoon-like rain and knee-deep mud when you're bone-tired. Or seeing all the awful things I saw in Tokyo," she said. "I certainly can't share all that with my aunt and uncle—they'd think I was complaining."

"Or exaggerating," Dot said with a rueful laugh. "Donna's husband—who just got back from Guadalcanal—understands. But Donna looks at me like I'm either lying or crazy if I talk about how hard it was sometimes."

The three friends looked up as Donna and Marge approached. "We just heard about a new club a few miles from here," Marge said. "They're supposed to have a great dance band and reasonably priced drinks. Do you kids want to go over there with us tonight?"

"Sure, we do," Shoe said, then turned to Dot and Louise. "Don't we?"

Dot and Louise nodded.

"Great!" Donna said. "Mom's grilling chicken for dinner. We'll go right after we eat."

"We'd better start getting ready if we all want to take showers," Dot said. "There are only two stalls in the bathhouse."

"You two can go first," Louise said. "My hair's shorter and will take less time to dry."

While her friends went to shower, Louise took out the new dress she'd purchased in La Crosse right after Christmas—a flowered silk jersey with a pleated skirt. The store clerk had assured her it was flattering and in fashion, but now Louise wasn't sure. *What's fashionable in small-town Wisconsin is probably very different from what is in Florida. I hope I don't stick out like a sore thumb.*

Later, when she came back from the shower, Louise found Dot and Shoe agonizing over what to wear. Each had two dresses to choose from but voiced fears similar to hers. "I feel so hopelessly out-of-date," Shoe moaned. "These dresses were brand new before the war, but I'm afraid I'll look like a frumpy old maid in either of them."

"Don't be silly," Dot said. "Wear the orange one, though. It brings out the color of your eyes and flatters your figure—which does *not* look like an old maid's."

"That one's cute," Shoe said when she saw Louise's new dress. "Want to let me borrow it?" she teased.

"No, thanks," Louise said. "I spent three hours in the dress shop trying on everything in my size before I found it."

They dried their hair, finished dressing, and applied makeup, feeling more confident as they went along.

Dot's father gave a wolf whistle from his lawn chair as they approached the trailer. "You girls are gonna turn some heads at that club!"

Louise blushed.

The White Sands Ballroom sounded exotic but left a lot to be desired. Its neon sign hadn't yet been hooked up to electricity, the walls were still unpainted and unadorned, and the bar was only half-stocked. "I wonder why they opened before the place was finished," Shoe commented.

"I heard the band is in demand and they decided to book it before realizing how long construction would take," Marge said. "Look how many people are here already."

"It is pretty amazing," Louise said, glancing at the tables surrounding the dance floor. "And most of them are women."

Dot looked deflated. "Everyone told us it'd be different when we got home and weren't vastly outnumbered by men…"

"Oh, c'mon, gals," Marge said with evident exasperation. Around forty and never married, she took pride in her independence and singlehood. "Surely you can't believe you need a man to be happy. In my experience, they're often more trouble than they're worth."

Sounds like Etta, Louise thought.

Marge led the group over to a table and ordered the first round of drinks—Mai Tais for all.

The fifteen-piece band *was* good, and the dance floor filled up quickly. When they began playing "In the Mood," two blond-haired, deeply-tanned fellows—probably only twenty-one or twenty-two years old—came and asked Louise and Dot to dance. The women nodded and followed them to the floor.

Swing music not being conducive to conversation, the men didn't bother to introduce themselves and merely mumbled, "Thanks," when the song ended.

Louise and Dot made their way back to the table, chuckling. "Mine was a terrible dancer," Louise said.

"Mine too, and he still had pimples!"

After their second round of drinks, the women began to dance with each other, taking turns staying to mind the table. When the group rejoined Shoe after her turn, she commented to Louise, "In the service, a gal sitting by herself would've attracted about ten boys. It's certainly different stateside."

"You don't need to remind me."

Back at the cabin, the three friends sat on the front porch drinking beer and talking. As the hours passed and the temperature dropped, they wrapped themselves in blankets. "It's been way too long since I've had so much fun," Dot said, "I don't want this night to end. But I need to use the little girls' room again and get another blanket."

"Me too," Louise said. "And maybe if we drink less beer we won't have to go so often!"

"Okay," Shoe said, "let's split the next one."

"I wish I could be more like Donna's friend Marge and not be concerned about being an old maid," Louise said when they'd settled in again. "I was so worried about finding a husband while I was in the service that I let myself be bamboozled over and over again."

Shoe nodded absently. "I can't believe how relieved I was when Del asked me to marry him..." Her face fell and she paused.

Louise and Dot waited in silence and watched a tear meander down their friend's cheek.

Sitting on the porch swing with Shoe, Louise put her arm around her and drew her close. "What do you mean about being relieved?" she asked.

Shoe's shoulders began heaving with sobs. "I don't want to talk about it!"

"Sorry," Louise said gently, "but that's not an option. Something's upsetting you, and it won't do any good to hold it in."

Still crying, Shoe refused to speak or look at them.

Louise pulled her into a firm hug and held on when Shoe tried to break free. "Does it have anything to do with the enlisted man who attacked you on the beach in Townsville?" she asked.

Shoe managed to extricate herself from the hug, then nodded silently.

"Let me guess," Dot said. "Louise and I *didn't* get there in time to stop him, did we?"

"No..."

"Oh, honey," Louise said, "I wish you would've told us."

"It was so disgusting and it hurt so bad...I just wanted to forget about it," Shoe mumbled. "But then..." She began crying harder and couldn't seem to catch her breath.

"But then you were afraid you were pregnant?" Louise asked.

Shoe took a deep breath and sighed. "Uh-huh," she said. "I had never been regular, but my period was really late. I didn't know what to do."

Louise and Dot exchanged a brief look, a tacit agreement to let Shoe tell it at her own pace.

After an interminable pause, their friend swallowed twice. "And then I met Del, and when he said he wanted to marry me, I let him go all the way. You know—thinking maybe he'd believe he was the father." She buried her face in her hands and wailed, "How could I even think of doing that to him?

"...And when I finally got my period, it was like the weight of the world was lifted. I vowed I'd never again refer to it as 'the curse,'" she said with a rueful smile. "And I've kept that promise."

"Do you think you miscarried?" Dot asked.

"Probably not," Shoe said. "Aside from being late, I never had any other signs—certainly not like Frankie, who was always nauseous."

"And," Dot said with a smirk, "who went from an A-cup to a C in a matter of weeks."

"Did you ever tell Del you thought you might be pregnant?" Louise asked.

"No, thank heaven. But, it's weird. Even though I'd thrown myself at him out of desperation—and even though I hardly knew him—I was devastated when Del stopped writing to me."

"Let's face it, women are castigated for being single," Louise said.

Shoe snorted. "I'm not familiar with the term, but it sounds about right!"

"It means berated or frowned upon," Dot said.

"Thank you, Mrs. Webster," Shoe shot back. "I figured as much."

They drank in silence for several minutes.

"Hey, why don't we make another pact?" Shoe suggested. "We'll each promise not to settle for just *any* man—we'll wait for the *right* man."

"Great idea," Dot said. "I promise."

"Me, too," Louise said.

Chapter Forty-Five

THE WEATHER WAS STILL FRIGID IN LA FARGE WHEN Louise returned in late January, tanned and less anxious than she'd been a month earlier.

Better yet, Etta—now also a civilian—came home a week later. They shared a room at Margaret and Chuck's and spent hours talking about their experiences and grousing about how Cousin Donald had swindled them.

"You girls are welcome to stay here as long as you want," Margaret told them whenever they broached the subject of moving on. They knew she meant it but couldn't help feeling they were imposing.

"You don't seem all that disappointed about us not having enough money to move to San Francisco," Louise said to Etta one day. "I thought you enjoyed living in Northern California."

"That was kind of a pipe dream. It was beautiful there and all, but it never really felt like home."

Pipe dream? Louise felt bile rising in her throat but forced herself not to react. She waited a few beats.

"One of the gals from my unit moved to Madison," she finally said. "I think we've got enough money to get ourselves set up there if we want. My friend says there are plenty of jobs and the city's nice."

Etta looked dubious. "I know Madison's only about a hundred miles from here," she said, "but that feels pretty far away right now."

Louise tried not to look incredulous. *Good heavens,* she wanted to say, *you were a thousand miles from home when you were stationed in New York and two thousand when you were in Oakland. What happened to your sense of adventure? What happened to the self-confidence you had to have developed along the way?*

Still, she pushed down her disappointment. "Vivian Vogel says they're hiring nurses at St. Francis Hospital in La Crosse. We've definitely got enough money to rent an apartment there."

Etta's relief was palpable. "Let's try La Crosse first," she replied.

WITHIN THE MONTH, THE TWO SISTERS HAD MOVED into a second-floor apartment in downtown La Crosse. Louise was able to walk to the hospital, and Etta could easily catch a bus to her new job in the registrar's office at Viterbo College.

But Louise was assigned to work the evening shift and rarely saw Vivian. Their occasional get-togethers left Louise feeling let down: Vivian—though sweet as ever—was wrapped up in planning a summer wedding and a move to St. Louis, and the blind dates she and Jimmy arranged for Louise were disheartening.

"Maybe I'm being too picky," Louise told Vivian after one uncomfortable double date.

"Don't be silly," Vivian replied. "If there's no spark, you can't pretend otherwise."

Louise nodded. "It sure seems like all the good guys are already taken."

"I can't believe that," Vivian said. "But I do believe many of them are sitting at home trying to get their bearings again."

Louise gave her an inquisitive look.

"You know how many men were shell-shocked after the last war?" Vivian continued, pausing while Louise nodded. "Well, a lot of our boys are having the same kinds of trouble. Jimmy says he wakes up in a cold sweat about once a week, usually after dreaming of getting shot again. I'm just happy he and I have been able to talk about how hard the adjustment is to come back from war. And he's glad my experiences over there give me a little better understanding of what he went through. He says that without me he'd be psycho."

"It *is* good that Jimmy's able to talk about it. I remember some of those boys we treated refused to say a word about what was troubling them—they'd just shake and cry."

"Right," Vivian said, "and most of them still got sent back to the front to be scarred all over again. Heaven only knows what kind of shape they're in now."

Vivian gave me a lot to think about today, Louise wrote in her diary that evening. *I've been so wrapped up in my own loneliness and restlessness I haven't spent much time thinking about what all the men who saw actual combat are going through. Lots of them are feeling pretty unsettled. But still, I've got to do something different or I'll end up in the psycho ward.*

IN THE EARLY SUMMER, LOUISE BOARDED A BUS TO travel to Madison to spend a couple of days with Shoe and Dot. They'd written back and forth several times and had done significant finagling to get the same days off from their respective jobs.

Shoe and Dot were due to arrive from Walworth about half an hour sooner than her, but Louise stepped down from the bus and couldn't locate them among the waiting group of people. She retrieved her suitcase from the driver and went inside the station, glancing around somewhat anxiously.

After a few minutes, she approached the counter person. "Excuse me, has the bus from Walworth arrived yet?"

"It's pulling up right now," came the reply.

Louise turned to exit the station just as Shoe burst through the door. "Louise!" she yelled, then dropped her bag and ran to hug her. "It's great to see you, but I badly need to use the little girls' room! Watch my suitcase, okay?"

Louise nodded and looked around for Dot, who was nowhere to be seen. Finally, she pushed Shoe's suitcase and her own over toward a bench and sat down to wait.

Shoe plopped down beside her a few minutes later. "Thanks! That feels much better," she said with an exaggerated sigh.

"You're welcome," Louise said with a grin. "Where's Dot?"

"'Fraid she stood us up."

"What? Why?"

"Don't be mad at her," Shoe said, nudging Louise's shoulder. "She started dating a boy a couple weeks ago who she's 'pretty sure' is 'the one,' and he asked her to go to a family wedding with him tomorrow. She felt guilty about not coming, but I told her you'd understand."

Louise swallowed the lump in her throat. "Of course, I understand...Have you met him yet?"

Shoe nodded. "Let's go check in to the hotel," she said, "and I'll tell you everything I know over a beer and some lunch."

The friends walked to the twelve-story, red-brick Belmont Hotel on the Capitol Square. It wasn't as luxurious as the Monterey Hotel where Louise and Dot had spent the snowy night in January, but it had a large, comfortable lounge and an English-style dining room.

"Looks great," Louise said as they dropped their luggage in the room. It was small, but removing the rollaway bed they would've needed had Dot come gave them latitude to move around.

"Having an adjoining bathroom sure beats what we would have had at the YWCA."

"And what we had our whole time in the jungle."

Half an hour later, over cold mugs of beer, Louise leaned back contentedly. "I've missed this so much," she said.

Shoe reached over and patted her hand. "Me too. I know I'm lucky to have Dot around, but she doesn't always have your sunny disposition."

"Maybe her new beau will help," Louise said. She paused to light a cigarette and inhale and exhale slowly. "Tell me about him."

"He's Dot's sister's friend Marge's little brother Danny," Shoe said. "He's your age—a couple years younger than Dot. Works at the Chevrolet plant in Janesville. Not the smartest guy you'll ever meet, but he's cute and so swell to her. He's always cheerful, and everyone likes him. I think they're made for each other."

"Hmmm," Louise replied, "'Danny and Dot' has a nice ring to it..."

The waiter brought their lunch—a hamburger and French fries for Louise, and a roast beef sandwich with potatoes and gravy for Shoe—and they nodded when he inquired whether they'd like more beer.

Between bites, the friends caught up on the whereabouts of their mutual acquaintances.

"Will Rogers moved from Miami back to Oklahoma last month," Louise said casually. "He's still flying cargo planes but managed to get himself based there."

"Didn't you tell me he had a gal in Oklahoma?" Shoe asked. "Is that why he went back?"

Louise took a sip from her new mug of beer and blotted the foam from her lip with her napkin. "He's never mentioned her to me," she said. "His former roommate was the one who told me about her after Will got sent home."

"Oh, that's right. He told you all about how confused Will

was. Well, if he's still corresponding with you, there's a good chance she's long gone."

"I guess so. But it's not as though he's writing me romantically or anything," Louise said. "We just exchange occasional friendly letters—like two people who happened to have shared the same world for a while."

"Are you still pining for him?" Shoe asked.

Louise shrugged. "I'm pining for *something*, but I'm not sure what. A change of scenery? The camaraderie we had in the Army? A fellow who makes me feel special? I don't know."

Shoe paused to take a bite of food. "Are you thinking of re-enlisting too?" she asked.

"*Too?* Don't tell me *you're* thinking of it?"

Shoe nodded. "I think about it every day, and I'd sign up again in a minute if it weren't for my mother," she said ruefully. "She had a hard enough time coping when my father died, but my brother's death pushed her to the breaking point. I'm afraid I'm stuck here for the foreseeable future."

They ate in silence for a while. "Didn't you say you'd never go anywhere again without your sister?" Shoe finally asked.

Louise fidgeted in her chair before answering, "That *is* what I always said. But the truth is, Etta and I aren't nearly as close as we used to be. She took to life in La Crosse like a duck to water. Made friends with Dorothy Collins, another WAVE veteran who works in the Viterbo admissions office. They do everything together, eating dinner, and attending movies and musical and theatrical performances at the college. We talk and all, but she never tells me how she *feels* about anything and always seems pretty distant. And to be honest, she doesn't need me anymore."

"Really?"

"Really," Louise replied. "We share an apartment, but Etta's already talking about asking Dorothy to move in. I don't think she even notices that I'm at work almost every night."

"Well then, you *should* re-enlist. I got a letter from Ruth Ziegler a little while ago and she's happy she did."

Louise lit another cigarette. "That's what I'm thinking."

Louise returned to La Crosse two days later, determined to tell Etta about her plan as soon as the time felt right.

Chapter Forty-Six

In July—her appointment with the recruiting office still days away and her disclosure to Etta still on the back burner—Louise finished her evening shift and left the ward. Her footsteps echoed in the dim, mostly deserted hallways, and raindrops trickled down the darkened windows. It wasn't until she was halfway down the marble stairs to the lobby that she realized she'd left her umbrella in her locker. By the time she retrieved it and reached the front door, the other second shift workers had already departed.

Louise startled to see a man in a raincoat standing outside beneath the massive portico, his unfurled umbrella at his side. *He's probably harmless,* she thought. *Just waiting for a ride out of the rain.*

She almost collapsed when he held the door open for her and said, "Louise Dietrich! As I live and breathe!"

"Will Rogers! What on earth are you doing in La Crosse?" she shrieked as he threw his arms around her.

"I'm on a two-day layover in Minneapolis. They've got a little airport here, and I managed to hitch a ride over—I can take the train or a bus back if I can't catch another plane."

Louise felt her eyes welling with tears and tried in vain to blink them back.

"Don't tell me you're sad to see me, little chick," Will said, reaching in his pocket for a handkerchief to blot her cheeks.

"Oh...no...I'm happy. I just never expected it."

"Well, you seemed a little down in your last letter," he said, "and you were talking nonsense about re-upping. I just had to come and make sure you were okay."

"H-h-how did you know I was at work?"

Will winked. "I called the head nurse several days ago and sweet-talked her into telling me your schedule. I told her I was your cousin—just released from Walter Reed Army Hospital—and wanted to come surprise you."

"And she believed you?"

"She must've, since here I am." He nodded toward a taxi at the curb. "The cabbie said he'd wait a bit, but he's anxious to go off duty. He'll drop you at your apartment and then take me to my hotel to check in."

"Why don't you stay at our place? My sister won't mind, and the couch is so comfy I fall asleep there several times a week."

"Well, if I wouldn't be interrupting anything—"

"If my boss told you my schedule, you know I have the next two days off," she said.

"You're right, but I meant interrupting your social life," he said shyly. "I didn't ask her if you were going with anybody."

Louise blushed and shook her head.

They hustled to the cab, and Will gave the driver her address. "Turns out we'll both be going there," he said.

When Louise looked in the rearview mirror and saw the driver give Will a surreptitious smile, she couldn't help but smile herself.

THEY LEFT THEIR WET UMBRELLAS IN THE HALLWAY AND tiptoed up the steps to Louise and Etta's apartment, where a living room lamp emitted a welcoming glow. "You're shivering," Will said as they entered the room. He pulled her close and began rubbing her back. "This damp weather chills you to the bones. It's not this cold in Oklahoma."

"I've got a bottle of brandy that might warm us up," Louise said reflexively, then thought, *What am I saying? I'd rather stand here in his arms.*

"In a minute, okay?"

She nodded and rested her head on his shoulder.

After several moments, he pulled back from the embrace and held her at arm's length. "Just look at you—all grown up!"

"What d'ya mean?" she sputtered. "I wasn't some *kid* when I met you!"

"No, but you were cute as a button, and now you're a beautiful woman. I don't want to take my eyes off of you."

She felt her cheeks flush. "Well, if your goal in coming here was to cheer me up, you've certainly done that. Have a seat and I'll go get the brandy."

They talked for hours and as they did, the twenty-some months since they'd seen one another melted away. They spoke of the fun times they'd had together, the movies they'd seen, the friends with whom they'd double- and triple-dated. They told each other about their respective homecomings, the awkward moments when they couldn't remember people's names, the glorious food they'd eaten since the war. They gossiped about who'd broken up, who'd married, who'd had children, and who'd not been heard from since they mustered out.

I haven't felt this alive since I got home, Louise thought. And, as though he could read her mind, Will grinned.

Around dawn, their conversation became more serious. "When I got stateside," Will said, "I missed my unit so much I practically ached. If you remember, I tried to re-up and rejoin them when they got sent to the Philippines."

Louise nodded.

"Thank God the powers that be didn't let me—it would've been a big mistake. I needed to lick my wounds and move on rather than putting on a bandage and reentering the fray."

"I understand that you're saying I shouldn't reenlist," Louise said, "but I'm not sure I understand your reasoning. We *weren't* wounded, after all."

"Not physically, we weren't," Will said. "But believe me, this war wounded us mentally. All the close calls we had, all the people we saw die, all the deprivation we experienced. They're like festering sores that we try to ignore by focusing only on the good times."

Louise remained silent, wondering if she should tell him about her experience in Tokyo.

"I didn't see it at first," Will continued, "but my roommate, Andy, helped me to understand. He'd been a pilot in the European theater, and once he finished his thirty proscribed missions, he got sent stateside—all in one piece, fit as a fiddle. After we were discharged, we both got hired by Eastern Airlines and moved in together in Miami."

"Oh! At 'Sleepy Hollow—The Home of the Near Great'?"

Will laughed. "Uh-huh. And I'm impressed that you remembered!"

"I remember many things about you," she said, then flushed again at her own forthrightness. "But continue with what you were saying about how he helped you."

Will took another sip of brandy and began. "Andy's a swell guy —handsome, intelligent, funny. Seemed like he was on top of the world, being a commercial pilot like he'd always dreamed. But a couple months after we started living together, he changed. He didn't sleep much, was always distracted, and lost weight. I could tell something was wrong, but he's kind of private and I didn't want to pry.

"Then I convinced him to go to the VFW club with me one night. We sat at the bar with several other fellows I knew and after a few beers, the guys began telling war stories. Andy was quiet for a while but then got to talking about the B-17 missions he'd flown. About how the 'flying fortress,' as the plane was called, had a non-retractable ball turret jutting out from its belly, which was protected only by a glass bubble. A machine gunner would be assigned to sit in the turret and twist and turn around, trying to spot and shoot down enemy aircraft. These daytime bombing raids were always terrifying, but Andy said that when they returned to their base after one particularly harrowing mission, the turret was gone—along with the crew member who'd been manning the machine gun. All that was left was mangled metal, broken glass, and blood."

Louise grabbed his hand. "How awful..."

He went on, "Pretty soon, Andy had tears streaming down his face and started rambling incoherently about how he couldn't get the picture out of his mind. How he was afraid to go to sleep because he'd dream about it. How he'd recently started panicking every time he got into the cockpit and was sure he was going nuts."

Will paused to brush a tear from his own cheek.

"One of the other guys put his arms around Andy 'til he stopped crying and said, 'You're not crazy. You've got anxiety neurosis—like thousands of other guys who returned from the war scarred by their experiences.' And he told Andy about a psychiatrist at the VA hospital who was experimenting with hypnosis to help them cope. And Andy, to his credit, swallowed his pride and went and saw the guy."

"Good for him," Louise said. "Did it work?"

"Uh-huh. But he says the thing that helped the most was talking about the horrible things he'd seen. Instead of trying to be stoic and forget the unforgettable, he shares the experiences with other guys. And he laughingly calls his 1940 Packard 'TAS-FUIA'—you know, 'things are so fouled up it's amazing!'"

Louise nodded thoughtfully, remembering the M.P. who'd arrested the rapists in Tokyo had used the same expression. She lit a cigarette and tentatively began to describe the scenes *she'd* been trying so hard to banish from her mind. Half an hour later, she sobbed in his arms as she told of her breakdown—and her fears that it might have affected her discharge.

"Oh, my little chick," Will said, wiping her tears with the cuff of his shirtsleeve. "I'm so sorry you had to witness more horrible stuff than you'd already seen in that damned war ...especially on top of losing so many family members and your home and all. I'm glad you told me.

"I've started talking with other veterans—mostly just sitting around the VFW, but sometimes at family gatherings—about what scared and scarred me. Andy's right, it does wonders for me. I think it will for you too."

"But so many people don't understand what we went through," Louise said. "I read somewhere that only about twenty-five percent of military personnel even left the States during the war, and many of those folks never saw battle or adversity."

"All the more reason for you to find people who *do* understand," Will said. "And you don't need to re-enlist to find them. You could talk with me, for instance."

Louise leaned back against the couch. "Can you imagine the long-distance phone bills we'd have?" she said with a sigh. "And I haven't even told you about other awful things, like finding out that Shoe'd been raped, for example."

Will didn't reply. Instead, he took her hands in his, faced her, and looked into her eyes.

"Wait a minute," she said. "What are you saying?"

"I'm saying what I should've said two years ago. I want to marry you."

"I...I don't know what to say."

"You don't have to say anything right now," Will said quickly. "I'd never expect you to make a decision like this until we've had a chance to talk about it some more. And to meet each other's families. And until you see what you think of Oklahoma. And if Oklahoma doesn't suit you, we can find someplace we both like. Maybe La Crosse?"

Louise giggled and put a finger to his lips. "I think either the brandy or the wee hours of the morning are making you a little giddy. But I'd love to meet your family and see what I think of Oklahoma."

Will kissed her fingertip. "Could that also mean you love me?"

"We never said it before, but I realized tonight that I always loved you and I've never stopped."

"I feel the same way about you."

Their long, delicious kiss was interrupted by the sounds of Etta's bedroom door opening and her footsteps in the hallway.

"Speaking of meeting our families..." Louise said.

Acknowledgments

Like many members of what Tom Brokaw named *The Greatest Generation*, my dear friend Linda Colletti's mother rarely spoke about her experiences serving as an Army nurse during World War II. The pages of letters she sent to her younger sister back in the United States were newsy, but—perhaps due to censorship or to spare her sister from worry—they omitted the difficult details. *Love in a Time of War* is loosely based on the text of those letters, with particulars drawn from my imagination, accounts of others in the military, and various historians.

Once again, thanks to Corinne Hollar, who read every draft of this novel and gave me confidence and excellent suggestions.

My loyal group of beta readers contributed in countless ways, and I cannot thank them enough: Linda Colletti, Steve Cone, Jean Baptiste Medreaux, Kent Miller, Bobbi Eich, Catherine Spinelli, and Nick Spinelli. I'm very grateful to all of you for sharing your time and talents with me and for your honest opinions.

Thanks to my editor, Victoria Curran, whose insightful comments and recommendations proved beyond valuable.

Kudos to Casey Niederwerfer for creating an awesome cover conjured from my imprecise vision and notes. Thanks to Linda Colletti for granting permission to use the primary cover photograph—a real treasure.

And to my husband, Nick, and children, Carlos Spinelli and Lauren Truman: your steadfast love and support mean more to me than words can express.

Sources

I relied heavily on the following sources, but please note this does not represent a full bibliography.

Condon-Rall, Mary Ellen and Cowdrey, Albert E. *The Medical Department: Medical Service in The War Against Japan.* Washington, D.C.: Center of Military History - United States Army, 1998.

Fessler, Diane Burke. *No Time for Fear: Voices of American Military Nurses in World War II.* East Lansing: Michigan State University Press, 1996.

Gladwell, Malcolm. *The Bomber Mafia: A Dream, A Temptation, and The Longest Night of the Second World War.* New York: Little, Brown and Company, 2021.

Monahan, Evelyn M. and Neidel-Greenlee, Rosemary. *And If I Perish: Frontline U.S. Army Nurses in World War II.* New York: Knopf, 2003.

Pullman, Sally Hitchcock. *Letters Home: Memoirs of one Army Nurse in the Southwest Pacific in World War II.* AuthorHouse, 2004.

Rogers, Michael H. (editor). *Answering Their Country's Call:*

Marylanders in World War II. Baltimore: The Johns Hopkins University Press, 2002.

Schnoor Family Collection. Wisconsin Veterans Museum, Madison.

Teague Family Collection. *Papers and Photographs, 1943-2005: United States Army, General Hospital, 44th*. Wisconsin Veterans Museum, Madison.

Tomblin, Barbara Brooks. *G.I. Nightingales: The Army Nurse Corps in World War II*. Lexington: The University Press of Kentucky, 1996.

About the Author

Leslyn Amthor Spinelli is the author of four novels in the Caroline Spencer series, all influenced by her former career in the criminal justice system and that of her husband Nick, a retired private investigator. This is her first historical novel.

Leslyn and Nick live in the Minneapolis area and spend winter months in San Diego.

LeslynAmthorSpinelli.com

Also by Leslyn Amthor Spinelli

The Caroline Spencer series of novels:

Taken for Granted

Taken by Surprise

Taken for a Fool

Taking My Chances